E.   ᴹᴾ

B.

MOONLIGHT ON THE MERSEY

MOONLIGHT ON THE MERSEY

Anne Baker

HEADLINE

Copyright © 1996 Anne Baker

The right of Anne Baker to be identified as the Author of
the Work has been asserted by her in accordance with the
Copyright, Designs and Patents Act 1988.

First published in 1996
by HEADLINE BOOK PUBLISHING

10 9 8 7 6 5 4 3 2 1

British Library Cataloguing in Publication Data
Baker, Anne
    Moonlight on the Mersey
    1. English fiction – 20th century
    I. Title
    823.9'14[F]

ISBN 07472 1679 7

Phototypeset by Intype, London
Printed and bound in Great Britain by
Mackays of Chatham PLC, Chatham, Kent

HEADLINE BOOK PUBLISHING
A division of Hodder Headline PLC
338 Euston Road
LONDON NW1 3BH

This book is for my son David

CHAPTER ONE

July 1976

Jillian Ridley told herself it was silly to be afraid of going home. It wasn't as though she knew what she was nervous about.

She should be pleased. She wanted to see more of her father, didn't she? She'd come home for a weekend only two months ago, and she'd been in a state of trepidation ever since.

As she drove along the leafy roads of Prenton Ridge, she caught a glimpse of the Mersey. She was almost there.

Through the gateposts of Links View then, and at last she could see the long, low house, set back by itself amongst tall trees.

The half-grown Virginia creeper she remembered from her childhood had bloomed to luxurious maturity and now covered the front of the house.

She drove round the side and left her car by the double garage, because her stepmother didn't like cars left in front of the house.

The garden slumbered in the mid-afternoon sun. The back door as well as the french windows stood invitingly open, as though the house had nothing to hide. Jill dragged her suitcases from the back seat, her throat tight with tension.

She was surprised to see a hose pipe snaking in untidy coils across the patio, with the sprinkler spraying its cooling haze over a rustic seat. She ignored that, stepping eagerly over the threshold.

The kitchen had been recently refitted with smart new units. A pile of string beans on the table had been abandoned in a half-prepared state.

The light, airy hall seemed hardly to have changed in the many years since she'd last lived here. A middle-aged woman stood with her back to her, talking on the phone, metal curlers bulging through a headscarf. Jill knew she was one of the pair who came in for a few hours each day to help with the housework.

'Still out on her rounds? What about Dr Meadows? I must speak to someone.'

Jill felt a trickle of unease. 'Hello,' she said, afraid now that something bad had happened. The woman was too engrossed to hear her.

1

'Any doctor will do.' She could hear the growing desperation in the woman's voice. 'Her mother's had an accident. It's urgent. You'll let Dr Benbow know?'

Jill had to go closer and touch the woman's arm. It made her spin round.

'Hello. It's Mrs Moon, isn't it?' They'd met briefly when she'd come on that flying visit, two months ago. 'What's happened?'

'Jill – thank goodness you've come. Your mother said to expect you.' Once the woman had got over the shock, her face was shining with relief. 'You're a doctor too, aren't you?'

Jill saw Mrs Moon's eyes fix in disbelief on the jeans and T-shirt she was wearing.

'What's happened to Gran? Is she hurt?'

'Not ten minutes ago. Tripped over the hose pipe on the patio.' Mrs Moon was wiping sweating palms down her floral pinafore.

'Where is she?'

'In there.' She was pointing to the sitting room.

Jill rushed to the door. Her grandmother's eyes were closed. She was lying on a new cretonne-covered settee, cradling her right arm. The room was elegant, with long windows overlooking the lawn.

'Gran?' She looked at the putty-coloured face, took a deep breath, then knelt to kiss the slack cheek. 'It's Jill.'

Gran's dark eyes jerked open. She screwed them up to peer at her. 'You've got here then?'

'Yes, I see you've hurt your arm. Is it very painful?'

'Better now. I've taken something.'

Jill could see them both reflected in the Queen Anne gilt-wood mirror of which her father was so proud. A withered old lady with her white hair drawn up into an elegant bun, and her own hot, anxious face and wind-tossed hair that was almost but not quite blonde.

'Silly woman, that Mrs Moon. I told her Lois would be out visiting.' Gran's voice was fretful. 'She won't listen. It's a Colles fracture.' She offered her arm up to Jill. 'I'll have to go to hospital.'

'Gran! Are you sure?'

'Of course I'm sure. I might be old but I'm not senile.'

Jill smiled. She was proud of the fact that the women of her family were all doctors. Well, step-family really. Stepmother, step-grandmother and step-great-grandmother.

Her great-grandmother Evelyn had qualified in 1904 at the age of thirty-six. Jill had been brought up on stories of the difficulties she'd faced and how she'd led the way for the rest of them. Gran had qualified in 1917, and it still hadn't been easy for women then.

Now Jill examined Gran's arm and had to agree with her diagnosis. Even at eighty-three, she still had her skills.

'No point in waiting for Lois. Call a taxi for me.'

'My car's outside. I can take you.'

2

'Can you drive? It seems no time since you were a toddler.'

'Gran, I'm twenty-six. Almost twenty-seven.'

The dark eyes strained up at her face. 'You still look a slip of a girl to me.'

'Come on, hardly that. I'm a doctor too, remember? That's where I've been all these years, training to follow in the family footsteps.'

As a child, she'd felt very close to Gran. Closer than she had to her stepmother. In those days Gran had had a flat of her own, but she used to come to look after Jill in the school holidays.

'Don't you wear glasses now? You don't look as though you can see properly.'

'There they are.' The old lady nodded towards the mahogany sofa-table. 'I broke them when I fell.'

They were in two pieces, the frame snapped at the bridge. Jill tried fitting the pieces together and decided she could tape them if she had to. 'Do you have a spare pair?'

'Yes.' Gran brightened and pulled herself up a little against the cushion. The effort made her gasp with pain. 'In the drawer by my bed.'

'I'll get them for you.' Jill got to her feet. 'Then I'll take you to hospital.'

As she picked up the suitcases she'd left in the hall, she could hear the sound of beans being chopped again in the kitchen.

A strange feeling closed round her as she went up to the bedroom she'd used as a child. It was not nostalgia, she could remember so little of her early years. It was fear. These last few years, she'd felt haunted by the strange blanks in her memory that she couldn't fill.

There was a faint smell of fresh paint. Lois had had her room redecorated and all the furniture was new. The bed was made up with a crisp new duvet cover.

Her dolls' house had been put up in the attic after her first year away at school. All the books and toys and ornaments she'd had as a child had likewise been banished.

In the wardrobe there was nothing but a row of empty coat hangers. It was as impersonal as a hotel room, except for the new silver-backed dressing-table set and the tasteful paintings Lois had hung on the wall. It was almost as though her stepmother did not want anything to remind her of her childhood.

Something very strange and frightening had happened then. Jill couldn't remember what it was but it had caused a family upset, and she'd suddenly been sent off to boarding school.

She'd never felt comfortable in this house since. Never felt at ease with her stepmother either. She'd dreaded coming home for the school holidays; really, had been a little afraid of doing so.

She'd tried to talk to Dad about it, and to Gran, and they'd put her off with reassurances.

'Lots of children have nightmares,' they told her. 'You must forget

3

it. Don't worry about what happened all that time ago.'

But whatever it was, it still bothered her, which was why she'd so rarely come home once she'd grown up. Jill felt there were things in the background that her family were keeping from her.

She felt she was old enough to understand now. She wanted to lay this ghost in her past, rid herself of this nervous fear. She didn't think she was neurotic, but it was making her act as though she was.

The upstairs landing seemed bigger than she remembered. There was new carpet here, and less furniture. Not at all as it had been when she was young.

In her grandmother's room, there was a Victorian dressing table with bottles of lavender water, and a snowy candlewick bedspread on a single bed. The filmy curtains moved in the slight breeze. She went to the bedside cabinet and opened the top drawer.

There were a lot of loose photographs in it, as well as other odds and ends. Her fingers were closing over a red spectacle case when she saw that the picture on top was of her stepmother as a young woman, cuddling herself as a baby.

Suddenly she was boiling with curiosity. Here was evidence of those early years she couldn't recall. Jill picked the picture up for a closer look.

She wanted to be part of the family again. She envied people with strong family ties, it seemed to give them an added strength.

She looked about three months old in the picture, but it told her nothing; all babies looked pretty much alike at that age. Her stepmother's chin was at the arrogant angle she remembered so well. Lois was inclined to congratulate herself on what she'd achieved in life.

Jill turned the picture over and read the fading scrawl on the back. 'Lois with baby Phoebe.'

She gasped aloud. The picture was not of her? She burrowed into the drawer again and found another, clearer picture of the same baby. Somebody had written on the back: 'Phoebe aged two months.'

Who was Phoebe? Here was clear evidence that her family were keeping things from her.

There were other photographs, many of them. Of her stepmother, her step-grandmother and her step-great-grandmother, all with the same young baby.

Of course it wasn't her. What had she been thinking of? She did remember some things. Her father had not married Lois until she, Jill, was three years old.

Jill felt her heart thudding with shock. She'd never heard mention of any other child. She'd assumed Lois hadn't wanted children of her own, that her career was more important to her than a family.

She pored over another picture, and found yet more to compare. She remembered that Lois had been married before, but was Phoebe

4

older or younger than Jill was? And was her father also Phoebe's father? He didn't seem to be in any of these pictures.

How could she have forgotten she'd had a sister? Jill felt perplexed. It drove home just how little she knew about her family. Suddenly she didn't seem part of it at all.

She shut the drawer with a slam. She had no time to deliberate on this. She'd been telling herself she was looking forward to being one of the family again. Now, suddenly, she wasn't so sure where she fitted into it. They all seemed strangers.

She found a coat for her grandmother in the wardrobe. The afternoon was quite hot but Gran's hand had been icy. It could be shock after her fall. And one thing she did remember was that Gran never went out without a hat. Jill picked out a grey toque.

Gran was shakier than she'd first seemed. Mrs Moon helped get her dressed and out to Jill's car. It was a slow process.

'What a good job you're a doctor too,' Mrs Moon said. 'It makes things so much easier if you know what to do.'

Jill sighed. It had not been easy for her, though she'd always wanted to follow in her step-family's footsteps.

'It's not in your genes,' Lois had told her when she had reached the age of sixteen and there had been talks at school about careers. She'd been home for the summer holidays at the time. 'Your natural mother worked in the chocolate trade. That might suit you better.'

'No,' Jill had protested. 'I want . . .'

'You might not be able to cope with a profession like medicine. Still, there's always nursing if you can't get into medical school.'

Dad had been about to take her to a concert. She'd wanted his support. On the way she'd asked: 'Do you think I could be a doctor?'

'You must think about it carefully, Jill. It's a big decision to make. You've a real head for figures, you know. Wouldn't you like a career using them?'

'You mean, be an accountant and work in the chocolate business like you?'

She remembered Dad's gusty sigh. 'I suppose that's what I do mean. It's the best training there is for running the business and I'd like to think I was just looking after it until you're old enough to take over.'

'I want to be a doctor.' She'd been stiff with determination.

Dad had talked to her about her real mother, his first wife, Sarah Lambourne.

Jill had been four months old when her Lambourne grandparents had wanted to take her mother with them on holiday. The birth had been a difficult one and Sarah had been ill afterwards. They'd said that ten days in Italy would do her good, get her on her feet again. Instead, it had cost Sarah her life.

5

She knew that the Lambourne family had started the business making up-market chocolates, and had employed Dad as their accountant. He'd gone on to marry their only child. Since the accident, he'd had to run the business by himself.

'Then you must go ahead. You'll succeed, if doctoring is what you really want. I know you will.' He'd grinned at her then with encouragement.

'What a nice new car,' Mrs Moon enthused as she handed Gran into the passenger seat. The sun was sparkling on its bright red paintwork.

It wasn't all that new now. Jill had started her general practice training with an old banger, but she'd had to have something more reliable. She'd bought a Mini with a bank loan so she wouldn't have to ask her father for money. He'd already been over-generous through all the years of her training.

'You're going the wrong way.' Gran pulled herself up in the seat beside her. 'Left here, down to the motorway. Isn't that the way you came this morning?'

It was, but before the new roads had been built they'd always gone the other way.

'You've stayed away too long.'

Then she had to concentrate on driving, conscious all the time of Gran sitting beside her nursing her wrist. Her eyes were closed now, but she knew that they snapped open every so often to make sure Jill was going the right way.

It was a relief to get to the accident and emergency department at Clatterbridge Hospital. Jill had spent enough time in places like this to feel at home; the smell of antiseptic, the rows of chairs in the waiting area, mostly occupied, the nurses scurrying round.

She booked her grandmother in. 'Dr Victoria Benbow,' she said when asked the patient's name. Then she sat down beside her to wait their turn. Gran's eyes were closed again behind the spare pair of glasses.

Now at last Jill was free to mull over the strange phenomenon of the baby Phoebe. Perhaps she was making a mountain out of a molehill. Phoebe was just another of those gaps in her memory. She'd ask about her. Find out all about her own family's history. Straighten herself out on this.

'Gran?' But Gran's eyelids didn't flicker. The painkiller she'd taken had made her soporific. She'd not want to talk about it now.

Even Dad had never so much as mentioned baby Phoebe's existence, and Jill had always felt close to him. He'd told her at a very early age that her real mother had died when she was tiny, and that Lois was his second wife.

6

Jill thought fondly of him. Dad was retiring by nature. He would have liked her to work in his business, but he hadn't tried to persuade her.

Her memories of childhood were so few. Long ago, she had sorted out in her own mind exactly where those gaps were. She could remember very little from the time her father married Lois until she went to boarding school at the age of eight. Her doctor's training made her question this.

Had she been jealous? Afraid that her father loved Lois more than he did her? Or was it stories like Cinderella and Snow White that made her imagine that all stepmothers were wicked?

She wanted to believe that her silly, half-formed fear of Lois wasn't justified. Perhaps, as a child, she hadn't given Lois a chance. After all, she'd wanted to follow in her footsteps and be a doctor. She had admired Lois for what she'd accomplished. How could she both fear and admire her?

She'd talked this over with a special friend she'd had, a fellow houseman in the psychiatric hospital where she'd worked for six months. He already knew something of her home circumstances.

'Your mind has closed it out,' he said. 'Something happened that you didn't like. Some trauma. Your way of dealing with it was to blank out all memory of that time in your life.'

'But I can remember things from when I was very young.'

'Clearly, you mean? Everything that happened?'

'Not everything, but as much as an average toddler. I remember my father's wedding. I wanted to taste the champagne and he let me have a sip, but I didn't like it. I had a blue velvet dress. I was three at the time.'

'The trauma happened after that. Something you couldn't bear to think about. It was too painful.'

'I don't think I had a traumatised childhood.' Jill had laughed at the very idea. 'I'm a fairly normal person. I've got my feet on the ground.' She laughed again. Normal, apart from this neurotic fear of the house and of Lois. 'For goodness' sake, I'm emotionally stable.'

'I'm not saying you aren't. You know as well as I do that when the mind shuts things out it's a protective device. Your way of dealing with the trauma succeeded. You shouldn't seek to fill the gaps.'

But curiosity was needling her. She wanted to know what had happened. She felt love for her father and grandmother, but she'd had to learn to hide her fear of Lois.

As a child, she could not have seen very much of her stepmother. In the evenings, when she would have been home from school, Lois would frequently have had an evening surgery to do.

With her stepmother working in a demanding profession, it must have suited family circumstances that Jill should go to boarding

7

school. She did remember overhearing her father's objections to this. It had made her feel better.

'I shall miss her. She's company for me when you're out. The house will be quiet without her.'

'You spend too much time with her, Nat.'

'I can't spend it with you if you're working. She's perfectly happy at school here. Why disrupt both of us? Besides, boarding school is expensive.'

'It'll be better for Jill in the long run.'

'But not better for me, Lois. I like having her here.'

Jill closed her eyes and thought of St Hilda's. It had taken her a long time to settle in.

It had been her father who had visited the school on prize days and sports days, her father who had taken her there and collected her, until she was old enough to make the journey on her own. She'd seen less and less of her stepmother.

Boarding school had done her no harm, not really. Sometimes she'd felt at a bit of a loss in the school holidays, having no friends nearby to play with, but often she'd been invited to spend part of the holiday with her school friend Jane, who lived near Manchester and had the same problem.

There had never been a convenient time to invite Jane back, because two children would be too much for Lois when she was working.

Dad had done his best. When Jill was at home, he'd come back early from the office to be with her. There was always a visit to the pantomime at Christmas, and occasionally to the cinema. She'd often spent a half-day with him at the chocolate factory. And Grandma had come to stay and taken her out and about.

But she'd never really known what was going on at home. As she'd grown older, she thought Lois rather strange at times, and noticeably less welcoming when she did go home. That caused her to make every effort to spend her holidays elsewhere.

Her father started taking her abroad for two weeks every summer. They both enjoyed dinghy sailing in the warmer waters of France and Greece.

She'd let them know she hadn't changed her mind about a career in medicine. She'd been almost eighteen, having a last meal with the family before returning to school for her last term, when she'd said:

'It's time now for me to apply for a place at medical school.'

'You'll want to go to Liverpool?' Her father had been eager that she should. 'It's got an excellent reputation, hasn't it, Lois?'

'It's not the only good medical school,' Lois put in sharply.

'Both Lois and her mother went there.' Nat beamed at his daughter. 'You'll be able to live here at home with us for a change.'

Lois had said coldly: 'Perhaps she'd prefer not to.'

Jill was left in no doubt that Lois would prefer that she did not. For her own part, she'd already made up her mind to go elsewhere. She felt she had to. She'd spent only four nights at home this holiday; she didn't feel she could face living with Lois for five solid years.

She applied to the Royal Free Hospital School in London, and breathed a sigh of relief when she heard she'd been given a place. Her step-great-grandmother Evelyn had trained there all those years ago. Only Dad seemed disappointed that she wouldn't be coming home.

Since then, she'd gone home less and less and hadn't felt part of the family.

Recently Dad had been writing to her more often. She had the impression, though he didn't say so directly, that he was less content with his life. He seemed unhappy, sometimes even depressed, as though things were no longer going his way.

A few weeks before she completed her training as a general practitioner, Jill had been looking round for a job. She wanted to settle into something permanent now, rather than do a series of locums.

For the first time ever, Lois had written to her, suggesting she join the practice in which she was a partner. Jill hardly knew what to make of it. It seemed a complete turnaround on her stepmother's part.

By the same post she'd received a worrying letter from her father. It was not what it said, exactly – it had been full of trivia about his business. But the last page had only two or three lines at the top, and below that the indentation of other words in his heavy hand showed up clearly. As though he'd originally written something quite different and then had had second thoughts and torn up the page.

She could read the first indentations. He'd said: 'I want you to come home, Jill.'

She'd studied the page then, even taken out a magnifying glass, and had eventually managed to decipher some more.

'Things are getting out of hand. The business just won't stand the . . . I just can't cope with the demands for . . .'

It had made up her mind for her. She must come back and stay. If she found living in the house with them too oppressive, she could find a small flat for herself. If Dad needed her help, she had to give it. Her mind made up, she'd written to Lois showing interest in her suggestion.

Jill hadn't heard much of her stepmother's voice recently, but now she recognised it instantly. Rather strident, with clear diction, the sort of voice that carries well. She could make out every syllable that Lois said from the other side of the department.

She couldn't drag her eyes away from Lois's ramrod-stiff figure, and the way she stabbed her long, thin fingers in the air. She was asking a nurse where Gran was and whether she had been treated yet.

9

At fifty-seven, Lois was tall and thin with grey hair cropped short. Her bearing was commanding, her style mannish. She wore a very formal grey chalk-stripe suit that had a certain elegance.

The nurse was indicating the waiting area. Jill caught her eye, and waved. The next moment her stepmother was striding across to her.

'How fortunate you came home this afternoon.' Jill felt a cool peck at her cheek. 'How are you feeling, Mother? You've hurt your wrist, I hear.'

'A Colles . . .' Jill began.

Lois was already examining it. Closer to, her dark eyes prickled with impatience and her lips were a thin, determined line. Jill knew she couldn't ask about Phoebe now.

'Have you spoken to the sister in charge? Asked her to push you through quickly? We can't just sit here and wait. Such a waste of time.'

Jill watched her stepmother stride off again and wondered why she'd ever wanted to be like her. Moments later, she knew: Lois was effective. Jill found herself escorting Gran into the examination room.

The houseman who came to attend to them was Asian. He seemed less than confident.

'A Colles, by the look of it,' Lois informed him airily before he'd had time to examine Gran's wrist himself. 'I'm Dr Benbow, by the way. General practitioner.' Jill had known that her stepmother used her maiden name to practise. 'We're all doctors of one sort or another in our family. My mother was too before she retired.'

The houseman opened his mouth to say something.

'I think we need an X-ray first, to confirm diagnosis,' Lois told him. She had the sort of personality that steam-rollered over everybody else. Jill marvelled at the self-confidence that enabled her to do it.

The Asian doctor looked as though he'd like to tell her to go to hell but didn't dare. Didn't ask her to wait outside while he saw to Gran, either.

Jill closed her eyes in embarrassment. She'd forgotten what her stepmother was like. She had never seen anyone quite so insensitive to other people's feelings.

Gran went through the X-ray department in record time and was soon having a plaster cast put on.

'I'll stay to run Mother home,' Lois announced.

'There's no need if you're in a rush,' Jill said. 'I've got my Mini here.'

'You were in too much of a hurry getting that. Your father would have bought you something better.'

'The Mini's fine. I like it.'

'Yes, well, now I'm here, I'd better take Mother home. My car will

10

be more comfortable for her. I'll just be able to fit it in before evening surgery.'

When the time came, Jill helped Gran into the passenger seat of Lois's large green Rover. It was parked under a sign saying that the space was strictly reserved for the hospital's senior medical staff.

Lois said: 'I've rung your father. Asked him to come home early to see to Mother, but he says he can't.'

Jill felt a stab of disappointment. She'd been looking forward to seeing him again. 'I'm here . . . Gran won't be alone.'

'He said to give you his love and that he'd be back in time for dinner. He's arranged something special to welcome you back, so he won't be late for that. Follow me home.'

Jill would have complied, but by the time she reached her Mini at the bottom of a distant car park, there was no sign of the green Rover. It left her wondering if coming to work in the practice with Lois had been a wise move.

CHAPTER TWO

Jill found the late afternoon uncomfortable. Lois had gone back to the surgery as soon as she'd settled Gran in bed and given her more painkillers.

Gran has asked for tea, and Jill had taken a tray up and had a cup with her, but the old lady's eyes had been ready to close, so she'd left her to rest.

She'd unpacked her suitcases feeling like a visitor in the house, then took a shower and changed.

She was crossing the landing when she noticed that one of the bedroom doors was ajar. She could see a man's dressing gown slung over a chair. Financial and trade magazines were piled up beside a double bed.

Jill pulled up in surprise. The well-worn slippers must belong to her father. Did her parents no longer sleep together? There was nothing belonging to Lois here, and besides, when she'd come up on that flying visit, she'd seen Lois heading towards the front bedroom that she and Nat had always used.

Jill hesitated a moment and then peeped into the main bedroom. It was a huge room, with two windows and a glass door opening on to a balcony. She could see face creams on the dressing table, medical journals by the king-size bed, velvet mules and a satin robe.

Poor Dad, it didn't say much for the state of his marriage. No wonder he'd sounded upset in his letters. She looked in on Gran, and finding her asleep, tiptoed downstairs to wait.

She felt restless and unsettled. This was her home, yet the feeling of not quite belonging, of not being at ease, was not new to her, which was why she'd come so seldom in recent years. She hoped it wasn't a mistake to have come now.

She went into the dining room to see the painting of her step-family again. It was a collective portrait of three generations of doctors. This was how she'd pictured her family while she'd been away. They had been painted larger than life because the picture had been designed for an earlier and larger house. Here at Links View it hung over the sideboard, dominating the room.

Lois looked unbelievably girlish; Victoria had been in her prime when it had been painted; Evelyn looked very much like Victoria did now. They reminded Jill of the goals she'd set for herself. They had blazed the trail and she'd wanted to be like them. She hoped she'd do as well.

She could hear Mrs Moon clattering about the kitchen, and the most heavenly scents were drifting out. Four places had been set with the finest linen, glass and cutlery on the polished mahogany table.

She heard tyres crunching on the gravel outside. She went to the window and saw her father getting stiffly out of his old Wolseley. He seemed to have aged since she'd been home two months ago.

'Dad!' She rushed out to kiss him. 'Lois said you'd be late, I didn't expect you yet.'

He swept her into a bear hug. It was what he always did when they met. He smelled deliciously of chocolate.

'I'm later than I wanted to be. We've got a big order from Harrods to make this week. I got away as soon as I could.' Her father whole-saled Lambourne's Luxury Chocolates through fifty shops up and down the country. He also owned two shops on Merseyside that retailed them.

She put her arms round him again and gave him another hug, and felt the emotional tug. The bond between them was as strong as ever.

'How are you, Dad?'

'Fine. Busy, of course.'

For the moment she was glad to have him to herself. They talked about her journey and Gran's accident. She noticed that he had bags beneath his eyes, rather like a lovable basset hound. And when he wasn't making an effort, when he was lost in his own thoughts, there was a melancholy droop to his mouth that she hadn't seen before.

Sympathy for him overflowed but there was no need to probe on her first night. She could take her time now she was back for good, let things come out gradually. The problem was something he couldn't easily tell her about, otherwise he wouldn't have rewritten that letter.

As soon as Lois came home, she went to the kitchen to check on the meal and send Mrs Moon home. Then she whisked upstairs to change.

She came down looking more elegant than ever, in a formal black dress, to announce that the meal was ready. When they reached the dining room door she was sweeping one place setting from the table.

'Mother won't be coming down tonight. Have you looked in to see her, Nat?'

'Yes, when I went up to change. She was asleep.'

'I think the least you can do is apologise. Leaving the hose where she could trip . . .'

'Of course I'll apologise, but the hose is always there when the sprinkler's on. It has to run from the tap. And I did point it out to her.'

14

'All the same, you could . . .'

'She's getting old, Lois. Sometimes she forgets . . .'

'Nonsense! Not Mother. I do hope she'll be all right.'

'Has she broken anything else?' Dad's face showed concern. 'Her wrist, you said. Is there more you haven't told me?'

'No, Dad,' Jill assured him as she carried dishes to the table.

As a child she'd thought her father besotted with Lois, but now things had definitely cooled.

'Just a broken wrist. She's shaken up and it's painful but she'll be all right. Won't she, Lois?'

'I expect so. It worries me so when Mother's ill. Nat, aren't you going to open . . .?'

Her father fetched a bottle from the fridge. Only when she heard the cork pop did Jill realise it was champagne. She felt touched that they'd provided it for her homecoming.

'Here's to you, Jill.' His smile wobbled a little as he raised his glass. 'Lovely to have you home.'

Lois raised her glass too. 'All the best for tomorrow in the new job.'

'Thank you. You're both very kind, putting on a delicious meal like this.' Jill was savouring the lobster thermidor.

She watched the bubbles rising in her own glass, and felt that they were both trying very hard, but the welcome, the *bonhomie*, seemed a bit forced. Even from Dad. He looked tired and his face was more heavily lined than it should be. He was only eight years older than Lois, after all.

Jill studied him as she ate. He'd changed out of his hot business suit and wore an open-necked shirt and slacks. His hair was still dark but heavily streaked with grey. He'd pushed it off his forehead in an effort to keep cool and it stood up in an untidy tuft.

His grey eyes smiled at her over the rim of his glass. Champagne froth showed on his upper lip. She remembered how he used to be, alert, on his toes, high-spirited. Tonight he was struggling.

'It's good to have you back and know you're staying this time.'

Lois's sloe-black eyes met hers across the table. 'Nat, we don't know that Jill wants to live here with us. Not permanently.'

Jill tried to smile. Tried to still the unease she felt. The trappings of welcome were here, but Lois was hardly hiding the fact that she didn't want her.

She said: 'When I've settled into the practice I'll look round for a small flat for myself.'

Dad was quite upset. 'Jill! This is your home. We want you to stay here, don't we, Lois?'

Lois's eyes were cold. 'Of course.'

'You'll be working hard, Jill. It'll be easier for you here, where meals are laid on and the cleaning done.'

Jill knew she'd be more comfortable with distance between herself and Lois. She didn't like this house, and she'd been looking forward to cooking for herself, being independent.

'Do say you'll stay. I've been so looking forward to having you back.'

Jill wanted to stay close to her father. If she was to help him, she had to.

'Of course I will, Dad. If you and Lois can put up with me.'

'You know we'll love having you here,' her father grinned.

Lois's smile was brittle. Jill didn't know what to make of her. It had been Lois who had suggested she join the practice. Lois who had pressed her to accept the position when it was offered. She'd thought Lois had changed, that she wanted her here. That as adults they could be friends. For Jill, that had tipped the balance. It had given her another reason to come.

But Lois seemed to be playing fast and loose with her. Now, having her here seemed the last thing she wanted.

The anecdote Lois was telling them about a patient she'd seen in the surgery that morning came to an end. Jill wanted to ask about Phoebe.

She said: 'When I was looking in Gran's drawer for her spare spectacles, I came across some photographs of a baby called Phoebe.'

Before she'd finished the sentence she felt the atmosphere chill down ten degrees. Lois was staring at her, the colour draining from her cheeks.

Jill added lamely: 'I just wondered who she was?'

She saw Lois swallow. She seemed dumbfounded. Neither she nor her father answered.

'I mean, I've never heard of her. Did I have a sister or a stepsister?'

Her father recovered first. 'A stepsister, she would have been. Yes, a stepsister.'

Jill looked from one to the other. Neither seemed to want to add to that.

'It's just that I find it strange that nobody has ever mentioned her existence.'

'I expect you've forgotten,' Lois said.

'You've been away so much,' Dad added, not looking at her.

'Well . . . Now I'm here, won't you tell me? I'd love to know more about her.'

'It was all so long ago.' Lois was uneasy and trying to dismiss the subject.

Jill said: 'When was it?'

'I suppose it would have been . . .' Her father seemed to go into some sort of reverie. 'She was younger than you. Just a few months.'

Lois was rattling the lids of the vegetable dishes. 'More beans, Nat? Jill? They're the first this season.'

'Thank you, they're a treat when they're fresh like this. The whole meal is delicious.' Jill helped herself.

'Out of the garden,' Lois said. 'Your father is taking more interest in it now.'

Jill said slowly: 'I feel so silly sometimes, knowing so little about my own family. How did Phoebe die?'

'A cot death.' It was her father who answered. 'You'll understand how upset Lois was. A painful experience for her.'

Lois's dark eyes were suddenly bright with unshed tears.

Jill knew that a cot death could bring searing grief to parents; she understood how bereft Lois must feel. In her job, she'd seen mothers devastated by it, had tried to help them come to terms with it.

'Very painful memories,' Lois said stiffly. 'I haven't been able to bring myself to talk about it.'

And still can't, Jill thought. Lois was the last person she'd ever expected to see near tears. This afternoon she'd seemed as hard as nails, so bombastic and full of her own importance with the Asian houseman.

This seemed abnormal behaviour for her stepmother. Not at all in character. Jill had the feeling that Phoebe had not died a straight-forward cot death. There must be more to it than that.

'It's not that I mean to pry,' Jill wanted to explain how little she remembered of her childhood. That she needed to know more in the hope it would scotch her silly fears. 'Please forgive me, but . . .'

'Do you mind if we don't talk about her?' Lois's voice was agon-ised, and she was gulping her champagne as though it were water. 'I can't bear it.'

'Lois, don't take on so.' Dad put a sympathetic hand on top of his wife's. 'If Jill wants to know, there's no reason why we can't tell her that . . .'

'Now don't you start.' Lois whirled on him in fury. 'There's no need for the whole world to know every detail. It's all in the past and I won't have it raked up.'

'Jill isn't the whole world,' Dad was saying gently. 'It isn't just idle curiosity . . .'

'That's enough, I've said!' Lois screamed.

Shocked, Jill looked at her father. His eyes were brimming with concern. Whether for her or for Lois, she didn't know. Suddenly her fear of her stepmother seemed more rational.

'I'm sorry, Lois,' she said. They finished the meal in an uncomfort-able silence.

'An early night?' Dad suggested as soon as they'd drunk their coffee. Lois was already hurrying up to her room.

Jill went up more slowly. Her mind was boiling with questions. She felt wide awake and on edge. She'd thought that once she was home

17

she'd easily fill the gaps in her memory. But nobody wanted to tell her anything.

She could understand Dad's reluctance to talk about Phoebe in Lois's hearing. He must have known it would upset her. She'd had to drag out of him the fact that Phoebe had been a few months younger than herself.

But she couldn't understand why Lois was still so uptight about it. Or why the atmosphere in this house felt so heavy and full of ghosts.

It wasn't as though it was an old building. It stood high on Prenton Ridge, newly constructed when her father and Lois had bought it at the time of their marriage. It looked well established, with the leafy creeper covering the front and spreading round the sides. Other people thought it a comfortable family home of five bedrooms and three bathrooms. Downstairs, the living rooms were all large and well proportioned.

Jill threw open her bedroom window. Here were far-reaching views over the trees in the garden, across the descending roofs and roads of Prenton. Tonight, she could see the rising moon sending a gleaming swathe of yellow light on to the black water of the Mersey.

From the rear, the house looked down over more descending roofs to the golf course, with semi-rural views beyond that to the Welsh hills. There should be nothing at all to make her nervous. Yet she couldn't rid herself of this prickling apprehension.

Two months ago, and for the first time in years, Jill had come home one Friday evening for the weekend. Lois had written to her a second time.

'You'll want to meet the partners. See the practice premises. Find out what things are like before you commit yourself.'

Dad had told her he'd meet her at Lime Street Station.

Her train had been late. At the terminus, passengers had streamed up the platform and out into the station. She'd been looking for him but failed to see him in the crowd. At last she'd heard him call her name, then felt his arms crushing her to him. When she lifted her eyes to his face, she'd hardly recognised him. The change had shocked her.

In the two years since she'd last seen him, his heavy, handsome face seemed to have slackened and crumpled. He looked so much older. He'd lost weight.

'How are you, Dad?'

'I'm fine,' he said, but he didn't look it. And he didn't look her in the eye. Jill felt guilty because she'd come home so rarely in recent years.

On the Saturday morning, Lois had taken her down to the surgery to meet Cuthbert Meadows and Miles Sutton, who would be her partners, and also Bill Goodbody, who was retiring and whose place she would take.

It hadn't been just a matter of meeting them. It had turned out to be a tough interview. She'd had to answer probing questions.

'Choosing the right partner is almost as difficult as choosing the right wife,' Goodbody had smiled at her. He was seventy-four, his almost bald scalp was darkly tanned and leather-like. A prominent blue vein snaked across his temple. 'Got to be just as careful. It causes problems if we don't have the same ideas about money and the same clinical standards. You mustn't mind the third degree.'

Lois said in her brisk way: 'You'd better start by telling them about your training.'

Like all doctors, following her five years in medical school Jill had worked for two years in hospitals.

'Some call it training,' Miles Sutton added sourly. 'Others call it paying junior doctors a pittance and working them to death.'

The hours Jill had worked had been both long and unsociable. She'd had to give up things other girls took for granted: parties, outings, theatre visits and boyfriends. She'd told herself that once it was over she'd make time for life's pleasures.

She told them about her first six months as a trainee general practitioner with an Edinburgh practice. She was just coming to the end of her second six months, with the practice near Exeter.

This was the last stage of hands-on training. Now she was expected to get on with the job. In fact, her trainer had gone away on a two-month trip. She'd discovered that night calls and evening surgeries fell heavily on the shoulders of the most junior.

The questioning had gone on all morning. She told herself they had to satisfy themselves that she was competent. All the same, she'd felt pressurised.

To gain a breather, she asked them what the practice did by way of preventative medicine.

'All for it,' they agreed unanimously, but it turned out to be the usual: immunisations for children, taking a few blood pressures, and the odd smear.

'It's the time,' Miles had said. 'Acute cases have to come first.'

'How do you feel about maternity work?' Cuthbert Meadows had a slow, gentle smile and sympathetic brown eyes. He was softly spoken, a gentle giant of a man, six foot three tall with broad shoulders in proportion. 'By the way, you must call me Titch. Everybody else does.'

'Titch?' She had to smile. No need to ask how he'd got his nickname.

'Can't stand being called Cuthbert. Fashions in names have changed in my time. Makes me feel ancient.'

'Titch suits you better anyway,' she told him.

'Do you feel capable of coping with maternity cases?'

'Yes.' Jill felt on firmer ground here. She'd enjoyed her six months' training in maternity.

'Neither Miles nor I are keen. We'll want to leave them to you and Lois. What about paediatrics?'

Jill liked young children. She'd taken a special interest in their illnesses.

'You need to be a bit of a vet to deal with the very young. They can't tell you much.'

Titch told her he was sixty, but she thought he looked younger. His hair was dark and showed no sign of grey; his moustache was thick and glossy. He wore heavy horn-rimmed spectacles and seemed friendly and kind. Yet behind the open manner Jill felt a wall of reserve.

She thought she'd get on well with him, but of Miles Sutton she was not so sure. She got the impression he didn't want her in the practice but was being overruled. She didn't think the others got on well with him either. She had the feeling that they ranged themselves against him.

Miles was standing alone. His manner was that of a man fighting with his back against the wall. He was being unpleasant to her as a matter of principle. His whole bearing reflected his feelings of antagonism.

He was tall and lean; blond and broad-shouldered. At forty, he was the youngest of the partners, a handsome man with a commanding presence. Jill also thought he felt superior to most of the human race.

'We've a lot of social and socio-medical problems on the practice,' he told her. 'I hope you're long on patience because they can be very time-consuming.'

'I think I am.'

At lunch time, Lois had brought them all home. They'd sat round the dining room table and the questioning had gone on.

Jill had had no appetite but anyway she hardly had time to eat. They were making her do most of the talking.

Did she take a moral stance over prescribing the pill to under-aged girls? And what about abortions? Had she given euthanasia any thought?

Just when she was beginning to relax, thinking the questioning over, Cuthbert Meadows said: 'You seem very confident. Is there nothing about general practice that makes you nervous? Nothing you fear?'

Jill took a deep breath. There were hundreds of things. The confidence was a protective veneer she'd had to adopt. It was easy to be confident about treating conditions she'd seen before but there were many things she hadn't yet met.

'I'm afraid of not asking the patient the right questions. Of missing signs. Of making mistakes. Of doing harm instead of good.'

Titch had smiled in his benign way and said: 'We're all afraid of that.'

But Miles Sutton sniggered. 'You'll do that sooner or later. Drop yourself in it. Almost a certainty.'

'Nonsense,' Lois retorted. 'Jill understands she has to be careful. We all need to be careful.'

The ferocity with which she glared at Miles made Jill guess that they'd had arguments about this before.

Miles said: 'Some you win and some you lose. You'll drive yourself into the ground if you think you can win them all.'

Jill knew she must have acquitted herself adequately because the terms on which she could join the partnership had then been outlined to her. Standard terms, what she had expected. She'd applied for her contract with the National Health Service.

Jill stirred and pushed her bedroom window further open. She wanted to catch more of the soft breeze coming off the river.

The moon was climbing higher in the dark sky, more light was sparkling on the water. It was brighter than the lights of Liverpool beyond.

That weekend visit here two months ago had awakened disturbing memories. She'd been worried about her father, and while he wasn't about she'd gone to the study to have a private word about him with Lois.

It was a large room. Lois was working at a pretty mahogany Carlton House desk in front of the window. It was pushed against another desk that her father used; bigger, workmanlike and of recent manufacture.

'Lois, is Dad all right?'

Lois's thin, elegant legs straightened and re-crossed themselves. 'Yes, why?'

'He doesn't look well. He's changed.'

'He's working too hard. He never lets up.'

'He says he's all right but I thought he looked ill.' She met Lois's sloe-black eyes.

'He had a hernia repaired last year, but he told you about that.'

She had known. She'd sent a get-well card to the hospital. Now she wished she'd done more.

'Some men do go to seed fairly early. I've told him it's time he retired.'

Jill thought Lois sounded unsympathetic. Worse, as though she knew she was wearing better and exulted in the fact.

'Surely it's more than that?'

The phone went, Lois reached across to answer it. Jill wanted to ask her if she would persuade Nat to have a check-up. She stood looking round.

This room, more than any other in the house, brought back ghosts of her childhood. Whatever it was that had frightened her had happened here. She'd no idea what it was, but it had involved Lois. It was a memory that wouldn't quite come. It was there, just like a word on the tip of her tongue that she couldn't quite recall.

She ran her hands across the red velvet of a Victorian armchair, one of a pair placed each side of the gas fire. One was dainty, designed to be used by ladies. The other was much larger, meant for gentlemen, with great wings to keep out the draughts of old houses.

Behind that, in the corner of the room, the sheen of a large copper urn drew her attention. It cast a glow across the carpet.

Inside was a pot containing a large plant. What had her father called it? Yes, an old-fashioned Japanese aspidistra. It must have been smaller all those years ago, but she'd thought of it as a tree. Now, its lush, broad leaves were touching the walls.

She could see her legs reflected in the urn's polished surface. Legs distorted by curves. They were slim now, in dark stockings and plain court shoes, but they triggered a vision of short, sturdy limbs encased in the scarlet woolly tights of childhood. Her own. She'd worn a kilt of red tartan too.

Jill bent down and looked underneath the leaves, at what she'd called her secret garden. A dark circle of root-riven soil. She felt a leaf tickle her chin, a feeling she remembered well. How many times had she squeezed herself into the corner behind the plant and played quietly with the tiny dolls that were meant to inhabit her dolls' house?

Often she'd creep in without her father knowing. Wanting to be near him. Unwilling to be parted when she knew he was home from work. She used to peep out at her father's shoulders bent over his work at the desk. Waiting for him to finish, and have time for her.

When she saw him lean back in his chair and stretch, she knew he was about to close his ledgers, and she would come out. Then he would smile at her and take her on his knee. Asking her how long she'd been there, and telling her she was a good girl to play quietly while he did his work.

Something made her put her hand down between the plant pot and the inside of the urn. Her fingers drew out a pipe cleaner twisted into the shape of a dog, now filthy, damp and disintegrating. Then she found, blackened with damp, a toy garden seat.

That brought memories in a rushing torrent, making her catch her breath.

It was a dark winter afternoon, and evening was drawing in. Her father sat at his desk with his back to her, the soft glow of the lamp

22

lighting up the papers he was working on. She'd grown tired of her games and had sunk back on the carpet behind the urn.

Jill heard the front door click shut. Lois's steps came across the hall. It was unusual for her to return home as early as this. The study door was thrown open, sending a cold draught across the floor.

'Nat. Such luck! You know how disappointed I was when we couldn't get tickets for Saturday?'

She could see Dad's face now; tired but lighting up with welcome as he turned to Lois.

'The ballet?'

'*Les Sylphides*. Janet Goodbody has managed to get four tickets for tonight. She wants us to make up a foursome. Have supper afterwards. Bill's booked a table at . . .'

Dad was suddenly frowning. 'What about Jill?' His voice was gentle but admonishing. 'Have you arranged a baby-sitter?'

Jill felt a stab of disappointment that Dad was going out again after all.

'Oh! No! Not yet.'

'Mrs Crookshank can't come. I've already asked her. That's why we decided the ballet wasn't possible.'

Mrs Crookshank cleaned up three mornings of the week. Jill liked her; she was plump and jolly, and usually came to stay with her when Dad went out. Mrs Tighe came in on alternate days and cooked dinner when Lois did evening surgery. She was thin and impatient.

'Mrs Tighe?' Lois's voice was more shrill.

'She isn't on the phone.'

'We can get Selma.'

'You might have asked before you left the surgery. There's only an hour before we'll need to leave.'

'No, not Selma. She's doing evening surgery and won't be able to leave there until seven. It'll have to be one of the other receptionists.'

Lois sat down at the desk and reached for the telephone directory. 'What's Paula's name? Hill?'

Jill heard her father sigh. 'You're asking her to drop everything and rush up here. She'll probably be cooking an evening meal now.'

'Yes, well, I don't often ask them to do anything for me.'

Jill could feel the tension between her parents tightening. She remembered sitting as quiet as a mouse, hardly daring to breathe.

'Damn. She's not answering the phone.'

'Lois, it's difficult to go out on the spur of the moment.'

'What a nuisance! I really wanted to see *Les Sylphides*.'

'You go with the Goodbodys. I'll stay here with Jill. I'm tired anyway. Could do with a quiet night.'

Jill remembered the jerk of pleasure that had given her. Dad was

23

choosing to stay with her rather than go out with Lois. He loved her more after all.

'Oh, for heaven's sake, Nat! I'll ring Esme Meadows. She won't mind if we drop Jill off for tonight. We can pick her up in the morning.'

'Jill's never stayed with her before. Not overnight. She might be scared in a strange place.'

'You coddle that child too much. I wish she'd grow up and get off our backs.'

'She can't grow up any faster than she's doing.'

'She stops us having any sort of life of our own. Any pleasures. We always have to stay home and look after her. She's always between us. It's not as though she's grateful for what I do. She hates me. I wish her mother had taken her with her on that plane.'

The years rolled away, Jill was back crouching in the corner behind the aspidistra, a child again in red woolly tights. She could feel her eyes prickling with silent tears and their salty wetness as they had rolled down her face. The awful feeling of not being wanted.

It hadn't come as a shock. She'd known what her stepmother thought of her for a long time, but this was the first time she'd heard it put into words.

'Lois, you know that isn't true. You're just tired and disappointed. She's a lovely little girl, easy to love if you'd just let yourself. I'd hoped you would by now.'

'How can I love her? You heard what she said, in front of the whole family. She made me feel guilty.'

Jill had crouched lower, not wanting to be seen. She knew exactly what Lois was referring to.

It had been just before Christmas, on one of the rare occasions when the family was gathered together. They were all having tea round the sitting room fire when Great-Grandmother Evelyn had said: 'Jillian, what would you like Father Christmas to bring you?'

She'd thought about it, then replied gravely, 'A mummy who loves me. A real mummy.'

She lived again through the shocked silence that followed, with four pairs of horrified eyes regarding her.

'Lois is your mummy.' Daddy had swept her up in his arms. 'You've got a real mummy, darling.' He'd laughed with embarrassment. 'Here is your mummy.'

She'd wanted to cling to him but he'd handed her over to Lois. She'd sat uncomfortably on the bony knees, Daddy's loving arms exchanged for Lois's cool grip. One hand on her back, the other on her knee holding her in position.

Jill knew she'd disgraced herself further by struggling to get down.

'Let her be,' Victoria had advised, and Jill had crawled behind an

24

armchair and sat apart, hugging her knees. Hurt as she always was that Daddy had aligned himself with Lois.

But there had been something worse. Much worse. Bad though this had been, it didn't account for the terror that she felt Lois had stirred up in her all those years ago.

She was quaking beside the copper urn when Lois put the phone down. Her stepmother's black eyes seemed to pin her down.

'Did you want something else?' she asked.

Jill felt the hairs on the back of her neck stand erect as she groped mentally for what exactly it was that had terrified her. It wouldn't come. There was just this awful, cold, crushing fear.

This was no childish phobia caused by fairy tales about wicked stepmothers. This was for real. She stared at Lois's cropped grey hair and flat masculine body. This was to do with Lois herself.

Jill rushed to the door as another wave of dread swept through her.

CHAPTER THREE

The day had come when she was to start work. This morning, her short honey-blonde hair was neat and shining. It curved towards her chin, almost straight, with a feathery fringe across her forehead. Her green eyes stared gravely back at her from her mirror.

The trouble with a style like this was that it made her look younger than she was. The rounded rosy cheeks didn't help either. She didn't look like a doctor. How could she expect older people to take seriously the advice she gave them when she looked positively adolescent?

When she'd first started general practice she got herself a pair of plain glass spectacles. Large, owlish ones that made her look more the part. But she'd found it impossible to manage a fashion accessory when she was putting her mind to medical problems. She had to concentrate on those.

She bought herself executive clothes and they helped. No short skirts, but no ultra-long ones either. No fashion statements; middle-of-the-road classic styling and good-quality cloth.

Jill put on a new blue cotton dress; high at the neck with elbow-length sleeves, the dress of a professional woman. She wanted to look the part.

At breakfast Lois said briskly: 'You'd better follow me down to the surgery. Or can you remember the way?'

Jill wanted to be on the safe side. 'I'll follow you.'

This was Dr Goodbody's last day at work, and she had arranged to sit in with him for a few hours this morning. There was a host of things she needed to ask about: the patients he was handing over, which consultants he referred on to, and such like.

Her stepmother's Rover was travelling at a good pace, and in the heavy traffic she had trouble keeping up. It took only ten or fifteen minutes, but the change from the comfortable detached houses around Prenton Golf Course to the surgery was dramatic.

It was near the edge of the Tranmere Hall Estate, which was the subject of a slum clearance scheme. New houses were being erected on it now and it seemed to be nothing more than a huge building site.

The surgery premises were in a gaunt Victorian semi-detached house of smoke-blackened brick, just outside the redevelopment area. Some time ago, the front wall and gate had been removed, and what had been a small garden had been tarmacadamed to provide parking space. It now had several pot-holes in it. An extension of raw-looking pink brick had been erected along the side.

The house to which it was attached looked even shabbier. It had been divided into flatlets.

The houses in the next road had already been demolished, and the grey mortar dust was trod into the surgery at every session.

Jill eyed the brass plate alongside the open front door. It listed Dr William Goodbody, Dr Cuthbert Meadows, Dr Lois Benbow and Dr Miles Sutton. It brought her a feeling of satisfaction to think that soon her name would appear on it.

'What a good job I've always practised under my maiden name,' Jill knew that Lois had noticed her glance. 'Better if we don't appear to be related. More professional this way.'

Jill peered into the dark waiting room as she went in. It was filling with patients.

A family doctor had been practising from these premises since the turn of the century, but in those days he'd also lived here. The waiting room had been his dining room too; the old oak dining table still stood in the middle, now covered with several piles of well-thumbed copies of *Woman's Own*.

The receptionist's office had been recently partitioned off. The fluorescent light was bright and harsh on the other side of the hatch. Even so, the receptionist seemed glamorous, with lots of dark curly hair.

'Hello.' She smiled a welcome to Jill. 'I'm Selma.'

Lois pushed forward. Her tone was cold.

'What have you got for me this morning?'

'These are yours.' Selma pushed a pile of patients' records towards her.

'I'll start straight away. Send the first in. I'll leave you to it, Jill.' Without another glance, Lois shot off towards her surgery in the new extension.

Through the hatch, Jill saw Goodbody emerging from amongst the filing cabinets. He came out offering a wrinkled hand for her to shake.

'Last day,' he exulted. 'Give us ten minutes, Selma, before we start.'

His face was crazed with lines and folds, and even at nine o'clock in the morning he had a five o'clock shadow. But his eyes were alert and kindly and his manner brisk.

'This is my surgery.' He ushered her in, and Jill looked round the room with covetous eyes. Once it had been the house's main sitting room; it was large, the ceiling high and ornamented with scrolls and ribbons in relief plasterwork. It was cool even on this midsummer morning.

28

Goodbody had started to clear out his personal belongings. Back numbers of *Pulse* and *General Practitioner* were crowding his desk.

'You don't want to keep these medical comics?' He swept them off and stacked them neatly in a corner where dusty piles of the *Lancet* and *Mims* were building up on the floor.

Now the big desk was cleared of its bric-à-brac, Jill imagined herself behind it. He seemed to read her thoughts.

'Miles Sutton doesn't like being upstairs. He has his eye on this room.' He smiled, showing sparse and yellow teeth.

'It won't be mine then? I thought . . .'

'It's the best room here. Titch won't let him have it, of course. The pecking order, my dear. There'll be a general shuffle round as soon as I'm out of the door. I'm afraid you might be the one to go upstairs.'

She tried to ignore the stab of disappointment. After all, what difference did it make which room she had?

They talked, and Jill elected to stay with him while he did his surgery. He told her about the patients, introduced them to her and then left her to get on with the consultation. She'd half expected that he would. He continued to clear out cupboards and drawers.

'You'll find this useful, I'm sure,' he said from time to time, as he pushed books, equipment and drugs over to her.

Two large cardboard boxes were filling up. One with torn paper and general rubbish. The other with ball-point pens, memo pads, mats, and penholders, all free handouts from the drug companies advertising their various wares.

When the waiting room had been emptied of patients, Goodbody took her to the kitchen for a cup of coffee. Miles Sutton was already sitting at the table puffing out clouds of smoke. There was a packet of Rothmans in front of him with a gold lighter on top.

'Sorry about this,' he said sourly. 'I expect you disapprove as much as the others, but I can't give it up.'

Jill hadn't taken to him when she'd met him at her interview. He was doing nothing to endear himself now. His handsome grey eyes raked her disdainfully.

'So you decided to join the circus? Hope you find it as rewarding as you expect.' Jill tried to ignore the sneer.

At her interview, she'd said: 'Once I'm qualified, I want a job I can get my teeth into. I'm keen to start work. Settle down in a practice. I want to work hard and do the best I can for my patients.'

Miles Sutton had pressed her and she'd said more, rather too much, perhaps. About questioning everything and reading meticulously to keep herself up to date.

Miles's pale supercilious eyes raked her again. 'You came over as a bit of a prig. Too much idealism and humanity.'

That made her gasp. Was she over-keen?

'What do you expect to get out of this?'

'A fulfilling career.'

He laughed cynically. 'Not here. You're at everybody's beck and call. They expect you to turn out in the middle of the night and they're not our sort at all, mostly class four and five.'

She thought him an unbearable snob. 'Aren't they the easiest to deal with? The working classes, the salt of the earth?'

'Working classes, that's a laugh. Actually, there's a growing underclass here, and they're all with this practice. A new classification of six. All on the social and intending to stay that way. There's a lot of drawbacks here and you won't earn any fortune.'

Jill turned to him and stabbed: 'What keeps you here then?'

Lois had told her: 'He wanted a friend of his to join the practice, but Titch and I had to put our feet down about that. The fellow was not at all the right sort. He'd been with three different practices in so many years, that's never a good sign. Miles can be a bit difficult, we certainly don't want another like him.'

'You don't like Miles?'

'The patients don't either.'

Jill thought she knew now why she'd been asked to join the practice. Lois hadn't wanted her for her own sake, but as her stepdaughter, and newly qualified, she was less likely to cause trouble for them. Titch and Lois had wanted to get their candidate in to block Miles's.

She got up and rinsed her cup at the sink. She was free to go home now for a few hours. First, she drove into town and walked down Grange Road to W. H. Smith to get herself a street atlas. Goodbody had offered her his, but the pages were loose and it was twenty years out of date.

Jill had made up her mind to ask Gran about Phoebe, in the hope that she would be more forthcoming. When she got back home, the old lady was still in her bedroom, but up and dressed.

'You can help me downstairs,' she said, but what Jill wanted was for Gran to get out all her old photographs and talk about the days gone by.

Phoebe was still on Jill's mind. The more she thought about her, the more intrigued she was.

Lois arrived home for lunch shortly afterwards, and they all ate a salad at the kitchen table with Mrs Moon.

Jill was steeling herself to tackle her grandmother as soon as Lois set out on her afternoon visits, but once in an easy chair in the sitting room, Gran disappeared behind a newspaper and Jill could hear little snores. Her arm was painful and the medication was making her drowsy. Sleep was probably the best thing for her.

A tea party had been arranged for three thirty to mark Dr Goodbody's retirement. Jill had been invited, and then at five she would take over evening surgery in his stead. Gran had been invited too, but after her fall, Lois insisted she spend the afternoon resting quietly at home. She woke up and decided to go into the garden in the shade of an old chestnut tree. Jill took out a garden chair for her but by then it was too late for a serious talk.

The Mini was hot and stuffy. Jill opened the windows as wide as she could. She wanted to arrive feeling bandbox fresh, not wilting.

Traffic was still heavy, but it was all going along Borough Road at a good pace. Jill's mind was on Phoebe again when suddenly, somewhere ahead, she could hear tyres screaming to a standstill. There was a deafening crash as metal tore apart. Instantly, brake lights were going red in front. She jammed on her own brakes and the Mini juddered to a halt.

A road traffic accident! And not very far ahead. Jill felt a trickle of perspiration run down her back. The Mini was sticky on hot days like this, but it was a nervous reaction too. She got out but could see nothing. When she stood on the door frame she could see a car slewed into the approaching traffic.

She reached for her bag in the passenger's footwell. She'd discovered it was rare for anything frightening to walk into a surgery, but an emergency like this still brought an unaccountable jerk of anxiety, because she didn't know what she'd have to deal with. It had taken years of self-discipline to get a grip on her own emotions. She'd had to do that, because she needed her wits about her before she treated a patient.

As she ran up the line of stationary cars, she could hear raised voices, harsh with shock, and screams of panic.

'Came straight for me, she did. There was nothing I could do.' The man was excited, red in the face and throwing his arms about. 'She slewed across to my side of the road and rammed me.'

Fortunately, she'd hit the rear door of his car. He was unharmed.

Jill looked at the car that had spun out of control. The window was open and the driver was screaming. She seemed to be covered with blood, and the whole side of the car was badly dented.

'We've phoned for an ambulance,' somebody told her. 'It's on its way.'

A burly man was trying to wrench open the car door but it was proving difficult. At last the lock gave, and the door swung open.

The driver, a young girl, almost fell into Jill's arms. She was streaming with blood, but was mobile and able to breathe.

Jill helped her to stagger as far as the pavement before she went down. Within moments there was blood everywhere; Jill was standing in it and could smell the hot, sticky odour. She wiped enough off the girl's face to confirm that it was a nose bleed. The driver had apparently banged her nose against the steering wheel; there was a tiny abrasion in the skin.

The damage was much less than Jill had at first assumed, though the girl would probably have a whiplash injury to her neck too. She made the patient lie back, and was ripping open dressings from her bag to absorb the flow when she caught the flash of a camera from the corner of her eye. It brought a feeling of outrage. She was used to treating patients in the privacy of a surgery.

'You're not taking photographs of this? An accident? Rotten bad taste.'

The first thing she noticed about the photographer was his agility. He moved from one side to the other, his camera clicking, letting off flashes. He seemed very supple, bending low, changing the viewpoint. Making sure he missed nothing. Jill felt a surge of annoyance.

'It's a bit ghoulish, isn't it? Not everyone wants to be caught *in extremis*.' The poor girl looked terrible but already she was losing less blood. She needed no other immediate treatment.

Jill saw another flash and knew he'd taken her picture too. 'Stop it,' she insisted, in tones that reminded her of Lois.

'Press,' he muttered, clicking away. 'Don't worry, all my pictures are tasteful.'

Jill was relieved to hear the ambulance arrive and see the onlookers part to let the paramedics through. She stood up, glad to relinquish her patient.

The man was at her elbow. 'I'm Felix Kingsley.'

She wished he would go away, but he grinned at her as he closed the shutter on his camera and swung it over his shoulder. He looked about thirty. Brown wavy hair, an overgrown schoolboy's face. Attractive.

'Yes,' she said shortly. 'Press photographer.'

'Journalist, actually. But I have to be both. Keeps the expenses down.'

Jill closed the bag, half interested in spite of herself. '*Birkenhead News?*'

'I'll offer this to them, but I'm freelance. Are you the new doctor?'

'Do you know all the doctors here?' Jill knew she sounded shorter than she'd meant to.

'I'm on my way to do a piece about Dr Goodbody's retirement. Nearly fifty years as a doctor. Stands to reason, if he's leaving, somebody will have to take his place.'

'You're right. I'm going to.'

'Dr Jillian Ridley, I presume?' He offered his hand in a theatrical gesture that irritated her anew.

'You do your homework, I have to admit that.'

'Come on, what's wrong with a picture of you coping with an

accident victim? A good way to introduce you to your patients.' He was beaming at her. 'Show you staying cool in an emergency. Giving first aid. Saving a poor girl from bleeding to death. Dramatic stuff anyway.'

Jill wanted to laugh. 'She was having a nose bleed. If you'd had a pad of cotton wool I'm sure you'd have managed just as well.'

'Is that all it was?' He was laughing too. 'Then you should have taken care not to get all that gore down the front of your dress.'

Jill gasped as she saw the extent of the stain on her smart blue dress. It was all down her skirt. She fingered it. It was sticky and stiffening as it dried.

The traffic was beginning to move. She ran back to her car. By the time she reached the surgery, there were so many cars outside she had to park her Mini in the road. Once inside, she ran upstairs to the bathroom to sponge the blood off her dress. She got the stain out, but it left a dark patch, clinging damply to her knees.

There were a lot of people standing about in the kitchen when she went down. Selma was pouring tea. She glanced up at Jill, and her hand wavered, filling the saucer.

'What on earth have you done to your dress?'

'Had to sponge it down. Should be all right when it dries,' Jill said self-consciously. Selma had changed into a smarter outfit since morning surgery and she was wearing scarlet slingbacks with four-inch heels. She looked more like a model than a receptionist.

She laughed. 'I used to baby-sit you when you were little. Did you know?'

'Really?'

'Don't you remember me?'

Jill studied the perfect features, the well-cared-for complexion, the beautifully manicured scarlet fingernails. She didn't. The awful blanks could be embarrassing in situations like this.

'How old would I have been?'

'I came off and on for years. Up until you went away to school.'

'I was eight then. I should remember you.' She had no recollection of ever being left with this woman. Selma stirred her interest. Here was an outsider who could tell her things about her past.

From a psychiatric standpoint she wouldn't advise a patient to probe, but it was different for her. She felt strong enough to cope with what might come out. All right, she had strange and unaccountable anxieties when she was near Lois. She wanted to know why.

She had other irrational episodes of fear too. She'd tried to talk about them to her fellow students. They'd laughed and admitted to panic attacks too, but Jill knew hers were different.

'I never thought you'd grow up to be a doctor.' Selma's brown eyes sparkled with life.

'Why not?'

She was shaking her head. 'Come and meet everybody.'

Jill was disappointed that she wasn't going to tell her. She sipped her tea while Selma introduced the three part-time receptionists. She made herself concentrate so she'd remember their names. Polly was red-haired, Marina dark and Edith middle-aged.

She'd just finished telling them about the accident and the blood on her dress when she heard Lois come up behind her to look at the table.

'What an inviting spread. Who are we to thank for all this work?' The patronising note in her voice grated on Jill.

'Selma mostly,' Polly told her. 'She organised it.'

'You all helped,' Selma laughed, tossing back her shoulder-length curls. 'We each made a cake. Whatever sort we're best at. I made the chocolate one.'

It was the biggest on the table and had pride of place on a board covered with silver paper. With a lot of hilarity, Goodbody was cutting it into generous slices. The legend on the top read: 'Happy Retirement Dr Goodbody'.

'Have some, Lois?' He put a slice on a plate for her. Lois's sloe-black eyes stared dubiously at it.

'I think I'd prefer a little of the plain sponge.' There was a piece already cut of that. Lois sliced it in two and slid half on to her plate. 'I do envy you all, having the time and energy to bake cakes. And being able to eat so much chocolate.'

Jill thought she pretended an aversion to chocolate because Dad made it. She said: 'The chocolate cake's delicious, Mother.'

'The sponge is lovely too.' Lois munched condescendingly. 'I'll have a cup of tea, Selma, when you're ready.'

Jill wanted to curl up again at the way her stepmother was treating Selma.

Lois turned to Dr Goodbody. 'The girls have certainly done you proud, Bill.'

'We wanted to give him a bit of a send-off,' Selma said through clenched teeth. Under her breath, Jill heard her add: 'Cat.'

She wanted to giggle, it seemed there was no love lost between Lois and Selma.

People were still coming in, and Jill said: 'You must tell me who everybody is.'

'You know the wives?' Selma indicated two grey-haired ladies in the passageway.

'No. Well, I've heard Victoria speak of them.'

Selma led her over to be introduced. 'Janet Goodbody and Esme Meadows.'

34

'Qualified now? Seems only yesterday you were a girl at school.' Mrs Goodbody had the beginnings of a dowager's hump and looked rather frail.

'Lovely to see you back here,' said Esme Meadows.

'Bill is so pleased. To have another member of the family in the practice.'

'We see ourselves as one big family.' Esme was much younger than Janet Goodbody. Shapeless and rather plain. Jill felt they were making a fuss of her. Both were tucking in to chocolate cake and praising it.

She'd been conscious of Felix Kingsley's presence from the moment she came downstairs, but she deliberately stayed away from him. She told herself she must take the opportunity of meeting the people with whom she was going to work.

She saw his camera flashing at Bill Goodbody, and when his colleagues were invited into the background, she crowded in with them.

His eyes kept meeting hers across the room. Holding her gaze longer than a chance acquaintance normally would. He was showing an interest beyond that of normal friendliness. It stirred something within her, and she was interested in spite of herself.

She went to get herself another piece of cake and found him at her elbow. 'How about coming for a drink afterwards?' he suggested softly.

'I'm doing evening surgery tonight.'

'After that?'

'I can't. My grandmother's not well and she's at home alone.'

She didn't want to. Tonight, her parents were taking the Goodbodys and the Meadowses to a restaurant. She wanted to talk to Gran without interruption.

His face registered disappointment. It made her add: 'Some other time, perhaps?'

'All right.'

Goodbody was holding forth, bemused at the thought of retiring.

'Seen a lot of changes in my time, I can tell you. We can do so much more now. I don't suppose you'll believe me,' he looked Jill in the eye, 'when I tell you that the best we could do when I first qualified was to make the patient comfortable and give sympathy to the relatives.'

Jill smiled; she was not unfamiliar with the history of general practice.

'Ninety per cent of our patients got better whether we treated them or not.' The old man beamed round at them. 'Two per cent died whatever we did. That left eight per cent on whom to practise our skills. We visited two or three times a day when they were very ill, but it was in the lap of the gods whether they got better or not.'

'Everything's changing,' Titch Meadows agreed. 'For the better, too.'

'So many diseases conquered. No more fevers. Diptheria was a real killer, terrible mortality some years. And no more TB. Now there are so many drugs that really work, I can hardly keep up with them.'

'Don't forget the operations on the kitchen table. Tonsils and all that.'

'You should have given up ages ago, Bill,' Miles Sutton said sourly. 'You could have enjoyed years of retirement instead of hanging on here. It's ridiculous working at your age.'

'I've enjoyed it.'

'Not that you've done all that much recently. You've been winding down. And really, we need younger doctors here who will put their backs into it.'

Jill found that his disdainful eyes had settled on her.

'By the way, you're having my consulting room, but I haven't cleared my things out yet.'

'Who's having Bill's old room?'

'Your mother's putting up a fight. She thinks she has the right to the best of everything.'

'Not Titch? Isn't he considered the most senior now?'

'I wouldn't mind it myself.'

'So it'll be a fight to the death?'

'No, not worth fighting for a thing like that. I'm going to tell your mother that I'll back down if she will. You can use it tonight, as a treat.'

A midwife came up and introduced herself, she was a bit of a gossip.

'Selma's a card, isn't she? Looks wonderful. Her husband was killed in a road accident a few years ago. She's over it now, thank goodness, and out to enjoy herself again. She loves parties of any sort.'

She went off to get more tea. Late-comers were clattering up the hall.

'This is Miles Sutton's family,' Selma was whispering.

Unaccountably, a silence fell on the room. Jill thought she saw Lois shiver. The atmosphere seemed to cool. She could almost feel the antagonism between the Suttons and the other partners.

Behind her hand, Selma whispered: 'His wife, Rosalie, thinks she's slumming when she comes down to the surgery. Doesn't often.'

Rosalie was dazzlingly attractive. Jill's eyes went first to her hair. It was several shades lighter than her own. Golden and shining, a real blonde. She had the very fair, translucent skin that often went with it. It made Jill envious.

But Rosalie also had a few faint lines round her eyes, so she'd be in her mid-thirties at least. It was not the sort of skin that lasted well. She was stylishly dressed in cream cotton.

'I saw that dress featured in last month's *Vogue*,' Selma went on. 'It's quite something, isn't it?'

Rosalie glanced slowly around the room in a manner that was downright contemptuous. Jill thought her eyes were strange. They were a very pale china blue.

'Sorry I'm late, Bill.' Rosalie had a plummy voice. 'Had to pick the girls up from school first.'

The two little girls wore the smart uniform of a private school. One of the receptionists urged them to the table, where they very politely helped themselves to one small piece of cake each.

'What a mess they're making outside,' Rosalie went on. 'Knocking everything down. It's like a desert. You can see the demolition dust being tramped in here.

'But they've got rid of some dreadful rat-infested housing,' Titch said. 'Needed doing. You can see the new ones going up. Proper bathrooms and decent heating.'

'We'll see an improvement in general health in this area,' Bill agreed. 'The new tenants love them. It'll make a big difference.'

'Really?' Rosalie asked, and then attached herself to Miles. They chatted and fussed over their children, staying aloof from the crowd. The other doctors seemed to be keeping their distance. Jill decided that Rosalie was no more popular than her husband.

When Miles was called to the phone and his wife was left to stare around the room, Jill went over to introduce herself.

'Sad to see Bill Goodbody retire,' Rosalie said. 'The place won't seem the same without him.'

Nearer to, Jill could see that Rosalie had very definite lines of discontent round her mouth. She started on again about the desolation round the surgery.

Jill's father came in then, to pump Bill's hand and to wink at Jill.

'We'd given you up, Nat,' Lois greeted him sourly. 'You're very late. And you've come smelling of chocolate.'

Selma laughed. 'You smell lovely, Nat. Don't let anybody tell you otherwise.'

'Got a bit held up, Lois, but you knew I wouldn't miss Bill's send-off.'

It was Selma who led him to the kitchen table. Jill heard him say, 'I hope I'm not too late for some of your chocolate cake?'

She couldn't stop her eyes searching for Felix in the crowd. He'd approached Lois, drawn her away from the others and was talking earnestly to her. Jill thought he had the sort of mouth that seemed always on the point of breaking into a smile, as though he found pleasure everywhere.

In the kitchen, the part-timers were beginning to pack what remained of the cake into tins and start on the washing-up.

Suddenly she heard Lois's voice loud and clear above the hum of conversation.

'Get off my back. Don't come here again prying into what doesn't concern you.'

Another sudden silence descended on the gathering. Jill felt electrified. Everybody seemed to hold their breath at the aggression in her voice as she shouted at Felix.

'You can tell him to get off my list. I'll refuse to see him again.'

'The trouble with you doctors,' Felix's voice was more controlled, 'is that you all think you can walk on water. Why shouldn't you be accountable for what you do? You're not gods, you know.'

That broke the tea party up. Guests hurried to leave the waiting room, calling their good wishes to Bill.

It was almost five and the first patients were peering round the front door. Selma went to deal with them.

'Time to move on,' Titch's voice carried through the premises now. Jill watched him take a couple of bottles of champagne from the fridge and usher Lois before him down the hall.

'Come to our place first,' Esme Meadows said, as the partners swept Bill Goodbody outside too. 'Goodbye, everyone.'

Jill watched Miles grind his cigarette into an ashtray. His eyebrows had lifted.

'Doesn't do to get on the wrong side of your mother, does it?' His voice told her he knew he was already in that position. 'Back to the grindstone for us.'

Here we go, Jill thought. It seemed that relationships in the practice were less harmonious than she'd first thought. And some of the patients weren't too happy either.

CHAPTER FOUR

Jill knew the job would be hard to start with. Every patient was a stranger and she had to get to know their problems. Even when sending patients for X-rays and routine blood tests she had to stop and think, because she didn't know the local routines.

Selma had helpfully drawn up a page of information she would need, together with useful phone numbers.

She drove home feeling more relaxed now that her first day was behind her. She was going to ask Gran about Phoebe and she hoped she'd get the full story this time.

As she let herself in, the house seemed too quiet, as though there was no one in, but the dining room table had been set for two people. She was afraid Gran had gone up to bed and she'd lost her chance.

She found her in the sitting room, fast asleep with an empty sherry glass beside her.

'Gran? I'm home. You haven't dozed off, have you?'

'No,' the old lady mumbled, and resumed her deep, even breathing.

Jill went into the kitchen. A note from Mrs Moon told her she had left two portions of casserole to heat up in the microwave. Scrubbed potatoes stood beside it ready to be baked, together with a covered bowl of garden spinach already seasoned and anointed with a knob of butter.

Jill started cooking according to the instructions in the note. She could appreciate the domestic arrangements at Links View now. They took all the hassle out of cooking a meal.

A half-empty bottle of red wine had been recorked and stood on the work surface. She poured herself a glass and went back to see Gran; she hadn't moved.

'Gran, wake up.' The deep breathing ceased, heavy-lidded eyes tried to open, and failed.

'Come on, Gran. It's supper time. Aren't you hungry?' Jill watched her pull herself up on the chair with her one good hand.

'Yes, I could eat something. I've been waiting for you.'

Jill made all speed to put supper on the table. When Gran tried to get to her feet, she seemed so shaky she had to help her. They started to eat, but she could see Gran was having difficulty.

39

'Shall I cut your meat up for you?'

'I feel so silly . . . I can't use my knife.'

'Not silly. Here, let me do it.'

The meat was soft because it had been casseroled. Jill scraped the potato out of its jacket and mashed it up for her too. Gran was more helpless than she'd expected.

As soon as Gran had cleared her plate Jill saw her half stifle a yawn. She refused the apple pie.

Jill said: 'I'll put the pots in the dishwasher and make us some coffee.'

'Malted milk for me, please, or I'll never sleep.'

'Right. Do you want to go up to bed? I'll bring it up to you in five minutes.'

'You'll have to help me.'

'Of course.' She'd forgotten Gran couldn't undo her buttons with one hand. She had to help her up the stairs too, because the banister was on the wrong side.

It wasn't just the few buttons on her dress. There were her suspenders, too, and a row of complicated hooks on her corsets. It was a long-drawn-out procedure, with the old wrinkled face showing embarrassment. At last Jill was helping the plaster cast through the armhole of a satin nightdress and readjusting the sling round Gran's neck to support its weight.

Gran insisted that she could wash her face and get into bed by herself. Jill raced downstairs, afraid she'd find her asleep again if she didn't hurry.

She got out the bed tray with legs that Gran used every morning for breakfast. She made the drinks. From the dining room she fetched the grapes that Lois had bought for her mother. The silver dish was piled high with both green and black, and furnished with silver scissors. She added the large box of chocolates she'd found on a shelf in the kitchen. Once there had been boxes of them all over the house. These were what Dad made. Lastly she took from her pocket Gran's spectacles in their red leather case.

Gran was sitting up in bed with a book before her, looking relaxed and drowsy. Jill set the bed tray carefully over her legs.

'You've had my specs repaired for me? That was thoughtful of you, dear.'

'They've put your bifocal lenses in a new frame.' Jill felt a niggle of guilt as she pulled up a chair to sit by the bed. She'd deliberately put off giving them to her until this moment.

Gran put them on. 'Much better for reading. They're almost new.' Jill put the discarded ones in the case.

'Shall I put these away for you?' She opened the bedside drawer. 'This is where I got them from, isn't it?'

40

She knew very well it was. This was her way of leading up to the subject she wanted to talk about.

'I noticed you have some photographs of the family here.' Jill brought out three or four black-and-white prints that had been taken in harsh tropical sun. Every detail was sharply distinct.

'Let me see.' Gran put out her hand. 'These were taken in Nigeria. Seems another life now.' She sighed.

'Grandfather worked there, didn't he?' Jill prompted.

'For most of his life. He was running the hospital before we were married. A mission hospital, miles from any town. Upcountry in the bush.'

'You have happy memories of Nigeria?'

'Sad ones too.' Gran seemed to go off in a daydream. Jill had to prompt her again.

'This is my grandfather, isn't it?' She put a photo into Gran's hand. The old lady seemed more awake now. Jill thought nostalgia a powerful force.

'Yes, in front of the hospital. With some of the staff. This was taken before we were married.'

All the men wore white coats over shorts and knee-length socks. They were standing on the veranda of a large building with a steep roof of corrugated iron.

'Poor Clive, he died very young. Only sixty. I still miss him.'

Jill knew he'd died suddenly of a heart attack not long after returning to England. Her grandmother had been alone ever since. She'd worked on for many more years.

'I was glad then I had a career of my own.'

'Gran, I think it's wonderful that there were three generations of women doctors before me in the family.'

Her grandmother was more interested in the photographs. 'This is more recent. Just after the last war it would be. You'll know some of the others here. They're in the practice with Lois now. Better to have partners you trust.'

Jill's eyes went along the row of men in white coats. She recognised Bill Goodbody's head, balding even then, and Cuthbert Meadow's height and bulk, but the third man was a stranger.

It wasn't these people who interested Jill, though. Her fingers were feeling inside the drawer again, searching for the photographs of Phoebe. This was what she'd been aiming to do all along.

She found one of Lois holding the baby and held it out for Gran to see. These photos had been taken some years later, in England. The light was softer.

Gran's face seemed to freeze. The hand that had reached so readily for the other snaps didn't move.

'I never knew I had a stepsister. Not until I saw this last night.'

41

Gran seemed confused. 'Stepsister?' Her gaze wavered, she was shaking her head.

'Lois's baby. She was my stepsister, wasn't she?'

'Yes, I suppose so.'

'Won't you tell me about her?'

'Not much to tell.' Gran was trying to cut grapes off the bunch. Jill reached out and did it for her.

'Nobody wants to talk about Phoebe, and I don't understand why.'

'Such a long time ago. Haven't thought about her for years.' Gran's manner told her this wasn't true. The old lady was suddenly stiff with tension. 'Phoebe died when she was a few months old.'

'But I'd like to know more. About how . . .'

'You're very curious.' Gran's dark eyes stared back at her warily.

'Naturally, I'm interested. What's wrong with that?'

Gran snapped out: 'The less you know about that child the better.'

Jill blinked. 'Gran, I'm grown up now. Why shouldn't I know all the circumstances. What is there to hide?'

Gran closed her eyes and shuddered. There was a grimace of fear on the old lined face. In spite of herself, Jill shivered too.

'Poor Lois, she's got to be protected.' Gran's voice was little more than a whisper.

Jill felt as though she was choking. Gran was almost tearful as she murmured, 'A terrible thing to happen.'

Then she seemed to pull herself together. 'I want to go to sleep now. Please go, and take this tray with you.'

'Sorry, Gran.' Jill bent to kiss the withered cheek and found the dark eyes full of suppressed fear.

Slowly, then, Jill collected up the old photographs and slid them back into the drawer. She lifted the bed tray and took it downstairs. When she cleared it in the kitchen, she discovered one dog-eared photograph hidden beneath the plate of grapes.

Someone had written on the back: 'Lois with Bill Goodbody, Cuthbert Meadows and Tom Sinclair'. They all wore white coats; all were smiling into the camera with eyes screwed up against the harsh African sun. She slid the picture into her pocket, marvelling that all but Tom Sinclair were still working together.

She'd hardly been able to believe her ears when Gran had said: 'Poor Lois she's got to be protected.' In her opinion, if anyone could look after herself it was Lois. Hadn't she seen her the other day bullying that Asian houseman?

How could frail, vulnerable Gran expect to protect Lois? The answer came easily. By keeping her mouth shut about Phoebe. It confirmed Jill's first instincts that there was much more to baby

Phoebe's death than she was being told. She felt more intrigued about her family than ever.

Victoria lay motionless until her bedroom door clicked shut. Then listened to Jill's footsteps descending the stairs.

When the sound had faded, she took a deep, shuddering breath and covered her mouth with her hand. She'd tried to warn Lois about letting Jill come back to live here.

Lois had said: 'Nat wants it. I can't refuse outright. Not without giving some reason.'

'Then make it clear to the girl that you expect it to be temporary. It's dangerous to let her stay.'

But Victoria knew she hadn't. Lois was afraid Nat might start asking questions.

And now she herself had done a very silly thing. Talked when she would have been wiser to keep silent. Allowed herself to lose her composure when confronted with a picture of Lois holding her baby girl. Jill must have noticed her strange behaviour.

Losing Clive at such a young age had not been the only tragedy in Victoria's life. She looked at the photo of him she still held, wishing he were here with her now.

She could no longer think quickly; she was a helpless old woman, and the past seemed suddenly more real than the present.

She pulled herself slowly up the bed. Poured herself a glass of water and swallowed the two tablets Jill had left out for her on the bedside table. She was tired and her defences had been down. She couldn't help wondering if the little minx had deliberately led her into that. And worse, she'd only just avoided falling further into the trap.

Jill had certainly seemed very curious about things that didn't concern her.

The next morning at the surgery, Jill watched Selma sorting packets of patients' records into four piles. It was routine for the partners to gather in the office before starting work.

They caught up with any gossip, found out if anything of note had happened during the night, and collected messages from Selma.

'We've had a bit of a swap-round,' Lois told her. 'You'll be using Miles's consulting rooms upstairs.'

'What's the matter with it?' Jill whispered to Selma. She'd peeped into it last night and it seemed better than those in the new extension.

'It takes the patients ages to get up the stairs, especially those with chest problems. Drags out the time it takes to do a surgery.'

'Better send the first one up right after me,' Jill told her.

The room was above Dr Goodbody's at the front, and was almost as large. The atmosphere was heavy with the scent of air freshener which didn't quite mask the cloying smell of Miles's cigarette smoke. She struggled to open the window that worked on an ancient system of sash cords.

Miles had made a token effort to collect up some of his belongings, but most remained. His desk drawers were full of letters he'd never filed, and medical magazines still tightly folded in their wrappers.

She found that Selma was right. Quite a lot of time was wasted waiting for the next patient to climb the stairs. She decided she could get over that by putting a couple of chairs on the landing and getting Selma to send them up sooner.

She wrote out a notice while she waited: 'Patients please wait here until called in.' She'd bring up a few magazines later.

Her pile of records seemed slow to go down. She knew that morning surgery was over for her partners. There had been flushings from the bathroom and much running up and down stairs. She heard the welcome chink of coffee cups rising up the stairwell.

This morning's patients had all been routine, with nothing she couldn't handle. She felt she was easing herself into the new job.

She was writing up her notes on the last patient when Selma put her head round the door.

'Will you see Felix Kingsley? He's asking if he can have a word with you.'

Jill felt the blood rush to her cheeks.

'Surprise, surprise, eh?' Selma laughed. 'Didn't expect him to darken these doors again. Not after the hassle Lois was giving him yesterday.'

'Since he has, you'd better send him up.' Jill knew she'd not been very polite to him yesterday. Seconds later she heard him bounding up the stairs.

'Come in,' she called before he had time to knock. He was beaming at her, radiating vitality and enthusiasm.

'Hello. My goodness, you look very professional.'

'Have a seat.'

'Those photos I took yesterday. I've brought them to show you. If you don't like them, if they interfere with the persona you want to project to your patients, then I won't offer them for publication.' He was opening his attaché case.

'This one, I thought.'

He pushed it across the desk to her. It was of herself at the accident. There was enough background to see that, but almost nothing of the poor girl having the nose bleed. Certainly not enough for her to be recognised, because she'd been holding a large pad of cotton wool over her face.

'You won't mind seeing that in the *News*?'

'Of course not.' In fact, it was quite a flattering picture of herself.

44

She felt that she shouldn't have made such a fuss at the time.

'This is what I plan to say about you. Go on, read it. It's a weekly paper, and comes out tomorrow, but I'll have time to change anything you don't like. I don't want to upset you.'

Jill hesitated. 'You must think I'm easily upset . . .'

'Doctors are different from the rest of us. Can be a bit sensitive.'

'We don't all think we're God, she told him, 'if that's what you mean.'

'I'm sorry. You must have thought me abominably rude yesterday to Dr Benbow. Let me explain. It's like this . . .'

'Don't tell me. I'd rather not know.'

He laughed. 'All right.' He was thumbing through the papers he'd brought. 'Dr Goodbody isn't here any more, or I'd show him the article about him too.'

'Do you always do this? Let people read what you say about them before it's published?'

'Sometimes – when I'm on my best behaviour.'

'You've been very complimentary. To both of us.'

'No reason to be otherwise. You didn't have to run to help that girl. And Goodbody's popular with his patients. The public needs to know the good things about its doctors.'

'As well as the bad?'

'Sorry . . .' There was something impish about his grin.

'Thank you for showing these to me. There's nothing I'd want to see changed.'

'There's something else.'

'Yes?'

'I'd take it as a great favour if you'd come out for a meal with me one evening. Any night you're free over the next month would be all right. But the sooner the better.'

She laughed. She liked his tongue-in-cheek manner. He was telling her he wanted to see more of her and was prepared to wait until he could. What else could she say but yes, and thank you?

'Tonight?' Again the wide, attractive smile.

'I've an evening surgery again and it's hard to say what time it'll finish. Tomorrow would be better.'

'Tomorrow it is, then.' His eyes danced with pleasure. 'I'll look forward to it.'

Lois wouldn't be pleased. It wasn't hard to guess that Felix had complained to her about the way she'd treated one of his relatives.

Well, that had nothing to do with Jill. She didn't want to know anything about it. Not from either of them. It was none of her business anyway. That was the way she was going to play it.

She went downstairs with him to see him out. She liked what she'd seen of Felix Kingsley. She had no friends here and she needed to make some.

She saw Miles talking to Selma as they passed reception. He smirked superciliously when he saw Felix.

On her way back, he said: 'You're pushing your luck, aren't you? Lois would consider that hobnobbing with the enemy.'

That pricked the bubble of pleasure she'd felt at Felix's invitation.

'You'd better be careful or you'll make yourself unpopular.'

'Like you?' Jill asked pointedly.

'Yes, you're going to find yourself outside the clique, just like me.' He laughed, picked up his bag, and went striding down the hall to start his round.

'Why does he stay?' Jill burst out at Selma. 'He knows nobody likes him. I don't understand why they let him in in the first place. He doesn't fit in here. I mean, they're all friends who go back years. And I'm family.'

Selma's long eyelashes swept her cheeks. She looked up and smiled. 'He's connected too in a way.'

'Really? Nobody told me.'

Selma's voice dropped, though there was nobody left in the surgery to hear her. 'By marriage.'

'Rosalie?'

'Her mother is Althea Meadows, a friend of Victoria's. Someone they knew in Nigeria years ago.'

'Meadows? Not related to Titch?'

'I believe she is.'

'In what way?'

'I don't know. Could be distant.'

Jill pulled a face. 'Doubly connected. Even so, they don't seem to like him much, and he positively bristles against them.'

'Althea isn't as popular with the others as she used to be. She's a patient of this practice.'

Jill brightened up. That meant she could find out more about her. 'Where will I find her records?'

'In Titch's filing cabinet.'

It stood open. Jill flicked through until she put her hand on the envelope labelled 'Althea Meadows'. She took it out to study.

'Bill Goodbody was her doctor,' she said in surprise. 'Shouldn't she be my patient now? How come Titch has taken her?'

'He kept a few of Bill's for himself. The favourites.'

Althea's envelope was bulging. That meant she'd given Bill plenty to do over the years.

'But she's in the Three Pines Nursing Home.'

'Yes, been there for years.'

'Don't they insist on their residents changing their GP when they

46

go in? There's usually one doctor who sees to them all.'

'Althea's a special patient. She doesn't go with the crowd. She'd only to ask for a visit and Bill was down there like a shot. Titch is just the same.' Selma's lush brown eyes smiled into hers.

Jill leaned back against the wall and scanned Althea's notes.

'I believe she's an invalid,' Selma said. 'Crippled now. Rather a sad case. Rheumatoid arthritis. Getting progressively worse.'

Breakfast was eaten in the kitchen at Links View, to save Lois the trouble of clearing the dining room table after the evening meal.

Jill spooned up muesli and yoghurt. Both her parents were reading newspapers while they ate. The room was filled with the scent of toast.

She said: 'I won't be in for dinner tonight, Lois.'

'You've soon got your social life organised.' Her father lowered the *Financial Times* for a moment. 'Going somewhere exciting?'

'I don't know exactly.'

'Here's the bit about Bill's retirement.' Lois held out the local paper. 'Good picture too. There's a bit about you on the next page.'

Jill scanned through both paragraphs; they were unchanged from what Felix had shown her yesterday.

'Let me see,' Dad was holding out his hand. 'That's a good picture of you.'

'Actually,' Jill said slowly, 'the person who took it ... Felix Kingsley ... he's asked me out for a meal tonight.'

'What, that journalist?' Lois was suddenly tense. 'I'd have nothing to do with him if I were you.'

Jill didn't need to ask why, but Lois told her anyway.

'He's a troublemaker. You heard him having a go at me at Bill's retirement party? You'd think he'd keep a rein on his tongue in public.' Lois's face was stiff with resentment.

'I thought it was you berating him.'

'Not at all. If you've any sense you'll put him off.'

Lois's sloe-black eyes were staring at her. Jill sensed that she was holding her tongue in check. She wanted to forbid her stepdaughter from seeing Felix. Now Jill was grown up she daren't. Jill meant to see him again whatever Lois thought of him.

'You can do better than a journalist on a local paper.' Lois's lips compressed into a straight line.

'He told me he was freelance.'

'Even more precarious. I don't expect he makes a decent living. I'll introduce you to men who have a future. We'll have a dinner party, won't we, Nat?'

'You don't have to do that, Lois. I'm quite capable of making my own friends.'

47

'I want to. It's the least I can do for you.'

'In Queen Victoria's day it might have been necessary, but not now.'

'We don't want you to get involved with the wrong sort of people.' Jill shivered. She could feel Lois's fear. 'It's just as easy to make friends with people who are making a success of their lives. Easier, they're more interesting.'

'Lois, I don't want . . .'

'You're a good-looking girl, Jill. At your age, men friends have a habit of developing into something more. We must think of your future. You'd be wise not to get involved with an aggressive fellow like Kingsley.'

Jill thought of Felix's boyish face and the smile that never seemed to leave his lips. He hadn't seemed aggressive to her, quite the reverse. There was nothing about him to frighten anybody. Lois was just afraid he was going to spill the beans about some mistake she'd made. Well, she needn't be. Jill meant to stay well clear of that.

She said slowly: 'I need to make up my own mind. I've agreed to have dinner with him tonight.'

'Don't bring him here then.' Lois's nostrils were flaring. She was angry as well as afraid now.

'He's coming to pick me up.'

'Then be sure you're ready and don't ask him in. I don't want him infiltrating this house.'

Jill swallowed uncomfortably, appalled at the strength of her step-mother's feelings.

'Anyway,' her father pushed the local paper back across the table and smiled at her, 'he's said some very complimentary things about you, Jill. And about Bill Goodbody, too.'

Jill hadn't had many visits to make and returned home early in the afternoon. She had hoped to spend an hour or so in the garden with Gran, but the old lady had gone up to her room after lunch.

Lois came home early too, and it was she who joined Jill in the garden. Lois was full of plans for inviting guests to Links View to introduce to her. She kept on talking about it.

'How else will you meet suitable men? You can't leave it to chance. You won't meet the right ones.'

Jill found it impossible to dissuade her. She was delighted to see her father's car return shortly after six. Ten minutes later and he was out in the garden, hoeing his vegetables.

Jill found another hoe and went to work alongside him. He was the reason she'd come to live at home and she'd barely had a chance to speak to him on her own.

'Nice of you to come and help,' he smiled. His face looked drawn with fatigue.

'I'm surprised you've the energy for gardening after being at work all day.'

'It gets me out in the fresh air. Lovely after breathing chocolate fumes all day.'

'How's the business?'

'Fine. I think I'll put another row of lettuces in here.'

Jill paused. How could she get him to talk about his problems? He looked as though he was weighed down by them and needed to open up, but somehow he couldn't get started. And it was time for her to go and change now. It seemed that if she wanted time to talk to Dad she would have to make an opportunity.

'I want us to go to a concert at the Philharmonic,' she said. 'You used to take me when I was a child. Now I want to take you.'

He looked up and smiled then. 'That would be lovely.'

'How are you fixed for Friday?'

He pulled a face. 'Friday is a bit difficult. Next week, perhaps?' Jill was left feeling even that was difficult.

By quarter to seven, her family had gathered in the sitting room to have a drink before supper. Jill couldn't sit with them. Lois was edgy, and kept getting up to look out of the window.

Jill said goodbye to them, picked up her jacket and went out to the front garden to wait for Felix there.

Exactly on time, a newish Triumph Stag nosed into the drive and pulled up in front of her. Lois had conditioned her thinking; she'd expected Felix to be driving an old banger.

'Hello.' He got out to greet her, the smile she remembered so well hovering at the corners of his mouth. His eyes raked the front of the house. 'Nice place you've got here.'

'I'm all ready.'

Jill wanted to be off. She was afraid he'd think it strange not to be invited in to meet her family.

She was going round to the passenger seat when her father came striding out of the front door with his arm outstretched. It made her feel better that she could introduce him to Felix.

'Excellent piece in the paper about old Bill Goodbody,' he said heartily. 'And about our Jill, too.'

'You must write for other papers?' Jill said as they drove off. 'Does living in Birkenhead make sense for a freelance writer?'

'I hope so.' He smiled, showing strong, even teeth. 'I'm a native of these parts too, and only recently returned.'

It seemed a shared bond. 'Where from?'

'London. I was working for *The Times*. I'm lucky, they still take some of my output. I came home because my father was ill. He lives here in Oxton. He needed somebody around and I'm the only family he has left. My mother died a couple of years ago.'

'Is it working out all right for you?'

49

He took a deep breath. 'I feel out on a limb. Away from what's going on in the world. Away from the people I know.'

'You seem to know everybody at the surgery.'

She knew as soon as the words were out of her mouth that she shouldn't have brought up the surgery.

'Not really. Lois Benbow was my father's doctor.' She saw his fingers tighten on the steering wheel.

Jill had meant to steer clear of this. She had more than enough troubles of her own to worry about. Yet here she was bringing it up within five minutes of meeting him. She needed to be more careful what she said.

'He sees Cuthbert Meadows now,' Felix added. 'He's still with the practice.'

Jill wanted to turn him off this. But there was something he had to know before he'd understand why.

'Lois Benbow is my mother.'

'Good Lord!' She felt the car swerve. 'I didn't know that!' He turned from the wheel to look at her, his mouth open, his brown eyes registering astonishment.

'My stepmother, actually. She practices under her maiden name, always has.'

He glanced at her again. 'I don't really know her. My mother and I were registered with a different practice – when I lived here, I mean.'

'I rather got the impression she knew you.' Jill couldn't help the wry note in her voice.

'I said a few words to her at the tea, that's all. Never spoken to her before that.'

'Are you sure?'

'Of course I'm sure. I rang her up. Tried to make an appointment to come in and talk about it, but she wasn't having any. Why do you ask?'

Jill shook her head. 'Nothing. I must have misunderstood.'

What she'd understood was that her stepmother was very jumpy abut the possible outcome. If there had been a problem with his father's treatment, the way Lois could have smoothed it out was to talk it over with Felix. It seemed she hadn't wanted that, and she certainly didn't want Jill to have any contact with him. She was afraid of something he might tell her.

'So that's a no-go area?' He was lifting one eyebrow.

''Fraid so.'

He took her to a bistro in West Kirby. The door pinged like that of a shop as they went in. Cast-iron kettles and pans decorated the walls.

'I heard someone recommend it,' Felix said. The place was almost full. 'Good job I booked a table.'

Jill sat opposite him. He moved the candle stuck in a bottle to the

50

edge of the red gingham cloth. 'Can't see you with that in the middle. Tell me about yourself. There's so much I want to know.' His brown eyes wouldn't leave hers now.

Jill tried. 'Apart from my training there's nothing much to tell. I'm just starting out.'

He ordered wine. Touched his brimming glass against hers and drank to her.

She asked: 'How about you?'

'I started work on the *Liverpool Echo*. Spent four years with them and then went down to London. I was doing all right. Enjoying life.'

Jill swirled the wine in her glass. I've met him at a good time, she thought. I don't have to work every hour in the day or worry about examinations now. I can spend my leisure as I wish. She wanted to spend all the time she could with him. He put out his hand and touched hers as it rested on the table.

There was a warmth about Felix. She liked his friendliness. Perhaps it was more than friendliness? His eyes, and the way he leaned forward on the table, made no secret of the fact that he liked what he saw.

A fat lady in a green satin dress began to play the honky-tonk piano, spinning out the tunes. There was life and jollity about the place. Jill's feet danced on the bare boards under the table. The steak was indifferent, but it didn't matter. Nothing could dim the pleasure she felt.

'We must do this again,' Felix said. 'What are you doing tomorrow?'

'Another evening surgery.'

'I can see you're one of those girls who has to be booked well ahead.'

She laughed. 'How about Friday?'

Dad had already told her he'd be busy, and she didn't want to spend a free evening at home with Lois and Gran.

'You're on.'

They sat for a long time over their coffee. When they finally got up from the table, Felix said: 'Let's walk off some of that food. The promenade isn't far and it's early yet.'

It was not quite dark, but the warmth of the day had gone and the few people walking along the front were going at a brisk pace.

They stopped to lean over the railings and look across the boating lake and the estuary to the Welsh hills. Lights were coming on.

Jill shivered and huddled against him in the lee of the wind. He put an arm round her shoulders and pulled her closer.

She held her breath, wondering if he meant to kiss her. She wanted him to. He bent his head to hers, and his warm lips touched her cheek and then found her mouth.

51

CHAPTER FIVE

Dr Lois Benbow rang the bell for the last patient in her morning surgery. She had a headache and she hadn't slept well.

Things had not run smoothly in the practice over the last decade. They'd taken on two partners and both had left after a few months. Until Miles Sutton had joined them, they'd had to fill in with a series of locums, none of whom had been very satisfactory.

They'd had such high hopes of Miles. They'd expected him to pull with them, share their aims. After all, everybody in the practice had done a good deal for the family he'd married in to.

But taking Miles Sutton into the partnership was the worst thing they could have done. He'd poked and pried into things that didn't concern him. Things they couldn't afford to have made public. It was like having a spy in the camp.

Lois shivered. Miles's manner was menacing when he wanted something. And anyway, he was a rotten doctor.

What was happening at the practice had become a terrible source of worry. It would be a huge relief to them all if Miles would go, but of course, there was no way they could budge him now.

She and Titch had clung to Bill. It was one reason he'd hung on so long, but he couldn't work for ever.

'What about your stepdaughter?' Bill had suggested. 'She's just qualified. One of the family. Probably the safest bet.'

Bringing Jill into the practice was a big step. Titch had pressed her to make the invitation, and somehow she'd been manoeuvred into organising it. She wished now she'd dug her heels in and refused. At the time she'd thought she could handle Jill, and having her seemed preferable to the man Miles Sutton was suggesting.

'The last thing you need is to let Miles get an ally in the practice,' Goodbody said. 'You two would have less say. You might have to dance to the Sutton tune; at times you'd have no choice.'

'We have no choice anyway,' Lois had said, but had allowed herself to be persuaded. Perhaps Jill wouldn't stay. Perhaps she'd marry young and give up the idea of a career? Lois hoped so.

She was a good-looking girl, not at all like Nat to look at. The sort that would turn heads.

Certainly, Lois should never have agreed to Jill coming to live at home. She hadn't talked this over with Victoria until it was all arranged.

'It's a very silly thing to do,' her mother had told her.

'I couldn't avoid it. Nat was very keen.'

'Anything could stir her memory. What were you thinking of?'

She knew she hadn't thought enough about the consequences.

'It's downright dangerous.'

It left Lois wondering if she'd opened the door to trouble. Jill had developed a will of her own. Not like her father in that, either. She had kept on and on about Phoebe, like a dog worrying a bone. Lois had felt edgy ever since.

She had to ring the bell a second time. Lois could never understand why it took so long to take the few steps from the waiting room to her surgery in the new extension. She looked round it with distaste. Purpose-built, it had everything necessary – desk, couch, washbowl, a couple of chairs – wedged into the minimum space.

She was reaching for the envelope of medical records, and trying to put a face to the name Jody Stubbs, when she heard a soft scuffling outside her door.

'Come in,' she called briskly. A thin schoolgirl with a washed-out, frightened face slid into the room and sat down. She looked shabby and undernourished.

'Hello, Jody.' Lois made herself smile. She'd last seen the girl when she had measles two years ago. 'What can I do for you?'

Jody wouldn't look at her. She was staring through the window. She wouldn't see much, just the blackened bricks of the house next door.

Lois remembered her now; the girl might look skinny but her mother was obese. She could see Jody's fingers shaking slightly against the arm of the chair and stifled a sigh. This wasn't going to be another case of the summer flu that was raging at the moment.

Lois's mind slid back to her own affairs. Sometimes she felt that she and Titch had their backs to the wall. With nearly eleven thousand patients in the practice, they had to have another doctor to replace Bill Goodbody, otherwise they'd work themselves into the ground.

'Please . . .' the girl was mumbling, 'I think . . . I think I'm going to have a baby.'

Lois knew that her lips had tightened with disapproval. The second schoolgirl this month! There had been two last month as well. She looked again at her records. The girl wasn't even sixteen.

'Tell me, Jody, what makes you think that?'

The girl's face registered alarm. 'Well, you know . . . I haven't had . . .'

'Since when? Can you tell me the dates?'

The girl stuttered, was hardly coherent.

54

'Do you have a boyfriend?'

'Of course.'

Her face now displayed disbelief as well as alarm, as though afraid Lois was about to suggest a second immaculate conception.

'Perhaps you'd better get on the couch and let me feel your tummy.' That was better; the girl hared behind the screen.

Lois prodded while Jody grimaced. She thought she could be pregnant; she might just be feeling the uterus growing up out of the pelvis, but it ought to be bigger if it was to agree with the dates the girl had given.

'At least you've come in time.'

Last month, one of her young patients had been taken short at a disco. She'd been lucky somebody had the sense to call an ambulance. It had been taking her to accident and emergency at Arrowe Park when the crew decided she was in labour and diverted to the mat. instead. The girl swore she'd never even suspected she was pregnant.

'We'd better do a test to make sure,' Lois said soberly.

'I am sure, Doctor. I wouldn't have come otherwise.'

Lois couldn't suppress another tightening of disapproval. 'Medically sure,' she said firmly. She wasn't going to refer anyone until she was quite certain.

'I don't know if I'll be able to get you an abortion on the National Health, Jody. It takes time to fix it up, and the sooner you have it done the better. It could be arranged privately through the Pregnancy Advisory Service if your parents are willing to pay.'

The girl's eyes widened with horror.

'Have you told your parents?'

Her answer was a long time coming and hardly audible. 'No.'

'I'm afraid you'll have to. Unless you want me to do it?' Already she was looking at the address on the card.

'No!' It was almost a shriek. 'And I don't want any abortion. I want to keep it.'

Lois stepped back with a jolt of frustration. The silly girl didn't know what she was taking on.

'Jody, you aren't old enough to bring up a child. Would your mother be willing to help you look after this baby? Care for it while you are at school?'

'School?' It was a frightened squeak. 'I'm finishing with school. I've had enough of that.'

'You're fifteen. You can't finish with it yet. To go back to studying later, with a baby to care for, is twice as hard. It will take double the effort and determination.'

'I'm not worried about that.' The girl was showing scorn. 'I won't be doing it.'

Lois tried again. 'Will your mother let you keep the baby at home?'

55

'I don't care if she doesn't! I don't want her help. I'll be able to get a flat of my own. I want to be independent.'

Lois couldn't control her snort of displeasure. 'On social welfare, I suppose?' It made her very cross indeed when a young girl proposed to bring up another generation to be dependent on the taxpayer.

'That is not what I call being independent. If you do that, you'll always be whining that you haven't enough money. Like the rest of them do. You'll never have anything you want. Always be dependent on handouts. Always at the very bottom of society.'

Lois felt her cheeks flushing with anger. It took a real effort to stop herself sounding off. Nothing she was saying was going to dissuade this stupid girl.

Instead, she said as calmly as she could: 'It will ruin your chances in life. You should be working hard at school in order to get yourself a good job. What do you want to be?'

This time Jody didn't attempt to answer.

'What school do you go to?'

More muttering, but Lois got the gist. A Catholic school. That made it worse. Usually the pregnancies came from the big comprehensives.

'I want to keep the baby.' Jody was defiant.

Lois tried again. 'It's very important to get your priorities right. A baby would be very hard work at your age. You'll have plenty of time for a family when you're older. Children will give you more satisfaction then.'

Lois looked at the years ahead for the girl and shuddered. She'd seen it all far too many times. Single parenthood was never easy, though they all thought it would be a delight. At sixteen, living on the state, it promised nothing but loneliness and poverty, a wasted life. Two wasted lives, if she counted the baby's. She had to make the girl see reason.

'What do you want from life, Jody?'

'I want to be happy.'

Lois felt rage spurting through her. 'Then this is no way to go about it. You can't be so blind as to believe you'll find happiness that way.'

Jody was on her feet, her pasty face turned grey, her eyes glassy with tears.

'Sit down,' Lois bellowed, but the girl didn't. She was cowering over the chair now.

'Listen to me. Take my advice, it's the best you'll get. An abortion is the only thing that makes sense in your position.'

'No!' The girl stared back at her with shocked, frightened eyes.

Lois was shaking with frustration. 'Then you're even more stupid than you look.'

'I'm going!' Jody was backing against the door.

Lois gave up in disgust. If the girl refused to be helped, then so be it.

'Wait. I'll arrange for a pregnancy test. If it's positive, I'll refer you to the booking clinic. That's what you want, isn't it?'

When she'd gone, Lois sat staring out of the window unable to control her anger. Jody Stubbs was facing a disaster that could ruin her life. What she found so frustrating was that the girl had turned down the help she'd been trying to give.

But there was no need for her to bother herself over a silly girl. Jody was one of the country's failures anyway.

Lois felt consumed by fury again. It was not only Jody. What had driven her to this point was that so many others were holding out against her. Miles Sutton, for instance, and his overbearing wife.

But she dared not think of them. She couldn't afford to. She'd never get herself back on an even keel to do her visits if she did.

Jill was on call all weekend. She'd planned to have a meal with Felix on Saturday night by leaving the restaurant phone number with her father. But she was called out early in the evening, and when she rushed home to change she found he'd already logged two more visits she'd have to make.

She had to ring Felix to cancel the dinner. He sounded disappointed. 'When will I be able to see you?'

'I've got Tuesday off in lieu. The whole day.'

'There's that new play at the Everyman Theatre you said you'd like to see. How about it?'

'I'd love that.'

'We could have a meal first.'

'Great.'

'I have to go over to Liverpool. To do some research. I could meet you after that.'

'What sort of research?'

'I need facts and figures for an article on the rise and fall of the port of Liverpool. I want to dig about in the local archives in the library.'

'Will it take you long?'

'Shouldn't be more than an hour. How about coming with me?'

'Would you mind?'

'What do you think? You can give me a hand.'

When they arrived at the reference library, Felix was handed a collection of books, pamphlets and reports, which he carried to a long table.

Jill sat down beside him. He'd given her the task of finding the relevant information and opening the books to the right page. Felix was reading and making notes.

Her job was finished fairly quickly. On the other side of her, further along the table, a woman was studying back numbers of the *Liverpool Echo.*

Jill pulled some of them closer, and saw that they dated back to the period April to June of 1953. Her first thought was that Phoebe had been alive then.

She knew a cot death would not be big news, but there might just be some mention of it. She could look under the appropriate dates in the births and deaths columns as well.

A front-page photograph caught her eye. Her heart began to pound. There could be no mistaking Titch Meadows.

He'd stood up straighter back in the fifties. He was thinner. Thinner in the face, too, and he wore rimless spectacles. But it was him.

Jill caught her breath as she read the caption beneath. The picture was said to be of Dr Thomas Sinclair and his lover, Mrs Georgina Scott-Temple, the wife of a well-known Member of Parliament.

That riveted her attention. She studied the woman photographed with Titch. It wasn't the same person who had been at Goodbody's retirement tea and who had been introduced to her as Titch's wife. She had been a plain dumpling. This woman was a sophisticated beauty.

She started to read. It was the report of a court case. There must have been enormous publicity at the time. The Member of Parliament had accused his wife of attempting to poison him and had also claimed she was aided and abetted by her lover, who was a prominent Harley Street doctor. Jill felt the blood running to her cheeks.

She knew the name Dr Thomas Sinclair. He was the one doctor she hadn't recognised on that photograph of Gran's.

She read on avidly, soaking up all the details. The findings of the case were reported daily and the newspaper carried the story for weeks. There were pictures of the wronged wife. Chloe Sinclair was made out to be a bitter woman.

Eventually both Georgina and Tom Sinclair were found not guilty. But the Member of Parliament was suing for divorce, quoting Sinclair as co-respondent. There were more pictures of Titch.

Evidence was put before the court that Mrs Georgina Scott-Temple was a patient of Sinclair's, and not the only one with whom he was said to have had sexual relations. Another name was quoted, another photograph in the newspaper.

The case had been a salacious one for the time. Jill could hardly get her breath when she read that as a result, Tom Sinclair's name had been struck off the register.

Her cheeks burned, she felt shocked. The man she knew as Cuthbert Meadows was actually Tom Sinclair. He was practising under a false name.

Even now, Jill found it hard to believe that Titch Meadows had anything to hide. He looked so honest, and was popular with everybody. She liked him herself.

What a mess he'd got himself into. The last person she'd have expected to do that. He seemed so normal, going about his duties in an unhurried, efficient manner. The one person in that practice she admired. And yet he was breaking the law by working at all. Not that his patients were in any danger from him. She'd trust him before Miles and Lois.

And after all these years? Names were removed as a disciplinary measure but were usually reinstated at some later date. Even in such a notorious case as this, Tom Sinclair's should have been. How had he managed to get away with the deception? And where was the real Cuthbert Meadows?

Goodbody, Lois and Victoria must all have rallied round Tom Sinclair. They must have invited him into the practice, covered up for him. Yet they'd kept her in ignorance. Matters were not at all as they'd seemed when she'd agreed to join the practice. There were things going on that would have made her think twice about it.

She felt a hand on her shoulders. Felix was standing behind her chair. Jill froze; she'd been so absorbed she'd forgotten Felix was with her.

'I'm ready. I hope I haven't . . .' Nervously, she began folding the newspaper.

'Phew, is that . . .?' She knew his eye had caught the headline too. He was tugging the paper round to see it better.

He whistled through his teeth. 'He's thickened out a bit with the years, and he wears heavy horn-rimmed specs now. Grown a moustache too.'

He bent closer and was reading as avidly as she had. 'It is him, isn't it?'

'Don't . . .'

'What a story it would be,' he marvelled, 'to resurrect this. It's the sort of thing journalists dream of.' An impish smile lit up his face. 'Such a scoop.'

'Felix! You mustn't.' Both her palms were covering her mouth. 'Think what it would do to Titch. You'll expose him. He could be charged . . .'

'I'd love a big story like this. It would make my name as a freelance. The national papers would jump at it. What a scandal . . .'

'You'd never have known about it if I hadn't come with you,' Jill said stiffly. She was agitated because of what she'd revealed to him. Titch would have good reason to blame her if this became general knowledge.

Felix was reaching for another paper, searching for more details.

'If you write one word about this, I'll never speak to you again,' she flared at him.

He jerked upright, stared down at her, his enthusiasm fading. He said: 'Don't worry. I won't say a word.'

'It's not what you'll say, but what you'll write that bothers me.'

'All right, I won't write anything. I've no quarrel with Tom Sinclair, or whatever he wants to call himself. In fact, he's been kind to Dad. Though if you'd turned up something like this on your stepmother, or even Miles Sutton . . .'

'That would cause terrible trouble for me, too.' Jill was folding the papers up neatly. 'You know it would.'

'Yes, well, I won't write about anything connected with that practice. Not without talking it over with you. Won't offer anything for publication that you don't agree to. How's that?'

'You will stick to that?'

'Of course I will.'

Jill sighed. She believed he'd keep his word, but it had put a barrier between them. She felt less at ease. She didn't enjoy the evening as much as she'd expected. She knew Felix didn't either.

When Jill finished surgery the next morning and went down to the kitchen, Lois and Miles were already there having their coffee.

'Has Titch gone out?' she asked.

'No, he's been caught by a drug rep. I'm going before he asks to see me.' Lois stood up.

'Don't rush off if you want a golfing weekend,' Miles told her. 'He's invited me to St Andrews in September.'

'Somebody has to stay and run the practice,' Lois snapped. 'We can't all go haring off to Scotland.'

The kitchen door slammed behind her and moments later swung open as Titch breezed in.

'Look what I've been given.' His large white hands fondled a coffee mug decorated with blue flowers. 'Gift from the rep.'

Jill read the message under the flowers: "Rinsol. Sterile normal saline solution for topical irrigation".

'Would be pretty without the advert. Rather spoils the effect.'

He grinned at her. 'You haven't seen the effect yet.' He was boiling up the kettle again, helping himself to the biscuits put out on the table.

'You heard there's a drug company lunch next Friday?' Miles asked.

Jill had already talked to the rep. She'd been invited to the lunch too.

'Are you coming, Titch?'

'No.'

'You should.'

Jill could see Miles was goading him.

'You don't know what you're missing. You get a jolly good feed and they aren't mean with the drink.'

'It's a form of bribery,' Titch retorted, putting in a rare barb.

'Makes you feel grateful, so you prescribe their drugs. And once you get used to prescribing them, you go on doing it.'

'How very high-minded you are,' Miles sneered.

'That's why they pay for luxury lunches, and you know it. It's their one sure way of pushing up sales.'

'This wouldn't have anything to do with the fact that you don't want to mix, would it?' Miles flashed. 'That you don't want to meet your fellow doctors?'

Jill had heard him say something like this before but she hadn't appreciated the point behind the jibe.

Miles got up to leave: 'You're scared of being recognised.'

She caught Titch's guilty glance. She wanted to talk to him about what she'd found out. Tell him that his secret was safe with her.

As the kitchen door slammed behind Miles and his footsteps retreated up the passage, Titch got up self-consciously to make coffee in his new mug.

He turned back to the table with it, chortling softly. 'Look at this. A technological miracle.' The blue flowers were turning pink with the heat of the coffee.

Jill said: 'Titch, I know.'

He froze. She pulled the photograph from her pocket, the one she'd found under the grapes on Gran's tray, and pushed it across the table to where he stood.

'You're Tom Sinclair, aren't you? Yesterday, I read about you in back numbers of the *Echo*.'

The impact of her words horrified her. The mug slid through Titch's fingers to shatter on the floor. She could see him shaking with shock. He turned on her angrily.

'Bring somebody new into the partnership and they're poking into every corner. This is my business, it has nothing to do with you.' His eyes, usually so gentle, burned with fury.

Selma came in, clucking at the mess on the floor. She started picking up broken crockery. Jill pulled herself together.

'I'm sorry, Titch.'

He snatched up the photograph and tore it into little pieces. With another angry grunt he dropped them into the waste bucket and stormed off to his room.

'Phew,' Selma breathed. 'What's the matter with everybody? I've never seen Titch lose his cool before. Takes a lot to drive him into a tizzy.'

Jill stared at her, aghast. Then she made another mug of coffee for Titch and took it to his room. He was at his desk, staring straight ahead. She put the mug on his blotter.

'Please forgive me, I didn't mean to upset you. I handled that very clumsily.'

He pushed his heavy horn-rimmed spectacles up his nose, didn't look at her.

'I was struck off, but I had to eat and I had to live. What else could I turn my hand to? This is the only thing I know.'

'Your secrets are safe with me. I won't be spreading any of it round. I thought I ought to tell you that I know.'

'Has Victoria kept cuttings? Of the old newspapers? Is that how you found out?'

'No, I saw them in the library.'

'What?' Titch looked horrified.

'The reference library. You knew they kept copies of old newspapers?'

He sighed. 'I've never thought about it. Not here in Liverpool. Silly, really. In American crime stories the sleuth often solves his case by reading old newspapers. Can anybody see them?'

'Yes, if they ask.'

'Oh, God!'

'I know you think I was prying into your affairs. I wasn't, Titch, honestly. I was just filling in a few moments. I did hope to find out something . . . But about the affairs of my own family. Once, I had a stepsister.'

'You know about her?'

Titch certainly did. But then he'd known Lois and Victoria for many years.

'I was asking Victoria about her, we were looking at some of her old snaps. That's where I first heard the name Tom Sinclair.'

'So now you know it all.' Abruptly, he got up and went to the window.

'Not everything.'

What had Cuthbert Meadows been doing all these years? Why had he allowed Titch to use his name?

'Enough to finish me.'

'Titch, I won't say a word.' She mustn't let him know that Felix knew too. That would upset him more.

He gave her a half-smile. 'What convoluted lives we all lead.' He'd recovered some of his usual gentle manner. 'It's probably unavoidable.'

'What is?'

'Getting involved in one's partners' affairs.'

She'd had enough and wanted to make her escape. 'I've got visits to do. Must get started.'

As she drove off, it occurred to her that doctors could cover up more than their medical mistakes.

CHAPTER SIX

By Wednesday, Jill had managed to pin her father down and buy tickets for a concert at the Philharmonic Hall.

When she phoned his office to tell him, he sounded pleased, and said: 'We'll get something to eat in Liverpool. Go over early and make a full evening of it.'

That afternoon, Jill had done the monthly baby immunisation clinic and made a couple of visits afterwards.

As she came up the drive of Links View, she saw a delivery van on the forecourt, and her father signing for a package at the front door. She was glad to know he was home before her and they could go as soon as they were ready.

He was putting the package on the hall table as she went inside. 'It's for Lois,' he said.

She took a quick shower and changed. She was ready before him. She met Gran at the sitting room door.

'I'd like to sit in the garden now that the heat of the day has gone. Get a breath of air.'

Jill erected a garden chair under the tree for her. Made a cup of tea and took it out. Had one herself. She couldn't close her eyes to the fact that Dad was slowing down, becoming less efficient at everything.

'I've mislaid my pen,' he said, patting his blazer pocket when he did come. 'But I won't need it tonight.'

'Did I see it on the hall table? Yes, here it is, Dad.'

She picked up the gold fountain pen. He'd had it for years; she remembered it from her childhood. He used to let her write with it sometimes. It was engraved with his initials, N.J.R.

'Wouldn't want to lose it. I must have used it to sign for that parcel. Lois gave it to me years ago.'

'Let's go.' They'd got as far as his car when she heard a woman call.

'Cooee. Anybody home?' A well-covered and shapeless figure came round the corner of the house, followed by a small white Airedale terrier.

Nat said: 'Hello, Esme.'

Jill recognised Titch's wife. Despite the heat of the day, she was

63

wearing a frilly blouse, a sensible skirt, and support tights with her open-toed sandals.

'Is your bell broken? Couldn't make anybody hear.'

'We've been in the back garden.'

'Victoria hasn't gone out?'

'No, she's in the garden too. She'll be glad to see you. She's getting a bit bored by herself now.'

'The ladies missed her at the lunch club today.'

Jill was surprised. 'She goes to a lunch club?'

'She helps me run one,' Esme laughed. 'In a church hall. Prides herself on being older than most of the old dears who come to eat. I'll be glad to see her back in her stride.'

'Good of you to call.'

'Nat, I only live in the next road and I have to take Trixie for a walk. Besides, I miss her.' She smiled at Jill again. 'We run a charity shop, too.'

'I'll get a chair out for you.'

'I can get it for myself, Nat. I know where they're kept. You'll want to be on your way.'

'She seems jolly,' Jill said as they started off.

'She's good for Victoria. She takes her out a lot. The people in the practice, they're like one big extended family. They look after each other.'

'Where shall we go to eat?'

Nat wanted Indian food. 'It isn't in Mrs Moon's repertoire,' he said, 'so we never get it at home, and I know a place that opens early.' Jill was prepared to go along with whatever he wanted.

'Dad,' she said, as they waited for their onion bhajis. 'I'm worried about you. You don't look well.'

'I'm all right.' His tone told her otherwise. 'I'm tired, can't do as much now I'm getting older, but there's nothing that needs doctoring.'

Jill pondered on that. Dad didn't seem to want to confide in her just yet. She couldn't help him if he wouldn't talk about it. Perhaps he'd let it come out in his own good time. There were other things she wanted to ask him about, but he was too uptight for anything at the moment.

'You're not that old,' she smiled.

The music swirled in Nathaniel Ridley's mind, building in a crescendo, lifting him. He always found Beethoven very moving.

He glanced down at his daughter and felt a rush of love. It brought with it an urge to confess. To tell her everything, to be honest and clear the air. He wanted to be rid of this gnawing guilt. But where did he begin?

He was glad they'd come, he hadn't had time to sit back and think for a long time. The music relaxed him. Not only was he enjoying it, but it was melting some of the stiffness between them. Jill had been away too long. He'd been afraid he'd lost the ease he'd once felt in her company. She turned now to smile at him and squeeze his arm. It pleased him that they were still on the same plane when it came to music.

Nat couldn't suppress a quiver of pride that she'd turned out so well. A doctor! That would have pleased her mother. Her natural mother, his first wife.

Now, for the first time, he could see Sarah's likeness in her. She had the same mannerisms. The same honey-blonde hair and level gaze from eyes the colour of jade. Jill was reminding him how different his life would have been if Sarah had lived. Sarah had been gentle and supportive, undemanding; the very opposite of Lois.

The concert ended, and Nathaniel joined in the rapturous applause.

'I did enjoy that,' Jill said in his ear. 'Just like old times.'

He held on to her arm in the crush as the hall emptied, not wanting them to become parted. They had to walk a little way to the car.

Liverpool seemed to throb with life and light. He felt exhilarated. Music had this effect on him. It helped him forget his problems.

'Dad,' Jill was hanging on to his arm, 'you know I've been poking for information about baby Phoebe? Well, Gran wouldn't tell me anything. Why is everybody so secretive about her?'

'Jill, I'd rather not . . . Lois doesn't want to talk to me about her problems. Especially those arising from the time before we were married.'

'But what problem can there be about Phoebe now?'

'It's always been my way to turn my back if it's not really my business. That's how Lois wants it.'

'I think problems should be faced, discussed and sorted out. That's the only way to settle them. Otherwise they have a habit of resurfacing when we least expect them.'

That was youth talking. Jill didn't know what problems were.

'I want you to tell me what really happened to Phoebe.'

That made his step falter. He should have known that what he'd said on her first night home would only whet her appetite for more. He'd had to watch his tongue then, because Lois was with them, and any mention of Phoebe always upset her.

'I told you. A cot death. Infant death syndrome, Lois calls it.'

'There was more to it than that, wasn't there?' Jill's voice was persuasive. 'I asked Gran about her and it made her very angry. She said she had to protect Lois. And that's what you're doing too, isn't it? Come on, Dad, Phoebe wasn't your child. Surely we can discuss her like adults?'

65

'I've told you all I know about Phoebe.'

Nat could feel his heart pounding. He wanted to tell her his real worries, he had to, that was the only way he'd ever be at peace with himself again. So why did he feel this reluctance even to talk about Lois's problems?

It wasn't a clash of loyalties, not any longer. Once he would never have spoken to anyone of Lois's private concerns.

'I'm a doctor, for heaven's sake.' She was pulling at his arm. 'Patients tell me things. Terrible things sometimes. It's Lois, then?'

'Yes,' he admitted. She'd be furious if she knew he was telling Jill.

'Why is everybody trying to protect her? What has she done? She strikes me as well able to take care of herself.'

'Not always.'

'You knew her when Phoebe was alive?'

'They lived across the road from us.' He'd never spoken of this to anyone.

'You knew her first husband then?'

They'd reached his old Wolseley. He unlocked it. 'His name was Graham. He was a surgeon.'

'Shall I drive, Dad?' He knew she wanted him to keep his mind on the story he was telling. 'We only brought your car because it's so old it's not likely to be stolen.'

He wasn't used to sitting in the passenger seat. And talking like this made the past rush back before his eyes.

It had been a long-ago autumn night. A cold night. He'd been tired after a long day at work and Sarah was very much on his mind. It was only a few months since the tragedy.

He felt her presence everywhere. He couldn't see her but she was always near. In the shop, on the premises where they manufatured the chocolates. She used to turn her hand to everything. There were times when he still found himself talking to her and waiting for the answer that didn't come.

He could hardly bear to think of the poor motherless babe in her cot. He found himself in tears sometimes as he looked down on her.

He let the nanny go out most evenings, resenting her presence in the house. If Sarah were alive, there would be no nanny.

'Graham used to come across from time to time. To have a drink.' He'd looked forward to Graham's visits.

'He was a friend of yours?'

'I think he came out of neighbourliness to start with. After the accident.'

He could see Graham now. Broad-shouldered, rather short for a man. He had a lot of glossy dark hair and sharp, intelligent eyes. It was Graham's intelligence Nat found attractive. He was interested in everything, he loved to talk about the chocolate business. Always, his mind had been one step ahead of Nat's.

'We got on well,' Nat added. 'I enjoyed his company.' It had helped to talk over his business problems. Graham had made several helpful suggestions off the top of his head.

Graham had been more a man of the world than Nat was, and Nat would have liked to be invited back to his home, but he was never asked. Instead, Graham would bring a bottle of whisky over with him once in a while, and not take it home.

'I used to watch Lois coming and going. I felt very curious about her. I knew the marriage was in trouble. He talked, not about anything too personal, but enough that I knew that.

'If I met her in the road, she'd say good morning but little else, though I tried to get her to talk.'

Nat stirred uncomfortably in his seat. That night, he'd felt very low. He'd been relieved when Graham knocked on his door.

'So what happened to Graham?' Jill asked.

'She divorced him.'

'Because she was in love with you?'

'No!' Nat knew his voice was an agonised wail. He went on more normally: 'No, Graham had another woman – a sister at the hospital.'

Graham had been distraught that night. He'd needed company himself and had not come to cheer Nat. He'd gulped at his whisky.

'I've asked Lois for my freedom,' he'd said, and his face had told Nat how painful an experience that had been. He wanted to marry his ward sister.

He had swirled the fluid in his glass before going on.

'I was sure Lois knew about Greta. She seemed to be suspicious, was always asking pointed questions, and I knew there had been a lot of gossip at the hospital. I thought she must have heard rumours at least.'

'But she didn't know?' Nat had asked.

'No, it all came as a dreadful shock to her.' Nat could see that Graham was still shaking. 'I meant to stay cool and calm but I couldn't. We ended up having a terrible row.'

Nat saw Jill shoot a glance in his direction.

'Not an unusual story, Dad. Rejection is always painful, but nowadays lots of people have to face it. It doesn't tell me why Lois needs protection.'

Nat tried to explain. 'Lois has an uncontrollable temper. The sort that sweeps all reason out of her mind.'

'Go on. What did she do?'

Nat shivered. It gave him the creeps just to think about it, even now.

'Graham and I were on our second drink and just beginning to talk freely. He was telling me about this girl he was in love with, when we heard a terrible screaming outside in the road. We went rushing out to find that it was Lois. She was like an animal in pain, screaming and sobbing and throwing herself about.

'Graham thought it was hysteria because of the showdown they'd just had. We managed to get her inside their kitchen. We had to bundle her in. Other people were coming out into the road to see what the noise was.

'Lois couldn't get the words out to tell us. She was choking with rage and panic.

' "What's the matter?" Graham kept asking. We were trying to quieten her and it took us quite a while to realise what had happened.

' "What is it, Lois?"

' "I didn't do it."

' "Didn't do what?"

'There was a sort of butcher's block in their kitchen, with a set of sharp knives hanging on it. Suddenly she snatched up the biggest and rushed at him.'

'She tried to kill him?' Nat heard the horror in Jill's voice.

'She cut his arm, that's all. She was too hysterical to make a decent job of it. It probably wasn't her intention to maim. She hadn't the strength anyway.

'All the time she was screaming and sobbing. She wasn't making sense, but I caught the word "dead". It was Graham who had understood first. "Is it the baby?"

"She's dead!" Lois had wept. "I didn't do it."

'He went rushing upstairs then to look. Lois and I followed. It horrified me to see Phoebe so lifeless and still. Graham was trying all the resuscitation techniques and shouting to me to get his bag from the hall.

'Shouting at Lois too, "What have you done to her? What have you been doing?" Panic stations all round.'

He saw Jill lick her lips. 'What did she say?'

' "I didn't do it. It's all your fault."

'Graham asked me to take Lois downstairs and try to calm her. I didn't make much headway with that. He came down eventually, and I asked him: "What has happened to the baby?"

' "A cot death, I'm sure. I think Lois went upstairs and found Phoebe dead in her cot. After the row we had earlier, it was too much for her."

'By then Graham was overwhelmed with grief and worried about the effects of this on both Lois's career and his own. He rang Dr Goodbody and asked him to come round as soon as he could.'

'Lois was working in the practice then?'

'She had been, before having Phoebe. Goodbody was their GP. He knew she wasn't finding it easy to cope with the baby.'

'Do you know if she had postnatal depression?' Jill wanted to know.

Nat shook his head. 'I heard Goodbody asking Graham that. He said no, she'd shown no signs of it, and despite her earlier history she seemed in good health.'

'What earlier history?'

'She'd been depressed before I knew her. Victoria told me.'

'Clinical depression, you mean?'

'Yes.'

'Treated by Bill Goodbody?'

Nat shook his head. 'I don't know. She had a second episode of it after Phoebe died. She was treated by a psychiatrist then.'

'Really? Then that could be why Lois doesn't want to talk about the baby.'

'Her death was so unexpected. Lois loved that baby, and any mention of her reminds her of how she attacked Graham. She feels very ashamed. Guilt-ridden. She doesn't want people to know.'

He could see Jill turning it over in her mind. She said: 'She'd have felt terrible when Phoebe died, of course. She'd have been torn apart with grief.'

'She was.'

'But I would have expected Lois to pride herself on putting it behind her. She'd know that was the best thing. To look to the future. Surely after a year or so she'd be able to think of Phoebe calmly and with love. Just at special times, such as on her birthday?'

'I think she saw it as a wasted life.'

'Not a total waste, Dad. If nothing else, it must have helped her show more sympathy and understanding for patients in the same position.'

Nat sat very still, thinking this over. He said at last: 'Lois is not as strong-minded as she seems. It knocked her sideways. They were both doctors, Jill. No patient wants to consult a doctor who rushes at people with a knife.'

They were in the Mersey tunnel now. He could see her face.

'What happened to Graham?'

'He moved out after that. I saw him once or twice but we lost touch. He married his ward sister soon after the divorce.'

'And Lois?'

'I suppose I looked after her. Saw her through. I thought he was a bit heartless abandoning her so soon after . . .'

'You weren't afraid she'd knife you?'

Nat smiled. 'I had no intention of giving her any cause.' He'd put his arm round Lois's shoulders to comfort her and had found love.

'Poor Dad.' He felt Jill's sympathy.

Life with Lois had not been easy. He hadn't expected it to be. Not after listening to Graham.

'I'm glad you've come home,' he said, patting his daughter's hand.

Jill made them a pot of tea when they got home, then she said: 'I'm tired, Dad. I'll take my tea upstairs and get to bed. Good night.'

Nat sat on alone in the sitting room, with one table lamp sending down a soft glow. The music played on in his head, and the memories, once started, could not be held back. Telling Jill about Lois had ripped the veils from his mind.

He'd gone to baby Phoebe's funeral. The tiny white coffin would have wrung tears from a stone, but Graham had been stern-faced and dignified, fully in command of himself. Lois, in floods of tears, had been well supported by her mother and grandmother. Graham had introduced Nat to them.

A week or so later, he'd been coming home from work and had met Lois in the road. Her smooth auburn hair was swinging about her shoulders, but he'd found the tormented gaze of her dark eyes heart-rending.

'Come inside and have a drink with me,' he'd invited, and she'd accepted. She'd been in a pitiable state, wandering round his sitting room and kitchen, unable to sit still.

She'd talked of Evelyn and Victoria, not of Graham and Phoebe. Her tears were only just under control, but he knew how much that awful night must have upset her. Having lost Sarah so recently, he understood how she must be feeling and felt a powerful stab of sympathy.

'Come whenever you feel like a chat,' he'd said when she was going.

He would not have been surprised if he'd never seen her again, but a few days later she was knocking on his door. She used to come then to see him much as Graham had previously.

She'd been white-faced for months, and he would see her fingers shake as she reached for the glass of wine she would sometimes accept. Her confidence was in shreds because her husband had walked out on her and her baby was dead.

He knew, because she talked a good deal about her career, that she was proud of being a doctor and of coming from a medical family.

'I worked for several years in paediatrics and at one time hoped to be a consultant,' she'd said.

Graham had already told him much the same.

'There was a clash of interests in our careers. Graham's pegged him in Birkenhead. He'd already had promotion, but I needed to seek it elsewhere. I was offered a job at Great Ormond Street but Graham talked me out of it.'

70

Nat remembered the night when Graham had told him that Lois had decided to be a general practitioner.

'She doesn't really want to,' he'd said, 'but I think it might suit her.' He'd said they were finding life stressful because they both expected too much from their careers.

Lois's haunted eyes made him feel compassion. He asked: 'Will you go back to work at the children's hospital when you feel better?'

'No, I don't think so. Work is easier to find in general practice. Even part-time work, if that's all I can manage.'

He hadn't pointed out that without a husband and child, she could concentrate on her career. Go anywhere. That would have been unfeeling of him. He thought that losing a child must almost be worse for a paediatrician than for anyone else.

On Sundays, he looked after Jill himself, giving her nanny the day off. One Sunday, he dressed her up in her best and took her round to Lois's house.

He wanted the three of them to share a walk. Then he would ask Lois back for tea and persuade her to feed Jill. He thought it might help if she were to share his baby.

Lois came out of the kitchen door to the pram. Jill laughed up at them both. He could see Lois trembling. It was a cool, blowy afternoon, but suddenly he could see moisture glistening on her forehead. It was only then that he realised the baby made her feel panic-stricken.

Lois refused brusquely to accompany them for a walk, and shot back inside the house. Victoria hovered uneasily, showing a polite interest in the baby.

'Lois is busy cooking at the moment,' she'd excused her. 'A special cake. Not a good moment for her to go for a walk, I'm afraid.' But it was Victoria's hands that were floury, not Lois's.

Lois drew back the next time he tried to take her near the baby. He'd blamed himself then, afraid he was rushing things; he shouldn't expect her to take to another child so soon.

He could understand that because he too had been bereaved. It was Sarah he wanted. Her loss gnawed at him. Loneliness was purgatorial. Baby Jill was a responsibility rather than a comfort. If he'd been given the choice in the early days, he'd gladly have given up Jill to have Sarah back.

At other times, Lois seemed in a frenzy of anger. She spoke of her loss, but it was the loss of Graham that she meant. She spoke of her grief, but she never mentioned Phoebe.

Nat felt instinctively that she was hovering on the edge of a nervous breakdown, but he didn't know what to do about it. He had to leave that to her family. They were all doctors and they'd rallied round her

71

from the start of her troubles. Her grandmother had moved in with her; her mother visited often.

One day Evelyn told him that Lois had gone into hospital and would be away for a few weeks, that it would be better if he didn't try to visit her.

Lois was better when she came out. It was only then that Victoria told him she'd needed psychiatric help to get over Phoebe's death. The invitations to supper came after that.

Nat felt that he was invited to cheer Lois. Evelyn and Victoria were always there and seemed to do all the cooking and serving. Lois's house was bigger and furnished in a grander style than his. He was flattered that she seemed to cling, to want him to come.

Lois had always had a slim, hard body and a worldly face. Had never seemed young, although at the time she'd been only thirty-two.

The only way he knew to offer comfort was to put an arm round her shoulders and pull her close. He hadn't intended to kiss her. Not the first time. He thought any woman's body would have inflamed him after all those months without Sarah.

Within two months of that first kiss, he was making love to Lois in Sarah's bed, half ashamed that he'd moved someone into her place so quickly. At the same time, he knew it was the right thing for him. Lois had bewitched him. Love had come again. Within weeks he'd been totally besotted by her.

He didn't think she'd ever felt that way about him, though she'd tried to pretend she did. She'd wanted him as a replacement for Graham. She'd wanted a man to run in circles round her. He'd felt disloyal about saying that, but he'd thought it for a long time.

CHAPTER SEVEN

The next morning at the surgery, Jill felt as if her last consultation was going on and on. She looked at the fraught face of the patient in front of her and tried to make up her mind what she should do.

She was consulted on so many things that were not strictly medical problems, and for which she felt she'd received no training.

Mrs Dunne was middle-aged and clearly at the end of her tether. She'd come in complaining of headaches, dizziness and sleepless nights, for which Jill could find no physical cause. Her story came out haltingly. Her husband had left her last year for another woman. For the past five years she'd managed a shop in Grange Road, but the business wasn't doing well.

'My boss is always pressing me. To re-dress the windows, or think of new ways of displaying the stock. He's on at me to keep the assistants on their toes and generally brighten the place up. The takings are going down. I think he's afraid of losing business.

'He gets mad at me if I have to take time off.' Her voice was lifting on a note of protest.

'What sort of shop?' Jill asked idly. Her father's chocolate shop was in Grange Road.

'It's Lambourne's,' the woman replied, pushing the grey hair from her forehead in a gesture of defeat. 'Do you know it?'

Jill was suddenly ramrod stiff in her chair. The takings were going down in Dad's shop? Was this why he was worried?

'Chocolates?'

'Lambourne's Luxury Chocolates.' Jill held her breath. What if the woman asked if she was related? The name Ridley was not that common.

Mrs Dunne's voice whined on: 'I've no energy to do any more, it's an effort to get through the day as it is.'

She was able to breath again, but found she was clutching the edge of her desk so hard she could see her fingers turning white. Dad had told her he had no business worries. If he mentioned his business at all, it was to say how busy he was, and that trade was buoyant.

She had known that something was wrong with Dad; he was in very low spirits. She hadn't thought it was anything as obvious as poor

73

business results. She'd been imagining something deeper, something connected with Lois. Unless, of course, he was going bankrupt . . .?

Jill took a deep breath. She mustn't think of Dad now. 'You live alone?'

'I've a fifteen-year-old daughter.'

'Still at school?'

'Yes, and I asked my mother to come and live with us. She's a widow, so it seemed sensible. I thought she could keep house while I continued to earn a living for us at the shop.'

'Very sensible,' Jill agreed.

'But now my mother and Colleen are fighting tooth and nail. There's never any peace. It drives me demented to hear them going on at each other. And they wait for me to come home to cook a meal for them every evening.'

'You must get your mother to do that.'

Mrs Dunne was grey-faced and sweating. She looked overworked and exhausted, and not far from a breakdown. In her present state, she wouldn't be able to insist on anything.

Jill pushed her prescription pad away. She didn't want to start the woman on medication. Nobody could do a good day's work if they were stuffed with tranquillisers. But what was the best thing for her?

She could give her a break from work, but that would mean she'd have to spend more time with her sparring family.

'Mrs Dunne, you need a holiday,' she said firmly. 'A complete rest. Could you get away for a while?'

'My sister has asked me . . . She lives in Llandudno.'

Jill felt relief that she'd found an answer.

'There's no treatment, Mrs Dunne,' she said with as much conviction as she could muster. 'Rest should cure you. Your body's telling you you've been doing far too much. You'll get no peace at home, so make sure you go away. I'll write you a note for two weeks off work.'

Jill sucked on the end of her pen. She must give the woman a reason for being off work, something to bolster her self-assurance. 'Nervous exhaustion,' she wrote on the sick note. It was the best she could come up with.

'You can't do everything. Let your family look after themselves. You need to relax. Come back and see me in two weeks.'

She looked up and saw such an expression of relief on the woman's face, she knew she'd done the right thing.

Jill didn't feel competent in cases like this. She felt too young to interfere in the lives of others. They should be making these decisions for themselves. She had to remind herself that Mrs Dunne was in no state to decide on anything.

Hearing about Dad's problems from a patient had almost thrown her. She'd been home all this time and had done nothing about getting to the bottom of his problems. When she'd had him to herself, curiosity had made her go on and on about Phoebe.

She must get her father to talk about his business. There was something very wrong somewhere. She could feel it everywhere in the house. An atmosphere of secrecy.

Jill did her home visits without stopping for lunch. Then she went to Lambourne's in Grange Road.

As soon as the shop door pinged open, she was sniffing the delicious scent of chocolate. Fancy boxes of all shapes and sizes were stacked on the shelves behind the counter. Dad had told her that once, Sarah, her mother, had designed the boxes and chosen the photographs and pictures that decorated them.

The shop was full of customers. Two smartly uniformed assistants were kept busy behind the glass counters, where chocolates were laid out on trays to be sold loose. There were dark, milk and white chocolates of every size and shape. The assistants used scoops to pick them up.

It didn't look as though Dad needed to spend much time overseeing the shop. It looked prosperous and efficient. She left without waiting to be served.

She knew where to find the manufacturing premises. Her father used to bring her here as a child. The building was only some four hundred yards away, in a quiet back street. She could smell chocolate as she got closer.

Once inside the door, the air was heavy and sensuous. The scent of chocolate almost seemed to wrap itself round her.

She found a cubby hole of an office, with a typewriter on the desk. His secretary wasn't in, but Jill could see her father in the cramped office beyond, hunched over his desk. A single electric bulb swung above it to augment the dearth of natural light. Machinery clattered close by.

'Not ideal working conditions, Dad.'

'Hello.' His crumpled face beamed with delight. 'Come to see the old place?' He leapt to his feet.

'Come to see you.'

'What about? It couldn't wait till I got home?'

'Your shop manager, Mrs Dunne. I've put her off work for a fortnight.'

He paused, rubbed his eyes. 'What's the matter with her?'

'Nervous exhaustion.'

'Is that an illness?' He was snorting with indignation. 'Then it must be catching! I think I might have a touch myself.'

'I know. That's one reason I came.'

'Really? I was joking. Nervous exhaustion indeed! She's always taking time off anyway. Never works a full week.'

'She's close to a breakdown, Dad.'

He seemed suddenly serious. 'I can believe that. She's been spiralling downwards for months. Not much good at the job.'

Jill remembered Mrs Dunne's lethargy and aura of defeat. She should have expected this.

'When she's off, it means I have to spend more time in the shop myself. I ought to sack her and take on somebody else, but these days that's difficult.'

'Dad! She could recover, work on for years, give you every satisfaction.'

'Because of your doctoring?' He let his breath escape through his lips in a low whistle. His expression said: Pigs might fly.

'Fortunately I've got two good girls there as assistants. I ought to make one of them manager to reduce my workload. Perhaps I will.'

'Don't, Dad. It won't help Mrs Dunne.'

'It'll reduce her workload and responsibilities. Make it easier for her to take a day off.'

'Reduce her self-esteem.' Jill met her father's gaze. His eyes were less than sympathetic today. 'And her pay, I suppose?'

'I'm trying to run a business, Jill. Not a convalescent home. Self-esteem indeed! We're on opposite sides of the fence here.'

'I'm just pointing out that your employees have difficulties. Do you know about her home life?'

'What do you expect me to do? I have to put the needs of the business first. It would go under if I didn't, then none of us would have jobs.'

'Is it likely to? Are you worried about it, Dad?' She was watching him closely.

'No,' he denied briskly. 'We're doing all right.' Something in his manner made her suspect that that wasn't the whole truth.

'Mrs Dunne says the shop takings are down. That you're pressing her to sell more the whole time.'

Jill knew she was handling this the wrong way the moment the words were out of her mouth.

His anger made him flash out: 'The Mrs Dunnes of this world have to be pushed to do anything. Otherwise she'd be asleep on the counter. Damn Mrs Dunne! She's neurotic. I'll have to get somebody else to run the place.'

Jill had to persist now she'd started. 'Did you tell her the takings were down?'

'It's her job to tell me what the shop takings are. But trade is seasonal, always has been. That's the way of it. The shop's doing all right.'

'And overall the business is profitable? You aren't worried about it?'

'It is profitable, Jill.'

She knew that there was something on his mind. He was blustering, losing his temper. He was finding it difficult to tell her.

And what was she doing pressing Mrs Dunne's case? She wanted to help her father. He needed efficient staff.

'How about some coffee?' He began fussing round with an ancient electric kettle and some mugs in his secretary's office.

'I've had no lunch,' she said. 'Am I allowed to have some of your chocolates?'

'I can do better than that.' He pushed a tin of oatcakes in front of her, then went to a rusting fridge outside in the corridor and found the heel of a piece of cheese.

'Did they never teach you anything at medical school about diet? You can't make a whole meal out of chocolates.'

'Is this what you eat?'

'Every day.'

Jill laughed. 'You should have more variety.'

'It's quicker than a pub lunch.'

'It isn't far to go home.'

'Yes, well . . . It's quicker than that, too.'

Jill wondered if he was avoiding Lois.

'Come on,' he said when she'd finished eating. 'I'll show you around and you can get some chocolates.'

The delicious scent was overpowering. Machinery hummed and whirred. She paused by a conveyor belt to watch pieces of fudge being cut to a precise size and then moving on to be immersed in a bath of chocolate.

'We've got ten people working in production,' her father told her. They were all wearing white coats and hats. He introduced them to her.

'We used to buy in some of the fancier fillings, but all our chocolates are made from scratch now.'

'Is that cheaper?'

'It will be eventually. I had to buy more equipment and it all takes space. We're pretty well automated. I brought over a French chocolatier last year to help us achieve the exact flavour at the most advantageous cost.'

'And it means that nobody else makes anything like yours?'

'Yes, we have to be different. I keep trying to develop new flavours. We now have a range of over fifty. Some are more popular than others, of course. Try one of these truffles.'

'Mmm, delicious.' She let the rich mocha melt on her tongue. 'I couldn't eat many of them, though.'

Nat laughed. 'These are less sickly. Try this lemon slice.'

It cleared Jill's palate. 'Wonderful tang.' She took another.

'We've just started making crystallised fruits and fruit pastilles, using real fruit and juice. They're going well and helping to keep sales up in the hot weather. Summer has always been our off season.'

Jill was impressed. Dad was putting thought and energy into the business. He still had bags under his eyes and looked exhausted, but he seemed to have more go here on his own ground.

'Of course, Christmas is our busiest time. I'm trying to decide what to do this year. We'll need to start making them soon.'

'I loved the new one you made last year called Wenceslas Cup.'

'Yes, we'll do that again. This is a new one I'm trying out. What's it taste of?'

'Hmm . . . Christmas pudding.'

'We'll shape them into balls and cover them with printed foil, so they look like Christmas puddings.'

'Should go well.'

'I'm hoping for big things. We have to keep searching for novelty. Wouldn't do for customers to get tired of our products.

'I need different ways of packaging too. I'd like you to look at our boxes and caskets and see if you can come up with something new. Your mother was very good at that. Sarah, I mean, not Lois.

'We've started making our own boxes. Unfortunately, there's no room for that here. We've had to take new premises in Liverpool.'

'Doesn't that make it harder for you to run?'

'I have to go over to our shop there anyway. The retail outlets make a big share of our profits. But I dream of having a purpose-built factory one day, with everything under one roof.'

The chocolates were not all new to Jill. Dad had kept her supplied with boxes of them all the time she'd been away from home. She'd handed them round to her friends, proud to say that Lambourne's Luxury Chocolates were made by her father. Even more proud when they reported seeing the boxes in Harrods and other big London shops.

She was telling him so when she heard the door bang shut and heavy footsteps coming up the passage.

'It's Ena coming back from lunch,' Nat told her. 'My secretary. I don't know what I'd do without her.'

She came to the door with easy familiarity and said: 'I'm back, Nat.'

'Come and say hello to Jill, my daughter.'

A large plump hand grasped Jill's. Ena had a fleshy, middle-aged face running into a thick neck.

'You're the doctor? He's very proud of you.' Ena's hair was short and mousy, like duck's down fluttering round her rubber-like face. 'He's been looking forward to having you home.'

Jill wondered if her father confided in Ena. She guessed he did when Ena added: 'You'll be able to help him now.'

'I'll help in any way I can.'

The tiny eyes under heavy lids glanced at Nat, showing affection for him. Jill was left in no doubt about Ena's feelings for her boss.

When Jill had gone, Nathaniel sat on in his dark office, staring at the wall. He should have told her. He could have had it all off his chest by now. He'd made up his mind to unload the whole sordid story on her, and yet when he had the chance, he'd got cold feet.

He hadn't handled it right either. There were lots of worries he could have told her about and still skirted over the worst part.

He could have said it was time he was thinking of retirement and that he needed to train somebody up to run the company in his place. That it was getting too much for him. He could have gone some way to preparing Jill. Instead he'd told her everything was fine.

But she'd come and caught him unawares, when his mind had been on other things. He hadn't been ready to talk about it. He was tired and not thinking straight. Guilt-ridden too, at what he'd done. And what was the good of making excuses now?

'Ena,' he called, 'have you seen my pen? I've mislaid it again.' He patted his breast pocket where he usually clipped it.

'I turned your office inside out yesterday, Nat. Have you left it at home?'

He'd forgotten to look last night. He sighed and reached for a biro, feeling worn-out and irritable. He wanted to make his peace with Jill, but he couldn't do that without making a clean breast of it.

What the hell was the matter with him?

A few days later, Felix held on to Jill's arm as they walked along the promenade at New Brighton. It was a bright and blustery Saturday afternoon.

Jill's honey-blonde hair was fluttering in the stiff breeze coming off the Mersey estuary. He noticed for the first time that she had a few freckles across her nose. She seemed to radiate good health and he found that very attractive. Spending so much time with Pa made him more sensitive to illness. It did him good to switch off from home and go out with her.

They had stood downwind of the donkeys until their acrid smell reached them. As they watched the animals set off along the sands, he told himself that Jill's company was exactly what he needed.

But Pa was beginning to come between them. Felix was very conscious of the fact that he hadn't taken Jill home to meet his father. He knew he would have done by now if circumstances had been different.

He hardly dared mention Pa to Jill. He was half afraid that he'd be drawn to say too much once he started.

Jill had laughed. 'For reasons of her own, Mother doesn't approve of you. She doesn't like me bringing my friends to the house.'

Felix caught his breath. It was on the tip of his tongue to tell her. To let it all come out.

Jill laughed again. 'I don't suppose you're sorry. You wouldn't find it much fun being polite to her.'

They'd walked out across the sands to see the old fort. They had stayed for an hour; Jill had been fascinated by the relics from the past. Then they'd watched two huge tankers come through the channel and into the river.

But all the time Felix's mind had been on other things. He knew so much about Jill and her relatives. He lapped up the smallest fact she dropped about the surgery and what went on there, but he dared not ask questions about it.

He couldn't speak frankly about his life and what he felt so strongly. He was sure he knew much more about her than she did about him.

Sometimes, as her jade-green eyes surveyed him, he thought he saw a puzzled look there. As though she'd noticed that he kept a tight rein on his tongue and thought him secretive. This wasn't getting him anywhere.

But there was worse. For months he'd been driven by an urge to take his revenge on Lois. His need for it was growing. It was not an attractive trait, and one he'd be ashamed to let Jill see.

Stamping it down, trying to turn his back on it, made his need to act all the stronger. Like unrequited love, it was burgeoning out of control.

It was holding him back, slowing him down. In this day and age, couples made up their minds quickly and without fuss. Half of them would be living together in less time than he had been taking Jill out to theatres and dinners and walks. It made him seem half-hearted about her, and that was the last thing he was.

He didn't dare think what might have happened had he not come home that night. He felt hot, burning anger rising in his throat every time he thought about it.

He was sure he had grounds for bringing a case for negligence against Lois Benbow. His father had also consulted Miles Sutton during the early stages of his illness, but both doctors refused to speak to him, and he couldn't get Cuthbert Meadows to discuss his father's previous treatment. They had closed ranks.

There could be only one reason, and that was to protect each other. That made him all the more certain he was right.

Now he was also being driven by a need to find out where he stood with Jill. He loved her. He wanted their relationship to be on a permanent basis.

It was like driving two wild horses. He wanted to discuss marriage with her. Why not? It was what he wanted. He'd never felt like this about any girl before. But he couldn't marry her without coming clean about Pa.

He stole a glance at her. She was gazing out across the Mersey estuary at the tankers. Each day that passed he felt more drawn to her. Outings with her went some way to compensate for giving up his job and coming home again.

It was a greater strain to earn a living this way. He'd had to keep thinking hard about where he could sell his articles. He spent endless hours studying possible markets. He daren't let up.

Felix felt the good parts of his life centred round Jill. It was on the tip of his tongue to tell her all this, but how could he tell the girl he loved that he'd asked her out that first time to pick her brains. That he'd intended to use her for his own ends?

He hoped Jill would never ask him whether it had been love at first sight.

Felix sighed as he stirred the spaghetti sauce. He used to enjoy cooking for himself, now he wasn't so sure. Pa didn't care for the sort of meals he made, yet he wouldn't come and do anything himself. He was sure his father would feel better if only he'd get out of his armchair and do something.

He felt for the cheese grater at the back of the cupboard. He knew where everything was kept in the kitchen. Nothing had changed since he'd grown up in this house. It was like being in a time warp. Everything was older and shabbier but otherwise had remained the same over a quarter of a century.

'Pa,' he went across to the sitting room door, 'I brought some whisky home. Would you like a glass?'

The heat in the sitting room overwhelmed him. Pa insisted on having the gas fire on all the time and sat right in front of it. He didn't even look round. His shoulders were bent, he looked torpid, numb almost.

'I don't mind.'

Felix went back to the kitchen, telling himself that he had to stay cheerful. He poured whisky for Pa and opened a bottle of beer for himself.

There were too many small rooms in this house, pantry, morning room, scullery, kitchen. They needed knocking together to make one decent-sized room.

It was a four-bedroomed family house, built after the First World War; mature, substantial, and far too large for his father on his own. But he wouldn't even consider moving anywhere else.

Felix took the drinks back and sat down in the chair opposite his father. 'There's a good programme on tonight.'

'I don't care much for television.' Pa sounded miserably apathetic.

'It's the history of the Second World War. You enjoyed last week's instalment.'

'I'm not in the mood for it tonight.'

Felix was finding it difficult to cope with his father. He seemed to have lost interest in everything. When his mother had died three years ago he'd insisted on taking Pa down to his flat in Streatham.

'You'll be better off there with me now,' he'd said. 'Come and try it. You're welcome to stay.'

Felix knew he had a good life in London. A comfortable flat, a decent social life. He was ambitious and everything was going well for him.

'Perhaps for a few days. I'll have to be back in time to start the new term.' His father was mathematics master at a local school.

'Why not try and get a job in London?'

'I'd rather stay with what I'm used to.'

Felix knew that his school friends had thought Pa a dry old stick years ago. He'd always been set in his ways, very formal. Even now, to sit about the house, he was wearing a suit with jacket and waistcoat. He had a black Oxford brogue on his one foot.

His father had come home to Birkenhead and the job he'd done for twenty-five years. Felix had telephoned once a week to see how he was getting on. In the school holidays, Pa would come down for a week or so, and Felix went home for an occasional weekend.

His father was never very cheerful. Felix knew that his mother's death had been a great blow and that he was lonely. He thought that in time, Pa would find life easier. Instead, he began to feel unwell.

His ill health dragged on for a long time and he seemed to be getting worse. One day, on the phone, he told Felix that his foot was very painful. Felix told him to be sure to see his doctor in the morning.

'I went yesterday.' He'd sounded so ill that Felix decided he must come up and see him straight away.

It was a Saturday, and he'd come on the train. It was less exhausting than driving both ways. He'd told Pa not to come and meet him, though he always had before. He had ridden up on the bus from Woodside. It had been pitch dark when he'd arrived.

He'd seen the light on in his father's bedroom as he'd come up the path. It had surprised him, because Pa didn't go to bed early. He'd been able to let himself in because he still had his key.

He'd run upstairs to see his father and found himself gripped with cold panic. Pa was confused and dazed. Writhing, almost crying out with pain. His foot was very much worse.

He couldn't stand the weight of the bedclothes on it. It was sticking out at the side. His toes were covered with a pad held on with stockinet, through which a foul discharge was soaking. With mounting horror, Felix realised he could smell it.

'What's the matter? What caused this?'

'Doctor thought my shoes – rubbing.'

'Do you have new shoes?'

He shook his head.

'Is it a long time since you had it dressed?'

'Never had it dressed.'

'But this dressing?'

'From the doctor. I put it on.'

'When?' Felix demanded.

Pa couldn't think.

'Recently?'

At last he mumbled, 'Yesterday? Or the day before.'

Between bouts of agonising pain, Pa struggled to tell Felix that he'd taken more than the prescribed amount of the painkillers he'd been given. They both knew they were having no effect.

Pa was so bad Felix couldn't see how he was going to get through the night. It was after eleven, but there was only one thing Felix felt he could do. He must get his father's doctor here.

He rang for Dr Lois Benbow. A voice on an answering machine told him that Dr Cuthbert Meadows was on call that night and gave him an alternative number. Felix rang that and asked for an immediate visit.

Cuthbert Meadows had been there within twenty minutes. He'd stayed with Pa until the ambulance came to the door half an hour later to take him to hospital. Felix went with him. He'd been stunned when he'd been told that his father had diabetic gangrene. There could be no delay. Pa's leg had been amputated later that night. Nothing else would have saved his life.

Felix had returned home by taxi in the small hours. He'd gone to bed but his mind had been on fire and he couldn't sleep. Pa had never been diagnosed as a diabetic. At the hospital they'd told him his father must have been suffering from diabetes for some time. Had it been treated, Pa would not have lost his leg.

Even now, Felix couldn't get over his anger and frustration when he thought about it.

Another trip to the kitchen told him the meal was ready to serve. Pa would only eat in the dining room.

'All ready, Pa,' he told him, and went back to dish up.

He couldn't watch Pa move about. To see one trouser leg flapping emptily brought a lump to his throat. Such an intense feeling of sympathy; of frustration that this had happened. That was why he kept on trying to give all the help he could.

Pa refused point-blank to have a wheelchair. He had learned to hop about the house, and could get around quite well on crutches. But he didn't like going out and displaying his infirmity.

Felix had taken him back to London to recuperate. But Pa hadn't been happy in the flat, though there had been a lift.

'Stay here with me,' Felix had tried to persuade him. 'We get on all right together.' He needed to make sure his father kept to his diet. He looked ill and frail and was despondent.

'I can't stand any more changes. Not yet, there've been too many since your mother died. And what if I'm passed fit for work?'

He'd just had his fifty-fifth birthday. Felix couldn't see him facing the hurly-burly of school life ever again. He expected him to be retired early on the grounds of ill health, but he couldn't say that. Pa had to have hope that life would return to normal.

So he'd given up the lease on his London flat and had come home to Birkenhead. After all, as a journalist he could continue to work as a freelance.

He'd been a bit nervous about that at first, but it was working out reasonably well. He felt a long way from the hub of the universe. Too far away from important happenings. He was missing stories because of that, but was getting the hang of writing about subjects of general interest.

Felix felt that his life had become a quagmire over the last six months. It had changed him, and not for the better. He'd never thought of himself as vindictive, but now he was boiling to exact revenge on those who by their negligence had allowed this to happen to his father.

The reason he'd gone to take pictures of Bill Goodbody's retirement was to get his foot in the surgery door. It helped that he'd been able to sell his work, but that had not been his main purpose.

The only good thing that had come out of it was that he'd met Jill Ridley.

At first it had pleased him that she was a doctor. He didn't trust his grasp on medical matters. He wanted desperately to discuss Pa's case with someone who could evaluate the treatment he'd received and give a fair judgement. That was why he'd asked Jill out for a meal. But once she'd told him that Lois Benbow was her mother, it had changed everything. In any case, she'd warned him off the subject.

The urge to talk about it hadn't gone away, but now he was afraid he'd spoil what seemed so promising. Afraid that Jill would do what the other doctors had done – refuse to talk about it. That she'd want no more to do with him and send him on his way. He didn't want to risk that. What he felt for Jill went too deep.

He wished she had nothing to do with that practice. It was a further complication he could do without.

The next afternoon, Jill had a patient to visit in Marion Street, which was close to her father's chocolate factory. She decided to call in and see him again. She felt that he wanted her to take more interest in his business.

There were several small businesses operating from premises close by, and she could smell peanuts being roasted before the cloying scent of chocolate took over.

She heard Ena laughing as soon as she opened the office door, and headed straight for the secretary's room. Dad was there too; she was glad he had someone to lift his spirits.

Ena was all cushions of fat, but she was tucking into chocolate along with a cup of coffee.

'Come and sit down, I'll make a cup for you,' she told Jill.

'We were just trying to come up with some new ideas for packaging.' Dad seemed to have recovered. 'You've come at a good time.'

'We're scraping the bottom of the barrel.' Ena laughed so that her layers of flesh wobbled. 'We've done it so often, it's hard to come up with anything new. We're just rehashing the usual stuff.'

'We need something different for Christmas,' Nat said, biting the end of his pencil. 'Some novelty that can be given to children, but not so Christmassy that we can't sell it afterwards. Our normal stock is very much for adults.'

Jill leafed through the books of samples her father kept as a record of every design he had used. She spent a lot of time over the first books showing her mother's designs.

She thought for a moment and said: 'What about a box of crayons? Stubby cylinders with a point at one end. Wrapped in coloured foil. Red for strawberry or cherry crème. Green for peppermint cream and so on.'

Ena sat up straighter. 'Lambourne's Box of Crayons. Just the thing, isn't it, Nat?'

'Lemon flavour could be yellow. Orange would be easy.'

'It's an idea we can work on.'

'Or you could call it a paintbox and have bite-size oblongs. Would that make them cheaper to make?'

'Wonderful stocking-fillers for children. It would be a change from chocolate Father Christmases.'

Jill was trying to draw.

'The paintbox,' Nat said, 'I like that.'

'We can use the standard box shape,' Ena added. 'Just alter the artwork. I'll see what I can come up with.'

'Jill, you must come more often with ideas like that.'

'Where are you going now?'

'Into the factory. We're working on a new flavour. Sort of bilberries in syrup. Come with me and see what you think.'

'You could wrap that in purple foil.'

'No, the filling isn't suitable for children. Need to keep that fairly plain.'

Jill was pleased to find her father in so cheerful a mood. He seemed better today. They went to his dark little office where the window looked out on to a brick wall only a few yards away.

'I'd like to come regularly, Dad. See if I can help in other ways. You often work on a Saturday, don't you?'

'Yes.'

'I could come then too, if you'll have me.'

'You know I'd be delighted if you would.'

Jill felt they were making progress. She was learning something about his business. She felt more hopeful, and decided there was nothing much the matter with him after all. Perhaps he was just in need of a holiday.

She'd get to the bottom of his problems sooner or later.

CHAPTER EIGHT

The following Saturday morning was dark and depressing. Jill could hear the rain lashing against her window. She snuggled down under her duvet, feeling heavy-eyed because she'd been out late with Felix again last night. She knew that Lois and her father had been downstairs for some time.

Much earlier, she'd heard Lois's voice on the landing, talking to Victoria.

'I've brought your breakfast tray. How are you this morning? Did you sleep well?'

Gran's voice had creaked wearily but Jill couldn't catch the words. It took Lois a long time to get her organised to eat. Now Lois was outside her door.

'Jill? Are you awake? It's gone half past eight.'

'I'm getting up.' Reluctantly she swung her feet out of bed.

As she went downstairs she could see Lois already at her desk in the study. 'Morning, Lois,' she called through the open door.

The scent of coffee filled the kitchen. Jill slid some bread into the toaster and went to kiss her father, who had the morning paper open across the table.

'There's a letter for you,' he said, nodding towards the official-looking envelope at her place. She ripped it open; she'd been half expecting it.

'Dad,' she started. It was a request from her solicitor to pay £6,000. She'd known it would be coming sooner or later.

Almost at the same moment, Lois's voice came peremptorily from the study. 'Nat? Can I have a word?'

He half smiled at his daughter before pulling himself to his feet and shambling out. Jill buttered her toast, pulled his paper towards her and started to eat.

She could hear their voices, lower now, murmuring together. She took no notice until she caught her own name.

'It's for Jill,' Lois was saying indignantly. 'Not for me at all.' Jill put her cup down and listened then. 'I did tell you.'

'No you didn't.'

'You've forgotten, Nat. I told you Jill has to buy her way in.'

'I thought doctors stopped buying and selling their practices years ago – when the Health Service came in.'

'Yes, they did, but I'm talking about our surgery premises, Nat. I did explain.'

'Does Jill have to? Can't she rent?'

Jill felt a stab of dismay. She knew exactly what they were talking about. She'd thanked her father for his help with this, but she'd known that his mind had been on something else at the time. She should have discussed it more fully with him.

'Some practices rent health centre accommodation from the council. But Bill Goodbody bought the house we practice in years ago.'

'So Jill . . .' She could hear the reluctance in her father's voice.

'You knew I bought a share of it when I became a partner.'

'That was before we were married.'

'Well, you knew I had to pay my share when we had the extension built.'

'You said something about a grant.'

'Yes, we got one but we had a loan too, to help us improve our practice premises. The partners own it between them; now Jill has to buy Bill's share from him. It's the way all partnerships work, Nat. You know that.'

At their first meeting, Lois had assured her, and all the partners, that Nathaniel would provide the money on Jill's behalf. That it would come from his business and there would be no difficulty. Now it seemed that there was.

Jill got to her feet and went over to the study door. Dad looked upset.

'Don't worry,' she said. 'I can get a mortgage or a bank loan or something.'

'Surely that won't be necessary?' Lois was affronted. 'Will it, Nat?'

'No, of course not.'

'If money is difficult to find at the moment, I'd rather . . .' Jill felt embarrassed. 'If business is tight, Dad. If it won't stretch to this, I'd rather go to the bank.'

'Don't worry,' Lois said firmly. 'Your father thought I wanted the money. Now he knows it's for you that's quite different.'

'It's a change for you not to want . . .' Nat began heatedly, and then pulled himself up. 'I've saved some money for you, Jill. It's in your name.'

He went to the safe and opened it. 'I have some securities here that you can liquidate to pay for your share.'

'Are you sure? Is the business all right, Dad?'

He'd already told her it was, but now it seemed that might not be the case. She'd meant to spend time talking to him today. Get him into a relaxed mood so he would tell her what was bothering him.

'Of course I'm sure.' Her father had taken a bundle of certificates from the safe and was sorting through them.

'Leave it with me for a while. I'll have to decide which of these are the best to cash in now.'

'I'm very grateful, Dad.' Jill hesitated. She didn't really understand what he was doing. 'Are you tying money up in my name?'

'Yes,' said Lois, tight-lipped.

Jill wondered if this was Dad's method of stopping Lois from getting her hands on it. There could be no other reason.

The episode seemed to sour everybody. Her father decided to go to work, though he'd agreed yesterday to spend the day at home with her.

'We've had two big orders in. Last-minute, of course. I've had to ask everybody to come in both today and tomorrow. The factory's running flat out.'

'But you don't need to be there the whole time, do you?' He didn't answer. 'Dad, you need a rest.'

'You said we could go for a long walk, but it's too wet for walking this morning,' he told her brusquely.

'I also said I'd come to the factory with you.'

'Better if you don't,' he said. 'I won't have time to be sociable. Sorry, Jill, but I'm not in the mood either.'

'Dad,' she protested, 'I want to help.'

The kitchen door slammed behind him, and she saw him striding out to his car. That left Jill feeling as touchy as he was.

When she went up to collect Gran's breakfast tray, the old lady said she wasn't feeling too good, and that she'd stay where she was for the time being.

'Is your wrist aching? Do you need more painkillers?'

'I just feel generally off. Heavy and headachy, and as though I could go back to sleep.' As Jill left, Gran was settling back on her pillows.

Her father came home for lunch and put a typewritten letter in front of her.

'Just sign this, and you can have the cash you need.'

'Dad, I don't want you to be worried about money. I'll borrow it. You don't have to provide for me now I'm working.'

'It's your money, Jill. It doesn't make sense to borrow if you have the capital.'

'But if the business . . .'

'This money is not coming from the business. I've already invested it in your name.'

'Why?' she asked.

He looked harassed. 'I haven't time to go into that now.'

'Thank you,' Jill said, and signed.

It was still raining. Dad was going back to the office and Gran was still in bed. She'd had her lunch on a tray upstairs.

Lois, who had invited a doctor friend for supper to introduce to Jill, was busy with preparations, though Mrs Moon was returning to do the cooking.

Jill decided she had to get out. Dad couldn't even talk about money. It had spoiled the whole morning for them. She was sure now he must have business problems.

She wished she'd accepted Felix's invitation to go swimming with him. She rang his home but nobody lifted the phone. She went down to Grange Road instead and bought herself a new pair of shoes.

Jill wasn't looking forward to the evening. Her father came home looking exhausted.

'I'd much prefer to have a light supper and watch the box,' he'd told her. But he didn't say that to Lois.

Now her family was gathering in the sitting room. Jill went downstairs to join them and sip a glass of white wine. Victoria had come down saying she felt a little better. They were waiting for their guest to arrive for dinner.

'You'll like him,' Lois told Jill confidently. 'He's a consultant anaesthetist. Very popular with the staff. Isn't he, Mother?'

Victoria agreed. Jill didn't share their confidence.

'Nat, could you change that tie? It looks a bit tired. I bought you two new silk ones, why don't you wear one of those? And a jacket. You must wear a jacket.'

'You said informal, Lois.' Dad sounded exasperated. 'And it's a heavy sort of evening.'

'Your blazer will do nicely. I don't want Robert to think your standards are slipping. The rest of us have tried.' Lois smoothed down her smart black sheath.

Jill watched uneasily as Nat left the room.

'He's going to seed,' Lois told her irritably. 'He never buys clothes for himself. If I didn't do it he'd look like a scarecrow. I do my best to keep him looking smart.'

It seemed that Lois and her father were on far worse terms than Jill had first supposed. Lois was henpecking him, and her dictatorial manner didn't help. Nat had been a handsome man in his youth but now his features were growing heavy and slack and he was taking less interest in his appearance. Jill felt sorry for him; she knew he wasn't happy.

I told you Robert was thirty-eight, didn't I? I think a man of that age is about right for you. He's had time to make his way in the world.'

'Lois, I won't be getting engaged to him tonight. It's not the way we do it these days.'

'I just want you to know how things stand.' Lois sounded testy. 'What's the harm in that?'

'He can afford to keep a wife in comfort,' Victoria added.

'Why hasn't he got one then?'

'Very upsetting,' Lois said. 'His wife left him last year. She wasn't a doctor. I think that's what he needs. It's another bond. Doctors understand each other.'

'He's here.' Jill watched a large grey Volvo pull up in front of the house. A very sedate car. The man who got out seemed stiff. He carried a bunch of flowers.

Her father was coming downstairs as the front door bell rang, and brought him in. Dad certainly looked spruced up. He'd combed his greying hair again. It was damped down and flat.

Robert Montgomery was a staid and serious man. He presented the flowers to Lois, kissed Victoria's cheek and offered his hand to Jill. It was limp. Jill sat down with another glass of wine.

Within five minutes their guest was holding forth about the latest techniques in anaesthetics. He seemed almost to lecture. Jill thought him very knowledgeable. She wondered what he'd say if she took out a notebook to record some of the facts he was spouting. She smiled at the thought. It was the only thing she did find to smile about.

As they went into the dining room, he did what every guest to the house did: he paused in front of the large oil painting hanging over the sideboard. It drew the attention like a magnet. In her youth, Jill had grown used to hearing them all say, as Robert Montgomery said now:

'How wonderful! Three lady doctors. A charming picture.'

They had been painted more than life size in the style of the Victorian school. The frame was six inches of ornate gilt curliques.

'When was it painted?'

'Just after the war,' Lois answered.

'Pity you aren't up there too,' Robert said to Jill. 'Wonderful to have four generations of doctors in the family.'

'I wasn't born then,' she retorted, but she couldn't take her eyes away from the picture either. It had always fascinated her.

Evelyn, her step-great-grandmother, seated very upright. Dark hair piled up on top of her head reminiscent of Edwardian days. A serious face, her jaw line heavy with determination.

Victoria smiling down, standing beside her mother's chair. More rounded and prettier than the older woman, her eyes almost coquettish.

Then Lois, still young, lolling on the grass, wearing a full-skirted dress. She'd been sharp-featured even then, so she lacked the family likeness. True, she had their sloe-black eyes, but in her they were wild and demanding. The set of her dark auburn head, everything about her, said quite clearly: I'm going to have everything in life. Succeed at everything. Drain life to the last drop.

It was lobster thermidor for dinner again; Mrs Moon's speciality, it seemed. Jill enjoyed it just as much the second time. It was beautifully set out in lobster shells and decorated with strands of fennel. There was chablis instead of champagne.

'For more sophisticated palates,' Lois had told her pointedly.

Robert Montgomery spent the entire meal explaining the latest factors in pain relief and its importance in keeping the patient relaxed. He seemed interested only in medical matters.

Jill began to feel she'd had enough of him. He was continuing to hold forth, becoming over-technical, reeling off new drugs until her mind refused to grasp any more.

She thought she'd given him a fair innings. As far as she was concerned, he was a non-starter. Felix was much more fun.

She looked round at her family again as they lingered over the cheese. Lois was in her element but Dad was bored with medical discussions. He'd given up trying to join in the conversation, and had poured port for those who wanted it and then got himself a bottle of beer. Lois's eyes were telling everybody she disapproved of that.

Gran was beginning to yawn. She looked very old tonight, very frail. She hadn't eaten much and seemed a bit switched off. She'd said earlier that she thought she was getting a head cold, and now she was using her handkerchief a good deal, so it seemed she was right.

Jill wanted to draw the old lady out. She was more curious than ever about her family, though of course she wasn't going to mention Phoebe again. She wouldn't push Gran, just try to get her to reminisce. Surely old people always liked doing that?

From her seat directly facing the portrait, she couldn't avoid the forceful eyes of her step-family. She knew that her grandmother was following her gaze.

'You were very pretty when you were young,' she said. 'Tell us about the old days, Gran.'

'I wasn't young then,' Victoria snorted contemptuously. 'I suppose to you, the end of the war must seem like the dark ages.'

Robert Montgomery was unexpectedly helpful and said: 'Medicine must have been very different. I expect it was hard for your mother in the very early years.'

Nat roused himself to say: 'She must have been one of the first women doctors in the country.'

'Don't be ridiculous,' Victoria flared. 'There was a school of medicine in London that trained women a hundred years ago.

'Very different for them when they came to practise. It was thought improper for women doctors to treat men. It would have caused a scandal then.'

'Men still ruled the profession in Evelyn's day. Women weren't generally accepted even then.'

'Come on, Gran. Tell us about her.' Jill felt mesmerised by the picture. Evelyn's fierce eyes were gazing straight into hers as though trying to tell her something.

Victoria said slowly: 'Even as a girl, my mother felt she was called to help the sick. That she had a gift for it. She thought of herself as a healer.'

'Something she could bestow with the laying-on of hands, you mean?' Jill asked.

'She had a fervour for it.' Victoria's voice creaked with weariness. 'She knew there was a scientific basis to medicine, and was desperately keen to learn all she could about it. And when she was qualified, she was even more desperate to be allowed to practise it.'

'That must have made her a good doctor.'

'One of the best. That was another thing that . . .'

'Let's go back to the sitting room,' Lois interrupted. 'More comfortable there.'

Jill carried round the cups of coffee Lois was pouring. Her father was pouring brandy for himself and their guest. She opened a fresh box of chocolates and handed those round too. Lois waved the box away imperiously. Robert was doing the same.

'These are what Dad makes,' Jill told him. He felt compelled to take one.

Jill savoured a chocolate fudge. What Gran had told them had whetted her appetite, but she hadn't got round to anything about her own experiences. She looked prickly now.

Robert was holding forth on anaesthetics again. Everybody but Lois had had enough of that. Dad's face registered resignation. He was sitting back with his eyes closed as Robert's voice droned on.

Jill helped herself to an orange cream. She thought it a little over-sweet for her taste. She ought to stick to the ones with nuts in, they were less rich, less sickly.

'You shouldn't gorge yourself on those,' Lois said disapprovingly. 'Not good for you. Chocolate can be addictive, you know.'

'I think it's already got a hold on me.' As Jill helped herself to another, she realised that Robert had paused for breath.

She said eagerly: 'Come on, Gran, tell us what it was like for you in the old days.'

'No,' Gran snapped, struggling to get up out of her chair. 'I think I'll go to bed. I'm tired.'

Jill was angry with herself for pushing too hard. Disappointed, too, but at least it made their guest stand up. Dad winked at her because she'd brought the evening to an end and they could all go to bed.

She sighed. She was finding it more difficult than she'd expected to get Victoria to tell her what she wanted to know. This was certainly a house for secrets. Everybody's lips were sealed.

Victoria felt as if she was half carried upstairs, by Nat on one side of her and Jill on the other. Lucky the stairs at Links View were wide enough for three people abreast, because the way she felt she'd never have made it on her own.

The climb left her feeling disorientated and weak. She sank down on the edge of her bed, struggling with the buttons on her dress.

'Let me help you,' Jill said, closing the door behind them.

'These fastenings . . .' Even before this accident it had been taking her longer and longer to get herself into bed.

She had no energy tonight. Jill was pulling her dress over her head. In no time at all, she felt the cool satin of her nightdress against her body. Victoria felt old and stiff, and so dreadfully tired, but she didn't need to tell Jill, who put two paracetamol in her hand and passed her a glass of water. It hurt to swallow, because she had a sore throat. Couldn't breathe properly, but she'd sleep all right.

Jill put out the light and tiptoed out. Victoria could feel herself sliding into sleep. She was absolutely dog tired.

She didn't know how long it was before she heard Lois's voice in a stage whisper from the door. 'Are you all right, Mother? You've managed?'

It was as much as she could do to grunt a reply.

'I had to say good night to Robert. I didn't want him to feel he was being pushed out. You shouldn't have shot off so suddenly.'

Victoria was more awake now, but she hardly knew who she was talking to.

'I was exhausted. Don't feel at all well.'

'I'm tired too. I've had a busy day. Good night.'

Victoria couldn't remember when she'd last felt so ill. She ached all over. It wasn't just her wrist now, though that was throbbing; her shoulders and her back were worse. Her head was thumping.

But worst of all was the heavy weight on her conscience. Her tears were salty as she wept for her poor, poor Lois.

She wished that the wrong she'd done her could be undone. But it was all so long ago.

Reliving those days now made her thrash about on the bed in agony.

Lois sat up in bed, her heart pounding in sudden alarm. A crash from her mother's room had woken her. She switched on her bedside lamp, blinking in the light. It was after midnight. She listened, half doubting her senses. Had she been dreaming?

A low moan came. That sent her scrambling from her bed, snatching for her dressing gown, her throat tight with apprehension.

Jill switched on the light in Victoria's room a second before Lois reached it. There was a twisted heap of satin, lace and old limbs on the bedside rug.

'Mother! What's happened? Are you all right?'

Jill reached her first and knelt beside her, but already Victoria's head was lifting. Bleary eyes looked up in an unfocused stare.

Lois was shocked. 'Are you hurt?'

The old lady was struggling to sit up.

Jill was tying the cord of her red dressing gown. 'She seems to be able to move everything.'

Together they helped Victoria back into bed. She felt hot and sticky.

'Her temperature's up,' Jill said.

'That's obvious.' Lois resented Jill's youth, the fact that she'd got here before her, and her calm, unhurried manner.

She demanded: 'What happened, Mother?'

Victoria let out a pent-up sigh. 'Fell out of bed.'

'Why? You've never done that before.' Victoria's head was settling back on the pillow, her eyes closing.

'Get my bag,' Lois said to Jill. 'It's by my desk in the study, where I always leave it.'

Trust Nat to sleep through all this, she thought as she heard Jill's bare feet pounding on the stairs. As far as she was concerned, she'd never got used to being woken in the night either. It was no fun.

When Lois read the thermometer, she found that her mother had a raging temperature. She listened to her chest but everything seemed all right there.

'Another case of the summer flu,' she told Jill. She'd been seeing a lot of it recently. 'Get a bowl,' she ordered. 'You'll find one in the kitchen. Tepid water. We'd better sponge her down to reduce her temperature.'

Then they were struggling to take off Victoria's sweat-soaked nightdress. She hardly seemed to know they were there, and kept muttering to herself.

'Clive, I'm sorry. I know it was a terrible thing to do. Forgive me.'

Lois felt a spasm of impatience. Clive had been dead for twenty-odd years. She had to bite back the words that would have told Victoria that.

'This will make you feel better, Mother.'

She could see goose pimples on the old flesh. Her mother was shivering now. Lois patted her dry, and shook on clouds of talcum powder. Jill found a clean nightdress. Victoria was comatose, only half with them.

'A terrible thing. Unpardonable.' The old lips were moving again.

95

'What was?' Lois asked without much interest. She thought she was hearing befuddled murmurs from a dream world. The high fever was making her mother delirious.

'What I did. Clive was such a good man.'

Jill was straightening the rucks out of the bottom sheet.

'Really it needs changing,' Lois told her. But it was asking too much at this time of night. She wanted to get back to bed.

'What did you do?' Jill was asking Victoria.

'There was no other way. I couldn't tell him. I went through dreadful agonies.' Lois saw tears ooze from under her mother's closed lids.

'What couldn't you tell him?' Jill's voice was gentle but persistent. Lois frowned, intrigued now despite herself.

Her mother moaned. 'I foisted another man's child on him.'

Lois heard Jill's gasp. She was filled with a terrible foreboding.

'What do you mean?' Jill asked quietly.

'Terrible thing to do to him. He was such a good man.'

Lois felt she'd been turned to stone. She was staring in disgust at the inert heap on the bed.

'Tell us,' Jill's soft voice was urging.

Suddenly Lois grasped Victoria by the shoulders and shook her. 'Which child? Which child, Mother? Do you mean me?'

'Lois!' Jill protested, trying to ease her back from the bed.

'I've got to know. You've got to tell me everything. Wake up and talk to me properly.' She couldn't believe this.

'Yes, Lois,' Victoria confirmed. 'Yes, my poor Lois. Such a terrible trouble. Never ending.'

Lois felt as though she'd been kicked in the stomach. She was winded and she knew she was taking too long to pull herself together.

Jill was staring at her aghast, her green eyes wide, her mouth open.

'You can go to bed now,' Lois choked. 'I'll sit with Mother until she goes off to sleep again.' She had to get rid of the girl.

'We ought to push Gran's bed against the wall. Stop her falling out again on that side.'

Jill's eyes levelled with her stepmother's again. Knowing eyes. It bothered Lois that the girl had heard more than was good for her.

'Then a chair on this side . . .'

'Of course,' Lois snapped, applying all the force needed to move the bed before Jill could get near. 'I can manage now.'

'Poor Gran, she must have been having a bad dream.'

Again a knowing look in Jill's green eyes. Lois was sure she didn't really believe that.

She was shaking as she pulled a small tub chair closer to the bed and lowered herself on to it. She couldn't believe what she'd heard.

Jill had left the bedroom door open, and no doubt her own door

96

too, so she'd hear more. Lois got up again and closed it quietly, though her mother seemed to be settling back to sleep.

She was tight with tension and burning with resentment. She took her mother's good hand in hers and hissed: 'Who was my father? It's no good telling me half the story. You've got to tell me everything now.'

It was like getting blood from a stone. Her mother knew now what she was saying. Her reluctance and her shame were obvious. Lois was appalled.

She wanted to hurt her mother. To strike back because she was hurt. She kept on at her, pressing her for more details, until her mother was in tears.

Lois wouldn't have believed any of it if she hadn't heard it with her own ears.

Mother had always seemed such an upright woman. A tower of strength telling her what she must do to save face. Telling her she must be careful not to tarnish the family name.

She felt tears scalding her own eyes. She'd loved Clive and thought him a wonderful father. She owed him so much. He'd always encouraged her. Told her she could cope with anything.

She'd been proud of what he'd done with his life. Now it seemed he was not her father at all.

'I've wanted to tell you many times.' The old voice creaked with emotion. 'I didn't dare. I was afraid you'd be upset.'

'Upset?' Lois felt sick. She'd never known her own father. Her mother had been just another slut, like all those she saw so often in the surgery.

She pulled herself to her feet. She'd never get over this. She was going back to bed.

'Can I have another drink, please?' Victoria asked weakly. 'Lois? Lois, are you there?'

Woken up for the second time that night, Jill propped herself up on her arm, feeling sleep-fuddled. Was Gran calling?

She heard the voice again, wavery and weak, yet with an edge of urgency. She half expected to hear Lois reply, but she didn't. Perhaps she'd fallen asleep in the chair. Jill got up again.

When she peeped out on the landing the house was in darkness. She opened Gran's door quietly, still expecting to find Lois in the room with her.

Her grandmother choked: 'Lois? Is that you?'

'It's Jill. Can I get you something?'

'Drink of water.' Jill put on the bedside light. The glass and carafe were empty.

'I'm so thirsty. I must have water.'

97

She refilled the carafe in the bathroom and then supported Victoria while she drained a full glass.

'I've been calling for ages. Where's Lois?'

'You're burning hot again.'

'It's always hot here.' Poor Gran was petulant.

Jill gave her more paracetamol to bring her temperature down, and she drank more water.

'Never feel cool. Not in Ekbo, but you get used to it.'

Jill sighed, Gran was back in the past now and ready to talk. But it was two o'clock in the morning, and she didn't know whether she had the energy to listen.

'Try and go back to sleep, Gran.'

She tied a dark scarf over the lampshade to dim the light, as she'd seen them do in hospitals.

'I'll stay with you so you don't have to shout for anything.'

'You're a good girl, Jill.'

She went across to her own room to fetch her duvet and pillows, and settled into a large armchair, putting her feet up on another.

Victoria was aware that Jill was trying to make her comfortable again by tucking the duvet round her plaster cast. She felt terrible. The room was beginning to spin round her.

She heard Jill's voice goading her again, as it had earlier: 'I'm proud of all the doctors in the family. You've all led such worthy lives.'

That had made her burn with shame. How could she talk about her past? She hardly dared think about it. The girl didn't know what life was.

But Jill hadn't left her alone.

'You and your mother must have made sacrifices to do medicine all those years ago.' That touched a raw spot. Her mother had made terrible sacrifices. 'It must have been hard for you.'

Suddenly Victoria was choking with emotion. She'd said: 'Harder for my mother. In her day, women were not expected to do anything other than keep house.'

She hadn't thought about her mother for a long time. Now she experienced a surge of love that left her aching. She'd always felt a fierce pride that Evelyn was one of very few women to be qualified at that time. She'd had to fight everybody to become a doctor.

'Tell us about her,' Jill had pleaded. Victoria knew she mustn't; she was afraid of betraying too much. Especially in front of Robert Montgomery. She'd managed to keep her mouth shut then.

But the girl had gone on: 'You must have sacrificed a good deal too. It can't have been easy for you, Gran.'

Victoria felt a tear run down her cheek now. She'd never sacrificed anything. She'd always grabbed at what she wanted. Indulged herself whenever she could. She'd not been like her mother in that respect.

'Lois? Another drink.'

'It's Jill, Gran.'

She felt herself being raised up. Felt the cold glass against her lips. It cleaned her mouth, made her feel better.

'More.' She dribbled a bit this time but it was wiped gently away.

'Always felt guilty about Lois,' she mumbled. 'But I tried. Time after time.'

'I'm sure you did. Why don't you tell me?'

Victoria sneezed. 'I've always loved Lois.' Her lips felt cracked and sore.

'Of course you have. She's your daughter.'

'I don't want to let her down.'

'You haven't let her down. You've been dreaming.'

She sighed. 'Not dreaming.'

'Tell me about it then. From the beginning.'

Victoria could feel herself being drawn back through the years to the time when she was young.

CHAPTER NINE

The new year of 1914 brought a cold snap to the weather. Snow had fallen the previous day and turned slushy before freezing hard overnight. This morning had brought another light fall on top.

'I don't know what possessed you, Vicky.' She knew her mother was feeling cantankerous as she teetered behind her. 'Buying a dress length of silk. I thought you had more sense.'

Victoria hitched her heavy skirt higher on her hips to keep it clear of the snow. She was enjoying this. The frosty air was burning the back of her throat and the wintry sun was making the snow sparkle.

'It's such pretty material, Mother. Mauve and white stripes, and so shiny the light seems to shoot through it.'

Victoria felt she could dance on the treacherous pavements. At twenty-one she was slight and slim and sure-footed. She swung the shopping bag that held the best end of neck they'd bought to make a warming stew.

She was fiercely proud of what her mother had achieved and understood why she was carping. Now that she was qualified and working as a doctor, she was struggling with feelings of disappointment that her high expectations were not being satisfied. She was afraid that Vicky, too, might be disappointed with her chosen way of life.

'A good wool serge I could understand, but silk? A party dress?'

Victoria knew exactly where her mother had gone wrong. She'd discounted the importance of money and turned her back on it. She'd thought she could manage well enough without, and now, too late, she was feeling the bite of poverty.

Evelyn was going on: 'Cotton would have been practical for the summer. And you'd have had enough money to pay the dressmaker. A dress length is no use unless you can get it made up.'

Evelyn never for a moment relaxed her grip on her purse strings and couldn't understand why her daughter didn't have the same self-discipline.

Vicky waited for her mother to catch her up again.

'Mother, that money was my Christmas present,' she reminded her gently. 'You gave it to me so I could choose something for myself.'

Evelyn steadied herself against the railings in front of a house. 'I'm sorry, Vicky, to go on so. It's just that we have to be so careful.'

Her mother was in her mid forties, and still slim, though she didn't seem so now, bundled up in shawls and scarves. Her grey tweed coat was seeing its fifth winter. Beneath it she wore a high-necked frilly blouse with a practical navy serge skirt. On her heavy dark hair was a large hat topped with fur and tied under her chin with veiling.

'Do slow down and let me take your arm.'

They were crossing Hamilton Square, one of the finest squares in the country and without equal in Birkenhead. The houses on three sides of it were all four storeys high, designed by Gillespie Graham, an Edinburgh architect, and built in the middle of the last century. All had iron balconies to the first-floor windows and cornices along the top, though they were not all identical.

Space had been left on the fourth side of the square for the more recently built town hall, and there were gardens in the centre which at one time had been for the private use of the occupants of the houses. Now they were in public use.

Vicky stopped and held her mother upright as they watched a chauffeur struggling with the starting handle of a very smart new automobile, while its passengers huddled together under a rug on the back seat.

She could see herself reflected in its window, her dark eyes sparkling with health, her rounded cheeks glowing and her thick dark hair piled high on her head under her heavy hat.

When the driver finally got the engine to fire, the slippery roads meant that the car moved round Hamilton Square at a pace no faster than she could walk.

Vicky was carrying the shopping on one arm and supporting her mother with the other as she slithered along. Ahead of them, she saw a stout, well-dressed woman, hampered by a large basket, trying to cross to their side of the square.

The road was wide and busy. Drays clattered past bound for the docks. There were hansom cabs heading to and from the ferry, the horses' hoofs ringing on the frozen road.

She could see a tub trap drawn by a mettlesome grey bearing down on the woman. The driver shouted a warning and the woman tried to hurry.

The next instant, she lost her footing. Vicky heard her mother's sharp intake of breath, felt her grip tighten on her own arm. Vicky's heart pounded as the trap swerved and skidded, but the horse recovered and went on.

The woman was sliding into the gutter on her back, her barathea cape trailing behind her. She ended up half lying, caught against the kerb and showing an embarrassing amount of black wool stocking above sensible button boots.

Evelyn hurried to help her. Vicky was already pulling down her skirts. Together they half lifted her on to the pavement and out of danger from other vehicles.

'Just sit there for a moment. Get your breath back,' Evelyn advised. 'A fall like that can shake you up.'

'I must get up,' the woman panted. 'I feel such a fool sitting in the snow.'

They helped her to her feet. Her heavy fur hat had listed to one side. Vicky set it to rights for her, then recovered the fur muff the woman had dropped and shook off the damp snow. She righted her basket and set about gathering up the articles that had been thrown out.

'Thank you. Such a silly thing to do,' the woman gasped.

'Not at all. It's treacherous underfoot.'

'Are you hurt?' Evelyn wanted to know. 'I'm a doctor.'

The woman put out a shaking hand to show her. The palm was grazed and covered with dirt from the road.

'Anything else?'

Vicky saw her mother's eyes go to the very wet patches across the back of woman's black dress where it had been in contact with the road. She'd also stepped on the hem and brought that down, and had torn a hole in her stocking, though that couldn't be seen now.

'Just a little shaky. And damp.' .

'And cold too, I'm sure.'

'I'll be all right.'

'Do you have far to go? We live just round the corner in Cleveland Street. If you'd like to come in with us I could clean up that graze and dry your dress. You'll feel better if you rest for ten minutes.'

'You're very kind, but my brother's house is even nearer. This is it. You must be neighbours of his.'

Vicky had walked past the house in Hamilton Square many times and thought it unoccupied. She'd never seen anyone coming and going, nor any lights inside. But the windows were curtained.

The woman paused at the door. 'I've been staying for a few days to open it up for him. He arrived home on leave yesterday. Strangely enough, he's a doctor too.'

'Alice, are you hurt? I was watching from the drawing room window and saw you fall.'

Victoria studied the man who came hurrying out. Despite the fact that they were only four paces from his front door, he was pulling on his alpaca overcoat and scarf.

'I'm all right, Clive. Just shaken up. These ladies have been so kind.'

'You must all come inside this minute. It's far too cold to stand about out here. Come in, Alice, you'll catch your death. I can see your breath hanging in the air. Yes, indeed, you must all come in. We must thank you properly for your help.'

Vicky was almost swept into the hall. He wouldn't take no for an answer. The first thing she noticed was that the whole house belonged to him, it hadn't been divided up into rooms like the house they lived in. A housekeeper took Alice upstairs to help her clean herself up.

Vicky would never forget her first impression of Clive Benbow. He was tall and slender when he took off his overcoat again, and seemed larger than life. His skin was deeply tanned by some hot foreign sun. He ushered them upstairs into a rather grand first-floor drawing room full of polished mahogany and red velvet chairs.

'I'm home on leave from Nigeria. From a hospital near Ekbo, but nobody here has ever heard of Ekbo. I'll never come home in winter again, the cold is an abomination.'

Victoria knew from the first meeting that Clive Benbow fascinated her mother. He in turn was so interested to find that Evelyn was a doctor that Alice's care was left entirely to the housekeeper.

'It's demanding work for a man. I've never met a lady doctor before.'

'Demanding for a woman too.' Evelyn had an attractive laugh.

'And much more difficult to achieve, I'm sure. Were there doctors in your family?'

'No.'

'Whatever made you think of medicine?'

'I caught measles when I was seven, and from then on it was what I wanted to do.'

'How did you manage it? Your family must have helped you?'

Evelyn was shaking her head. 'My father was very much against it.'

Vicky was afraid that her mother would not be able to talk openly about personal matters after such a short acquaintance. She was reticent, her answers becoming more reluctant.

Vicky laughed and told Clive: 'In those days, everybody knew their place in the world. Everybody except my mother. She was determined to prove she was as good as any man.'

Evelyn smiled. 'Medicine was a man's world then.'

As a child, Vicky had never tired of her mother's story. She'd made her tell it over and over. Now she said: 'Go on, Mother. Tell him.'

Evelyn's voice, low and rather husky, took up the tale.

'My father described himself as a gentleman. He lived on the farming rents of his small country estate in Shropshire. In Queen Victoria's time this had been sufficient to allow him to live well. He spent his days hunting, shooting and fishing.

'I had an older brother, James, who was sent away to school, but my father thought a governess more suitable for me. I pleaded with him to let me go to school too.'

'But you managed it eventually, Mother.'

As a girl, Victoria had known the story by heart. She felt like a girl again now.

Her mother said: 'I loved school when I got there, and I did well, but when the time came for me to go on to medical school my father put his foot down.'

Vicky smiled. 'He said he couldn't afford to pay your fees, didn't he?'

'Agriculture wasn't doing so well by then, but I don't think it was that. He said that as far as he was concerned, women should be wives and mothers and there was no need for me to work at all. He made me stay at home.'

'But Ledbury Park was a comfortable home. A lovely house.'

'I had nothing to do but arrange the flowers.'

'You had time to read.'

'Yes, Vicky, I did a lot of reading, and when my mother was alive she used to take me out in the carriage to pay formal visits.'

Vicky knew that shortly after Evelyn had finished school, her mother had fallen from her horse during a hunt and had never recovered from her injuries.

'You had more to do after her death, Mother.'

'I kept house for my father but nothing I did was right. I couldn't please him. He married again within a year.'

Vicky knew better than to remind Evelyn that her new stepmother was only seven years older than she was herself. Or that she'd bitterly resented having to hand over her domestic duties and accept a girl in her mother's place.

'But you had a good life, Mother. Your father gave you an allowance so you could have lots of pretty clothes.'

That was what Victoria craved. Money to buy clothes. Money to buy books and food, and more money to buy just about everything else.

'I wanted real work and independence.'

'But then your brother . . .' Vicky had to prompt.

'James was in the army by then and brought a friend home to join one of the shoots that father arranged.'

'And you fell in love.'

'Ye-es. Your father was a very handsome man. He certainly fell in love with me. When he asked me to marry him I jumped at it. It was the one way I could see to get away from home.'

'But Gerrard Ormond didn't please your father?'

'Not entirely, because he had nothing but his army pay. Father said he'd expected me to marry a rich man, but by then he just wanted me off his hands. He had a new baby son and I was a source of trouble to him, coming between him and his new family. He agreed to my marrying Gerrard.'

'But you still weren't happy?'

Vicky already knew that Gerrard Ormond had not turned out to be a good husband. He was given to heavy drinking and betting on cards; he spent too freely in the mess. There was little left over to keep his family.

She couldn't remember her father at all. He'd been away with his regiment most of the time. She remembered living with her mother in a succession of rented cottages and being perennially short of money. The Boer War came and both her father and her Uncle James had been killed in South Africa.

'I took you home to Ledbury then.'

'Mother, it was the most beautiful house I've ever seen.'

Even after all these years, Vicky carried in her mind a clear picture of that house, large and comfortable and gracious. She'd never been able to understand how her mother could bring herself to turn her back on that and choose instead to live in poky squalid rooms.

'I'd kept in touch with Father and thought he'd want to help us. Especially since James was gone too. We were the only survivors of his first family.

'Now that I was a widow and old enough to know my own mind, I was determined to become a doctor. I needed a means of earning a living for us and I hoped Father would agree to help me.'

Victoria had felt very much in awe of him, remembering only his forcefulness and the way he barked out his opinions.

'That was the only time I ever saw my grandfather. I must have been about ten at the time.'

'A doctor?' he'd said to Evelyn. 'Don't be ridiculous! I don't know where you get these wild ideas. It's a very unladylike thing to do. No, I will not help you.'

'My father left you no money and we had no home of our own,' Victoria recalled.

'As an army officer's widow, I received a pension, and I still had the small legacy my mother had left me. And I was free of my father's domination.'

'And strong enough not to let the fact that you had me to look after stop you doing what you wanted.'

Vicky knew they'd left Ledbury Park in a hurry and that Evelyn had taken her mother's jewellery with her and a few small but valuable knick-knacks from about the house.

'Strictly speaking they weren't mine to take,' she'd admitted later. 'But Father owed us something and Mother would have wanted me to have her things. I had to take them, Vicky, when I had the chance. I knew there might never be another.'

Evelyn had been right in her prediction. Her father had written to her demanding that she return what he called his property, and threatening that if she did not, she would never receive another penny from him.

'I had to sell my mother's things to pay my course fees,' she had told Vicky. 'Though I'd have dearly loved to keep them.'

As far as Evelyn was concerned the need justified what she'd done. There was no other way she could have become a doctor.

'I went to the Royal Free Hospital in London. It had been started expressly to train women because established medical schools wouldn't accept them. But of course women couldn't remain segregated, it would have looked as if there were two standards. So by my day, it took men too. I was in my element there.'

'And you became the first doctor in the family.' Vicky had felt very proud of her then.

'At the age of thirty-six, in 1904.'

'One of the first women doctors.'

'Hardly,' Evelyn smiled. 'Women have been qualifying since the middle of the last century.'

'One of the few,' Clive corrected now.

Victoria knew that her mother felt she should have achieved more than she had. Elizabeth Garrett Anderson, the first Englishwoman to qualify in medicine, had set up her own dispensary to treat women's problems. For Evelyn, lack of money had ruled out anything like that.

She smiled at Clive and said: 'The medical profession was dominated by men. Women doctors were still fighting to be accepted in it. Even when qualified my mother's problems were not over.'

'It took me nearly a year to get my first appointment,' Evelyn said quietly. 'And I only got that because I agreed to work without a salary. I just had to get experience.'

'And we came to Birkenhead because you were offered a job at the children's hospital in Woodchurch Road.'

Vicky knew Evelyn had received payment for her work then, though not on the same scale that a man would enjoy. She also knew that her mother would never mention remuneration to a man like Clive Benbow. For him, the account ended here.

When, as a girl, Evelyn had talked to her daughter about it, she usually went on to say: 'You had a poverty-striken upbringing.'

Then Vicky would add: 'But when I said I wanted to become a doctor too, it was taken for granted that one day I would. You were always prepared to spend what you could on my education.'

'We lived in rooms which I kept changing, hoping that each new place would spare us the difficulties of the last.'

'We scrimped and saved and made do.'

'We moved into rooms on the attic floor of a tall, narrow house in Cleveland Street. Just across the road from Hamilton Square, close to the church. We had had a bad experience . . . I had learned that it was essential to live in a good residential district. There, the houses were all classical Georgian terraces, built for rich shipping merchants in the last century.'

They had had a sitting room and a bedroom in which they both slept, but being on the attic floor the rooms had been intended for the use of servants and were not ideal. Even worse, they had to share the bathroom and kitchen with other lodgers.

Evelyn thought it was impossible for ladies to wash in a shared bathroom. They carried jugs of water to their bedroom instead. She found the shared lavatory one of the greatest privations she had to bear. The shared kitchen was difficult to cope with too. They cooked some of their meals on the sitting room fire.

Evelyn often said with a smile: 'The cramped conditions keep us close. We are more like sisters.'

'No.' Vicky couldn't agree with that. To her, Evelyn seemed very much the older generation, with her serious face and iron determination. 'You're so much stronger than I am, Mother.'

Clive Benbow turned his kind, benign eyes on Victoria when he heard she was already in medical school.

'It will be easier for you,' he said. He seemed gentle by nature, other-worldly almost.

'Yes,' Evelyn agreed. 'Because I can guide her. I don't want Victoria to have to fight for everything.'

Now he had them in his house, Clive was unwilling to let them go.

'You must take a glass of Madeira wine with me,' he insisted.

When Alice rejoined then, she ordered a pot of tea to be made for them because that was what she preferred.

Clive Benbow was an extrovert, he wanted to talk. He told them that he was forty-three. Vicky knew her mother was just three years older, and being only twenty-one at the time, she saw him as a father figure.

She was soon absorbed in the stories he told of foreign places and the diseases rampant there. She could see that her mother was hanging on to every word.

'I ought to know more about tropical diseases,' she said. 'Sometimes they're brought here by sailors.'

He was full of anecdotes and described some of the more interesting cases he'd treated recently.

'He does so much for the poor Africans,' Alice told them, and it was only then that Vicky understood he was a medical missionary.

Before they left that morning, they learned that Clive would be in residence for most of the summer. That Alice lived in Southport, her husband was a clergyman and she'd hired a cook and a housekeeper to look after her brother.

Clive was quite the opposite of Evelyn, the sort of man who talked openly about himself. Words tumbled from his mouth, he couldn't keep any fact hidden. He even held forth at some length about why he had never married.

'I wanted to, when I was younger, but there are no European women and children in Ekbo. A wife would have had to stay alone in England. I felt I couldn't ask any woman to share such a solitary life.

'Besides, I would not have been able to afford it when I was young. Not as a medical missionary. Only when my father died and left me this house and a modest income could I consider it, and by then it was too late for me. I was set in my ways.'

He went on about the isolation and the sticky heat of Ekbo, the lack of variety in the diet, but already Victoria could see that he'd captured her mother's interest. Evelyn was sparkling in a way she'd never seen before. Her seriousness had gone. She was more alive, laughing and talking more too, and it didn't seem to be the second glass of Madeira that was causing it.

Clive told them he had missed the company of women and they must forgive him for being so entranced with them.

When they finally got home, her mother could talk of little else but meeting Clive Benbow.

Victoria found the following weeks exciting and knew her mother did too. Clive was eager for their company. He said he'd have a very dull leave if they didn't take pity on him.

'Because I've spent so much time abroad, I've lost touch with my friends. I'm sorry to monopolise your time.'

They both told him they loved their new social life. Vicky had her mauve and white striped silk made up, and had plenty of opportunity to wear it. She told Evelyn she couldn't have managed without it.

Clive took them to concert halls and theatres, to lectures, museums and libraries. He loaned them books to read, and then later took pleasure in discussing them. He invited them to meals at his house.

Always he invited them together. If one was not free to go, the other did not.

'You are my chaperone,' Evelyn smiled. 'This way he knows he doesn't compromise me. Clive is very understanding.'

Victoria knew that as time went on, her mother was hoping for more. Clive spoke often of how much he had missed in life by not having a wife and family of his own.

'It would have meant long separations,' he insisted again. 'European women don't go out to West Africa. They wouldn't be able to stand the climate.'

'Are there no women there at all?' Victoria wanted to know.

'One or two. Wives of missionaries mostly.'

109

'What about nurses?'

'The hospital is run by an order of nuns.'

'They are women,' Evelyn smiled. 'If nuns can survive there, then it shouldn't be impossible for a woman doctor. She'd be able to work too, wouldn't she?'

He laughed delightedly. 'There's no shortage of work there. Plenty for everyone.'

Victoria saw her mother as a liberated woman. Even when things were at their most difficult, Evelyn had maintained that all the sacrifices she'd made were worth while. She said she preferred bringing her daughter up alone, rather than having Gerrard Ormond as a husband.

'Clive Benbow as a husband would be an entirely different matter,' Evelyn told her now. For her own part, Vicky heartily approved.

Money shortage dictated everything in their lives, but Clive was a man who considered money unimportant. He told them one day that he had been running the hospital at Ekbo for many years on a subsistence salary. A fraction of what was usually paid to expatriate junior doctors.

'I don't need it,' he said simply. 'but the others come out on standard Colonial Office terms and could claim their pensions at the age of forty-five if they didn't wish to stay. We missionaries go on longer.'

'How long?' Victoria asked. She knew that her mother would be desperate to know, but would not ask.

'As long as possible. As long as we can be useful there.' Clive, she could see, wanted to give of himself.

They discussed this avidly in bed that night. 'It's because he has enough money already.' Vicky said in amazement. 'By our standards he's frittering away a fortune to amuse us, and his house stands empty for years at a time while he's away.'

'He's not really wealthy,' Evelyn pondered. 'Just solid middle class.' Clive had told them his father had been a salt merchant and that he'd been brought up in the house in Hamilton Square.

'He doesn't have to think of thrift,' Victoria said with feeling. 'Other-worldly. Wants to do the best he can for his patients.'

'I don't mind being short of money,' Evelyn had said, but Victoria knew she did. Particularly now that Clive was reminding them of the pleasures it could buy.

For her own part, Victoria craved more. Poverty had dogged her all her life. Her mother barely earned enough for them to live on. She knew it was going to be a struggle to put her through medical school. She reasoned that if her mother married Clive, it would ease an impossible burden.

Besides, Clive brought more interest into their lives. He was a good man who gave generously to everyone. His manners were impeccable. The worst fault anyone could accuse him of was the habit of requesting dishes that were not on the menu when he took them for a hotel meal, thereby keeping them waiting while the food was cooked specially for him.

Vicky knew that her mother was in love with him. She was looking much younger and prettier than she used to. She seemed to have so much more vitality.

Spring came and brought warmer weather. Clive abandoned his alpaca overcoat and took to wearing crumpled linen suits with a Panama hat. Her mother no longer talked so much of him in the moments before they went to sleep.

They met him in Hamilton Square one afternoon as they were heading for the underground railway to take them over to Liverpool. They were going to buy a medical textbook for Victoria.

Evelyn had said to her when they'd first met him: 'I don't want you to make too much of our poverty. Don't ram it down his throat.'

'Don't mention it, you mean? Don't let him know we're poor?'

'Just don't talk about it.'

'Your father would have said it was unladylike?' Vicky teased.

'Perhaps he would.' Her mother flushed.

Vicky hadn't meant to let it slip that she was making do with her mother's old textbooks, which were more than a decade out of date. It hadn't mattered much for the first year or so. Human anatomy and physiology didn't change.

Now she was learning about diseases, though, it was a different matter. More was understood about them these days. Evelyn had saved to replace two books which they thought important.

But because she'd told Clive, he insisted on seeing her book list and then accompanying them to the university bookshop and buying every book on it.

'You can't expect Victoria to achieve the highest marks if she doesn't have the recommended textbooks,' he'd chided Evelyn.

Vicky was thrilled to see the books piling up on the counter for her.

'I can't possibly allow you to do this.' Her mother was choking with embarrassment because he hadn't said a word to put their relationship on a more formal footing.

'I insist,' he said, beaming like a conspirator at Vicky.

When they got back, he helped them carry the books upstairs to their attic sitting room. Evelyn was intercepted by their landlord on a lower landing. Vicky had three minutes alone with Clive.

'You're so kind,' she'd laughed excitedly, full of gratitude for his generosity. 'I want you to know I'll be delighted if . . . if we become related.'

His mild eyes looked at her in amazement. She tried to explain herself.

'I hope you don't think I'm talking out of turn. I just want you to

111

know I'm all for it. I won't have any trouble accepting you.' She meant as a father. 'I think you're wonderful.'

Over the next weeks, she began to feel less easy. When she first noticed the way Clive's eyes followed her about the room she felt she must be mistaken.

Then, when she was telling him and her mother about something that had happened in the school, she'd heard him laugh and looked up to find his eyes full of adoration.

It had come as a shock. It was only then she realised that Clive was smiling at her more than at her mother; that it was to her he directed his flow of anecdotes, and her he was trying to please.

She lay in bed that night wondering how she could say this to Evelyn. Her mother had told her so clearly that she thought she was the object of Clive's affections. That she expected him to propose to her.

Vicky couldn't bring herself to broach the subject. She knew how hurtful it would be for her mother. She thought Clive would go back to Ekbo soon, and she and Evelyn would be left to settle back into their old routine.

One warm Sunday in early summer, Clive hired a motor car and drove them out to Leasowe for a picnic on the sands. Vicky had never ridden in a car before, and she settled herself on the back seat feeling absolutely thrilled.

She knew that for her mother, too, it was a rare treat. She was in the front with Clive, talking more than usual, her cheeks pink with excitement.

Evelyn was wearing, for the first time, the new straw hat Vicky had persuaded her to buy for the summer. It was topped with poppies and had veiling which tied under her chin. She was looking young and stylish.

Clive seemed unusually silent on the drive out, but Vicky knew he was unused to cars and she thought he needed to concentrate.

He found just the right sheltered spot for their picnic, out of the stiffish breeze. They almost had the beach to themselves. Clive unpacked the three canvas chairs and the picnic table from the car. Victoria spread the checked cloth. She was kneeling on the rug as they unpacked the food from the hamper, when Clive said, self-consciously:

'I know I should have spoken to you sooner, Evelyn. Don't think I haven't wanted to.' Under his Panama hat, his face was flushed. 'It's just that Victoria is so young, and the last thing I want is to interrupt her studies at this stage. Do let me assure you that I'll always take great care of her. I love her deeply.'

Vicky couldn't get her breath. She felt shocked, appalled, acutely

112

uncomfortable. Clive was proposing at last. As she'd expected, it wasn't her mother he wanted to marry.

She saw Evelyn swallow hard and look at her. She could see her fighting for composure. Vicky sank back on her knees, nursing the cold chicken instead of laying it out on the cloth.

'I've been telling myself I'm selfish,' Clive went on, his face earnest. 'That it would be quite wrong to part you when you are so happy with your lives as they are.'

Vicky looked at him with fresh eyes. He wanted to marry her! She admired Clive, of course she did, but he was nearly forty-five and wore crumpled linen suits. And her mother must surely be devastated.

'But I do truly love her. I know I can't expect her to come out to Ekbo with me now. That's another reason I've delayed. But I would so like us to make it permanent. I want the security of knowing that when I come home on leave, and when I finally give up, Victoria will be here waiting for me.'

Vicky swallowed hard. She'd looked at herself in the mirror as she'd tied her hat on top of her thick brown hair this morning, and thought she appeared a child still, rather than a twenty-one-year-old adult. She dared not look at her mother.

'Perhaps sometime in the future she'll even come out to see me there.'

'Victoria?' her mother faltered.

Vicky knew they were both waiting for her answer. She couldn't trust herself to speak at that moment. She went to her mother and put her arms round her in a gesture of sympathy and affection.

She wanted to tell Clive that she thought Evelyn would make him a more suitable wife; that he would be able to take her out to West Africa straight away, that above all else, her mother wanted to work in his hospital.

'You see, even Victoria thinks I ask too much,' he said sadly.

She ought to protest. Of course she was very taken with Clive. He was a good man and he'd make a good husband. She admired his selflessness. She enjoyed his company. But she had her own ideas about love and marriage and Clive wasn't the right age to be her husband.

'We'll have to think about it,' Evelyn said quietly.

Vicky couldn't bear to look at her mother's face. Pale with shock and disappointment, grim with determination to keep her feelings under control. Evelyn, she knew, wanted to hide from him her own expectations.

'I know I shouldn't rush you into it, Vicky,' Clive said gently. 'The trouble is, I'm due to go back to Ekbo soon, and I'm so afraid that if I do you'll forget all about me. I'll have lost my chance. So you see, there's everything in this for me, and nothing for you.'

Vicky knew exactly what was in it for her. It would mean financial security for the rest of her life.

'I'm asking too much of you,' Clive said. 'I've agonised about what I should do. I know I'm selfish.'

'Give her a little time to think it over,' Evelyn pleaded, her voice anguished.

Vicky knew from her face that her mother was prepared to make yet another sacrifice. She would want her to marry Clive. He was generous, it meant financial security for them both. For Evelyn the result justified the means. It always had.

CHAPTER TEN

There were tears that night. Vicky knew from the half-stifled sounds when their bedroom light went out that her mother was weeping with disappointment. Her own eyes were wet with sympathy.

'Sleep on it,' her mother had advised, but she didn't sleep well either. She had her decision to make.

There was a fellow medical student she was friendly with; a Mr Oakley, who had held her hand once, and carried her books from time to time. He was more the sort of man she wanted for a husband. He smiled at her often across the lecture hall.

In the morning, she told her mother that she would accept Clive's offer.

'Love will come,' her mother assured her. 'Clive is a good man. I don't think you're making a mistake.'

'You make me very happy,' he told Vicky, as he kissed her cheek. 'Very proud. Very flattered that you care enough.' She thought she saw tears in Clive's eyes too.

But once she'd accepted his proposal, Vicky felt she was rushed to the altar.

'There's no time to drag your feet now,' Evelyn told her tartly. 'You know Clive has to return to Africa.' Her mother's youthful veneer was suddenly gone, leaving her pale and rather grim.

It was a very quite church wedding. Clive invited his sister and one or two other guests, but there was no pomp and little ceremony. Evelyn's thrift would not allow good money to be spent on a bridal gown that would be worn only once.

Instead, Vicky chose an ornate blue tea gown, with a large blue organdie hat covered with dark blue roses. It was the most expensive ensemble she'd ever had. Clive insisted on paying for it. In it, she felt even better than she did in her mauve and white silk.

Clive brought his guests back to Hamilton Square for the wedding breakfast. There were twelve of them round the dining room table for the most elaborate meal Vicky had ever eaten. There was champagne.

What did it matter that Clive's sister Alice seemed a little cold now, when she'd been so friendly earlier on?

Victoria had heard her say: 'You always were impulsive, Clive. I do

115

hope you've given this sufficient thought.'

Clearly she didn't approve of their marriage. Vicky was afraid that Alice thought she'd lured him into it.

All the same, for Vicky it brought satisfaction. She felt she'd banished poverty from her life. What was more, she had banished it from her mother's life too. She wanted to help Evelyn, who had done so much for her.

The guests started to take their leave. Vicky went down to the hall with Clive to see them off. She felt nervous when her mother kissed her and went too, leaving her alone with Clive for the first time.

He closed the front door and turned to face her. Vicky went to the hall mirror to ease off her hat. Etiquette demanded that she keep it on for so formal occasion as a wedding breakfast. She was pushing her fingers through her dark hair to fluff it out, smoothing down her blue dress. Her cheeks were rounded and flushed, her figure willow-slim. She looked younger than she really was.

She could see Clive reflected in the mirror beside her. Fine lines fanned out from his eyes that deepened when he smiled. His tan had faded now but the tropical sun had given him deeper lines across his forehead. She thought he looked old.

'Beauty and the beast,' he said sadly, meeting her eyes in the glass.

Vicky laughed. 'Clive, you're a handsome, mature man, and still in your prime.'

'I hope you'll always think that.' He bent to kiss her cheek.

Then he led the way back upstairs to his very comfortable drawing room. Ill at ease, Vicky perched on the edge of an armchair on the opposite side of the marble fireplace, wondering what would come next.

She need not have worried. Clive seemed to anticipate her nervousness. He poured them each another glass of champagne.

'I feel very honoured that you've become my wife,' he told her. 'I'll do my best to make sure you never regret it.'

He sat back and talked at length, as he always did. Vicky began to relax. They had always got on well, he was a good companion. Bed time was the only thing left to worry about. But it was just the unknown that bothered her. Clive was very gentle and very thoughtful for her.

'I love you,' he told her. 'You're a very beautiful girl. You've made me very happy.' She fell asleep in his arms.

Vicky was sorry when the time came for Clive to sail for West Africa. She'd expected to have only three weeks of married life, but he'd managed to extend it to five. The more she saw of him, the more she liked him.

She went across to Liverpool to see him off on the mail boat. He showed her his cabin and they walked round the ship.

116

Up on deck, they leaned against the rail, looking back over the swirling waters of the Mersey to Birkenhead.

'I wish I was coming with you,' she said.

Clive was sad. 'You must finish your training. I can't ask you to give that up now.'

Vicky knew it was usual for a bride to give up any career she might have. Marriage was considered a full-time occupation. It was another sign of Clive's generosity that he did not demand it. If she'd had time to think about it, she thought she might have preferred to do the usual thing.

'I hate parting from you, Vicky, and we're facing a long separation. But the time will pass. Once you're qualified it will be different.' He made her feel cherished.

'I'll be able to come out and work at your hospital then.' She felt at that moment that there was nothing she would like more.

'It would be wonderful experience for you.'

'But it's years off yet. Perhaps I should forget about being a doctor. Perhaps I should . . .'

Clive was shaking his head. 'I'm more than twice your age, Vicky. I'm afraid you'll have many years as a widow. Face it, because it's bound to happen. You'll need something to fill those years.'

She knew that for Clive, work and service to others seemed the obvious way to reach contentment.

'You're an old man's darling,' he teased her.

Clive showed his love for her so clearly, it was impossible not to love him in return.

Vicky felt lost without Clive. Her life seemed suddenly empty. The long summer vacation had started, she didn't even have college work to occupy her. The flat feeling of anticlimax wouldn't go away.

'The best thing for you to do,' Clive had told her before he went, 'is to ask your mother to move in here with you. You won't want to be alone.'

Evelyn was pleased. 'And silly to keep on two establishments,' she said.

Vicky was delighted to do something for her mother at last. They had a very comfortable house to themselves now.

'Seven big bedrooms,' Vicky marvelled. 'And servants' rooms.'

Clive expected Vicky to keep on the cook and housekeeper to look after them. He'd asked if they needed a ladies' maid too. He made sure there was always money available for Victoria to draw on and asked no questions about how she spent it. He expected to provide for them. At last she felt she had sufficient money.

She wrote to Clive every week, telling him everything that happened. Evelyn wrote to him too, showing the letters to Vicky first. It

117

seemed the least they could do for him.

On August the second, Vicky had gone into town to look for some new clothes for autumn. She'd bought herself two blouses in Lewis's and had walked up Bold Street to treat herself to a very expensive skirt from Cripps. She was on her way home when she saw the crowd around the news vendors outside Central Station.

'War coming, read all about it!' they shouted.

For years there had been rumours that there might be war. There was already fighting in the Balkans and the Archduke Ferdinand had been assassinated at Sarajevo back in June. Hatred amongst the countries of Europe seemed to be growing, but negotiations were carried on with so much secrecy, nobody knew what was really happening.

Vicky pushed through the crowd and bought a newspaper. It seemed that the Kaiser had asked Belgium for permission to cross her borders, and when this was refused, his troops marched in, overrunning Luxembourg as well.

She travelled home on the train to Hamilton Square in a daze, trying to work out what war would mean to her and her family.

She had no relatives who would be called upon to fight, but she soon saw the effects of war all around her: the casualties, the result of carnage in the trenches; and the shortages of food.

For Evelyn, the Great War brought acceptance of women doctors. Wanting to do more, she left the children's hospital and took a job at Liverpool Royal Infirmary. At last she was able to work alongside men on the same terms. Women were doing all kinds of work now their menfolk were away fighting.

She found treating the maimed and the blind, those disfigured with burns and affected by mustard gas, filled her with anger as well as pity. She worked very long hours, with little time off.

Victoria soon realised she was cut off from Clive for the duration. But she knew he was safe from the effects of war and separation seemed a small price to pay for that. She and Evelyn continued to write to him, but the post was almost non-existent. They would go for months without news of him and then receive half a dozen letters on the same day. It seemed he wrote many that never did arrive.

In 1917, Victoria obtained the qualifications of Bachelor of Medicine and Bachelor of Surgery, and went straight on to do her hospital courses. She chose paediatrics first. She didn't feel she was having a hard war.

Food grew scarcer and therefore very expensive, but Clive's money cushioned them. Both Vicky and her mother ate many hospital meals while they were on duty. Neither ever went hungry. Vicky knew she was seeing the agonies of war at second hand.

All the same, she felt the miseries of others not so fortunate and the war seemed to go on for ever. Life was duller because so many things were no longer possible.

The Armistice brought relief. Everybody was suddenly more optimistic. Letters from Clive began to come more regularly.

'So silly of me to be trapped here away from all the action,' he wrote. 'I feel totally isolated. Please, Victoria, will you take pity on me and come out for a visit?'

She felt her heart jerk with pleasure at the thought.

'I'd like you to see the place before you feel committed to staying with me for a full tour.

'I'm overdue for leave, of course. Very much so. But I can't come home at the moment because I'm the only doctor left here. The war made it impossible to recruit expatriates of any sort, and those we had drifted away over the years for one reason or another.'

He went on to explain that doctors were being recruited in England at the moment, and one, a Dr Jonathon Pine, had already been appointed.

'If you're willing to come, I'll write and ask him to escort you out. It's a long and difficult journey for a woman to make on her own, especially for the first time. I'll feel happier if I know you have somebody to take care of things.'

Victoria hardly knew what she felt for Clive now. She hadn't seen him for over four years and during that time her own life had changed. Now she was working as a junior hospital doctor. Since he'd gone, she'd been careful to conduct herself as a married woman and had kept aloof from the men in her classes. It hadn't been too difficult because most men had been away fighting in the trenches.

Now that Clive had suggested she go out to him, she badly wanted to. She hadn't been away for a holiday at any time during the war. Her mother had been unable to take more than a few days off in all that time. Vicky saw the trip to Ekbo as a great adventure.

It was decided that she would travel out, and return with Clive when he came on leave. She had one more hospital course to take before she could practise in England, but she could take a year off and return to that later. Clive told her she could work at Ekbo and that it would be experience that would stand her in good stead.

Vicky threw herself into getting a tropical wardrobe together. She had a letter from Dr Jonathon Pine, giving her details of the mail boat on which he had booked his passage. Vicky booked a cabin on the same sailing, and because he lived in Kent and would have to come up to Liverpool to catch the boat, invited him to spend the night with them at Hamilton Square.

'More comfortable for you than a hotel,' Evelyn assured him, when they met him off the London train at Woodside Station. 'And it gives us an opportunity to get to know each other.'

Victoria tried to hide her giggle when he immediately attached himself to her mother, assuming that Evelyn was Dr Benbow's wife.

'What's the joke?' he asked.

Then she had to explain, and say that she in her turn had expected him to be more Clive's age. He was only two years older than she was herself, and incredibly good-looking.

Once he realised it was Vicky he was to escort out, he was so obviously delighted that she was flattered. His dark eyes lit up, his generous mouth broke into a wide smile. After that she couldn't take her eyes off his strong features and thick wavy hair.

At the dinner table that night she was totally captivated. Jonathon was relaxed and began to tell them about himself.

'I know it's a mission hospital,' he said, 'but I'm not a missionary. I've been working round the clock in a hospital near Canterbury trying to keep up with the flow of war casualties. I'm going out for a bit of fun. I believe in enjoying myself in this life and taking my chances in the next.'

Although his words were rather too blunt for Evelyn's liking, his manners were charming, and he took pains to include her in the conversation. Vicky thought he was going to be a wonderful companion. She felt she had a lot in common with him.

As she was getting ready for bed on the last night she would be spending at home, her mother came to her room. She didn't give any direct warning, but her message was clear.

'I'm not sure that I approve of him, Vicky. You could have managed on your own. I can't see what protection he's likely to provide. What is Clive thinking of?'

Vicky laughed when Evelyn had gone; she'd been looking forward to the voyage, now she couldn't wait to get on the boat. Her mother came with them to see them off. Once on board, she went with Vicky to see her cabin.

Vicky had been disappointed when she found that all the single cabins were already reserved. Evelyn had suggested she request the use of a double one for herself.

Now Evelyn looked at the twin bunks and said: 'You might have enjoyed the company of another woman to share this.'

'Hardly any women go out to the Coast, Mother.'

'Even for part of the way. They might go to the Canary Isles.'

Vicky loved the scents of the ship. Below decks it pulsated with warmth, as though the temperature was already tropical. They peeped into the dining room and walked through the lounge and the bar.

'I'd stay away from here,' her mother advised. 'I don't think it's wise for a young girl like you to take drink.'

They never drank at home, but Vicky could remember the wine

Clive had provided. He believed in living well, even if her mother did not.

They were to sail on the afternoon tide. Vicky felt the ship's engines begin to throb beneath her feet.

'I'll have to go.' Evelyn led the way out on deck. Jonathon was waiting at the rail to thank her for her hospitality. Vicky stood with him to watch Evelyn go down the gangway.

The February afternoon was drawing in. They both waved when they saw Evelyn turn for the last time before being swallowed up in the winter dusk.

Vicky felt the cold Mersey breeze tugging at her hair as she watched the ship's hawsers being cast off. Moments later, the dark Mersey water was rushing between the ship and Princes' Dock. The gap widened until she could see the buildings on the Liverpool sky-line standing out stark against the darkening sky.

She felt excited, glad to be leaving. The ship was swinging in the river, nudged around by a tug. A deep blast from the funnel made her jump and grip the ship's rail.

'We're off,' Jonathon murmured beside her and turned to laugh down at her. She knew she'd find it difficult to keep him at arm's length. The throbbing engines seemed to echo the throbbing of her heart as they headed downriver and out to the Irish Sea.

Vicky had always taken her marriage vows seriously. It felt wrong to be alone with Jonathon like this, even though Clive had arranged it. He slid a warm hand over hers as it rested on the ship's rail. The physical contact made her catch her breath.

'Am I looking forward to this trip,' he breathed, as he bent to kiss her. His lips were warm against her cold cheeks. She felt on fire, her heart thudding.

'Hey,' she said, pushing him gently away, 'you're overdoing things. I'm Clive Benbow's wife, remember? He asked you to look after me, deliver me safely to Ekbo. That's all.'

'Sorry, Vicky,' he said. 'I forgot myself.'

Vicky hadn't resisted Jonathon's advances because she wanted to, but because she felt she had to. He kept his hands in his pockets for the first two days of the voyage.

Gradually the sea became calm and the sun began to shine. She found she was a good sailor and she enjoyed the sophistication of life on board. Jon introduced her to the cocktail hour and wine with every meal.

He seemed always to be at her side; ready to escort her in to meals, have a game of deck quoits or put a bet on the ship's mileage.

They took their meals at a table with six other passengers, but they were too engrossed in each other to need more companionship. They were as discreet as they could be in public and didn't talk of their own circumstances. They knew no other passengers. Nobody on board knew them except as Dr Benbow and Dr Pine, and no one else had Ekbo as their destination.

When Vicky found herself putting out a hand to touch him, she admitted to herself that she found him magnetic. Every time she met his gaze she felt the pull. She wanted to spend every minute she could with him. Soon they were inseparable.

'Perhaps they think we are a married couple,' Victoria said, as they sat in steamer chairs and watched other passengers taking their daily constitutions round the deck. After all, she was wearing Clive's wedding band.

She'd thought she loved Clive, but what she'd felt for him was nothing like this. As they sailed into the Bay of Biscay, Vicky knew she was in love with Jon and that temptation was spiralling. She felt it had been inevitable from the moment they'd met.

On some evenings, there was dancing after dinner to a duo: a piano and violin for romantic waltzes, and the violinist could play the accordion for polkas. Jon put his arms round her and pulled her close against him to dance every dance together. She could feel his body moving against hers. Vicky shut her eyes and dreamed. She felt she was being transported to heaven.

Jon heightened her senses, she could feel herself tingling. The intensity of her feelings made it impossible for her to draw back. It left her breathless and starry-eyed. He was equally passionate about her.

That night the ship was passing Cape St Vincent. The duo had stopped for a rest and the dancers surged on deck to catch their last glimpse of Europe. Vicky stood against the rail with Jon's arm still around her shoulders, watching the light flash out its signal.

She could see white foam curling along the side of the ship as the engines pounded on and on. There was no moon but the sky was bright with stars. Starlight glistened in the dark water below.

'You're very pretty.' His finger stroked the line of her chin. 'Why are all the attractive women already spoken for?'

Her memories of Clive were faded. She wanted Jon. His body was young, and so much more attractive. He had more virility. His needs were ever more urgent.

When he led her to his small single cabin high in the bows of the ship, she no longer had the strength to resist. She could feel the vessel lift and fall with the swell, and below the engines pounded, keeping pace with her heart.

'I'm in love with you,' Jon whispered. 'Head over heels from the moment I saw you. I don't know how I've held myself in check this long.'

He was raining feathery kisses up her neck and backing her towards his bunk. He'd kissed her in the darkness on deck many times, and she'd felt his passion, but this was the first time they'd had any privacy. He was stripping off his bow tie and his dinner jacket.

Jon's body was beautiful. He was tender, he was gentle and he loved her. Vicky knew she'd always given in to her own wishes. She'd never had her mother's self-discipline. She couldn't stop herself. She certainly couldn't stop Jon.

He lifted her to heights she'd never known with Clive. This time they were both truly in love. And having made love once, Vicky wanted more and more. She couldn't have enough of him.

The hot afternoons were given up to sensuous pleasures on Jon's bunk; with the waves gently lapping against the side of the ship, and sun and water dappling the ceiling through the porthole.

He came to her cabin every night and slipped out just before the stewardess brought her morning tea. Vicky felt on top of the world but the days were adding up. She wanted to stop time. A two-week voyage was not enough.

Soon she knew every line of Jonathon's body as well as she did his face. His healthy pink cheeks took on a light tan and became even more attractive. His quick dark eyes were telling her and everybody else just how much she meant to him.

From the deck of the mail boat Lagos looked a beautiful place. Closer inspection changed Vicky's mind. The heat wrapped itself round her like a steaming blanket. Even so, they were both pleased to find that they had three nights to wait for the cargo ship to come in and unload before it could take them on to Port Harcourt. It gave them three extra days together.

They booked into a hotel. Two rooms because Clive would expect to pay for separate rooms, but by then they had no intention of using more than one. They could no longer think of parting at night. Vicky unpacked her spine pad and pith helmet. They made her feel hotter than ever.

'We'll have time to look round Lagos,' Jon enthused. 'It's the biggest town on the West Coast.'

Vicky thought the marina was attractive but she'd seen all she wanted of Lagos in the first few hours. It seemed like the last outpost of the Empire. The dust and the squalor shocked her and the sticky heat robbed her of energy. She had to return to lie on her bed in the hotel. They spent most of their time there. At night, the mosquito net made it so airless and hot they couldn't sleep.

The freighter provided large, comfortable cabins and they were rid of mosquito nets while they were at sea. But they had only four more nights to spend together.

They left the sea and entered the narrow inland waterways of the

123

Niger delta. Because of the way the channels looped back and forth across reedy mud flats, when they saw a ship coming down channel to meet them, it seemed from a distance to be sailing on land. Jon kept exclaiming about the strange scenery, but Vicky was beginning to feel too guilty to enjoy anything.

On the last night of all, she had a panic attack as she lay cradled in Jon's arms. She knew she was about to rejoin her husband after almost five years' absence, and that she was bringing with her the man with whom she was deeply in love. She was afraid to think of the outcome.

'I'm shocked,' Jon whispered. 'I thought I could rely on myself to act like a gentleman. You've driven all reason out of my mind.'

The enormity of what they'd done was threatening to overwhelm Vicky.

'What are we going to do now?'

What they did was to make love again. It was the only way they knew how to comfort each other.

The town of Port Harcourt seemed to consist of little more than the docks and the railway terminus. The buildings were of concrete blocks, mostly single-storey. The roads were laterite tracks which had never been tarmacked. They had a train journey to make now. The closer they got to Ekbo, the worse Vicky felt.

'We have to hide what we've done,' she whispered to Jon. 'I couldn't bear it if Clive found out.'

'Of course we must hide it,' he agreed, fondling her hand.

Vicky was afraid it wouldn't be possible. Jon often stood so close that their bodies touched; sat too close if there was a sofa. He kept putting out a hand to touch her bare arm. They couldn't take their eyes off each other.

She thought of Clive and his goodness, and of how badly she had betrayed his trust, and was filled with remorse.

The railway line didn't go all the way to Ekbo. They had to get off at Oloka but found Clive had sent fourteen porters to wait for them.

They were carried on the last leg of their journey in mammy chairs. These were slung between two poles and carried on the shoulders of four men. There was a green gloom in the forest, but Vicky welcomed the shade of the trees. The heat was almost more than she could stand.

All she could see as she was carried along at a jog was the laterite path, an occasional huge ant heap and the feet of her porters. They chattered noisily all the time in a language she found incomprehensible.

It was a very different world from any she knew, and she felt she'd travelled half round the world to get here. She wondered, as she braced herself to meet Clive, how she'd ever get used to it. At last the poles were being lowered to the ground and Clive's hand was helping her out of the contraption.

Her first thought was that he was much older than she remembered. His skin was the yellowish-greyish-brown of one who has spent five years in a terrible climate without a break, and with an ever-increasing work load.

'Vicky! How marvellous to see you. You look wonderful. Have you had a good journey?' She recognised, then, Clive's exuberant manner.

'I'm thrilled you've come all this way to be with me. I can't wait to show you everything. Come and see your new home.'

Jon was arriving and the poles of his mammy chair being laid on the ground. Vicky couldn't meet the eyes of either man as she introduced them.

Clive was gentle and kind as always, as he hurried her into the cool bungalow and called for a pot of tea to be made.

CHAPTER ELEVEN

Victoria's first impression of Ekbo was that it had a certain charm.

There was a line of mud huts thatched with palm leaves strung along a rough track. Stalls had been set up in front of some of them, each with a small heap of tomatoes or a few bunches of bananas for sale.

Outside other huts, an oil drum bubbled over an open fire as rich orange-coloured palm oil was extracted from the fruit. This was their source of income.

It was fertile country. Behind the huts the trees had been cleared, and Indian corn and yams grew ten times bigger and faster in the tropical sun and high rainfall than did crops in England. The bountiful harvests supported a large population. Goats and pigs and chickens roamed at will.

There were no towns nearby. Enugu was sixty miles north, Port Harcourt a hundred miles south, and having seen the latter, Vicky hardly counted it a town. Hot rain forest surrounded them and seemed to stretch for countless miles.

Vicky had travelled the track through it from the railway thirty miles away, and had seen nothing but tall trees and thick scrub that seemed impenetrable. But Clive told her it was full of narrow winding paths and hidden villages. She thought the dark, silent forest had an eerie, sinister quality.

A few hundred yards away, more trees had been cut down to make a clearing for the mission hospital. Its steep roof of corrugated iron painted red overhung its mud walls to provide shady verandas which were always crowded. The sick were brought in in what seemed tens of thousands, and their families stayed to nurse them. The place was filled with their noise.

Divided from the hospital by a fence that grew eight feet high were the church and a nunnery, and five identical bungalows which were meant to house the expatriate staff.

She and Clive occupied one; George Draper, a white South African doctor who had arrived a few weeks earlier, lived in a second; Jon was allotted the third. The remaining two were empty.

They were unlike any other houses she'd ever known, built of concrete blocks with huge overhanging roofs of corrugated iron. The rooms were big and airy. Wide verandas ran round two sides. The kitchen was separated from the main building by a covered passage.

'How strange,' she said to Clive.

'It's a good idea. It keeps the heat of the wood stove at a distance. The chattering of the servants too.'

Clive had told her that the atmosphere was claustrophobic, but she had to experience it herself before she could appreciate just what this meant.

The nuns kept to themselves. Their lives were made up of prayer and their work with the sick. There was an Irish priest who called in for a drink and a chat once every few months.

The District Officer, a Scot, lived in a village about twenty miles away. Two or three times a year he would come over to have dinner and spend the night with them.

There were African helpers who lived in the village or in huts outside the hospital gates. These were the gardeners and the washermen, the cleaners and domestic servants. That left her and Clive, George Draper and Jon.

'We must ask Jon round, make him feel welcome,' Clive impressed upon her. 'It's all right for you and me – we have each other – but he must be feeling isolated. I know I did when I first came out. Too much solitude in one's off-duty hours is hard to bear.'

Clive had set up a billiard table on his veranda. He told George Draper and Jon to use it whenever they wanted. He usually offered drinks and a chat when they did.

Vicky was very careful not to give Clive any reason to think she was in love with Jon. She schooled herself to talk about him. Not to say anything after she'd spent three weeks in his company would surely arouse suspicion. She talked of the sightseeing they'd done in Las Palmas and the books they'd read.

'Did you find him a help on the journey out?' Clive asked. 'I was afraid, after I'd done it, that I might have saddled you with somebody you wouldn't like.'

'I would have been very nervous on my own. He was a wonderful help with the arrangements in Lagos.' She heard the tremor in her voice. She couldn't look at Clive's other-worldly smile.

'As soon as I saw him, I knew you must have got on well together,' he said with all his usual exuberance.

Victoria felt a surge of guilt so strong it was like a thrust to the heart.

'We did,' she choked. 'He was a very pleasant companion.'

'We'll have him round for dinner when you've both settled in,' Clive said easily.

She dreaded it. She was almost afraid to come face to face with Jon.

She never stopped thinking about him, craving his company and the feel of his firm, youthful body.

But when he came, Jon was careful too. His eyes didn't meet hers. His manner showed none of the intimacy she was used to. She should have felt thankful he had such control; instead she felt cheated of the love she wanted.

Vicky felt her life settling into a routine. Once a week, George and Jon came over to eat dinner with them. Once a week George entertained them at his bungalow, and on another night, Jon at his. Victoria found these occasions almost impossible to cope with.

She felt that it drove them in on each other, made them live in each other's pockets. In time they would know everything about each other that there was to know. Yet she and Jon must hide their secret from Clive for ever.

She asked Clive to show her round the hospital. She thought it might help if she could work. She didn't want time to think about what she'd done. But Clive was already taking Jon round. She tagged on behind.

The hospital was another shock. There was nothing of the quiet orderliness she associated with British hospitals. Every bed was always filled. Between the beds, there were patients on trolleys and more patients on mattresses on the floor. The verandas were crowded with more patients lying on the bare boards wrapped in blankets. Even more patients camped under the hedges round the compound, and their relatives stayed to care for them and lit fires at night to cook their meals.

'It's difficult to keep medical standards up,' Clive said wearily. 'The nuns do a wonderful job. Their standards of hygiene are of the highest, but we have so few facilities.'

They had kerosene lamps and wax night lights, but often both were in short supply. It wasn't easy to keep up the stocks of medicines they needed either. The one thing they could be sure of was a never-ending stream of patients.

Victoria was surprised and shocked at the amount and variety of work Clive undertook, but not at the affection which everybody seemed to feel for him.

She felt obsessed with Jon. There were days when she craved his company, and found herself watching him as he went about his duties at the hospital.

She knew she must put him out of her mind. Even if Clive wasn't about the bungalow, they had no privacy. Doors and windows were kept wide open to take advantage of any breeze. There were usually cooks and stewards, garden boys and small boys going about their duties.

One afternoon, over lunch, Clive said wearily: 'No rest for me today. I have to go back to do an emergency Caesarean section.'

Everybody took a rest on their beds at this time of day. Even the servants went off after they had cleared the lunch table.

'What's the matter?'

'The poor woman's been in labour for a long time, they tell me several days already. Her husband only started walking her here when it was obvious she wasn't going to deliver. We can't keep her waiting any longer. '

'Do you want me to give the anaesthetic?'

'No, you have your rest. George Draper's going to do it.'

Vicky finished her coffee on the veranda and went to her bedroom.

The bungalow had been quiet for ten minutes when Jon opened her bedroom door and slipped inside. Vicky hadn't heard him coming. Shocked at his audacity, she threw down the book she'd been reading and shot off the bed.

'It's quite safe,' he assured her, trying to put his arms round her.

She was shaking. 'What if somebody saw you coming over?'

'Nobody did.'

'One of the servants could see you leaving.' She was terrified they'd be found out.

'Come on, Vicky,' he urged. 'This is the first chance we've had in a fortnight.'

She was reluctant. For her, the consequences could be disastrous.

'I'll tell Clive I ran out of reading matter and came over to borrow a book. I'll tell him that anyway, then it won't matter if one of the servants says he saw me here.'

Her throat was tight with tension. She pushed his arms away and crept out to the sitting room. The house was deserted and somnolent in the afternoon sun. She hovered in indecision, then took one of Clive's books from his bookcase.

She couldn't relax. The magic she'd shared with Jon was gone. It seemed nothing more than a hot and hasty toss on the bed. And it was Clive's bed!

Afterwards, she threw on her clothes and, filled with dread, went out of the bedroom to make sure the coast was still clear. She felt sick with fear and not far from tears.

'Don't ever come again,' she told him. 'We have to stop.'

Victoria could see now that even without Jon it would not have been easy to slip back into the comfortable comradeship she'd known with Clive. She could see him striving to bridge the years of separation.

She struggled with the language, and with the presenting signs and symptoms of local diseases, but her biggest tussle was with her own feelings of shame, guilt and remorse. If that wasn't enough, she also had to appear to welcome Clive's lovemaking when all the time she was comparing his sagging body with Jon's firm youth. The only way she could get through it at all was to close her eyes and pretend that Clive was Jon.

There were times when she looked at Jon and crawled with frustration. Once or twice she was on the point of suggesting to him that they go back to England and set up home together.

Sometimes she felt a terrible urge to confess. Clive would surely be forgiving. But strongest of all she felt fear. The most awful fear that she would be found out. She was turning into a nervous wreck.

When she first had reason to suspect she might be pregnant, it brought on such a state of shock that it almost broke her. She was trembling with fear. She didn't dare tell anybody about it. If she were pregnant now it could only be Jon's child.

She felt that fate could not have treated her more cruelly and she was being pushed to the very edge of her endurance.

It made matters worse that she was a doctor and should have foreseen the possibility. With hindsight she knew she could have avoided it.

Contraception was not on the curriculum for trainee doctors but she'd been interested in the work that Marie Stopes was doing. Most women, even those who were married, did not concern themselves with such things until they already had a family.

She knew that Clive wanted children. She rather liked the idea herself. She hadn't wanted to avoid the results of married love. So no amount of forethought would have caused her to take such things on the voyage with her.

And she hadn't foreseen just how reckless her affair with Jon would make her.

Vicky had seen her mother cope with problems and knew what she must do. She pulled herself together. She started taking more clinics at the hospital, threw herself into work. It took her mind off her own problems. Soothed the guilt and resentment.

As soon as the minimum length of time had elapsed to make it possible, she schooled herself to tell Clive. She chose a moment when they were getting ready for bed.

'I have something to tell you.' She tried to smile. 'Clive, I think I'm going to have a baby.'

He turned to hug her, his eyes incredulous. Vicky began relating the early signs she'd noticed.

He was over the moon and had a broad smile on his face. 'So soon, too. Vicky, you don't know how proud and happy you've made me.'

She felt another surge of shame that she had to saddle Clive with another man's child. If he knew, he would think that unpardonable.

After what seemed long-drawn-out weeks, two more doctors arrived.

131

Everybody had been looking forward to their arrival, but for Victoria they spelled salvation. Their tiny social group was expanding.

Best of all, Clive decided that in another month, when the new men had settled in, he could at last have some leave.

'I must take you home, Vicky. You can't stay here now.'

It brought Vicky some respite to leave the claustrophobic atmosphere. A measure of relief to get away from Jon.

Back in the comfortable Hamilton Square house she began to feel safer. Things seemed more normal. Evelyn fussed round her, pleased about the baby. But Victoria knew she was by no means in the clear.

Her baby was gong to be born a month earlier than the date on which she was telling everybody it could be expected. She couldn't stop Clive monitoring her condition with close interest, and he'd already told her she was large for dates. There was the further anxiety that the coming child might look like Jon.

She was surrounded by doctors. They would know at one glance the difference between a baby at term and one that was a month premature. She certainly would.

As the time of the birth grew closer she became more agitated. Surely once the babe was here to be held and examined, Clive must question whether he could possibly be its father?

The last weeks of her pregnancy was one of the worst times of her life. She was heavy with dread and a guilty conscience, as well as with child. To make matters worse, Clive hardly left her side. He was very solicitous for her welfare.

The real date for her confinement came and went. She felt ungainly but it was what she had hoped for. It seemed that at last luck was on her side.

She was hoping to last out another two weeks, but she went only nine days over term. Clive sat with her during the early part of her labour. She made the comment that the child would be of thirty-eight weeks' gestation. She said the same to her mother, to the doctor who attended her, and to the midwife. Thirty-eight weeks was just enough for everybody to believe the child was Clive's.

Labour itself seemed easy. She was much more worried about other things. Although exhausted by the birth, she demanded to hold the infant immediately. She had to see for herself.

Baby Lois weighed in at just over seven pounds and looked like any other neonate. She wasn't a particularly handsome infant, being rather sharp-featured, and the down on her head looked distinctly gingerish. But Victoria couldn't see the slightest resemblance to Jonathan Pine.

What did scare her was to find that the infant had the long fingernails and flaking skin of the post-mature. The signs were there for everybody to see.

132

'She's absolutely beautiful.' Clive was delighted with the child and spent hours cradling her in his arms. Evelyn agreed. Vicky couldn't understand why they didn't comment on what seemed so obvious to her. It kept her on a knife edge.

The midwife said: 'She's lovely. Very well developed. Nothing of the pre-term baby about her at all.'

It took Vicky's breath away. She was thankful they were alone at the time, but after that she couldn't rest. She secreted a pair of nail scissors under her pillow and cut the child's nails on the first occasion she was left alone with her. She rubbed baby oil into Lois's skin until the flakiness was no longer noticeable.

As the days passed, she began to relax. The baby was growing and developing before her eyes. She could hardly believe it, but it seemed she'd survived the crisis.

Her confidence returned, and she felt that at last she could put the whole affair of Jonathan Pine behind her. What she wanted now was to turn over a new leaf and be a good mother to Lois and a good wife to Clive.

'I wish you didn't have to go back to Ekbo,' she said, as the months of his leave drew to an end. 'It's a place for the young.' He was nearly fifty by this time.

'If you want to work, you could get yourself a job either here or in Liverpool, but we would be very happy if you never worked again.'

Clive was not convinced. For him, the months of idleness at home had begun to drag.

'I can still do a lot to help at Ekbo. My life's work has been there. I'd love to go back if it weren't for the separation from you and Lois.'

As soon as Vicky saw the letter with Nigerian stamps on the hall table, she knew he would go.

'It's from George Draper,' Clive said, handing it over for her to read. 'He says that Jon has decided to go home and will not be returning. He can't stand the loneliness there. He says he's had enough.'

Vicky felt suffused with relief. If Clive had no further contact with Jon, if she had none, then her secret would be safe.

'They need me back now,' Clive told her sadly. 'And you have to do another six months' training as a hospital houseman.'

Vicky wasn't sure that she wanted to. She was more interested in her infant daughter now, and in Clive.

'You can't give up now. Not when you're so nearly qualified. It would be such a waste. Besides . . .'

'You're going to tell me I'll be a widow for a long time and will need something to fill my days.'

'Yes,' Clive smiled. 'Would you like to do tropical diseases?'

'Medicine,' Vicky said firmly. 'I've always intended that. It's more important for me to get a good grasp of basic principles. I suppose I'd better start applying.'

'You could do it at the General,' Evelyn told her briskly. 'Just up the road from here. We'll get a nanny for Lois and they can stay here with me.'

'I don't really want to leave her.' Vicky had her daughter in her arms; she cuddled her closer.

'Of course you don't,' Evelyn agreed. 'I didn't want to leave you when you were young, but it has to be done if you want to be a doctor. One of the sacrifices we have to make.'

Clive held her in his arms that night and said tenderly: 'This is one of the problems of mixing a career with marriage. I'm afraid you'll find it very hard to part with Lois now. I knew I'd give you this heartache, right from the start. I'm sorry, love.'

'I'll be able to come home and see her often,' Vicky said. She was repeating her mother's words. 'And it's only for six months.'

'I promised Evelyn I'd make sure you finished your training,' Clive said. 'I don't think she'd have let me marry you if I hadn't.'

'I didn't need her permission.'

'But I did, love. If I was to remain on good terms.'

Vicky felt full of remorse again. Here he was apologising as though it was his fault, when most men expected their wives to devote themselves to their home and family. It made what she had done to Clive seem ten times worse.

'Perhaps when my six months are up I could come out to see you?' Victoria whispered. If she were honest, she would have preferred to stay in Birkenhead with her baby, but she wanted to please Clive, and most of all she wanted a sop to her conscience.

Clive pondered for a long time. 'If the nanny settles down and you think she's good enough . . .'

Vicky was lonely without Clive. She gritted her teeth and settled into the General Hospital as house officer on the medical team for six months. She had to live in, of course, and the hours of work were long and hard.

She went home every free moment she had, and eventually felt she'd settled into this very different way of life. Lois thrived and Evelyn enjoyed being involved with a baby again. There were no problems.

When her six months were coming to an end, Vicky wrote to her husband and suggested again that she should come out to see him.

'There's nothing I want more,' he wrote back. 'I would love to have you here. I'm missing you terribly. But you must make sure Evelyn is prepared to act *in loco parentis*.

'I'm afraid Ekbo is no place to bring a baby. If you find you can't bear to be parted from Lois, you can always go home again. At least I'll have had your company for a little while.'

This time, Vicky travelled out alone, keeping herself very much to herself. She coped better with life in Ekbo, though everything there reminded her of Jon. She threw herself into work at the hospital.

Within a few months, she was pregnant again, and relieved that this time she could be sure the child was Clive's. She felt this would go some way to make things up to him, but she found it almost impossible to keep her mind off Jon.

During the months he'd worked in Ekbo Jon had been friendly with George Draper. George was still working here and from time to time he had a letter from him. There was so little news from the outside world, it pleased him to have snippets to pass on.

'Jon was doing orthopaedics in a hospital in Newcastle but he couldn't settle. He's now working as a GP in Edinburgh.'

Vicky found herself imagining the sort of life Jon would be leading. Imagined herself sharing it.

Then one day George received a white and silver box containing a piece of dried-up wedding cake and a photograph. He took them round to Vicky's bungalow to show her.

Vicky was stunned. At first she couldn't look at the bride. It caught in her throat that Jon had only been in Edinburgh for four months at the time of his marriage.

'He's not the sort to waste any time,' George laughed. 'The bride's name is Myra.'

When Vicky was over the first shock, and George had accepted a cup of tea, she took up the photo again to study it. Myra was not beautiful but Jon looked radiantly happy. She was burning with jealousy.

She suffered months of torment as a result of that. It did her no good to tell herself that Jonathan Pine would make a rotten husband. That he'd probably be off after other women in no time at all. He'd been a wonderful lover and she couldn't forget him.

The years began to pass more quickly and brought Victoria two sons, Keith and Barnaby, whom she loved dearly. They were gentle like their father, like him to look at too. They both had his slow, wide smile and his kind blue eyes.

Lois was different, and Vicky adored her. She wondered if the tight bond she felt with Lois was because she was her love child.

Neither she nor Clive had liked leaving Lois at home as a baby; now neither was prepared to be parted from their children. They brought them out to Ekbo, and the family stayed together until Clive could take home leave.

Their bungalow had not been designed for family use. Originally

135

there had been one enormous bedroom. In a climate like Ekbo's, all rooms had to be the full width of the building so that there could be windows on both sides to provide a cross-draught. Without natural movement in the air, rooms were uncomfortably stuffy to the point of being unusable.

Originally, there had been four windows in their bedroom. Clive had arranged for a partition to be erected down the middle to make two bedrooms each with windows on opposite walls. They had also had a store room and a linen room. Clive had them knocked together and more windows put in, to make a room for Lois.

These days, Victoria worked in the hospital only until noon and then spent the rest of the day with her children.

Over the years, she felt she'd grown very attached to Clive and settled down to married life. He was always kind and loving but his manner became less exuberant as he grew older. He was beginning to speak of retirement. Already he'd worked in the Ekbo hospital longer than any other doctor, but he said he still enjoyed his work.

Apart from Vicky, Clive had four expatriate doctors working permanently in Ekbo now. One, of whom he thought very highly, was called Bill Goodbody.

When Goodbody saw that Victoria and her children lived out in Ekbo, he persuaded his wife Janet to come out too. She was younger than Vicky but in time they grew very close. Janet Goodbody had been trained as a teacher and took it upon herself to teach all the children living on the compound. They built her a school room and she held classes every morning.

It pleased Clive that they didn't have to send the children away to school, as soon as they were five years old. Janet felt she could teach them until they were eleven, though Clive thought Lois would be ready for boarding school in England by the time she was nine or ten.

Occasionally a fifth doctor would join them but would be driven home by the climate, the monotony or the long queues of patients. The local population believed that the white man's medicine would cure them of the most dire ills.

Far from home and other people, the doctors were thrown together. It was still a tiny social circle from which there was no escape, but Vicky felt they were all firm friends now. For all of them, that made a big difference.

Clive adored his children. He taught them to play simple card games, draughts and dominoes. He went on to teach Lois the rudiments of chess.

'You gave me a good game,' he praised her. 'Soon you'll be able to beat me.'

One day, he pulled her onto his knee to replait her thin red hair, which was breaking free from its ribbon and said: 'Lois, you're quite the cuckoo in the nest.'

Vicky caught her breath. She'd long ceased to worry that Clive might find out he was not her father. The remark caught her unawares.

'What do you mean?' Her heart was pounding like a sledge-hammer.

'She's not like either of us. Where does she get these talents?'

'From you, Clive. You spend hours teaching her.'

'But where's this red hair come from?'

When Vicky had first seen Lois's red hair she'd taken comfort from the fact that Jon's hair had been brown. She'd told Clive it might be a throwback to her family, though Evelyn had contradicted her, saying that she knew of no red hair on her side.

'It's pretty,' Clive smiled, fondling it. 'Lois is unlike any of us in temperament too.'

Victoria knew what he meant. There was a ferocity about Lois; she could be headstrong and wilful. She often fought with Barnaby, but she was easily upset too, and took things very much to heart.

Vicky felt all her fears building up again, threatening to overwhelm her. It almost seemed as if Clive suspected her secret.

Suddenly, he was smiling at her. 'Evelyn thinks she takes after your father's family.'

Vicky swallowed hard. She knew that Evelyn believed Gerrard Ormond had been her big mistake.

CHAPTER TWELVE

Clive often told Vicky how much he loved her and how happy she made him by staying in Ekbo. How fortunate he felt to see his children growing up, and to have his wife working at his side.

They both knew it was rare indeed for English women and children to stay out in West Africa.

Vicky had stayed long enough to settle down. She'd wanted to repay Clive for his kindness and generosity, and to assuage her guilt about Jonathan Pine. Now she quite enjoyed the life, but she understood the risks.

She'd only to walk round the graves clustered behind the little church to know that West Africa was not called the White Man's Grave for nothing. It could claim its victims with appalling rapidity. She knew that Clive dreaded an outbreak of a major killer such as yellow fever or cholera.

One morning, during her clinic, she saw a middle-aged native woman called Comfort Jahodi who had been brought in by her relatives from a nearby village.

Comfort's husband told Vicky that his wife had had a fever the day before but she'd sweated and felt better by evening. She'd not been eating and had complained of pains in her back. To Vicky, she didn't seem too ill.

The woman had stretched out under the hedge in a corner of the compound, as was the custom, winding her lapper so it covered her head too.

Her relatives had kept watch and in the middle of the night had gone to one of the nuns on duty for further advice. After seeing the patient, the nun had come over to the bungalow.

Vicky happened to be awake and heard her footsteps approaching. Clive was snoring gently, she threw on a wrap and went out quietly. It was unusual for any of the doctors to be called out in the night. The nuns believed in letting them get their rest unless the need for their services was absolutely vital.

'It's one of your patients, Comfort Jahodi,' the nun told her. 'I'm worried about her. She's babbling in disjointed sentences now, and she's been vomiting. Her husband says she's been drifting in and out of consciousness.'

Victoria shivered in the night air. If the nun was worried, it probably meant she had good reason to be. Out in the compound, very few people were sleeping. They were sitting about in groups, chattering, and seemed alarmed. The nun had to part a group so that they could get near to the patient.

Victoria shone her torch at the black vomit on the hard ground, and then on her patient's face. The whites of Comfort's eyes were bright yellow. As soon as Victoria saw that, her heart pumped with dread. She looked carefully at the patient's skin then, and was reassured momentarily to find it a normal chocolate brown. It took her a few moments to realise that there was too much pigment in it for the jaundice to show clearly.

The woman had a raging fever and Vicky wrote her up for quinine to bring it down.

'Anything else?' the nun asked.

Vicky hesitated, frightened now. 'Better isolate her. Full barrier nursing.' There was a long row of cubicles at the far end of the compound where they nursed infectious fevers. 'Is there space?' Like the rest of the hospital, they were always full.

'I'll make space, Doctor.'

'And a mosquito net. She must have that.'

Victoria stumbled back to the bungalow. She was so worried she woke Clive.

'I'm afraid.' She whispered the dreaded words. 'Yellow fever.'

She'd never seen a case before but the signs were classic. He was wide awake in an instant.

'I hope you're wrong.' Vicky hoped she was wrong too.

Clive's face was creased with concern, making him look older than ever.

'We had an outbreak here in 1916. There were eighteen deaths. I'll have to go and see for myself, Vicky. I can't lie here worrying about it.'

It was a long time before he came back. When he did, his face was screwed up with tension.

'I'm right?' she asked. 'It is yellow fever?'

He looked dejected. 'Yes. We have to assume it is.'

In the morning, Vicky went across the compound before breakfast to find out how her patient was. She knew from the wailing as she neared the isolation cubicles that Comfort Jahodi was already dead.

She went cold with terror. Then ran back home in a panic, wanting to reassure herself that her children were all right.

Being a doctor, being surrounded by other doctors and having medicines available, had given her a false sense of security about keeping her children out here. There was no specific medicine known to cure yellow fever. She was fearful for them now.

Ruby, the African nursemaid, was supervising the children as they washed and dressed. She was stout, a huge mound of soft flesh, and wore her hair in tiny tight knots all over her head. She was in the bathroom, helping three-year-old Keith to wash.

He looked study enough. His chubby cheeks were tanned, his hair bleached to white-blond by the sun. But he didn't have the rosy cheeks that children brought up in England had.

In the bedroom her small sons shared, seven-year-old Barnaby was yelling for help. Nine-year-old Lois had him in a corner and seemed about to pounce on him.

'Lois,' Vicky said, distracting her, and with a whoop Barnaby leapt out of the way. 'What game is this?' she asked suspiciously. She caught her older son in her arms as he took a flying leap at his own bed.

'Mummy, he's taken my book. He's hidden it and won't give it me back,' Lois wailed.

'Where is it? What have you done with Lois's book?' She shook Barney, half playfully.

'Haven't got it.'

'He has. He's a liar. I hate him.'

'Lois!'

'It's true. I hate him.' Angry tears were filling Lois's dark eyes. For the sake of coolness, she wore her fine gingery hair in two plaits. She was thinner in the face than the boys, the only one with freckles.

'Barney? Have you taken her book?' Vicky turned him round to face her.

'No, Mummy.'

Vicky put Barnaby down and went to cuddle Lois.

'He's horrible to me,' she sniffed.

'What book have you lost?'

'The Christopher Robin book Auntie Janet loaned to me. I know he's taken it.'

'Haven't,' Barnaby yelled, and with another whoop pushed past them both and escaped.

Vicky called up her reserves of patience.

'Let's see if we can find it.' She took her daughter by the hand and led her to her own bedroom. Within moments she'd seen the book under Lois's bed.

'Are you sure you didn't drop it there when you finished reading last night?'

'It was Barnaby,' Lois cried. 'He hid it so I wouldn't be able to read. He doesn't like it because I can read better than he can.'

'He's only seven. When he's your age, he'll read just as well.'

'He won't. He's not as clever as me.'

141

Vicky's eyes came to rest on Lois's chest of drawers. 'What are these things?' She picked up a monkey's tail between her finger and thumb, then dropped it in disgust to prod the dried body of a chameleon and a bunch of feathers.

'They're mine.'

'They're horrible. Let's throw them away.'

'No! I want them.'

'What for?'

'They're for casting spells. Juju. It's like magic.'

'Yes, I know, but . . .'

'I'm going to put a spell on Barnaby so he'll never learn to read well.'

'Don't be silly, darling. Juju doesn't work like that.'

'It does. Juju can make anything happen. It can kill people.' Lois's pout was mutinous. 'I know it can. I heard Ephraim telling Nanny it killed his grandfather.'

Ephraim was their steward. He did the work a housekeeper would do in England.

'I've cast a spell to kill Barney.'

'You're casting a lot of spells.'

'Only on Barney. I hate him.'

'Lois, darling, you don't.'

Vicky's patience was exhausted. She swept the articles off the chest into a waste-paper basket, then found that a piece of what looked like decomposing leopard skin had stuck to her hand.

Lois let out a wail of protest. Vicky flounced back to Ruby with the waste-paper basket.

'Get rid of these dreadful things,' she commanded through clenched teeth. 'Do not allow the children to get any more.'

'I want them.' Lois's face was scarlet with rage, tears running down it unheeded.

'Lois, be quiet this instant. You have your book back and Barnaby says he didn't touch it.'

'You always take his part. You always believe him, not me.'

'No I don't. I do wish you wouldn't fight like this. Wash your face again and then come and eat your breakfast or you'll be late for school.'

Vicky was pouring her breakfast tea when Clive came into the dining room. Suddenly he pounced on the vase of canna lilies she'd placed on the table yesterday. He rushed out to hurl the water over the veranda in a silver stream. It soaked instantly into the dry ground. He came back grim-faced.

'No stagnant water, Vicky. We can't afford to have it anywhere near us. All tanks, gutters, tins and buckets must be emptied.

We mustn't let the mosquitoes breed and we must be particularly careful not to get bitten now.'

'The children . . .' Vicky worried, as she spooned porridge into bowls for them.

'They must go to bed earlier. They'll be safe under their mosquito nets. And spray their bedrooms at dusk. Ours too. The aedes mosquito bites a person suffering from the disease and spreads it by biting others.'

'I'll see to the spraying myself.'

Clive sat down but he was too worried to eat much.

She asked: 'Is there nothing else we can do?'

'I'll have to check our supplies of insecticide, order some more and get the garden boys to go round spraying every ditch and puddle.'

'What about the river?' Vicky asked. They called it a river but it was only the width of a stream, and since it moved very slowly, it was more a ditch filled with murky water. It was used by the hospital for personal washing and for laundry.

'We'll have to spray it. Every day.'

Vicky reminded him that Comfort Jahodi had come from a village eight miles away.

'I'll organise a squad to go in that direction,' he said, 'to spray all stagnant water. And I'll send somebody to talk to the local people, to explain what they must do to protect themselves. I do hope we aren't going to have an epidemic.'

In the next four days there were six more cases in the hospital. On the fifth day Vicky was doing a clinic when Ephraim, her steward, came bursting in, his black face shining with sweat. He could hardly get the words out.

'Baby not well, ma'am. Ruby want you come home one time.'

She dropped everything and ran home before him. Keith was having a rigor. He was shaking so much his bed was rattling, and his temperature was sky high. What she had feared most had happened.

Vicky stayed and nursed him herself. She felt helpless because she knew there was no medicine that could cure him. She sponged him down to keep him cool. He was delirious and very distressed. She gave him quinine and glucose drinks. She was very fearful for him; he was so young.

Clive set up an intravenous drip. 'To stop him dehydrating,' he said.

He hovered and offered advice. To see him so worried made Vicky more anxious. He told her the nuns were saying special prayers for Keith's recovery. They all knew that a quarter of all cases died.

On the third day, Vicky could see he was becoming jaundiced. She was sitting with him, holding his hand and trying to comfort him, when Barnaby crept into the room.

'I feel queer, Mummy,' he whispered. His eyes were half closed when she pulled him on to her knee. He felt boiling hot.

Vicky was horrified. Surely not both her sons? She questioned him. Barney could tell her how he felt.

'My head hurts and I ache all over.'

She knew he had yellow fever too, but he was older than Keith, and seemed to have a stronger hold on life. Vicky sponged him too, put him to bed and hoped for the best.

On the fourth day, Keith lapsed into a coma, and on the fifth, he died. Vicky cried for an hour. Then she pulled herself together and sponged Barnaby down and made him comfortable again. Both his skin and his eyes were deep yellow.

Clive came home and wept too. He looked bone-weary. She knew they were both physically and emotionally washed out.

That night they saw to Barnaby then left him in Ruby's care. They went to bed at eight o'clock, and Vicky fell asleep in Clive's arms. But at midnight a nun came to wake them. Clive was needed at the hospital again.

Vicky got up to see to Barnaby. He was delirious and seemed to be getting worse. She blamed herself for leaving him and going to bed for four hours. Life had become a nightmare.

'You must have some rest,' Clive told her wearily, but he was getting very little himself.

They both crept to the door of Lois's room, lingered for a moment by her bed. She was sleeping and her forehead felt cool. But Vicky knew that here in the African bush a child could be running about happily one minute and be very sick the next. Even Clive couldn't save them.

She noticed that the monkey tail and dried chameleon had not been disposed of. They were on Lois's bedside table now, surrounded by a row of pebbles.

The epidemic was reaching calamitous proportions. Many of the nuns had caught it. So had one of their young doctors who was due to go on leave next month. It raged in the villages around. Clive had to close the hospital to any more patients. Too many of the staff were ill and they could no longer cope. He had never taken such a step before.

When she realised that Barnaby was going to die too, Vicky felt her life disintegrating round her. He lapsed into a coma, and she sent Ephraim to the hospital to fetch Clive.

He came home and they clung together, watching over their son. Barnaby died in his father's arms that night.

'I'm sorry, Vicky.' She had never seen Clive so upset. 'I blame myself, I should never have allowed the children to stay out here.'

'It was my decision too. I wanted it.'

'I knew this climate could kill. Goodness knows, I've seen enough of it.' He covered his face with his hands and wept. 'I thought I could keep you all well. Or if you became ill, I thought I could cure you, and I can't.' He lifted his ravaged face to hers. 'I shouldn't have let you stay.'

Victoria was past grief. She couldn't even cry. She was at the end of her strength. Clive insisted that she go to bed.

She feared for them all, especially for Clive. He was too old to work like this, going without proper sleep night after night. She knew that Ruby, the nursemaid, was ill, and so was Bill Goodbody.

Vicky woke in the middle of the night in a feverish sweat. Clive was not with her, so she knew he must be over at the hospital again. She needed to tell him that she had a raging thirst and an agonising headache, and that she'd caught the fever too. She needed all the comfort he could give her.

She was very frightened; she didn't want to die, she was too young. But she knew Keith and Barnaby had been even younger, and that hadn't spared them.

The next day she had the pains in her back that all the victims complained of, but she felt a little better and her temperature was down.

The next time she woke up, Clive was taking off her nightdress because it was stained with black vomit. She felt him gently sponge her down. The water was cool enough to bring her out in goose pimples. She felt too weak to tell him so.

'Darling Vicky,' his cheek brushed hers, 'you must fight this. Be strong. I couldn't bear it if anything happened to you.'

She seemed to float away from him, then come back. She heard him imploring her: 'Don't die. Please don't die.'

He was by her side when she woke the next time, tenderly wiping the sweat from her face and offering her sips of water. She saw the bottle of intravenous dextrose and saline swinging above her, felt the needle in her arm.

'Another sip, Vicky, it will clean your mouth, make you feel better.'

She felt herself drifting off and fought the sensation. 'Am I yellow?'

'I'm afraid so.'

She knew that there were times when she cried out for Clive, when her head swam with the fever. On the fifth day of her illness Vicky lay exhausted and sweating in the smothering afternoon heat.

The following day she felt better, and knew she had won the battle and would live.

'Thank God.' Clive didn't leave her bedside then. He looked grey and ill. 'Thank God you're better.'

She was well enough to smile and ask, 'Are you all right?' He was nodding. 'And Lois?'

'She's not caught it. There are fewer cases now. I think we're over the worst. It's taken a terrible toll.'

'Bill Goodbody?'

'He's better.' Clive looked haggard. 'So is Ruby, but we've lost five nuns and three more are very sick. They're all devastated.' His voice was barely above a whisper.

'And we've lost twenty-two of our hospital patients as well as one of our doctors.' They were such a close-knit group that to lose a doctor was like losing a member of their own family.

Michael MacAllister had been thirty-six, and had had everything to live for. His wife, Mary, had been out for a long visit with their daughter of about Lois's age. They had gone home a month before the outbreak to rent a house for Michael's leave, and to find a school for Esme.

'Poor Mary.'

'I've had to write and tell her. Such a shock, to get my letter. Terrible loss.'

Victoria was close to tears again. 'Keith and Barnaby too.'

They'd lost the sons she'd given him to assuage her own guilt. She knew what that loss must mean to Clive.

'We still have Lois,' he said simply. 'And we still have each other.'

Vicky let the tears run down her face. Only Lois left of her children. She felt more guilt-ridden than ever.

The days were passing but Victoria still felt very weak. Clive kept telling her that everything was back to normal at the hospital, but she knew it wasn't. None of them had been able to get over the horror. The epidemic had left them all in a state of nervous exhaustion. Now she felt worried about Lois.

'She's never been an easy child to manage,' she said slowly. She and Clive were waiting for supper to be put on the table. 'But she used to be very rewarding. Such enthusiasm for her school work. Such hugs and kisses for me. She was reading a Christopher Robin book, was halfway through when . . .

'I thought, if I read a little with her she'd take it up again, but no. She just sits about moping. She stays by herself in her bedroom. She's there now.'

'She's lost her brothers,' Clive reminded her gently. 'It's bound to take time for her to get over that.'

'She didn't play with Barnaby. Never seemed attached to him.'

'But she must have been. We must be patient and loving with her.'

'I try to be,' Vicky said wearily.

'I know, and it's hard for you to find the energy just now. When you're well enough to travel, you could take her home.'

'Can't you come too, Clive? You're due for leave. You need a rest.'

He sighed. 'We're all in need of rest. If I can get a replacement for MacAllister . . . I can't leave them short-handed.'

'I'm no longer working either . . .'

146

'You can't go back to work. Not yet.'

Ephraim came to the sitting room door to tell them supper was ready. Vicky pulled herself to her feet.

'Lois,' she called. There was no answer. 'Lois?'

She went down the passage towards Lois's bedroom. Her daughter was lying face down on her bed.

'Lois, supper is on the table. Wash your hands and come now.'

She didn't answer. Vicky put a hand on her shoulder. 'You're not asleep?'

'Don't want any,' Lois mumbled.

'You must eat something.' She and Clive were concerned because Lois's appetite seemed to have gone. 'It's meat pie. Your favourite.'

'Don't want any.'

Victoria heard the tears in her voice then. She sat down on the edge of the bed and pulled Lois up. Her face was agonised and wet with tears, her eyes red.

'What's the matter, love?' Full of sympathy, Victoria wrapped her arms round the child and hugged her.

'I'm sorry, Mummy.' The small body was racked with huge sobs.

'What for?' Victoria rocked her gently. Clive came to hover in the doorway.

'I did it. I killed them. It's all my fault.' Lois was crying more noisily, burying her face in her mother's shoulder. Victoria could feel her dress growing damp from her tears.

'I put a spell on them. I made them die.'

Vicky felt sick with horror. She could see the bit of leopard's skin, drier now, and the monkey's tail, still laid out on a banana leaf on the bedside table. Why hadn't she disposed of them herself?

'You think that because you put a spell on your brothers you made them die? Is that what you're saying?' Clive was loosening Lois's hold and pulling her on to his own lap. 'Now, love, let's get to the bottom of this.'

Lois's small body heaved. She flung both arms round Clive's neck and clung to him like a limpet.

'I know I've been very naughty, Daddy. I killed them.'

'No, love, you didn't,' he soothed.

'Yes I did. Ephraim told me how to do it.'

'Did he get you these things?' Vicky got up to look at the articles laid out on the banana leaf.

'Yes, from the market. He said they'd work and they did. He knows a witch doctor, a juju man, who showed him how to cast spells.'

Clive got up to look, swinging Lois up with him.

'Dried chameleons and feathers won't hurt anybody. You didn't kill them. It was the fever.'

Lois sniffed in disbelief. 'The fever didn't kill Mummy when she caught it.'

'Mummy is stronger than Keith and Barnaby were. She fought the fever off. They couldn't.'

'Ephraim said . . .'

'We believe in science, Lois. Why would so many people come to the hospital if their own witch doctors could cure them?'

'Witch doctors are different from ordinary doctors like you,' Lois cried. 'You don't ask a doctor to kill people.'

'You shouldn't ask that of anybody.'

'You can ask a witch doctor for anything you want.'

'Juju is black man's magic, a sort of witchcraft. It doesn't work for Europeans like us.'

'What does work, then?'

'We say our prayers. We ask God for what we want.'

'But He doesn't answer mine,' Lois said sadly. 'I've tried Him, many times. Weren't the nuns asking for Keith and Barnaby to be spared and He didn't . . .'

'He answers our prayers in His own way,' Clive tried to explain.

'But I wanted things done my way,' Lois said stubbornly.

'This is something new.' Vicky touched another disgusting object. 'What is it?'

'A hornbill's beak. Ephraim said it would bring them back to life, but it hasn't. He told me how to do it but it didn't work. He thinks I need an ape's skull too but there wasn't one in the market, and anyway, I've no more pocket money.'

'Lois, nothing will bring your brothers back,' Clive told her gently. 'And none of these things had the slightest effect on what happened to them. What you did didn't hurt them. It was the fever.'

'I didn't kill them after all?'

'No, Lois. No. Now take those things and put them in the bin.'

Slowly she folded the banana leaf over them. Vicky watched her take them and put them in the bin outside the kitchen door.

'Poor Lois,' she said. 'It was on her conscience. She must have felt dreadful, thinking she'd killed them.' She knew she'd said the wrong thing as soon as the words were out of her mouth.

'I should never have allowed the children to stay here with me,' Clive said slowly, with agony in his eyes. 'Look what happened to my sons. Look what it's doing to Lois.'

Vicky felt agonised too. She'd known Lois was jealous of Barnaby. She'd heard her say she hated him and wanted to kill him. She'd taken that as childish overstatement, the result of some petty quarrel. Now she knew Lois had really tried to do it.

That was the awful part. That Lois had really wanted to kill Barnaby.

CHAPTER THIRTEEN

Vicky insisted on waiting until Clive felt ready to go home with her. She was afraid he'd stay for many months longer if she left him on his own. That he'd never feel he could be spared.

'I want to go.' Lois's eyes became more haunted. 'I want to go back to England. I don't feel safe here.'

That seemed to make Clive's mind up for him. Victoria was relieved when, two months later, they were all able to leave together. She felt that once they were home they'd all feel better.

'One of the first things we must do now we are back is to call on Mary MacAllister,' Clive said. They were sitting round the dining room table in the Hamilton Square house.

Victoria was reluctant; she wanted to forget the yellow fever epidemic and the terrible tragedies it had caused.

'We must offer sympathy,' he insisted. 'Try to provide comfort. Talk about it. Help her come to terms with Michael's death.'

'He has a daughter called Esme, just a year older than you, Lois. We'll take you with us so you can tell her you lost two brothers, and how sad that has made you.'

'No!' Lois shrieked.

Clive took both her hands in his. 'If we try to help others, we often find we've helped ourselves.'

'No!' Lois cried again. 'I don't want to talk about it. I can't.' She pushed herself up from the table and rushed upstairs to her room.

'I'm afraid we've already put her through too much,' Clive mourned. On the day they went to see Mary MacAllister, they left Lois with Evelyn.

Mary MacAllister lived in a cottage in Maghull, on the outskirts of Liverpool. She sat on a settee with her arm round her daughter. They both wanted to hear every detail of the epidemic. Esme asked tearfully about her father's end.

Victoria found it harrowing. The family had been out in Ekbo for a year and she'd grown fond of them. To talk about it brought back to the forefront of her mind all the things she wanted to forget. She clung to Clive as they went back into the centre of Liverpool in a taxi.

'I thank God that we still have Lois,' he whispered, and Victoria felt the same.

Before the fever, they had decided that the time had come to find a boarding school for her. She was very interested in her schoolwork and quick to learn. Clive was afraid she wasn't being stretched enough by what Janet Goodbody could provide.

But when Vicky started to send for prospectuses, he pleaded: 'Not yet. We must keep her with us a bit longer. Give her time to get over the loss of her brothers. Give me time too.'

He seemed very wrapped up in Lois, hardly wanting to let her out of his sight. Nothing was too good for her. Together, they took her to the shops and bought her clothes and books and toys, indulging all her whims, giving her the attention she craved. In time, Lois grew more rounded and looked the picture of health and happiness.

They decided they could not part with her to boarding school, and instead entered her in Birkenhead High School.

Clive kept telling her: 'You're clever, Lois. Above average in everything. The world is your oyster. If you put yourself out, you can do anything, and have anything you want in this life.'

Lois believed him. It gave her tremendous confidence in her own abilities. She was sailing effortlessly through her lessons, always top of her class.

She was still fierce and headstrong and had to have her own way in everything. If it wasn't given, she fought for what she wanted and usually got it. She made up her mind to follow the family tradition and go to medical school.

'You'll be the best doctor the family has ever turned out.' Clive told her, pleased that she had come to this decision by herself.

Out of school hours, he took Vicky and Lois on a round of pleasures. To theatres and museums and to the new talkie films. To anything that might interest Lois. 'Widening her scope,' he called it.

They invited Mary and Esme MacAllister over to stay with them in the school holidays and share their expeditions. The girls seemed to get on reasonably well together.

Esme was rather a plain child, with straight mousy-brown hair and a dumpy figure. But she was chatty, with a bubbly personality. Victoria knew that Lois wouldn't see her as a rival for their love.

'There was so little for children out in Ekbo,' Clive mourned. 'They were there because I wanted their company, not for their own good.'

Vicky felt better once they had settled back into the house in Hamilton Square. Her hair grew glossy again and her cheeks pink beneath their suntan. Clive persuaded her to buy the latest fashions. Her willowy figure suited the short, slim dresses of the period. She was thirty-five but still looked younger than her age.

Clive got out his creased linen suits and the Panama hat Vicky remembered so well, and settled back into what she hoped would be retirement.

His health did not pick up. She was upset to find that he still looked grey and pinched six months after returning home. He was almost fifty-seven.

'I won't go back to Ekbo again,' he said. 'I'm too old.' Retirement age for expatriates working there was between forty-five and fifty.

'I haven't the energy to work as I did. I can't risk your health again and I don't want to go back alone.'

Vicky felt she'd had more than her fill of Ekbo. She wanted them to stay at home.

Evelyn moved out of the Hamilton Square house, deciding to get a small place of her own now they were back for good. She had retired, but still had a lot of friends who worked at the children's hospital in Woodchurch Road.

But after eighteen months, Vicky suspected that Clive was growing bored with his life of idleness. It was Bill Goodbody who changed his plans.

As soon as she saw the envelope with the Nigerian stamps on it, she was afraid that Clive would want to go back there.

'What does Bill say?' He gave her the letter to read.

Bill wrote that once again they were desperately short of doctors in Ekbo.

'Don't go, Clive,' she pleaded. She knew by the look on his face that he was tempted.

'I'm needed,' he said simply. 'But I'll not stay long. Just until Bill can get somebody else.'

'What about me?' Vicky demanded. 'I don't want to stay here without you.'

'You'll be safer here,' he said sadly.

'But not happier.'

'There's Lois to consider.'

They pondered for a long time about what was the best thing to do.

'Mother is too old to be saddled with the responsibility of looking after her now.'

'We can't take her with us,' Clive said. 'Her education would suffer. Besides, I don't think Ekbo suited her. All those ideas about juju. They upset her.'

Clive arranged for Lois to go to Liverpool College as a boarder, so that Vicky could return to Ekbo with him.

Once there, Vicky went back to work in the hospital and soon settled in. They renewed their friendship with Bill and Janet Goodbody, but Ekbo didn't seem to suit Clive any more. He never seemed really well.

They stayed six months. They both knew by then that he had a

151

problem with his heart from which he could not recover.

'I'm too old for this,' he said at last. 'I've got to accept it.'

Even back home, he didn't seem to pick up. He no longer had any energy. Vicky thought he'd never quite got over the deaths of his sons.

He died in his sleep one night only eight weeks after they got back to Hamilton Square. Vicky woke up in the morning to find him dead beside her.

She was prostrated by grief and shock. She kept telling herself that this way was better for Clive, he had not suffered, but she was left totally bereft by it. She learned then how much she'd relied on him, and how much she had loved and needed him. Not to have Clive beside her was the end of an era. For weeks she felt like a rudderless ship, unable to decide what she should do next.

Evelyn was so upset she took to her bed for a few days. Vicky was glad to bring her back to the Hamilton Square house so that she could look after her. It gave her something with which to fill her days and it meant she wasn't alone.

Clive had conditioned her to expect widowhood. 'You're an old man's darling,' he'd told her many times. 'It's certain to happen.'

Lois sat at her father's Carlton House desk, running her fingers over its polished surface.

She felt she'd been fighting her tears for weeks. She couldn't get them under control. She couldn't believe that he had died; it had happened too suddenly for her to take it in.

Her eyes went round the familiar sitting room, drawing comfort from its solid furniture and red velvet chairs. She'd thought of this room often when they were away in Ekbo.

She tried to take comfort from her father's photograph smiling up at her from a silver frame. To think that she'd never see him again left her shaking with panic. She didn't know if she could manage without him.

She must do what Clive had taught her to do at moments like this.

'Concentrate on your successes,' he'd told her. 'Forget those things that don't go your way. That's the secret of self-confidence, and a doctor must have that at all times.'

'Divide your mind into compartments like I do. I have one for my home life, and one for work. Then I divide my work compartment into little boxes. One for each sort of case that I treat.

'If I make a mistake or do something wrong, then I think about why that happened and make up my mind never to make the same mistake again. Then I pull down a mental roller blind on that box and refuse to think about it.

'No doctor must let his failures worry him or he'll never have the confidence to carry on. Confidence in yourself is very important, Lois.'

'So in my school compartment, I must have a box for every subject?'

'That's right. You did very well in your biology exam.'

'Top of the class.'

'Excellent, so your biology box brings huge confidence.'

'But history . . .'

'When you have a history lesson you must concentrate wholly on what's in the history box. But you know you are top at biology and some of that confidence goes into history too, because the blind is up.'

'I'll try.'

'And we both have so much to be thankful for in our home compartment. I have a little box for you, and one for Mother, and one for the house. All my home boxes are always open because I'm happy at home.'

'What about my brothers?' she'd asked. 'If they had boxes in your mind, they must be closed now because you couldn't cure them. You let them die.'

'No, I couldn't stop them dying, but I did everything humanly possible to prevent it. I shall never pull a blind down on them.'

At the time she hadn't thought that logical, but Clive went on: 'I loved them and their lives were gifts to me. I shall value them always and derive pleasure from having had them.'

Lois sighed, a gusty sigh of childhood. She hadn't had the courage to tell Clive that her box for Barney must stay closed for ever. She would never think of him again. It would leak away her confidence, and Clive said that that was what she must hang on to.

Clive had been a wonderful father. Even now she gained strength from his ideas. If only he hadn't had to die. She missed him more than she'd ever thought possible.

There were too many boxes in her mind with the roller blinds locked down. Everything was going wrong. She felt she was on a downward spiral and didn't know how to stop it.

Lois's anguish made Vicky throw her arms round her. She felt overflowing with love for her daughter.

'There's no need for you to board at school any longer, Victoria told her. 'I won't be going away again. You can live at home with me. Go back to the High.'

It disconcerted her to see Lois draw back. 'I don't know, Mother . . .'

Vicky had been going to say how much she'd love having Lois at home with her, but she could see Lois wanted things to stay as they were.

'I like this school and I don't want to change again. There's less to distract me if I board, and no time wasted travelling back and forth.'

Perhaps in her grief she was swamping her daughter with her own needs? Lois was in the grip of adolescence and needed some independence. She needed to find her own feet.

Victoria loved her more than ever, but she disciplined herself not to demand any show of affection in return. She mustn't expect too much.

'After all, Mother, you'll want to work now, so you won't be home all that much.'

Evelyn's friends invited Victoria to join their team at the children's hospital. Victoria was in her prime. She didn't want for money – Clive had left her adequately provided for – but she needed to make a new life for herself now that she didn't have Clive.

As the years rolled on and gathered momentum, Lois grew to womanhood. Vicky knew that Clive would have been proud of her; she and Evelyn certainly were. She was sailing effortlessly through medical school.

The Second World War came and went. Once again, Victoria marvelled that she had no relative of an age to be embroiled in it. She would have worried for Keith and Barney had they lived.

But perhaps Barney, like Lois, would already have been in medical school when it started. That might have kept him safe.

She knew that Bill Goodbody was caught out in Ekbo, just as Clive had been during the Great War. Vicky didn't have such an easy time of it as she had then. Civilians were caught up in the mayhem. Many children were injured in the bombing. It broke her heart to see them suffer and be left with permanent disabilities.

When it was all over, the Goodbodys came home on leave. Victoria met them from the mail boat and took them back to Hamilton Square to stay with her for a week. She was shocked at how much they had aged.

Bill had the same yellowish-grey look Clive had had, and his head was almost bald. Janet's skin was rubbery and her hair was grey now and looked very different.

'I had it cut and permed on the mail boat,' she laughed. There were no hairdressers in Ekbo. 'Felt I had to smarten myself up.' But their easy relationship remained. Victoria felt immediately comfortable with them.

She pressed them to stay longer, but they wanted to visit other friends.

'You must certainly spend the end of your leave with me, because it's so handy for the return journey. You'd have to stay in Liverpool if you didn't stay here.'

'You've been a wonderful friend,' Janet said, as she kissed her goodbye. 'Why don't you come out to Ekbo for a visit? You know we'd love to have you.'

When Victoria had left with Clive, the last thing she'd thought she'd ever want to do was to return. But that had been seventeen years ago, and she'd worked very hard throughout the war with no real holiday.

In the postwar years, England seemed a place of grim shortages. Lois would shortly finish her last six months as a houseman and be fully qualified.

'Wouldn't Lois benefit from a few months' experience out in Ekbo?' Bill asked. 'It would liven the place up if you both came out for a visit.'

Lois was enthusiastic. 'How exciting! I'd love to see Father's hospital.'

'You must remember it?'

'Yes, but to see it again – and where we lived . . . Do say we can go, Mother.'

Vicky felt a trickle of excitement. She never denied Lois anything. For her own part she would treat it as a pilgrimage to what Clive had built up. It would be good to see more of Janet and Bill and find out how the hospital had fared.

Full of anticipation, they prepared for the voyage.

'It does me good to see you like this,' she said to Lois, who was filled with zest and rushing round the shops getting her wardrobe together.

They both enjoyed the sea voyage. Lois threw herself into all the activities on board.

As soon as they got off the train at Oloka, Victoria was afraid it had been a mistake to come. Too much had changed. There was a motor road from Oloka to Ekbo. They covered it by car in less than an hour instead of the long-drawn-out trek in mammy chairs. The forest, though, still seemed brooding and sinister.

Vicky had been looking forward to the sun, but she'd forgotten its damp, broiling heat. Her body trickled with sweat at the slightest exertion.

Bill and Janet Goodbody greeted them with hugs of delight. 'Life is so much easier here now,' they enthused. 'So many improvements since you left, you won't know the place.'

The bungalow Bill and Janet occupied had once been Victoria and Clive's. She had planted the hydrangeas in the big clay pots along the veranda. The sitting room was bright with new chair covers.

'It all seems smaller than I remember,' Lois said. But they were both delighted to see again the geckoes scurrying up the walls to hide behind pictures and furniture.

Over tea, taken on the veranda, Bill went on to explain that the hospital had been taken over by the Nigerian Government.

Victoria was just having her tea cup refilled when a young woman came down the path. She had a baby in a pushchair and three other children scampering round her.

'This is Althea Meadows, the wife of one of our doctors.' Janet was on her feet and calling to her.

'You must stop for a moment, Althea, and say hello to our visitors.

'Such beautiful children.' Janet was smiling round at them.

Victoria looked at their white-blonde hair and suntanned skin and had to agree. But they were stripped to the waist. In her day, she had covered up her children to protect them from the sun. Lois had never gone out of doors without a hat.

'Times have changed,' Bill said. 'It was the war. The British tommies stripped down and wouldn't wear their pith helmets. Now everybody does it, much more comfortable.'

'It's good to see young children out here, isn't it?' Janet said. But Victoria didn't agree. She should never have allowed her sons to stay here.

'We're just out for a month in the school holidays.' Althea Meadows had a girlish giggle. 'I don't think I'd like to stay longer. I'm not a doctor so I can't work here like you did.'

'Do you work at all?' Lois wanted to know.

'What, with these four?'

'I tell Althea they're like a set of jugs,' Bill chuckled. 'Identical, but different sizes.'

They were very much like their mother. All had blonde ponytails and round blue eyes.

The eldest attached herself to Janet, who put an arm round her shoulders and pulled her forward.

'Rosalie is six and she's reading a book of Nigerian fairy tales,' she told Vicky.

'She loves it,' Althea said.

'How far have you got? Have you read the one where the children suck sugar cane in the fields?'

The child nodded solemnly. 'Yes, and it changes them all into frogs.'

'I remember reading that to my children,' Victoria told her.

'I can read properly by myself,' Rosalie said proudly. 'I don't need grown-ups to read to me.'

'You're very good at it,' Janet said with approval. Althea sat down next to Lois on the settee.

'I could read at her age,' Lois told her, unimpressed.

Victoria pondered on the difference in the lifestyles of the two young women. They were much the same age. From what Althea Meadows was saying, her existence was totally filled with child care and domesticity. She had blonde curly hair and a sweetly pretty face.

Lois was not so good-looking. Her features were sharper, but her hair, which had been gingery in childhood, had darkened to an attractive auburn shade. She wore it short, styled to compliment her face.

She seemed more confident than Althea. Victoria thought she had more purpose to her life because she'd trained for a career. They were as different as chalk and cheese.

The children were delightful, well mannered and well behaved. Lois was indifferent to them, Althea entirely engrossed.

'We've just been out for a walk,' she said.

'Where do you go?'

'Round the hospital compound and the church, then along the river bank for a few hundred yards.'

'I used to walk Lois along exactly the same path donkey's years ago,' Victoria told her.

'There's nowhere else. Sometimes we go round it twice. I'm afraid they'll get run over on the road.'

Other things had changed. Victoria's children had been taken down the road to the market. There had been no traffic to worry about then.

Althea stood up. 'I'll have to go. I need to get my brood started on their baths and bed-time stories. Bertie and I are invited here to dinner tonight. If I'm not careful you'll be fed up with my company.'

'Nonsense, Althea,' Bill told her. 'I only wish you'd stay out here longer.'

After she'd swept her children to the bungalow next door, he said: 'She'd be a great asset, she's always so cheerful. They're a lovely family.'

'We still take it in turn to invite the others to dinner,' Janet told Victoria.

'Every week?'

'Better than eating alone every night. With our fellow countrymen, we're on the same wavelength,' Janet explained. 'We do ask the African doctors from time to time and they ask us back, but they don't play bridge or take an interest in the London newspapers.'

Lois folded the paper she'd been scanning and said in her superior way: 'But they are weeks old when you get them.'

'Tom Sinclair will be coming tonight too. So you'll meet us all.'

Victoria went off to take her bath, thinking how stiflingly narrow their social life still was.

Later, as they waited for their guests to arrive, Janet sat back in her armchair, nursing a glass of sherry, talking about the other doctors.

'They're both married. A good thing for men out here.'

'Why?' Lois wanted to know.

'It settles them down.'

Tom Sinclair was extremely good-looking, even though he wore spectacles. He was six foot three and had broad shoulders in proportion. His large hand clamped painfully on to Victoria's.

'We all call him Titch,' Janet said with a smile. 'Because he's twice the size of the rest of us.'

'The Africans call me Dr Titch,' he grinned. 'I blame Bertie, he started it.'

He turned back to Victoria. 'I've heard so much about Clive Benbow since I've been here. About how much he did for the hospital. It's a great pleasure to meet his family.'

It gave Victoria a warm feeling to know that Clive was not forgotten.

'He enjoyed his time here,' she smiled. 'Are you enjoying yours?'

'The work is very satisfying.' Titch Sinclair had a slow, deliberate manner. 'Everything else, well . . . no. I'm not enjoying it any more.' He glanced apologetically at Bill Goodbody.

'It was fine when I was single and had no ties, but I've made up my mind, Bill. I don't want another contract. This is no place for me now I'm married. It's not fair on Chloe for me to come back again.'

Victoria knew from Bill's face that this was the first he'd heard of it. Clive had hated being told that his staff meant to leave. It had never been easy to replace them.

'What will you do?' Bill's face was stern, as though he was struggling to hide his resentment.

'I shall try to get rooms in Harley Street. Set myself up to treat the rich instead of the poor.'

'You're too good a doctor for that, Titch. Pampering to the rich.'

'The rich get ill too. They suffer from the same problems.' He smiled in his disarming manner. 'I'll need to polish my bedside manner a bit, though. I need a change. I'd done my bit for the poor and needy. I shall try for the opposite end of the spectrum. Chloe will like that.'

He smiled at Lois and went to sit at the opposite end of the settee she occupied.

'Lovely to see a new face out here,' he told her. 'Apart from other men's wives, you're the first white woman I've spoken to since I came here.'

Janet had told them that Sinclair had a reputation as a womaniser, and Victoria could see how he'd earned it.

She heard shoes crunching on the path outside, and laughter at some shared joke, then Althea and her husband came inside the circle of light and into the room. She led him forward to be introduced. He had a lean, handsome face, with dark blue eyes and an engaging smile.

Althea was wearing a little make-up now and looked very pretty in a full-skirted pink dress. Victoria didn't approve of its low neckline and short sleeves. Nor of her bare legs and high-heeled sandals.

She had provided Lois with mosquito boots and impressed upon her that she must cover up after dark to avoid being bitten. Everybody else was suitably garbed. Victoria watched as the new arrivals turned to Lois.

'My husband, Cuthbert Meadows,' Althea said.

Lois smiled up at him and giggled. 'Sorry, I shouldn't laugh at your name. It's ridiculously old-fashioned.'

'I did complain to my mother.' He giggled too. 'Cuthbert was my father's name. He was killed before I was born, in the Great War. She named me after him.'

Althea drew Victoria's eye like a butterfly. She was the only fashionably dressed woman in the group.

'Rather sad really,' she said. 'His poor mother, she's passed on too now.'

Her husband's laugh was hearty. 'You'd better call me Bertie,' he said, all his attention on Lois. 'Everyone else does.'

Lois moved up the settee, making room for him to sit beside her, totally ignoring Titch. Within moments, she and Bertie were talking together instead of joining in the general conversation.

Victoria watched Cuthbert nervously. The strong sun had tanned his skin, and had bleached his brownish hair three shades lighter than its natural colour. He was shorter and of a slighter build than his colleague, but he still topped Lois by a couple of inches, and she was tall for a woman. She hoped Lois wasn't as dazzled by his intense blue gaze as she seemed.

She had been edgy, tired after the journey, but now she seemed to sparkle. Bertie was devoting all his attention to her, taking more interest in her than he should. Or was Victoria imagining it?

Was this cold premonition a product of her own guilt? For her, things had been different. Clive had awakened her feelings, while Lois didn't know what married love was. But Lois was older than she had been, and hopefully wiser.

Titch had moved closer to Victoria and was telling her how much he missed the shops and theatres and restaurants in London.

'I feel quite cut off from life here,' he said, before changing tack. 'What do you think of the new Health Service they're bringing in? Will it make a lot of difference to the way you work?'

Victoria settled back to tell him. These people were so hungry for news of home, they were falling on her and Lois. That was all it was. They wanted to know exactly what was happening in the rest of the world. She was forgetting how much she'd looked forward to visitors when she'd lived there.

CHAPTER FOURTEEN

The next morning, Bill Goodbody took Victoria on a tour of inspection round the hospital, pointing out the improvements he'd made and the new equipment he'd installed.

Lois was tagging along behind them. Her face told Victoria that she thought the improvements were basic necessities, and she couldn't imagine being able to cope without them.

Victoria knew her daughter was put off by the heat, the lack of space, the queues of patients waiting for attention outside the clinics and their continual noisy chatter.

'Have you got over the journey, Lois? Would you like to stay and give a hand?' Bill asked. Now it was a Government Hospital, nobody was expected to donate their services for nothing.

'Spend an hour with Bertie Meadows, he'll show you the ropes. Then you could run a clinic alongside him.' Lois seemed enthusiastic.

Victoria had had no intention of working while she was out this time. She had meant to go back and ask Althea in for coffee, but seeing the hospital working again brought back the early years she'd spent here with Clive.

Janet still devoted most of her mornings to the school. She had the children of some of the Nigerian staff as pupils, and the older members of Althea's family attended to fill their mornings.

Bill had to push his way through the crush of patients round the clinic door. Victoria and Lois followed behind. The room was just as close and fetid and shabby as she remembered it, filled to capacity with furniture and people.

'There's talk of getting air conditioners for the clinics as well as the rest of the place,' Bill told her. She could see the sweat standing out on his brow.

She saw Cuthbert Meadows' eyes light up when he saw Lois. He was wearing shorts with long woollen stockings to the knee, a short-sleeved shirt and a tie. The doctors here had always dressed like that. Clive had.

'Hello, Lois, come to join the mêlée?' Lois was about to sit on the bench next to the interpreter. 'Can we have another chair?'

Both nurse and interpreter rushed to take one from a waiting patient. Here, patients did not expect to be seated.

'Yes, here beside me.'

Victoria sank down on the bench at the back. 'I'll just sit here for a while, Bill,' she said. 'Soak up the atmosphere.'

She felt disquieted by Lois's flush of excitement. Titch Sinclair might have the reputation of being a womaniser, but she was afraid Lois was finding Bertie more attractive. Her smile seemed to say she was bowled over by him.

She watched Meadows dealing with the queue of patients just as she used to.

He said to Lois: 'I suppose it seems primitive, that medicine as we practise it here has regressed by fifty years?'

After an hour he asked the interpreter to find a small table and a few instruments for Lois. There was so little space it had to be set up on the veranda outside.

'Shout out if you want help,' he told her, as he diverted some of the queue in her direction.

'I'll give you a hand to get started,' Victoria said, going with her. 'I'll try and act as interpreter. I used to get by in Ibo in the old days.'

She was trying to make things as easy as she could for Lois. She could still remember how disorientated she'd felt when she'd first come out. She thought Lois did well. She knew how pleased Clive would be to see her here, totally engrossed in the job.

There was more air outside, but as the morning progressed it got hotter. They had to close their ears to the restless chatter from the queue, and Bertie's consultations not far away. It took a lot of concentration, and soon she could see Lois's dress sticking to her back.

They were dealing with their last patient when Bill Goodbody returned with another European. Bertie had already finished his morning's work and was stretching himself in the clinic doorway.

'Hello, Johnny,' he said.

'This is Johnny Walsh, the District Officer.' Bill introduced them. 'Now there's a road, he comes up to see us about once a month.'

Victoria felt her hand gripped in a sunburned fist. Stern blue eyes were assessing her from under a bush hat.

'A special trip this morning,' he said. 'Not social.'

'He's brought a body in,' Bill told them. 'Wants our opinion. Come to the morgue when you've finished here.'

'What's the problem?' Bertie asked.

'It's a young girl, said to have been killed by a leopard. Wants our opinion on that.'

'I'll wait for the ladies,' Bertie said. 'We'll take a look later.'

'Lunch at our place today,' Bill said. 'You can tell Johnny what you think then.'

When they'd finished, Victoria went into the clinic to wash her hands in the newly installed washbowl. She heard Bertie say to Lois: 'Do you want to see this body?'

She turned round to see him running his eyes over her daughter, who replied: 'Of course. Why not?'

He shrugged. 'Could be a gruesome sight.'

'I hope you aren't trying to protect me. You wouldn't say that to a man, would you? I am a doctor too.'

'Sorry,' he grinned. He dropped his voice, but Victoria's hearing was good. 'I'm seeing you as a woman, and I can't get beyond that. Doctors are two a penny here.'

'I'm coming too,' Victoria said, joining them.

'Come on then, let's see what Johnny's brought us.'

The morgue was a small building at some distance from any other. Nothing had changed here, not even the stink. Even the strong pall of disinfectant couldn't cover it. The floor was of concrete, with a drain running down the middle.

The body was laid out on a central slab and covered with a sheet. Bertie folded it back in businesslike fashion.,

She saw Lois swallow hard before looking at what was beneath it.

'Aged about seventeen,' Bertie said. 'She was probably a pretty girl.'

Victoria studied the body carefully, taking in the facts. The flesh had been scraped from the head and the left arm. The girl was badly mutilated.

'What are we looking for?' Lois asked.

'I expect Johnny is looking for confirmation that it was actually done by a leopard.'

'Aren't those claw marks on her arm?'

'They could have been done with knives,' Victoria said slowly. 'Particularly just here.'

She pointed to the plump and rounded arm. 'I think this is a blade mark. What do you think?'

Lois choked out: 'You mean, is it murder?'

'I bet that's what he wants to know.' Bertie was putting everything back as he'd found it.

'Right then, lunch,' he said, taking Lois's arm companionably. 'Janet always does us proud when Johnny comes over.'

Victoria walked behind them. They hardly seemed to notice her presence. Lois was quiet; she thought she was trying to banish from her mind the disturbing sight she had just seen.

At the lunch table, Johnny Walsh asked: 'What do you reckon?'

He was looking at Lois. She shook her head numbly. 'I've never seen what a leopard can do. I'd be guessing.'

'I agree with Victoria. More likely knife marks,' Bertie answered. 'What's the story?'

'The number of people killed by leopards is rising steadily. Statistics

163

have shown it over the last few years. It puzzles everyone because statistics also show that the number of wild leopards is falling.'

Victoria thought of the silent, eerie forest. She saw Lois shudder again.

Johnny went on: 'The villages say this girl was killed by a leopard, that her mother saw it running away, but I've seen several bodies like this recently. They're mostly women, usually young girls, and it happens in the early evening between five and seven when they're coming home from tilling their fields.

'What makes me suspicious is that all the bodies I've seen are mutilated in the same way. The flesh is always scraped from the head and an arm, usually the left.

'I'm sure this girl was murdered. You've all agreed that the marks could have been made by a knife.'

'Ugh,' Lois said, pushing the food about her plate.

'You did insist on seeing her,' Bertie said. 'I told you she wouldn't be a pretty sight.'

'You mean a lot of people are being murdered?' Janet asked in horrified tones.

'That seems to be the only conclusion, yes.'

'But why?' Victoria was losing interest in her salad.

'I've been reading about it,' Titch said. 'They do it to obtain human fat for juju purposes.'

'Human fat?' Lois echoed in disgust.

'There have always been leopard societies . . .'

'Thousands of miles away in Sierra Leone,' Janet interrupted. 'And in the last century. This is 1947.'

'Well it seems that leopard societies have arrived here now. They're terrorising the local population, and they're very powerful.'

Johnny Walsh explained: 'It seems they kill a leopard, cure the skin and shape it to fit a man. Then they make a three-pronged knife, shaped so the wound it leaves is like that from a leopard's claw.'

Lois put down her knife and fork. 'What can they possibly want human fat for?'

'They make a parcel of magic ingredients, such as the skin from the palm of the human hand and sole of the foot, and various human organs, the liver for instance.'

Victoria watched Lois's face screwing up with disgust.

'These are added to ingredients such as a cockerel's comb and claws, or a few grains of rice, and the concoction is all wrapped up in leaves.

'In the native mind it makes the owner rich and all-powerful. He is respected. He can do anything he wants. It helps him in the white man's courts and hospitals.

'To retain its potency the package has to be anointed with human fat and blood at regular intervals. If this isn't done, it can turn against its owner.'

'How horrible,' Lois said. 'You mean a member of this society dresses up in the skin to attack its victim?'

'Yes, so that if they are seen or disturbed in the act they can escape, and the story spreads that a leopard made the attack.'

'The victims are always young,' Titch said. 'It's thought that if all goes well, the society feasts on other parts of the body.'

'Eats it, you mean?' Lois was choking.

'Yes. It's well known that older men believe that to eat human flesh increases their virility.'

'I thought cannibalism was extinct,' Victoria said crisply. 'It was thought so in my day.'

'Here, old customs die hard,' Bill said quietly, forking up his egg mayonnaise.

'I shall have to take some photographs and let the police know,' Johnny said.

Once Johnny Walsh had taken the body away, normality quickly returned. Over the following few days Victoria watched her daughter blossom. She took to putting on more make-up and refused to wear her mosquito boots because they made her look dowdy.

Her features seemed to soften. Victoria couldn't help but notice that Bertie was turning to her more often at the dinners they ate in each other's houses.

'Ekbo suits Lois,' Janet said. 'She's enjoying the work here. Bill says she soon got the hang of things.'

Victoria hastened to agree, but she didn't think it was the work. She was afraid her daughter was making the same mistake she had.

With hindsight, she knew that the weeks of reckless passion she'd shared with Jonathon had never been worth what they'd cost her. It had taken her years to get over him. The affair had spoiled what she'd had with Clive. She didn't want Lois to go through the same agony of remorse, guilt and fear.

And worse, Lois was not trying to hide what she felt. Her feelings for Bertie were written on her face, and Bertie's were even more obvious. Victoria was afraid that when they all realised what was happening it would blow this tight community apart.

Althea gave a farewell dinner. Victoria saw Lois looking round Bertie Meadows' bungalow with heightened interest. Bertie spent a good deal of the time showing her his books and records, leaving Althea to see to the needs of his guests.

'I wish I wasn't going now,' Althea told Victoria. She seemed less bubbly. Was the glance she shot in Lois's direction uneasy?

The next day, Bertie drove his wife and children to Oloka, then went with them on the train to Port Harcourt to see them safely on board the ship. With four young children, the youngest only eighteen months old, it was not easy for Althea to manage alone.

When Bertie came back he joined them in Bill's sitting room for a drink. He seemed subdued.

Afterwards, Janet said: 'It must be very hard for him, parting from his family.'

Victoria had always thought the round of entertaining turned like a wheel. Titch and Bertie vied with each other to put on a different meal each week.

At the Goodbodys' they were in the habit of playing bridge after dinner. Now, with Lois and herself, it meant they were two people over.

Lois was not a practised player and hated not to shine at what she did.

'I'd rather sit and talk,' she said. 'Count me out.'

Bertie elected to sit out with her. They were sitting on the settee when play had started. Victoria didn't notice them moving out on to the veranda but later she could hear them talking softly out there.

Bill smiled and said: 'I'm glad Lois is here to take Bertie's mind off his family. It's such a wrench, knowing they'll be parted for a year.'

It was unusual for anybody to sit outside after dark. There were too many flying insects and in the wet season the frogs croaked so loudly you could hardly hear yourself think.

Victoria told herself that Lois wasn't the sort to be swept off her feet by passion. She wasn't the demonstrative type who threw her arms round people giving them hugs and kisses. Hadn't she wished Lois would be less aloof with her?

Her boyfriends had never lasted long, her feelings had never seemed deeply involved. Lois had told her mother they didn't measure up once she got to know them.

In a way, that had surprised Victoria. Jonathon, her natural father, had been a passionate man. Passion was in Lois's genes on both sides; could she really be as cool and aloof as she seemed?

Another game of bridge was under way. Victoria was dummy; as she laid her cards down on the table it seemed that Lois and Bertie were no longer on the veranda. She murmured an excuse and got up. She was right.

There were lights on in Bertie's bungalow next door. She knew that Lois would count it as prying if she went to see what they were doing. She went anyway. She was getting more worried. She didn't want Janet to remark on their absence.

The sky was black, there were a few stars but no moon. Cicadas rustled in the oil palms. The hospital was brightly lit now they had electricity. All round it in the compound, little wax night lights flickered like fireflies.

She trod softly so as not to sound a warning on the path, though there was still noise coming from the hospital.

There was no light on Bertie's veranda. As she got closer, she could see that the chairs were empty. The table gleamed with dew in the night air.

The doors and windows stood wide open to catch the breeze, and there was a light on in the sitting room. She went quietly up the steps and looked inside.

Her stomach was knotting in pain. They were not here either. Surely he hadn't taken Lois to his bedroom? She listened. The buzz of the air conditioning was just audible over the chatter from the compound and the distant drumming in the forest.

Surely Lois wouldn't dare? But she herself had dared when she was young. She desperately wanted to know for sure. But she backed off. Outside, she looked for other lights in the house. There were none. She didn't know what else to do but go back to the Goodbodys'.

Janet, her partner, was flushed with excitement because she'd made a grand slam. It was Victoria's turn to deal the next hand. She had to get on with it before they missed Lois and Bertie. She let two cards slide face up on to the floor. That meant the pack had to be reshuffled and recut. She was glad of the diversion. She could see her fingers shaking as she started to deal once more.

From then on her game went to pieces. She couldn't concentrate, not even when she realised that Lois and Bertie had come back to the veranda.

She felt that things were blowing up in her face. She wished Lois would confide in her so she could help. But Lois had never confided her more intimate feelings. She loved Lois, but her daughter seemed always just out of reach. As though she kept herself at arm's length.

Victoria knew that she would have to raise the subject when they were alone together in the bedroom they shared. She had to know how things stood.

They were getting ready for bed when she asked: 'Where did you and Bertie go?' She knew she shouldn't sound angry, but she couldn't help it.

'We didn't go anywhere, just out on the veranda.'

'You didn't stay there,' she retorted sharply. 'I couldn't help but notice.'

'Oh, that's right.' Lois stopped smoothing cream on to her face and looked up, her eyes disarmingly innocent. 'We went to get a book from Bertie's bungalow. He's just finished reading this and recommended it to me.' She held it up as though offering proof.

Victoria felt her stomach turn over. Hadn't she and Jon thought up a similar excuse all those years ago? And that had been to hide . . .

She turned on her daughter angrily. 'I wasn't born yesterday, Lois. You shouldn't be looking for excuses to be alone with Cuthbert Meadows. Particularly not here.'

'I don't know what you mean, Mother.'

Victoria felt her spirits sink further. She knew a guilty conscience when she saw one.

'He's not for you. He's a married man with four little daughters and a lovely wife. How do you think Bill and Janet will feel if they find out?'

Lois's dark eyes were defiant, her lips a straight line. Victoria could read the signs. Lois wanted Cuthbert Meadows just as she had wanted Jonathon. History was repeating itself. And Lois didn't care if she broke up a happy family. She was used to getting what she wanted in life.

'Take a grip on yourself, for goodness' sake,' Victoria said more harshly. 'It's just an infatuation and you'll find it isn't worth the trouble it'll bring you.'

'How would you know whether it's worth it or not? You've had a blameless life. You've never felt any temptations.'

Victoria swallowed hard. It was on the tip of her tongue to tell her daughter about Jonathon, in order to make her understand.

'I'm not a saint like you,' Lois flared.

Victoria knew that she couldn't tell her Clive was not her father. She owed it to Clive's memory never to do that. She found it hard to say anything more.

'Bill and Janet have high standards of morality. You'll upset them. You must stop seeing Bertie.'

'How can I stop seeing him? We're thrown together all the time here.'

Victoria felt torn in two. It was second nature now for her to give Lois what she wanted. But not this. It would bring her heartbreak and unhappiness in the long run. And a terrible searing guilt.

She said firmly: 'Then we'll have to go home.'

Lois flew at her in fury. 'We've only been here three weeks; we agreed to stay three months. I want to stay.'

'Better if you don't.'

'Look, Mother, I've kept my nose to the grindstone for years. All those dreadful war years, I had no holidays and no fun.'

'We none of us had fun then.'

'Mother, they'll hear us if you don't keep your voice down.'

'Not above the buzz of the air conditioning.'

'I need this holiday. I need more sun. It lifts me. Makes everything look so much better. Makes me feel better.'

'It's not the sun that's doing that. Anyway, you'll have those things on the boat trip going home.'

'It's a whole new world here. I'm learning a lot. I'm even earning my living.' Lois was glaring at her, at her most mutinous.

'You can do that back home.'

'You go home, Mother, if you want to. I'm twenty-eight, for good-ness' sake. I'm old enough to make my own decisions and to look after myself.'

That shocked Victoria. To leave her here with Bertie was the last thing she should do.

'I'll ask Bill for a permanent job. A bungalow of my own. I was thinking of it anyway.'

'What do you expect to get out of it? Bertie can't marry you. And what will they think of him when they find out?'

'Nobody will find out.'

'I have. You won't be able to hide it. Not here. Everybody lives in each other's pockets.'

She and Jonathon had hid it, but she'd lived in terror of being found out. And Bill was more worldly-wise than Clive had been, less inclined to think well of other people.

'Janet feels very strongly about moral lapses. You know what she thinks about Tom Sinclair's womanising ways.'

'This is different,' Lois said in her arrogant way. 'I love Bertie.'

Victoria's self-control snapped. 'In what way are you different? Your face tells everybody that you want him to kiss you, that you long for it.'

Lois was silent, her sloe-black eyes wide with shock, but Victoria didn't stop herself now.

'Oh, I know how you feel. That it was inevitable from the moment he told you to call him Bertie. I was watching you that first night. I know he exudes attraction for you, and that the longer you're with him the more attractive he seems. I've seen him run his fingers up your arm. What did you feel then? It made you tingle, didn't it? And his deep blue eyes excite you.'

Lois was choking in protest: 'You make me seem . . .'

'You're nothing but a wanton harlot. You must stop before you get in too deep. It's not love, it's lust and that's like quicksand, Lois. One toe in and the next minute you're being sucked under, out of control.'

'Bertie and I will go back to England. Nobody knows us there.'

'You'll get caught up in a nasty divorce case, and what good would that do you? You're both doctors and the mud will stick. Have some sense before it's too late.' Victoria felt she was breathing fire.

'How selfish can you get? Doesn't he feel any obligation to Althea? You're breaking up a family, Lois. Think of those little children instead of yourself. Now, before it's too late.'

'I'll try,' Lois choked, humbled at last. 'I'll try and cool it down.'

In the days that followed, Victoria was watching Lois like a cat wat-ches a mouse. She wasn't aware of it until Lois turned on her.

'I can't stand it, Mother. I can feel your eyes on me all the time.

And you should see your face when Bertie comes anywhere near. You've got to stop, you're drawing attention to us.'

Vicky tried to appear more relaxed. She felt she was walking on eggshells.

As far as she could see, Lois and Bertie were no more careful. If it was obvious to her, then soon Janet and Bill would notice. They were all living too close for it to stay hidden.

A few days later, when they were all due to go to Titch's bungalow for dinner, Victoria had her bath early to leave the one bathroom free for others to use.

Bill was still over at the hospital when she took her book into the sitting room, meaning to read until the others came for their pre-dinner drink.

'I'd better have my bath next,' Janet said, rolling up her knitting. It was a cardigan she was making for one of Althea's children. Stifling a yawn, she headed slowly towards her bedroom.

Moments later, she came rushing back, her face grey, her mouth working with shock.

'I've just seen Bertie . . .' Her voice was a harsh whisper. 'Through my bedroom window. I was closing it to put the air conditioning on.'

Victoria's mouth went suddenly dry. 'With Lois?'

'On his veranda. In each other's arms. It's still broad daylight!'

Victoria was stricken. She could think of nothing to say. The way Lois was carrying on, she'd known it was only a matter of time. Janet slid on to the chair next to her. She couldn't hold the words back.

'I have thought once or twice . . . they seemed very interested in each other, but I didn't think Bertie . . . Oh, poor Althea. And those lovely children.'

Victoria was embarrassed and said stiffly; 'I'll take Lois home.' It seemed the only thing she could do. 'If we go straight away . . .'

Janet pushed her fingers through her grey hair. 'You can't go straight away,' she pointed out. 'The mail boat leaves every two weeks from Lagos. You'll just miss one if you go now.'

'I'll phone tomorrow,' Victoria said. 'Find out about connections – when the next cargo boat is expected in Port Harcourt.'

'Unless you fly,' Janet said.

'I've never flown.'

'It's possible now to fly to Lagos from Port Harcourt.'

'No, I don't think I could fly.'

Lois was coming to the door, looking on top of the world. She beamed in their direction and said: 'Is it all right if I have my bath now?'

Without another glance at them, she seemed to dance on her way.

Lois was already putting the plug in when Janet managed to gasp: 'Yes!'

CHAPTER FIFTEEN

Victoria felt very much on edge as they all gathered round Titch's table later that evening. The comfortable, easy-going comradeship of the tight circle had been shattered. It seemed that an extramarital affair was too embarrassing a subject to discuss openly.

Janet and Bill were trying to pretend that nothing had happened, but they couldn't bring themselves to speak directly to the culprits and were generally quiet and withdrawn.

Lois and Bertie both seemed uneasy, as though aware that their affair was no longer a secret. Victoria knew she wasn't the only one watching them now.

The atmosphere must have seemed unaccountably flat to Titch. She watched his gentle brown eyes blink round at them through his glasses.

The leopard killings had engrossed everybody's attention over the last few days. They'd talked of little else. Tonight Titch had more news for them.

'I've been talking to Johnny Walsh on the phone.' His voice was soft. 'He says there's total panic in the villages around him. Another body has been found with imitation claw marks. More police are being sent in.'

It hardly raised a comment. Titch seemed disconcerted. He moved his giant frame up the settee to be closer to the rest of the group.

He was doing his best to keep the conversation going. The evening dragged, and as soon as the clock struck ten, Bill stood up to take his leave.

By then, Lois could no longer look at Bertie. She thanked Titch and said good night to them all, then hurried across to the Goodbodys' bungalow and went straight to the room she was sharing with Victoria.

At the front door, Janet put a hand on Victoria's arm and drew her into their sitting room.

'We'd like a word.'

Victoria didn't sit down. 'I'm sorry. I feel we've taken advantage of your hospitality.'

'Not you.'

'I'll take her home, Bill, as soon as I can.'

'Such a shame,' Janet said, 'to cut your visit short like this. I'll be sorry to see you go.'

Victoria guessed they wouldn't invite her again, but after this, she didn't think she'd want to come.

'I'll have a word with Bertie,' Bill said grimly. 'Remind him of his obligations.'

So they were not going to say anything to Lois. They were leaving that to her. They didn't realise she'd already had her say, and a fat lot of good it had done.

'I'm sorry we have to impose on your hospitality a bit longer.' Victoria knew that they wanted Lois gone. 'As soon as I can get berths . . .'

'I hope Bertie will have the sense to stay away from her over the next few days.' Janet was full of disapproval.

'I can make sure he does,' Bill told them. 'I'll send him off for a few days. He can go round the outlying clinics.'

Victoria remembered that there were nine of these, and that every two or three months a medical team toured round them. Once Clive had taken her with him. It had been an experience she remembered well. They had taken a pharmacist with a trunk full of medicines, two male nurses, a cook with boxes of food, stewards and small boys, camping equipment and porters. They had travelled miles, setting up camp in remote villages.

'It's really the turn of one of our Nigerian doctors, but I'll put it to Bertie that he ought to go instead. That should keep him out of mischief.'

'We used to be away for a month or longer.'

'They use a pick-up truck now. There are roads but they aren't all tarmaced, just hard-packed laterite with terrible ruts. Still, it's a lot quicker than the mammy chair.'

Victoria went to her room feeling ruffled and upset. Lois was already in bed and apparently settled for the night.

'It's no good pretending to be asleep,' she told her. 'Now everybody knows that you and Bertie are having a torrid affair, we'll have to go home.'

Lois lifted her head off the pillow and mumbled: 'I don't see there's any hurry.'

Her mother felt a spurt of anger. 'The Goodbodys find your behaviour unacceptable. They think you're taking advantage of their hospitality. They don't want you here any longer. Don't you under-stand? You're an embarrassment to them.'

She tried to convey how shocked they were, and how protective towards Althea and her children.

Lois began to cry. 'I love Bertie. I couldn't help myself.'

Victoria felt her anger melt and pulled out the mosquito net to put her arms round Lois. She knew exactly what her daughter was going through. She'd only just managed to avoid this outcome herself.

'We'll go home as soon as we can. You'll get a job and settle down,' she tried to soothe her. 'You'll forget Bertie – he isn't for you. I told you that in the first place.'

Lois was pushing her away impatiently. Her sharp features were red, tear-stained and defiant.

'And I'm telling you, Mother, we love each other. If you make me go home now, Bertie will follow. He won't give me up.' She pushed her mother aside and got out of bed. Victoria hurt her hip against the bedside table.

'Nonsense, Lois. You've only known him a month.'

'That has nothing to do with it,' Lois snapped, striding round the room. 'You don't understand. What you felt for my father and what I feel for Bertie are not the same thing.'

Victoria froze. Once again she was tempted to tell Lois how she too had loved with passion. But she couldn't, it was too late for that.

'I know it's wrong, Mother, but I can't stop myself, and neither can he. We aren't going to try. We're going to be together, whatever happens.'

Two days later, the red pick-up truck had been packed and the medical team were ready to start on their journey at first light. Victoria knew that both Bill and Lois meant to get up to see Bertie off, so she did too.

In the cool, grey dawn light, Bertie was checking that they'd loaded all the essential equipment. He was wearing a bush hat with his usual outfit of shorts and knee-length socks, and he looked subdued. She could tell by the set of his shoulders that he was not leaving by choice.

'Right,' he said at last. 'I think we've got everything.'

He glanced in Lois's direction, but because Victoria and Bill were there, there were no special farewells. No handshakes for anybody, nothing.

The pharmacist was also the driver. Bertie climbed into the passenger seat, and the rest of the team piled into the back. Lois held her chin up proudly. She tried to smile.

'Goodbye,' Bertie called as the wheels started to turn. He turned to wave then, head and shoulders out of the window, his blue eyes fixed with open longing on Lois.

Victoria heard Lois's gasp of anguish as the vehicle turned on to the road and disappeared from sight. Then she went striding ahead of them, her head held high, back to the bungalow for breakfast.

Victoria had booked passages to Lagos on a cargo ship that was

173

expected in Port Harcourt any time now. It was never easy to tie the journey in because cargo vessels didn't run to an exact timetable. It depended at which ports they had to call and how much cargo they had to load and unload. Every morning she rang the agent in Port Harcourt to find out if it had arrived.

She had packed most of their baggage, and hoped they would be on their way before Bertie came back.

Lois had been in a sour mood when he'd gone, barely civil to any of them. Now Bertie was due to return, she seemed more cheerful, no doubt hoping he'd come before they left.

With Bertie gone, Titch was having dinner with them for the second night in a row.

'If Emmanuel is cooking for four,' Janet had told him, 'it's no more trouble for him to make enough for five.'

To Victoria, it sounded as though her friend felt the need of Titch's company to dilute theirs.

'Bit of an imposition otherwise.' Janet smiled at her. 'He has to feed four of us and gets only one meal in return.'

Now dinner was over and they were back in the sitting room with their coffee. Titch and Bill were discussing a case of leprosy that had turned up at the clinic that morning.

Victoria sat back, half listening. It was a hot, clammy night and she could feel herself perspiring.

Every night, as soon as it was dark, tom-toms would start drumming in the forest around them. Talking drums, they called them. First, a message would thump out from a village on one side of the hospital. Then an answering burst could be heard from another place.

Tonight, the rhythm of the drums was pounding in her head, resounding round the hospital and filling the night with sound. They were louder than usual. The message seemed more urgent, more pervasive. The answer came thumping out. The drummers sounded excited, even frenzied. The message seemed to have an ominous note.

The steward came from the kitchen to take his leave of them.

'We finish, ma'am. Good night.' Usually, his black face beamed above his white starched uniform. Tonight he was unsmiling.

'What are the drums saying?' Janet asked.

'Palaver. Big palaver.' His dark eyes had a wild look.

'Trouble, you mean? Fighting?'

'No, killing. Too much.'

Victoria thought immediately of Bertie. Felt a shaft of fear for him. Something out of the ordinary was happening.

'Where is this trouble?' she asked, but the boy would only shake his head.

'I heard rumours going round the hospital.' Titch was frowning. 'More leopard murders down near the Cameroon border. The villagers are terrified of the society.'

'I heard it was nearer than that,' Bill said soberly. 'Near Alasi. It seems the police have rounded up several suspects.'

'How far away is that?' Lois demanded.

'About a hundred miles.'

'Bertie wouldn't be near there, would he?' She looked anxious now.

'It's one of the places he would visit, but he could have left before there was any trouble. He should be nearly back by now.'

'If the trouble started while he was there,' Titch said, 'he might stay longer. The presence of a European calms them down in that sort of situation. They know juju doesn't affect white men.'

'I hope he's all right,' Lois burst out.

'There's no reason to suppose he isn't,' Bill said firmly. 'He's not alone, there are eight men from the hospital with him.'

When Victoria telephoned about her passage to Lagos the next morning, she heard that the ship had passed Bonny and was on its way up the channel. It was expected to arrive within the next five hours and take another twenty-four to discharge and reload.

She was glad they could be on their way, Lois was disturbing her sleep; she seemed to toss and turn for hours every night.

'Bertie was only sent away because I'm here,' she mourned. 'If anything has happened to him . . .'

'We don't know it has,' Victoria told her firmly.

'Some sixth sense tells me. Bill should never have sent him out into the bush.'

'Lois! Your father used to take me. If it was safe thirty years ago, it's safe now.'

'There were no leopard murders then. Bill shouldn't have sent him. If the leopard men believe human fat provides the magic, it seems to me they'd believe fat from a white man would be twice as powerful.'

It made Victoria feel sick to hear it put like that. But what Lois said was true.

'There's no point in getting worked up until we know definitely,' was the best she could manage.

Victoria hoped there would be news of Bertie before they went. She was quite anxious herself about him and understood how tormented Lois must feel.

She was half afraid that Lois would refuse to leave until he did return, but when the time came, she compressed her lips and carried her hand luggage out to the car. Bill drove them to Oloka to catch that evening's train.

Janet came to see them off. 'We mustn't let Lois change anything between us,' she said, hugging Victoria. 'We've been friends for too long for that.'

'It won't,' Victoria assured her.

For her, it was a miserable trip home. Lois was very low in spirits, and didn't want to join in any of the sporting or social activities on the ship.

Mostly she sat in a steamer chair on deck, keeping a book in front of her which she didn't read. At meal times, she didn't join in the conversation, and she refused to go to the Captain's cocktail party or make any effort for the fancy-dress party.

Victoria began to feel more worried about Lois than she was about Bertie. Then one night Lois fell ill with a sudden acute fever. Victoria recognised it as a malarial breakthrough, and dosed her on mepacrine as well as the Paludrine she had been taking. Her temperature was normal the next morning, as Victoria had expected, but it left Lois feeling weak.

Other things began coming out during the night hours when Lois couldn't sleep.

She was afraid she'd made some bad mistakes at the hospital. 'I saw a patient in clinic who had yaws and I didn't recognise it.'

Victoria knew she had to offer comfort, 'Well, how could you, if you've never seen it before? All you had to do was to ask somebody else to take a look at the patient.'

'Yes, but I didn't,' she muttered.

'Nobody's blaming you, are they?'

'No, but Bertie said a course of penicillin would produce a clinical cure and I sent him away without it.'

The following night Lois brought out another reason for her depression.

'I tried to do a Caesarean section on a woman and I must have nicked the bladder. I was horrified to find she was leaking urine afterwards.'

Victoria had frowned. 'Are you sure you did anything wrong? So often, the women have been in labour for days when they're brought in. Husbands only bring them when they've given up hope that they'll deliver normally. The baby's head can squeeze the bladder against the pelvis in those circumstances. That can have the same effect.'

'That's what Bertie said.' She saw relief in Lois's eyes.

'Bill repairs bladders like that. He gets plenty of practice. Didn't you watch him do one?'

'Yes, on this particular patient. But he didn't succeed. She was still leaking.'

Victoria lost her patience. 'Lois, at Ekbo it's a miracle any of them can be cured. They don't come soon enough. 'Usually they try their own medicine man first, and it's only when he fails that they think of us. Then they have to walk or be carried on someone's back.'

'They can't all be cured. Advanced illness is easier to diagnose but it's harder to treat. Everybody knows that.'

Lois could only sniff in her distress.

'Bill will try again. Sometimes it takes two goes.'

'So he said.'

It was only then that Victoria realised Lois had not found her feet at Ekbo. She hadn't gained confidence from being able to handle illness and disease in its late stage. She hadn't had time. Victoria had brought her back too soon for that.

When they got home, Lois threw herself at the pile of post that had accumulated while they'd been away. There was nothing from Bertie, nothing from Ekbo at all.

'The post takes a long time,' Victoria said. 'You know that. There'll be letters from them in due course. What you must do now is find yourself a job.'

She thought that Lois would be better if she was busy; it would take her mind off Bertie. Her stay in Ekbo had pulled her down further than Victoria had first thought.

'I don't think I'm cut out to be a doctor after all,' Lois said miserably.

'Nonsense,' Victoria said briskly. 'You've made a good start. You were enjoying it.'

Evelyn was even more brisk. She had worked for most of her life at the children's hospital and was on good terms with the medical superintendent. She told Lois there were vacancies there for which she should apply. Victoria decided she would like to work with children again too.

The day before they were both due to start work, Victoria heard from Ekbo. Janet had written:

Such sad news for you, I'm afraid. We've heard nothing more of Bertie. We're all worried stiff but keep hoping he'll turn up.

Bill has been out with the District Officer and the police to look for the medical team. They asked in all the villages and it seems Bertie visited seven of the nine clinics, and that they set off for Alasi at about the time one mutilated body was found there.

Bill is afraid now it could have been one of the team, but at this stage there's no way of knowing. Johnny said the face was mutilated beyond hope of anybody recognising the body.

The forest is full of rumours. A white man in a red pick-up has been sighted in every village between here and the Cameroon border. Bill could find no trace of it, though he followed the rumours. He found a burnt-out metal box which he thinks is the one they used to carry drugs, but the people told him it had been there in the river for the last five years.

Nobody admits to seeing them come to any harm. Always they were seen driving somewhere else.

Johnny is very upset. He particularly looked for their clothing. He says they'd value that too much to destroy it, especially Bertie's shoes, but they found no sign.

I've had to write to Althea. She's out of her mind with worry. She says she feels so remote from it all. That it might have been easier if she'd been at Ekbo when it happened. There's nobody she can talk to about this. No near relatives either, I'm afraid.

We do feel so sorry for her. Guilty too, that we let it happen. The four little girls keep her so busy, and she's expecting a fifth. She couldn't be in a worse position, poor girl.

I enclose her address, I believe she lives quite close to you. If you could find the time to call and have a chat, I'm sure she'd appreciate it. And if you would take her some flowers from us all, we'd be very grateful.

After all this time, we have to presume Bertie has been killed. He was only thirty-two, with his whole life before him.

You can imagine how we all feel here. Titch has decided to cut his tour short, and even Bill says he's had enough and would like to end our connection with Ekbo.

We are all sickened by the loss. We live in hope, of course, but it seems less likely as time goes on.

'He's dead,' Lois wailed. 'I knew it from the start. He'd have come back to see me before we left. He promised he would. He'd write to me now if he was alive.'

Victoria put her arm round the shaking shoulders. The news was worse than she'd expected.

'That girl they brought into the Ekbo hospital,' Lois sniffed. 'She'd had all the flesh clawed off her face. I couldn't bear to think of Bertie mutilated like that.'

'Lois! They wouldn't, not to . . .'

'Of course they would, Mother,' she said fiercely. 'And if eating human flesh makes old men more virile, then eating a white man's flesh makes them more powerful.'

Over the years she'd lived in the country, Victoria had heard this said before. Now she felt even more revolted. 'You're going too far. We don't know that cannibalism goes on.'

'We didn't want to know.' Lois's sloe-black eyes burned feverishly in her white face. 'The authorities know it does. They passed that law, didn't they? That all meat sold in the market must have its hide left on. To prove it's sheep or goat or pig.'

Victoria stiffened. She remembered Bill telling her that the law was to stop the trade in human flesh. The farmers had been angry; it reduced their profit because their animal hides could not be used for making leather.

'Mother, you understand the way the people think better than I do. Power and wealth are what they seek above all else. They believe the white races have it and that by ingesting . . .'

Victoria clapped her palm to her mouth, feeling appalled and sickened. She couldn't admit the truth of that. Not now. Not when it could involve Bertie.

Next morning Lois got herself up and dressed but said at breakfast that she didn't feel well. Victoria put it down to the news from Ekbo, and thought she'd be better if her mind was kept firmly on other things.

She'd believed Lois to be a competent doctor. Now, when she started to work close to her, she was shocked.

Lois had done six months' hospital work in paediatrics and said she'd particularly enjoyed working with children. Now she hardly seemed to know where to begin. Her self-confidence and arrogance were gone. She looked pathetic, had no energy; in fact, she looked downright ill.

Victoria went home that night and thought long and hard. She was afraid Lois had psychiatric problems, but she didn't want to admit it. Two days later, Lois had another acute attack of fever and was unable to get out of bed.

Victoria was scared. Things seemed to be going from bad to worse. She had to unburden her worries on somebody. She telephoned her mother.

'I'll come and look after Lois,' Evelyn said. 'I'll get her physically well. She'll cope with medicine again, don't worry. You leave her to me.'

Victoria knew that her mother wouldn't find it easy. She was nearly eighty and there were too many stairs in the Hamilton Square house for her now. For herself, she was struggling with a new job and a growing anxiety about her daughter. It had been a mistake to take her to Africa.

Lois's fever abated but she didn't pick up. She didn't want to get out of bed. Evelyn looked exhausted when Victoria came home from the hospital the following night.

'Come and sit down and have a glass of sherry.' Victoria took her to the first-floor drawing room that was still furnished with Clive's mahogany furniture and red velvet chairs.

'You're right, Lois is depressed,' Evelyn said. 'Clinically depressed.'

'What can we do?'

'Get her the best treatment. A good psychiatrist. I know just the man. This is the last thing I would have expected of Lois. What's happened to her?'

Feeling heavy with guilt, Victoria told her about Lois's affair with

Bertie. She'd thought of it as a mirror image to her affair with Jonathon Pine. But this was turning into a disaster for Lois. She related Bertie's subsequent disappearance.

Evelyn was censorious and pursed her lips.

'A violent love affair that she knew was wrong? A married man!'

'She couldn't say no to him, you see.'

'Then she doesn't have the self-discipline she should have.' Evelyn had always had iron control and expected the same from her relatives.

'It's the emotional upset,' Victoria tried to explain. 'The conflict between duty and desire.'

'She should have known where her duty lay. She knew it was wrong. But surely the rest of it, the leopard men and juju, is all make-believe? She doesn't seriously believe that's possible?'

Victoria leaned forward in her chair, her voice urgent. 'You've never been there, Mother. If you had you wouldn't say that.'

Evelyn snorted with disbelief. 'It's just fairy tales and magic.'

'I've watched a healthy man die, Mother. His relatives brought him to the clinic at Ekbo and told me some witch doctor was practising juju on him. They asked for my help, but they all believed nothing could be done once the spell was cast.

'I checked him over. He was wasting away but otherwise every-thing seemed normal. I got Clive to look at him, we ran all sorts of tests. Nothing.

'I told him there was nothing wrong with him, that I didn't believe in juju, it was for children. Clive talked to him for ages but he still died. They believe they'll die, so they do.'

'So Lois feels it's her fault Bertie was sent out into the bush? That if it hadn't been for their affair he'd have stayed safe in Ekbo?'

'I'm sure she feels guilt. And we don't know exactly what happened to him, that's the horrible part. It leaves so much to be imagined. The emotional strain of that explains her breakdown.'

'Of course it does. Even so, she should have had more backbone. More emotional balance.'

'It can happen to anyone, Mother. You know that.'

'Not to me,' Evelyn retorted.

'Not to you,' Victoria agreed. 'You're one apart.' But she knew she'd been near it herself, when she'd first gone out to Ekbo. And again in the yellow fever epidemic. It had been touch and go at other times, too.

'There's never been anything like this in our family,' Evelyn went on. 'And she couldn't have had a better father than Clive. If anybody had emotional strength it was him.'

Victoria felt a hot surge of guilt. She didn't know what Lois had inherited from Jonathon Pine. His genes were an unknown quantity.

For years that had been gnawing at her conscience. If Clive had been Lois's father, would she have been stronger? She took a deep breath.

'Clive was not her father,' she choked.

Evelyn's facial muscles tightened. She was staring back at Victoria in shocked surprise.

'Mother, you're the only person I can tell. You met Jonathon Pine once.'

She let the whole story come out then. Even after all these years, what she'd done appalled her. It was still having an effect on her and her family.

'But what about Clive?'

She could see the outrage on her mother's face. Past agonies were resurfacing. She remembered how her mother had stood back when she'd loved Clive herself.

'I tried to make it up to him. He never knew.'

Victoria felt overcome with remorse. She knew that her mother thought she hadn't valued Clive enough.

'He adored Lois. Always made such a fuss of her. Built up her confidence.' She straightened up in her chair. Perhaps he'd understood more about Lois than she'd supposed?

'It's a relief to talk about it.' How many times had she suppressed the urge? 'So you see, Mother, Lois is not the first in the family to have an affair she knew was wrong.'

'You could cope with the emotional turmoil it brings. Lois can't.'

Victoria looked at her mother. She was old and frail, but her mind was still incisive and her spirit stronger than ever.

'Jonathon Pine was clearly no gentleman,' she snapped. 'What happened to him?'

Victoria had shut her mind to that. She couldn't say he'd soon married another. That still hurt.

She got up to refill their glasses. She hadn't thought about this enough. She hadn't realised, until now, that emotionally Lois wasn't on the same even keel that Evelyn was. Victoria placed herself somewhere in between; this could have happened to her. She took a strengthening gulp of amontillado.

'Ekbo didn't suit Lois. She'd had no experience but her hospital courses and none at all of tropical diseases. She was young and untried, and the queues of waiting patients were never-ending.'

'You were younger, with even less experience,' Evelyn retorted. 'You hadn't finished your hospital training when you first went out.'

'But I knew that, and I had Clive. He supported me through the first months and I'd ask his opinion when I was unsure.'

'Lois isn't the sort to ask for help,' her grandmother said. 'She doesn't like admitting she doesn't know, or that she could be wrong. And she has an air of assurance that could mislead.'

'Perhaps we all thought her more competent than she is.'

With hindsight, Victoria could see now that Lois had wanted to impress Bertie and Bill. If she'd worked at the Ekbo hospital herself, Lois might have been able to ask her for advice.

And they had not stayed long enough for Lois to settle down and learn how to cope out there.

Victoria knew that for her daughter, she'd played it all wrong.

Victoria had wanted to phone Althea, but couldn't. Now it was on her conscience because she'd put off going to see her.

On Sunday, which was her day off, she took a bus from Woodside and went out to Bebington, the outlying newish suburb where Althea lived. She left it until mid-afternoon, to give Althea a chance to get the lunch cleared away, and hoped she wouldn't have taken her brood out for a walk.

She found the house with the aid of her street guide. It was of pretty pink brick and very new; bigger than most of those she'd passed on the way, detached, when most were semis, but still a modest house on an estate.

The front garden had weed-ridden borders and few flowers. The lawn was thriving, with grass eight inches high. Next door's garden looked manicured, with a good display of roses.

Victoria knew that it meant Althea was fully stretched by her indoor duties.

She rang the doorbell, and heard the sound of children scampering up the hall towards her. A tot with a blonde ponytail stood on tiptoe to open the door. Two other blonde heads crowded close.

'You must be . . .?' Victoria sought for a name but it wouldn't come. Three pairs of round blue eyes stared up at her with interest. 'Is your mother in?'

They were beautiful children, but not quite as clean or as well dressed as she remembered them.

'Who is it?' Althea came to the hall, carrying her youngest child.

Victoria had never seen anyone change so much in a few short months. Althea was noticeably pregnant now, and her face was pale and drawn.

'Hello, Althea. Remember me?' Althea looked blank. 'Victoria Benbow – Ekbo.' She was shocked to see Althea's tired eyes glazing over with tears.

'Of course.' Her face showed no pleasure at the visit. 'Do come in.'

Victoria had a glimpse of a chaotic kitchen; dishes and food on the table, dishes in the sink. Clothes on maidens, toys everywhere.

She found herself in an untidy sitting room. New furniture, new carpets but with toys and children's belongings littering everything.

Althea hurriedly dropped the infant in a corner of a settee. She removed a child's cardigan, a book and a doll from an armchair for Victoria to sit down.

'Sorry. You've caught me in a bit of a muddle.'

'I would have rung first if I . . .'

'I've applied for a phone, but there's a waiting list. Aftermath of the war. Perhaps it's just as well now.'

A thought seemed to grip Althea. Her face brightened. 'Is there news? Of Bertie? You've come to tell me . . .?'

That horrified Victoria.

'No.' What else could she say? She watched hope fade from Althea's face. Tears welled up again, and this time one rolled down her cheek. 'No, I'm so sorry.'

The infant on the settee started to snivel. Another child was pulling at Althea's skirt.

'Terribly difficult. It's a nightmare. To lose Bertie like this.' Althea sounded desperate.

Victoria felt sympathy flooding through her. She could remember what she'd felt when she'd lost Clive. And he'd had a decent span in the world and a peaceful death.

'It must be very hard for you.'

'If I knew whether he was dead or alive . . . If I knew definitely, one way or the other . . .'

Victoria had to stay silent. How could she tell her that everyone else was giving up hope?

'Is there anything I can do to help?'

Did she need to ask? The girl couldn't cope with the housework and four young children. Not now she was pregnant and on her own.

But Althea was shaking her head. Her hair needed a trim. The apron she was wearing could have done with a wash.

'I want Bertie, and there's nothing anyone can do about that.'

'No, I'm very sorry, there isn't. But a little help with the children? So you can get some rest?'

Althea's eyes fixed on her as though she'd taken leave of her senses.

'I can't afford anything like that. Do you understand what Bertie's death means? There's the mortgage to pay. The bills. We've all got to eat. I'll have to get a job.'

Victoria felt cold. The poor girl was in a worse position than she'd supposed.

'You've no money of your own?'

What a stupid, heartless thing to ask. She of all people shouldn't forget what poverty meant.

'I'm getting the allowance Bertie arranged for me. His salary is still being paid into his bank, Bill Goodbody is seeing to that. But if Bertie is dead, he won't be able to keep on paying him. Not for ever.'

Victoria suppressed a shudder and put an arm round her shoulders. By comparison with this, Lois was making a fuss about nothing.

'What am I going to do?' Althea's eyes searched the older woman's face. A few short months ago, Victoria had thought her pretty: she wasn't pretty now.

'We'll think of something.'

'If only I wasn't pregnant.' It sounded a heartfelt wish.

'Don't say that.'

'But what am I going to do? I wanted to have it here, but the doctor thinks I should have a rest in hospital. He's booked me in. He says social services will look after the others, but they'll be upset.'

Victoria tried to think. 'When is it due?'

'Ten more weeks.

Althea took out a handkerchief and scrubbed her face.

'We didn't plan it, we wouldn't have been so mad. It was just one of those things. Bertie said not to worry, that he wanted a son anyway and one more try wouldn't hurt. He said we'd cope. But without him, another is the last thing I need.'

'What you need is a nanny,' Victoria said firmly. 'I'll see if I can find one for you.'

'I can't possibly afford it. It's not so bad on a weekday when the two older ones are in school.'

'In the short term, there's no other way. I'll pay a nanny's wages for six months. I want to help. It's the least I can do.'

Althea was sobbing openly now. A larger child had climbed up on her lap and was crying too. Sticky fingers were clawing Victoria's arm.

'Don't you see, if we can get somebody now, the children will be used to her. She can manage when you go into hospital. In the meantime, you'll be able to get some time to yourself to rest. Six months would see you on your feet again.'

'You're very kind. I don't know where to turn.' Althea was drying her eyes.

'You'll feel better when the baby is born. Have more energy.'

'I'll get a job then.'

Victoria sighed. 'What sort of job?'

'I was going to be a medical secretary. Did most of the training, but I married Bertie instead of getting a job.'

Victoria's heart sank. No experience, training well behind her. And even if she did manage to get a job, it wouldn't bring in enough to keep six people and pay the mortgage.

It made her feel guilty because of the part her daughter had played in this tragedy. Lois's lot looked infinitely better than Althea's.

CHAPTER SIXTEEN

Victoria started making enquiries about a nanny and found that a New Zealand colleague was cutting short her stay in England because her mother was ill at home. She was taking her children back with her and was seeking an alternative job for the nanny she'd employed.

Myrtle Stott had worked as a nanny all her life, never married and was now middle-aged. She was old enough to nanny Althea as well.

Myrtle preferred to live in, but having no home of her own made it difficult for her to change jobs at the drop of a hat. She came with the highest possible recommendation. Victoria decided she was exactly the right person for Althea, and took her to see her new charges.

Althea seemed a little more organised this time. She was wearing a little make-up, and went out of her way to welcome Myrtle and show her round. Three days later, Myrtle moved in.

Victoria continued to visit from time to time, and was glad to see the look of desperation fade from Althea's face. She continued to grieve for Bertie, of course, but she was brighter, and looking forward to the birth now she had somebody else in the house.

Victoria wished she could solve Lois's problems as quickly.

Lois didn't improve much. Her grandmother was her doctor, nurse, and occupational therapist.

She took her out for walks round the square, to tea shops and, on days when she was a little better, on shopping expeditions. They listened to the wireless together, and she tried to interest her in embroidery and books.

Evelyn looked exhausted by it all, but she didn't complain.

It was during this time that they heard of another tragedy. Mary MacAllister, the widow of the doctor who had died of yellow fever in Ekbo, was knocked off her bike by a delivery van and never recovered from her injuries. Victoria went over to Maghull to the funeral.

She knew Esme, Mary's daughter, better than she did Althea, and thought she had more in common with her. Esme had qualified as a doctor and had a job in public health. She was unmarried and had been living with her mother. Victoria thought she'd grown up to be a thoroughly sensible girl.

'It's come as a terrible shock,' Esme said. 'So sudden. It's shaken me.'

'Don't stay here by yourself,' Victoria said. 'Come and stay with us for a week or two, until you feel better. You know we have plenty of room.'

'Thank you. My mother was very fond of you all. She was always saying we could rely on the friends we'd made in Ekbo.'

'You can.'

'I'm going to take a few days off work, but my job . . .'

'Esme, you'll find it quicker to get to work from Hamilton Square than it is from here. Think about it anyway. We'd love to have you.'

It was what Clive would have done, and she felt it might help both Esme and Lois to spend some time together. She also hoped it would ease the burden on Evelyn.

Esme telephoned her a few days later.

'Hello? Victoria? I would like to come and stay. You were such a comfort to us when my father died. Such a source of strength. And I'm finding it hard, being on my own here at the moment.'

Esme was very pale when she arrived. She'd always been rather plain, with a dumpy figure; now she seemed to take no interest in her appearance at all.

'She could do with pulling herself together,' Lois said, rather spitefully.

Esme fitted in to the Hamilton Square household and stayed for several weeks, taking much of the work of caring for Lois off Evelyn's shoulders.

Victoria took her to see Althea, mainly to give her a break from Lois. They seemed to get on well together and enjoy each other's company. That pleased her. They each needed a friend.

When Althea went into hospital and gave birth to a seven-pound son, Esme went every evening to her house in Bebington to make sure the little girls were all right. And then, more often than not, on to the hospital to report their doings to Althea.

'He's a beautiful little boy,' she told them at supper back in Hamilton Square.

'How you do all fuss over Althea,' Lois said resentfully. 'Rushing backwards and forwards, buying her books and flowers.'

'She has no husband to make a fuss of her,' Esme said, causing Lois to slam out of the room in a temper.

'I'm afraid she's a little jealous,' Victoria whispered to Esme. 'We mustn't talk about Althea in front of Lois.' She understood only too well why Althea and her new son upset Lois.

Esme continued to visit Althea regularly. She reported to Victoria on the progress she was making. Althea was home again and looking rested. She was taking an interest in her family again, even sewing dresses for the little girls.

It was many months before Esme moved out. She decided to sell her parents' cottage in Maghull; it held too many memories for her.

'I'd rather stay this side of the river,' she said to Victoria. 'All my friends seem to be here, and you're right, it's as easy to get into central Liverpool from here as it is from Maghull.

'I'll buy myself a flat in Oxton, or a little house in Bebington. Haven't quite decided yet.'

'There's no hurry,' Victoria assured her. 'You're a great help to us here. I don't know what I'd do without you.'

It was months before Lois began to improve.

'I think it would be a nice idea to have our portraits painted,' Evelyn said one evening at the supper table. 'What do you think?'

'A good idea for you and Lois. You've both got the time to sit for it.' Victoria smiled encouragingly at Lois, thinking it another idea to interest her.

'I thought one large picture to hang there over the sideboard,' Evelyn said. 'The three of us together. We are three generations of doctors.'

'Well, yes.' Victoria wasn't sure she wanted to spend her scarce leisure time that way.

'While we are all here together,' her mother said, as though that might not be the case for much longer. Victoria was persuaded.

There was a portrait of Clive's mother over the fireplace in the sitting room. She'd always liked it. It was all she'd ever known of her mother-in-law, and it was a reminder that this had been a family home for several generations. In future years, she'd value a portrait of her own mother in the same way.

'I think it's a good idea,' Lois said.

'I know just the person to do it.' Evelyn was enthusiastic. 'You know Dr March? His son is an excellent portrait painter, but he's not finding it easy to get commissions. An artist's life can be hard these days. It'll help him and please his mother. I've known Vera March for a good many years now.'

Work on the portrait started. Victoria went with Evelyn and Lois to Dr March's house in Noctorum for the first sitting. Justin March took some photographs of her so that he could manage with fewer sittings.

Evelyn enjoyed the whole process. 'It's somewhere else to take Lois, and Vera March gives us tea afterwards. Lois is showing more interest in things but she's very dependent at the moment. She won't go anywhere alone.'

'We'll give her another month or so, then we must try to get her back to work,' Victoria said.

187

When they put it to Lois, she was adamant.

'I don't want to go back to work.' All the stuffing seemed to have been knocked out of her.

'You can't spend the rest of your life sitting about at home,' Evelyn told her firmly. 'You're getting better now. Once you have your health and strength back, your confidence will follow.'

The day Justin March brought the finished portrait and hung it in their dining room, Evelyn said to Victoria: 'The children's hospital is the best place for her. She'll be amongst friends and you're on the spot to keep an eye on her. If she doesn't go back soon she'll never practise medicine again. She's getting cold feet about it.'

Lois was persuaded to try. Evelyn's friends were sympathetic and eased her into the work. After the first week or so, Victoria was convinced they'd done the right thing.

Lois began to pick up more quickly. She was enjoying outings to the theatre and the cinema. The colour was coming back to her cheeks.

'She needs more of a social life now,' her grandmother said. 'You and I can't keep pace with a young girl like Lois.'

Esme had joined the tennis club, and tried to persuade Lois to join too.

'You'll meet people of your own age,' she told her. 'It's good fun.'

Lois went with her one evening, and discovered that Althea had also been persuaded to join.

'I don't think it's my sort of place,' Lois told them.

'Perhaps it's just as well,' Victoria said afterwards. 'If Althea's a member.'

'She's jealous,' Evelyn said. 'She thinks you make more fuss of those girls than you do of her. And she's afraid they'll be better at tennis and better at making friends than she is.'

Victoria sighed. 'What more can we do?'

'We've got to find her some friends of her own. Men friends.'

'Lois can't afford another affair like the one with Bertie.'

'A love affair is exactly what she does need,' her grandmother said. 'It would put her back on her feet.'

'We'll have to vet them carefully. Make sure they're suitable.'

'Who do we know?'

'She needs a man who will support her.'

'A man near her own age so that she won't be left high and dry too early. It won't suit Lois to be an old man's darling.'

Victoria still missed Clive and wished he were here to help now. They took their time, discussed all the possibilities.

'We'll invite them here to dinner. Just tell Lois we're having a dinner party. And not Esme. She's no beauty, but Lois sees her as a competitor.'

They decided on two men who might do. One of them was Graham Challoner, a consultant surgeon working at the General Hospital. Evelyn invited a life-long friend, a man of her own age, to balance the numbers.

Lois made an effort. She bought herself a pretty tulle dress with a tight-fitting bodice and a long, full skirt. It was the very fashionable New Look.

Victoria and Evelyn took great pains with the food and the table settings. The evening looked like being a great success.

Graham Challoner arrived first. He had served in the army during the war. He was tall, with a military bearing and a commanding voice that left nobody in any doubt that he was born to lead. He accepted a glass of sherry and sat himself down next to Lois, giving her all his attention.

Victoria watched them from the other side of the fireplace and was pleased. Lois was laughing and seemed more animated than she had been of late.

Graham was a good-looking man with a pencil moustache. Victoria didn't know how old he was but he looked about right for Lois.

He was a widower twice over. His first wife had been a doctor. She'd been killed in an air raid early in the war. His second had been a major in the QAs and had died on active service during the D-Day landings. There were no children from either marriage.

Victoria thought they had had a very pleasant evening. The following week Graham invited all three ladies to a meal at the Bowler Hat, and a few days after that he took Lois to the theatre in Liverpool.

Evelyn and Victoria were satisfied then that they had given Lois every chance to make a full recovery.

Victoria came home from work a few days later to meet Evelyn in the hall.

'There's another letter from Janet Goodbody waiting for you,' Evelyn whispered. 'Lois has seen it. She's turned it over and over. I think she's desperate to know if there's any news.'

Victoria snatched it up. She was burning with hope for Bertie as she ripped it open. Janet's large hand scrawled down the page.

We've heard nothing more of Bertie Meadows or the others in the medical team and must stop hoping that we'll ever see them again. They must have been killed. It's been desperate here waiting for news that doesn't come.

Titch Sinclair went home some time ago. We've heard from him, he's taken rooms in Harley Street just as he'd planned. No doubt he'll have a brilliant future. He was cleverer than the rest of us.

189

We are leaving Ekbo for good ourselves. Bill can't stomach any more. We're just waiting for his replacement to get here so that we can show him the ropes. There will be nobody left here then of the old crowd we all knew so well.

Victoria looked up to find that Lois had heard her come in and was hurrying downstairs. Without a word, she handed the letter over for her to read.

She watched Lois's face. Hope died from it as she read the bit about Bertie. She could see tears glistening on her daughter's lashes when she'd finished.

Victoria said hesitantly: 'About Bill and Janet. How would you feel if I were to invite them here to stay with us for a while? They've no home of their own in England and they'll need a base. Just for a few weeks, until they decide what to do.'

'I don't mind.' She could see that Lois was trying to hold herself in check. 'You don't have to protect me from every connection with . . . I was just hoping that perhaps Bertie . . .'

Evelyn had said to her: 'Lois has got to put Cuthbert Meadows behind her and get on with her life. She must stop brooding about him.'

Lois added: 'It's just that I blame myself for his death, you see.'

'Lois, Bill Goodbody is blaming himself too. We are all sickened by what happened to Bertie.'

Victoria was trying to find a balance between the needs of her daughter and those of her friends.

'I don't think Bill and Janet have any relatives left in this country now.'

'Ask them here if you want to, Mother.' Lois handed the letter on to Evelyn. 'You know I'm perfectly all right now.'

'We have plenty of room. Janet has been a very good friend to me, I'd like to help them. I think perhaps I will.'

It was another three months before Bill and Janet were able to return to England. By then, Esme had her own flat in Oxton and Evelyn and Victoria were congratulating themselves that they had succeeded in what they'd set out to do for Lois.

She was continuing to make good progress. She was working hard at the hospital and seemed to be coping.

Graham Challoner was escorting her out and about. They were seeing more of him at the Hamilton Square house.

Victoria thought him an ideal choice for Lois. He was authoritarian in manner and left her in no doubt as to what he expected of her. He was sweeping Lois along with him. Nobody had to concern themselves with occupational therapy for her now. Lois had changed completely and seemed a normal, happy girl again.

'I think I'll go back to my own little flat,' Evelyn told Victoria wearily. 'I feel in need of a rest after running round with Lois so much. Besides my place is warmer and suits me better than all these stairs.'

'You've done a lot for her. I'm very grateful, Mother.'

Victoria was afraid Evelyn didn't feel up to entertaining the Goodbodys. In some ways it suited her to have her friends to herself. She was out at work most days, which meant they could please themselves.

It seemed Bill and Janet hadn't recovered from what had happened to Cuthbert Meadows either.

'A horrible thing.' Janet shuddered. 'It soured everything for us. I hope Bill will be able to forget all about it now that we've come away. It's been giving us nightmares.'

'Have you heard from Titch Sinclair?'

'Yes, he sends his regards to you and Lois. I think it changed everything for him too. He keeps writing to ask if we've heard anything more of Bertie.'

'How is he getting on in Harley Street?'

'Settling down and doing well, he says. Probably has a big future there.'

'He was right to get out as soon as he could. Though he left you and Bill to soldier on by yourselves.'

'The number of suspicions deaths went up and up after you'd gone. There was a feeling of terror in Ekbo village.

'The local police force was greatly enlarged. They called it the "leopard force". Their main duty was to seek out members of the leopard society and destroy their shrines.

'It racked the whole of the Eastern Region. The whole country really. None of us could talk of anything else.'

Victoria shuddered. 'I never liked the bush. Despite the height of the trees, it was almost impenetrable. Threatening too. I never went in without Clive.'

'There have been almost two hundred highly probably leopard murders. Ninety-six persons have been convicted, of whom seventy-seven were hanged.'

Victoria shivered. 'What about the rest?'

'Over a hundred have been acquitted and two died in custody. There were countless more deaths in the bush which could have been caused by genuine leopards.

'All these are native deaths, of course. Nobody knows what happened to poor Bertie.'

'What is Bill planning to do now?'

Janet sighed. 'He thinks general practice would suit him best.'

'Will you go back to Bristol? That's where you come from, isn't it?'

191

'I do, but Bill comes from Plymouth. We've both been away so long and we've no ties there any more, so we've decided we might as well stay here in Birkenhead. Most of our friends seem to be here now.'

'Bill is going to look round for a practice here?'

'Yes, and for a house,' Janet added.

'I shall be delighted if he gets fixed up,' Victoria exclaimed. 'What could be better? I want you to stay here in Hamilton Square with me until you get yourselves settled.'

For Victoria, 1949 turned out to be a good year. Bill Goodbody settled into a practice in Tranmere and bought a house in Oxton.

Graham asked Lois to marry him and bought her a large and impressive solitaire diamond. Victoria thought how her daughter's life continued to mirror her own. Even though Graham might be second best, she thought Lois would settle down as she had done.

At the wedding Lois looked lovely in her bridal white.

Evelyn whispered to Victoria: 'A quiet wedding would have been more appropriate, and she should have worn a pastel-coloured dress.

'I shall close my eyes to this, of course. No point in upsetting Lois when I've taken so much trouble to get her back on an even keel.'

Victoria felt she'd had to close her eyes to quite a lot of things for Lois's sake.

'We've both done the best we could for her.'

'At least we can now hope Lois will live happily ever after.'

Bill Goodbody had settled into his practice in Tranmere and was trying to persuade Victoria to join him.

'I need a partner, Victoria. How about it?'

'I thought you had a single-handed practice?'

'It's been that for the last fifty years, but patients are flocking in. There's more work than I can cope with. What do you say?' She was tempted.

Bill said, 'I've worked with you. I know we'll get along together.'

Victoria had had a difficult day. She was no longer a spring chicken able to rush up and down those wards. She'd worked at the children's hospital on and off for more years than she wanted to count.

Here she was at fifty-seven, feeling at a crossroads in her life.

Lois was married, her mother had already moved back to her own flat. Esme was gone. Bill and Janet had found a house of their own and were gone too. Victoria counted herself lucky that they all lived nearby, met often and remained close friends.

If she were to tell the truth, the thought of giving up work altogether appealed to her. But she hadn't as much to occupy her at home as she'd once had. Sometimes she felt at a loose end. She'd surely compound the problem if she had no job to go to.

She decided she must carry on for the time being, but she wanted less hassle. Perhaps doing morning surgery for Bill Goodbody would be easier?

Bill was pleased when Victoria told him she'd join his practice. Evelyn thought it was a good idea. Only Lois came out against it.

'General practice! Whatever for? You've let yourself get into a rut, that's your problem. They're going to need another registrar at the hospital. Benton is leaving.'

'Yes, I know.'

'You'd do better to apply for his post. I thought you would.'

'No.'

'Why not?' She'd been querulous. 'You'd stand a good chance of getting it. Think of all the experience you've had. If you'd sought promotion you could have been a consultant by now.'

'Perhaps, but I want less work, not more. I don't want new challenges and more responsibility. I want time to do other things. Sit around and talk to Janet when I feel like it.'

Lois's eyebrows had gone higher. 'You've worked there for years, always at the bottom of the ladder.'

'Yes, and on the whole I've enjoyed it.'

'Grandma was a consultant.'

'We're all different, Lois. Anyway, I spent too much time abroad. I let promotion pass me by.'

Victoria sighed. She'd never been all that interested in medicine. Neither had she been ambitious. What she'd done was to plod along in her mother's footsteps.

Marriage had suited her better. She'd wanted to support Clive in his career and bring up her family. If things had been different – if Clive had lived longer, if she'd had the boys to bring up – she might never have gone back to work.

Lois was glowering at her. 'I don't know what's the matter with you, Mother. You neglect your own career.'

'No. I just want more time . . .'

'Oh yes, I know what for. So you can interfere in my affairs. I think you do it to humiliate me.'

Victoria felt her spirits sinking. Lois was agitated again. 'That's the last thing I want.'

'Then why go behind my back?' Why discuss what I do, or don't do, with Graham?'

Victoria was fighting to stay calm. She ought to have realised Lois would resent what she'd done.

'I was trying to help. Your grandmother and I, we were both trying to help.'

At Lois's wedding reception, Evelyn had let their glasses clink together in congratulation.

She'd whispered: 'We've got Lois up and going again. What we

193

have to do now is to make sure she stays on an even keel over the next few years. She'll need a protected environment, but Graham is very supportive.'

There seemed to be every reason to believe Lois would settle down and be happy. Graham had bought a modern house in Oxton. When he and Lois moved in after their wedding, Lois invited Victoria and Evelyn up to see it.

'Ideal,' Evelyn had said. It was light and warm and easy to keep clean. The newly-weds were engrossed in choosing furniture for it.

But within a few weeks, Graham called on Evelyn and asked for help. He said he didn't want to upset Lois, but she was having trouble coping with the housekeeping as well as her job.

In the first month she'd had an argument with the daily help Graham had employed for five years, and dismissed her on the spot. She was making no effort to replace her, though he'd urged her to do so. By then the domestic chores were getting out of hand.

'I should have noticed sooner.' He'd been apologetic. 'It took me by surprise. At Hamilton Square everything seems to run like clockwork.'

'That's Victoria's house. She organises it. We'll have a word with Lois, see what we can do.'

Graham had been used to an orderly life and expected Lois to keep his home clean and tidy and put food on the table when he needed it.

Victoria had been upset when Evelyn told her about it. Perhaps it was a setback they should have foreseen? Lois had never concerned herself with what went on in the house.

'Perhaps Graham expects too much.'

'Only what a husband should expect. Lois has no sense of duty.' Her grandmother had been cross. 'She does only what she wants to. Thinks housework is beneath her, I'm sure.'

'She needs time,' Victoria had pleaded.

'She needs a few lessons.' Evelyn had been less sympathetic. 'But I'll teach her.'

'Do be gentle with her, Mother. We mustn't upset her, remember what you said.'

'Sometimes I think she should have been given a good spanking when she was younger. You and Clive were too indulgent.'

It was Victoria who found Lois two daily women to work alternate mornings. Evelyn drew up a timetable for them, and explained to Lois exactly what she must ask them to do. Graham was grateful and said things were much improved.

But Lois was enraged. 'Going behind my back. Taking Graham's side against me. I expect some support from you, Mother. Why do you keep letting me down? Spoiling everything for me?'

Victoria had had a busy day. Bill and Janet had gone away for a holiday. She'd been late finishing evening surgery and was an hour later than usual coming home.

Feeling exhausted, she'd walked slowly across Hamilton Square. It was almost deserted at this time of the evening, the houses closed up and dark.

Because of its central position in the town, the whole atmosphere of the district had changed since she'd first come to live here. Once it had been residential, but since the last war, the houses were almost all used as offices of one sort or another.

Solicitors particularly favoured them, but there was a dentist, and a restaurant. The house next door to hers had sold recently to an insurance company.

The brass plates beside the front doors were restrained, and she didn't object to them, but some houses sprouted neon signs advertising their business.

She reached her own front door and turned to survey the square. Now, in the fifties, her house must be just about the last still being used for the purpose for which it was designed. Many had had their rooms rented out singly before being taken over for commercial use. Clive wouldn't know the place.

She let herself into the hall and closed the front door behind her. Nothing had changed inside. The grandfather clock ticked just as loudly.

Victoria sighed. This was the first time she'd ever lived alone in this house. It was far too big for her. Far too difficult to cope with all the stairs and the seven bedrooms.

It must be about a year since she'd gone up to the attic rooms that the servants had once used. Since the war she'd counted herself lucky to get daily help. The worst thing about the house now was its still, quiet loneliness.

She'd changed nothing at all in the years she'd been mistress of it. She still had the huge pieces of heavy Victorian mahogany furniture. They suited the place.

When new carpets and curtains had been needed, she'd chosen similar designs and colours. When Clive's red velvet armchairs became threadbare with use, she'd had them re-upholstered in velvet of the same shade. His books still filled the shelves. The atmosphere had not changed at all.

In a way Clive still lived here. Tonight, Victoria was aware of his gentle presence all round her. She asked herself whether he would still be living here if he were alive today. She didn't think so.

She went to the kitchen. Her daily woman had left a casserole in the oven for her lonely dinner. Clive wouldn't know this part of the house.

She'd had to have a modern kitchen installed on the ground floor to save Evelyn yet another flight of stairs down to the warren of kitchens, pantries, store rooms, laundry rooms and wine cellars in the basement. They had been designed a century ago to house the small army of servants thought necessary to run the place then.

Victoria turned on her electric hotplate under the pan containing one potato. There was a small amount of chopped cabbage in another. She went back to the dining room at the front of the house, poured herself a glass of sherry and sat in the armchair by the window to think.

She'd seen quite a lot of modern property recently. She'd gone with Janet Goodbody to look at houses. The one they'd chosen was small compared with this, but it was so cosy. Here the ceilings were three feet higher and the central heating cost four times as much to run and provided a fraction of the warmth.

It would be a great wrench to leave Clive's house. She'd admired it, and if the truth were to be told, she'd married Clive so that she could live in it.

But now the time had come to go. Victoria felt depressed. She would find herself a flat like her mother's. If she hadn't been so attached to this place, she'd have moved long ago. She got up and helped herself to another glass of sherry from the decanter on the sideboard, then opened the newspaper that had been delivered that morning and at which she'd barely glanced at breakfast.

Titch's face smiled up at her from an inner page. She felt her heart turn over as she read the article about him.

They'd kept in touch with Titch. Stayed in his splendid house when they went down to London. They were all very impressed at the rapid success he'd achieved in his career. Now all that had gone.

Long ago, Janet had said he was a womaniser. It seemed she was right.

Victoria was sorry to see him in such terrible difficulties. Particularly because they were so unexpected.

Of course, they'd all had their problems since they'd left Ekbo.

She considered her biggest worry to be Lois. Without the help she and Evelyn gave, she was sure Lois wouldn't have coped as well as she had.

Althea too. She'd continued to pay for a nanny for her. Janet went to see her and the children often. Bill was helping with her household expenses. Althea had a job but it didn't begin to pay for the needs of a family the size of hers.

Yes, they all had their difficulties. For herself, Victoria had learned to be content with the minutiae of life as the years began to pass more rapidly.

CHAPTER SEVENTEEN

Jill stretched and tried to turn over. She banged her knee against something hard before she realised she was not in her bed.

She peered over her duvet. Gran's room was a mess. There were towels and other oddments tossed on the floor. Her bed was pushed against the wall and she was still snoring softly.

A shaft of brilliant sunlight was coming through the curtains. Slowly and quietly, so as not to disturb her grandmother, Jill climbed out of the chairs.

It was after nine thirty and she'd heard none of the usual morning sounds.

Jill yawned, feeling heavy-eyed. It was as though she'd lifted the lid of Pandora's box last night. She'd been needling Gran to tell her about the old days, without success.

Then, when she'd least expected it, it had all come pouring out. Things that Victoria considered were dark secrets; things she'd suppressed for years, things of which she was ashamed.

Gran had talked for much of the night. Now Jill understood the sacrifices her great-grandmother Evelyn had had to make to become a doctor, and all she'd given up for Victoria's sake.

She'd learned of Victoria's two sons who had died of yellow fever in Ekbo, and how the lonely life there had welded together the people who lived there for the rest of their lives.

Instead of clearing the air as she'd expected, it had made matters worse. She was afraid that so far she'd only scratched the surface; that there was more Victoria was keeping hidden. This morning, the house seemed positively eerie.

She went downstairs and found her father having breakfast. He said: 'What's the matter with Lois? She never stays in bed, says it gives her a headache. She won't even talk to me.'

Jill poured herself some tea. She hadn't considered the effect Gran's revelation would have on Lois.

'Victoria's upset her. She was delirious last night. She talked a lot, hardly knew what she was saying.'

The bags below her father's tired eyes seemed bigger than ever.

'She told Lois that Clive wasn't her father, that she'd had a lover.'

'Good God!' Nat's heavy features seemed to crumple. 'Lois wouldn't like that. She was very close to her father. Can't believe it of Victoria!'

It had shocked Jill. Victoria was respected, held in high esteem. Revered almost. Today, when to conceive such a child was commonplace, to foist it on one's husband was still a terrible sin.

'I knew there were things they didn't talk about. I've always felt it,' her father said slowly.

Jill shuddered. She'd felt it too.

'Lois is in a very bad temper.'

'I'll take her some tea and toast,' Jill said.

She found Lois still lying flat, with the duvet pulled up to her chin.

'Morning, Lois.' She opened her curtains to let the daylight in.

'Don't do that,' her stepmother spat. 'I've had a terrible night and I've got a headache.'

'It's getting on for ten.'

'I don't care what time it is. I need more sleep.'

Jill drew the curtains again, left the tray and went out.

Jill looked in on Victoria, who was just waking up. As she was drawing back the curtains, a voice made gravelly by flu croaked: 'Where am I?'

'At home. In your own room.'

'No, this isn't . . .' With glazed eyes, Victoria was looking round her without recognition.

'You're in your own bed, Gran. Safe and sound.'

Jill started to put the room to rights. All the furniture had been moved last night; no wonder Gran didn't recognise the place.

'No,' Victoria protested. 'Not safe.'

'Of course you're safe. What makes you say that?'

'Feel on the edge. A precipice. I've nothing left.'

'Everything's still here. We just moved it. I slept here in these two chairs last night. In case you woke up and wanted something.'

The old lips pursed. 'No money left. I don't know what we'll do now. All gone.'

'Gran, you've lots of money. You told me last night Clive had left you well provided for.'

'All gone now.' Gran's dark eyes looked up into hers.

'You sold your house in Hamilton Square. You must have the money from that.'

'All gone, I said.' She sounded irritable.

'It can't be. Anyway, you don't need money here. Lois will look after you.'

'Lois is the one who needs it.' Her voice was sharper, more emphatic. 'Lois hasn't any left. If she has to find more . . .'

'Lois has plenty,' Jill assured her easily.

She knew exactly what the practice earned and what Lois had drawn from it over recent years, because they'd shown her the books when they'd made her a partner.

The agreement was that Jill would draw only two-thirds of what the other partners did for the first three years, and she was feeling fairly rich on it.

'What Lois earns should provide generously for anything she needs.'

'No, I tell you . . .'

'Gran, there's no need to worry about money,' Jill said firmly. 'Nat has plenty too.'

'Nat won't part with it.'

That made Jill straighten up. It made her think of what she'd over-heard yesterday. Dad and Lois had been having an argument about money.

From what Dad had said, Lois had asked him for money in the past. That was why he'd invested it in securities in Jill's name – so Lois couldn't get her hands on it. But none of that had made much sense to her.

Jill found it hard to believe there was any shortage of money. They were living well, but surely they could afford to? Apart from Lois's earnings, Dad had his business. He'd told her that was earning a good profit.

'I feel strange . . . light-headed,' Gran complained. This was easier to understand.

'It's flu. The summer flu. You were pyrexial last night.' Hyper-pyrexial, in fact. Jill felt her forehead. 'It's down this morning. Are you feeling better?'

'Just a bit fuddled.' Gran began to cough. Her wrinkled face looked haunted.

'Any pain in your chest, Gran?' Was she getting a chest infection?

Jill went to get her stethoscope from her bag and listened to Victoria's chest. She could hear a few rales but nothing full-blown as yet.

Perhaps they should have started her on antibiotics last night. she didn't usually prescribe them for flu, but in view of Gran's age . . . It would prevent her getting complications, if nothing else.

She kept a few samples in her bag. She'd start her on them now just in case.

But perhaps she should mention it to Lois first? Jill didn't want anything else to upset her stepmother.

She went to see Lois again. The tea had been drunk but the toast hadn't been touched.

'Antibiotics? For heaven's sake! I don't care. Do what you like.' Jill went back and gave Gran her first dose.

199

'Would you like some breakfast?'

'A drink.'

'Tea? There's some freshly made.' She ran down to the kitchen to get it.

Lois humped herself over in bed. She was in a boiling rage that her mother had done this to her. She bashed at her pillow and pulled herself up the bed. Her head was throbbing. She couldn't believe, didn't want to believe, that Clive was not her father.

Everybody had admired Clive. She remembered all the gentle love he'd shown her. His kindness and generosity. He'd thought she could achieve anything she wanted, but he hadn't known he wasn't her father!

She could feel the bile rising in her throat every time she thought of that.

She leapt out of bed. Dragged on her dressing gown, rushed up the landing and threw open her mother's door. Victoria's frightened face lifted off the pillow, grey and drawn.

'Call yourself a mother? You've made a rotten job of it.'

'Lois?'

'How dare you say Clive wasn't my father? Such awful lies. Why do you do it?' Lois felt humiliated, debased. 'I hate you.'

'Lois, no!' She rarely saw her mother with her wispy hair loose about her shoulders. It made her look older than ever.

'You pretend to be a saint, but you've cheated Clive and you've cheated me. You even killed my two brothers.'

'No!'

'If you'd had any motherly instincts at all, you'd have stayed here in England with us children, instead of exposing us to the horrors of Ekbo. All that juju business terrified the life out of us. Keith and Barney too. No child could survive that unscathed.'

Her mother's lips were moving. They looked blue. No sound came.

'I hated Africa but you hauled me back as a young adult. At an impressionable time of life. Just when I was beginning to get over my childhood nightmares. It was the worst thing you could have done to me.'

'You wanted to go.'

'No. If you'd left me at home to get on with my life, I'd never have met Bertie Meadows. Nor would I be blighted with memories of those awful murders. Poor Bertie wouldn't have died that way.'

'Please, Lois . . . Don't . . .'

'It was an evil place but you couldn't get enough of it. It suited you. You didn't care that it was ruining my life.'

She hovered closer. Victoria flopped back against her pillows and raised her arm to protect her face.

'You needn't be afraid I'll hurt you!' Lois grabbed at her mother's shoulders, lifting her, forcing her arms away from her helpless, frightened face. Pushing her own closer.

'I hate you. With a mother like you, everything was stacked against me from the start.'

'Lois . . . Tried my best,' Victoria panted.

Lois could hear footsteps running upstairs. A gasp of horror.

'Lois!' She was aware that Jill held a tray that had tea slopping all over it. 'Leave your mother alone. Can't you see she's ill?'

'If only she'd left me alone. I'd have been fine. She's always been selfish.'

'No, Lois, you're upset.'

Lois felt strong hands turning her round, pushing her back to her own room.

She shouted: 'It's all her fault. She's ruined my life!'

Lois flung herself back on her bed. She could see again the house Graham had bought in Oxton. A modern box. She should never have settled for that. She'd wanted something larger, something to reflect their status.

It was breakfast time in the poky dining room. All she could see of Graham was the back of his newspaper. But through the door to the kitchen, last night's dinner dishes faced her, stacked on the sink in gravy-stained piles.

She'd felt the first stirrings of dissatisfaction within weeks of her marriage. Back home in Hamilton Square, her mother and grandmother had fussed round her, letting her know how pleased they were with the work she was doing at the hospital.

And her clothes had been washed and ironed, and her meals prepared and put on the table with no effort on her part. She did not belong to the class that had to concern themselves with such matters.

Graham demanded a lot more of her. He'd made such a fuss about her housekeeping, she'd been driven to ask: 'Was Mary better at it than I am?' Mary was his first wife.

'How would I know? I was in the army then.'

'I expect Charlotte was?'

'She was in the army too. She'd have loved to have had a home of her own. We didn't get the chance to try it.'

Lois had seen censure in his eyes then, but he'd said: 'This is my first marriage under normal conditions, Lois. I do want us to make a success of it. Forget what's gone before.

'Twice I was married, and twice I lost my wife within a year. I spent only weeks with Mary before we were separated. About two months altogether with Charlotte.'

'I'm sorry.'

She didn't know why she felt threatened by his war-time tragedies. She didn't like to think he'd had other wives.

His newspaper rustled now and sank to plate level. His stern, dignified face looked up.

'Would you take a suit to the cleaners for me, Lois? I've left it on the bed.'

The surge of resentment she felt at that prevented her from answering.

'It is your half-day, isn't it?' Graham prided himself on always being calm and polite. He had what Lois called a polished bedside manner, and he used it on friends and relatives too.

'Yes,' she managed, but with a certain shortness. She had so little time off, and so much to get through now.

'You might as well take two while you're at it. The grey with the faint pinstripe could do with cleaning too.'

'And where am I likely to find that?' She couldn't stop the hint of sarcasm creeping in.

'Hanging in my wardrobe. There's a love.'

He refolded his paper and started to read again. All she could see were his well-manicured hands protruding from his immaculately ironed shirtsleeves, with the gold cuff links she'd give him last Christmas.

She was relieved he knew how to organise the laundry service and didn't try to involve her in that.

Graham was a perfectionist and expected the same of her. She felt he'd been hypercritical of her first efforts at household management. High-handed to make such a fuss.

If he'd really loved her, he'd not have asked Evelyn to sort things out for him, saying her housekeeping standards fell short of what he expected. He shouldn't have exposed her, made her lose face.

After all, she was still doing a great deal more for Graham's comfort than he was doing for hers.

In the first weeks of their marriage he'd driven her to work, because once she'd moved to this house she was no longer on a direct bus route to the children's hospital, and it was further for her to go.

'No point in relying on other people to drive you round,' he'd smiled. 'Besides, it increases my journey to work fourfold. I'm going round in a circle.'

Graham had insisted on her having driving lessons and had then bought her a smart Morris Minor. She'd had to master that, as she had to master everything else.

Her mother had been very impressed that she'd learned to drive and immediately started learning herself.

Lois couldn't stop herself fulminating. Everybody seemed to think she'd found it easy to cut herself free of Africa and free of her mother. She still thought of Bertie. He'd have been a more caring husband than Graham. Less selfish.

Graham attached too much importance to his own career. He published papers regularly in the *Lancet* and other medical journals to keep his name in the forefront of the profession. He did everything to enhance his reputation.

He saw her career very differently. It didn't matter how much of her time, attention and energy he sapped. If she hadn't married him, she could have been a paediatric consultant.

Lois felt more confident about what she did in the hospital. Unlike housework, it was something she wanted to do. She derived satisfaction from it, she was ambitious and meant to go far.

'Must be off.' Graham's cup clattered back on to its saucer. He came round to her side of the table and dropped a kiss on her forehead.

His dark grey suit was in the best possible taste. Just a hint of sportiness in the double vent at the back of the jacket. He wore sober ties in silver and grey and highly polished black Oxford shoes. This was his workaday image. He aimed to look the professional man through and through.

Off duty, he could be quite different. He liked bright pullovers, cravats and hand-made brogues. He still looked sophisticated but he liked simple fun.

He enjoyed a drink and a laugh. Above all, he loved the company of women and any sort of social gathering. He was a bit of an extrovert and liked the sound of his own voice.

Her mother had told her that other women admired Graham, that most thought a husband necessary to get the best from life. Even Evelyn thought Graham was desirable.

Lois knew he'd wanted her and that had warmed her response. He might not be perfect, but he was a husband she needn't be ashamed of.

'See you this evening. I won't be late. Would you like to go out for a meal?'

'Yes.' Anything to save herself the trouble of having to cook it and put it on the table.

'We might have something to celebrate by then.' His eyes twinkled down at her.

'Perhaps,' she agreed. It gave her a lift to think of that.

She'd started working at the children's hospital as a supernumerary. As Evelyn had told her at the time, they had wanted her enough to take her on when there was no real post for her. She was graded as a house officer, the only one not on a six-month training course.

At the hospital, Victoria was not directly involved with her. Lois worked under the supervision of a different registrar. But now that registrar was leaving to take promotion at Myrtle Street, and she had applied for his job.

'Do you think you stand a chance?' Graham had asked her. She had thought that a little condescending, since she was doing so much of the registrar's work and had been doing it for the last few months.

'Be quite a feather in your cap if you get it. You're still very young and you haven't had much experience in paediatrics.'

'You were made a consultant at thirty-two,' she reminded him shortly. She couldn't help but feel a twinge of envy at that.

'I was lucky. In the right place at the right time.'

'I've applied for a registrar's post, nothing so grand as a consultant's,' Lois retorted. 'I've worked hard.' Why shouldn't she get it?

She was up in her bedroom getting ready for work when she heard the post flop through the letter box.

As she rushed downstairs, she could see the envelope lying on the mat, and knew immediately it was the one she'd been waiting for. Her fingers were shaking with anticipation as she ripped it open.

The black letters leapt off the page. 'Dear Dr Benbow . . .'

Lois felt her stomach turn over, the bitterness of bile was on her tongue. She was suddenly dizzy and had to sit down. No, lie down.

She collapsed on the settee in the sitting room, her head thumping. She'd been passed over for promotion.

She was overwhelmed by feelings of failure and disappointment. After all the years Victoria and Evelyn had worked at the hospital, they weren't prepared to give her a chance.

Lois was convulsed with envy. Graham's career was going so well when hers was not. This was another slap in the face.

Graham was more sympathetic than she'd expected. Her mother and grandmother fussed round her too.

'It's just that they don't think you're quite ready for it yet, Lois dear.'

'But they've given the post to some outsider who nobody knows,' she'd wailed. 'It's because he's a man.'

'No,' Graham had said in his calm manner. 'He's had a lot more experience than you, love.'

'Carry on for another year or two,' Evelyn advised. 'Then, when another post comes up, you can apply again.'

But none of that really helped her. Over the following months, she knew she was losing interest in her career. She was no longer getting the satisfaction from it that she should.

Lois had soldiered on, feeling vaguely discontented with everything.

'If that's the way you feel,' Graham said, 'give it up. There's no need for you to work.'

The message from the media was that a woman's place was in the home. Every magazine and newspaper she opened seemed to have an article driving that into her mind. Most of Graham's colleagues had wives who didn't work. She knew he wanted her to be a full-time wife.

'I want children and a real marriage this time.' he pleaded. 'I wanted them before, but it was an impossible indulgence in the middle of a war.'

She'd seen a good many children during the course of her work, but she'd never felt particularly drawn to any of them. She saw what children meant to other women but she'd never felt any urge to have any of her own.

Until she saw Peter Pelham. She came back from a weekend off to find Peter in her care. He was an eighteen-month-old infant who had been admitted following an accident involving his parents' car. He had several fractures and both his legs were in plaster when she saw him.

He was still deeply sedated. Lois stood looking down at his white-blond hair and fair skin. His long, pale lashes lay across chubby cheeks, his limbs were rounded. She thought he was the most beautiful baby she'd ever seen.

Within a week, he was smiling up at her when she leaned over his cot, and she felt the first stirrings of mother-love.

She understood then why women wanted children, and began to think she was missing out on satisfactions other people valued. A husband was not enough for a complete and fulfilling life. She needed a family as well.

On Victoria's birthday, she invited her family and friends to a meal at her flat. Bill Goodbody was there and suggested that Lois might like to try general practice.

'I'd need to think about it,' she told him. 'I've never done any.'

'I think it might suit you,' her mother said.

Lois felt wary. It was unknown ground.

'No need to be nervous. Very rare for anything frightening to walk into surgery. Mostly trivial stuff, coughs and colds.'

'You might find it less exacting now you have a home and husband to care for.'

'Now I'm coming up to sixty,' Victoria told her, 'I'd like to retire and have more time to myself.'

'Would you like to take your mother's place in the practice?' Bill asked.

'A good idea,' Graham enthused. 'You're finding it hard at the hospital. You'd have more energy for other things.'

'I don't work a full day.' Her mother was smiling at her.

'Come and do your mother's hours to start with and see how you get on,' Bill said. His bald head caught the light, making it shine.

'Sooner or later, I'll have to get a full-time partner though, because the practice is growing.'

Lois felt disenchanted with her job at the hospital. She'd seen enough to know it was not for her. Not now she had so much to do at home.

Working mornings only, this could be her chance to have a child. She'd manage with a nanny. It was what Graham wanted.

And Bill would give her a chance to work full-time again when she wanted to. She could still have a career.

'I've made up my mind, Bill,' she said as they were finishing off the roast chicken. 'I'll come to the practice.'

Graham smiled at her from across the table. He seemed to know she wanted to do the other thing as well.

Lois thought she settled easily into doing a morning surgery. She was soon convinced that it suited her and she'd made the right choice. Bill was already a family friend. She knew she could get on with him.

Getting pregnant wasn't quite so easy. It took her six months to achieve that, but then she knew she was going to have everything life could offer.

She worked throughout her pregnancy, leaving only three weeks before the baby was due. Her daughter, Phoebe, was born in The Elms, a private nursing home in Liverpool. Graham knew the owners and thought Lois would be more comfortable there than in Grange Mount maternity hospital.

When Lois held Phoebe in her arms for the first time, she marvelled at the miracle she'd produced. Graham brought in a bottle of champagne and drank most of it himself.

'Wonderful, darling,' he kept saying. 'She's a beautiful baby.'

Lois wasn't so sure. She found breast-feeding not to her liking, and anyway, Phoebe couldn't get the hang of it. Despite what she'd advised other new mothers to do, she changed her to the bottle.

Phoebe seemed to cry more than she should, but the nurses took her away to the nursery so that Lois could rest. She lay back in bed and entertained her visitors, accepting flowers and gifts for her tiny daughter.

It was only when she got Phoebe home that she realised just how much work a baby made. Four-hourly feeding seemed a treadmill, and she had all the bottles to sterilise and feeds to make up in between.

The two daily helps her mother had found for her continued to come on alternate mornings and do most of the housework. But they couldn't stop the sitting room, which used to look like an illustration from *House and Garden*, becoming strewn with infant paraphernalia.

Graham came home from work and had to remove napkins and

matinée jackets, feeders and bibs from his chair before he could sit down.

'I think you ought to advertise for a nanny, Lois,' he said, getting up again to dislodge Phoebe's silver-backed hairbrush which had slid down the arm of his chair.

Graham said he adored his daughter, but he didn't want too many signs of her about his home. Lois felt he was being selfish because he wanted his comfortable life to continue. He left all the baby care to her.

'You know more about babies,' he explained. 'All that time doing paediatrics must be a great help to you now.'

Lois sniffed back her resentment. As if experience in dealing with children's ailments was any help at all when it came to this endless round of feeding and napkin-changing. She knew that when it came to motherhood, there was a huge gap between her expectations and her actual experience.

She might just have been able to bear it if Phoebe had slept between feeds, but she cried endlessly. It drove Lois to frenzy, and nothing she did could soothe the child.

The broken nights were the worst part. Graham began to grumble if she didn't get up quickly to see to the baby in the night. It didn't matter how many times Phoebe woke them, he expected Lois to go to her.

'I've got a busy day ahead,' he'd mutter from the pillow without opening his eyes. 'You'll be able to have a rest when she has her nap tomorrow.'

Lois could feel anger building up inside her. She needed more support than she was getting. She hated being at her baby's beck and call.

To make matters worse, Phoebe had eczema on her face and napkin rash on her bottom. As a doctor, Lois felt she ought to be able to cure both. When other mothers had brought their babies in like that, she'd put it down to poor hygiene and lack of care. Now she found that she couldn't cure Phoebe and she was exhausted by it all.

Her mother was working down at the surgery again. Standing in for Lois, she'd said, so that she could return to her job when she wanted to. But of course it was for Bill's convenience she did it.

'You need a nanny to help you,' Victoria told her. 'Have you tried to get one?'

'Of course I've tried.' Lois snapped back. 'I've interviewed four and each one seems worse than the last. I even offered the job to one, but she had another baby to see before she would commit herself.'

'And she chose the other?' Victoria shook her head in despair. 'Help of any sort in the house is difficult to get these days, but it's not impossible. Keep trying.'

'Bringing up a child seems like a twenty-year sentence,' Lois burst out petulantly. Her mother gave her an odd look.

'More like a lifetime's sentence,' she returned. 'I'll see what I can do about a nanny.'

Her grandmother came to see her from time to time, but she sat down in an armchair and offered advice instead of practical help. She expected to be served with tea and cake and wanted Lois to sit down and chat with her, as though she had all the time in the world.

Graham still expected her to run a trouble-free home and have a meal ready to put on the table when he came home. She couldn't do it.

'A baby will turn us into a real family. Bring us much closer together,' Lois had whispered to him when she was pregnant. Now she found that the very opposite was happening. She was always carping and miserable; Graham was not enjoying himself either, and began to make excuses to go out without her in the evenings.

Lois began to feel cut off from real life. She was far too intelligent to get down to the level of looking after babies. It was a waste of her education.

She looked a mess. She had no time for hairdressers and beauty care now. She hated not to be dressed up and out and about.

She'd thought when she had her baby she'd have everything life could offer. Instead, she felt she'd made big sacrifices for nothing.

Now it was too late, she knew that motherhood didn't suit her. She'd made a mistake. This wasn't what she wanted from life at all.

CHAPTER EIGHTEEN

On Monday morning, Jill got up a little earlier than usual and took Lois a cup of tea when she took Gran's breakfast tray up.

Lois hadn't got out of bed at all the day before, and had hardly eaten any of the food Jill had taken up to her.

She asked: 'Are you well enough to go to work this morning, Lois?'

It was perfectly possible for the rest of them to do Lois's work between them, but Selma needed to know because she'd have to reschedule the appointments.

'Of course I am.' Lois was aggressive. 'Perfectly well.'

She'd come down to breakfast looking grim and white-faced.

'Gran says she's a bit better,' Jill told her.

Lois barely spoke to either of them. She picked up her medical case and went out to her car.

'Not in a very good mood.' Nat lowered his paper, and smiled sadly at Jill.

As soon as she set foot on the surgery steps, Jill could hear Lois's voice raised in complaint.

'What's the matter with you this morning?' she was shouting at Selma.

'I won't be a minute.' Selma was flicking through the filing cabinet, getting out records. 'Not quite ready yet.'

'Where's my coffee? Isn't that ready either? I don't know what you're thinking of, Selma.'

Lois turned on Jill and hissed: 'Too busy painting her fingernails. Could do with keeping her mind on the job.'

'We're early,' Jill tried to placate her.

The phone rang and Selma turned away to answer it. Lois clucked with impatience.

Polly came from the kitchen. 'Here's your coffee, Dr Benbow.'

'Thank you.' Lois snatched the china cup and saucer from the tin tray, leaving three mugs.

'I might as well start work.' She took her pile of records. 'You can bring the rest in, Selma, when you've got them organised.'

When Lois had gone, Polly's lips formed the words: 'What's upset her?'

Jill helped herself to a mug of coffee. 'Lois isn't very well.'

'Your stepmother . . . She and Selma . . .' Polly was whispering.

'She's giving Selma a bit of stick? I had noticed.'

'They used to get on.' Polly's pale face turned pink with embarrassment. 'Selma's very easy-going . . .'

'Lois hasn't been well over the weekend.'

'Been going on longer than that. Haven't you heard?' Polly whispered. 'It's Selma's new boyfriend. Well, man friend really. Your mother's bound to take it hard, isn't she?'

'What do you mean?'

But Titch and Miles were clattering up the hall. Polly offered them the coffee she'd made earlier and they went off to make some more.

As Jill sipped hers, she watched Selma writing in the appointments book, and wondered why Lois could care who her men friends were.

Suddenly she was almost choking, unable to take her eyes from the pen Selma was using.

She recognised it instantly. There were not many pens like that about. Engraved gold case. Expensive. Not new. Dad had been complaining he hadn't seen his pen for several days.

Jill was trying to weigh up the significance of finding that Selma had it. She'd never mentioned Selma to her father, but of course he knew her.

So far as she was aware, Dad hadn't been here in the surgery since Bill Goodbody's retirement. He was hardly likely to have been in Selma's flat recently, unless . . .

Did this mean a new and closer relationship? She found that hard to believe. She held her breath, hardly daring to look at Selma now.

Polly had been embarrassed and hadn't wanted to say too much. Was this what she'd meant?

It could be. Jill felt the blood coursing through her veins. Dad wasn't sleeping with Lois any more. Often he was out in the evenings, until very late. He said he was at work, but . . .

If this was his problem, Selma's position here would make it doubly embarrassing for Lois. No wonder he couldn't talk about it. Jill had been seeking problems in his business, even though he kept telling her it was making a healthy profit.

This would explain why Lois was agitated and upset, and why she was hateful to Selma.

Was Dad in love with Selma? She still couldn't believe it. But if Selma was what Dad wanted, Jill couldn't blame him. She was chatty and outgoing, friendly and easy to get on with. The very opposite of Lois. She could understand the attraction.

Selma looked up and saw her staring at the pen.

'Yes,' she smiled. 'Silly to use it here, isn't it?'

Jill took a deep breath. She had to know. 'Better not let Lois see it. You don't want her to know how things stand. Only make it more obvious.'

Selma pulled a face. 'Yes, you've heard rumours then? He warned me they'd be rife.'

She opened her desk drawer, found her handbag, put the pen safely inside. Then she reached for a ballpoint. They kept a mugful by the phone, each one advertising some drug company product.

Jill didn't know what to say. She felt overwhelmed. It put a new light on Dad's problems. She wasn't going to think of him and the complications this affair could bring to her own life. It could break up his marriage, yet leave her as Lois's partner in the practice. She still couldn't believe it.

She swallowed hard. 'I might as well start too.'

She scooped her pile of records from Selma's desk, collected her first patient from the waiting room, and led the way up to her room.

Morning surgery was over for Jill. She went down to the kitchen for coffee and found that Titch and Miles had already had theirs and gone out.

'Your mother's still at it,' Selma said. 'Two more to see. I've never known her to be so slow.'

'As I said, she's not well.'

Jill hadn't had time to think about what she should say to Selma. She still found it hard to believe.

Neither did she want to sit and chat to Lois. She took her coffee back upstairs to her desk.

When, a few minutes later, Selma buzzed through to tell her that Felix was on the phone, she was glad she was upstairs where she could talk to him without Lois overhearing what she said.

'Hello. How do you feel about coming swimming with me tonight?' Felix sounded energetic. 'I thought of going to the pool at West Kirby.'

Jill wanted a break from her family, and he couldn't have suggested anything better as far as she was concerned.

'Love to. You said you were going on Saturday. Did you?'

'No, it wouldn't have been any fun without you. I took my father out instead. We'll have a swim, then a bite to eat afterwards. There are lots of little restaurants round there.'

Jill felt cheered. She looked forward to it all afternoon. Felix was in the car park of the sports complex when she drove in, and beamed with pleasure when he caught sight of her. He indicated a space at the far end where she could park, then ran after her.

The kiss he gave her as she got out of her car left her in no doubt that he was equally delighted to have her company. Then, after a hot day in the surgery, it felt wonderful to be pulling herself through the cool water.

Felix was forcing the pace, trying to overtake her, feet flailing, arms curving through the water, splashing up a huge amount of foam. All the agility he showed on dry land had gone. He was using brute strength now.

When he reached the shallow end, another swimmer got in his way, balking his progress. Felix was laughing when he turned to look for her.

'I can beat you if I really try,' he said when she caught him up. 'For a girl you can certainly swim.'

The male body was made familiar by her work. Mostly the ones she saw sagged with disuse, age or illness. Felix was strong, with broad, muscular shoulders. With his hair plastered to his head and rivulets of water running down his face, he radiated health and vitality.

There had not been many men in her life. A few that hadn't got going. Casualties of the long hours she'd worked and the studying she'd had to do.

She'd had only one serious love affair, and that was long over. Mark had never been like Felix. A fellow medical student he'd been as eager as she was and he'd made all the running. They'd both understood the way the human body worked and felt there was no point in beating about the bush. It hadn't lasted, but it had been good at the time. They'd parted without too many regrets.

After her first evening out with Felix, she expected to be bowled over. She'd thought that just possibly he might become a permanent fixture in her life. It wasn't the sort of thing she could be absolutely certain about, not without knowing him for longer, but she was hopeful.

She was glad to find he didn't want to leap into bed after having a couple of meals with her. She wouldn't have thought highly of him if he had. But now, well, the sixties' sex revolution had certainly passed him by. He was going no further than a chaste kiss.

She'd been out with him many times and enjoyed his company. She needed somebody uncomplicated and open in her life to counterbalance the new job and the heavy going at home.

Everything about Felix pleased her, but he was holding back, and it wasn't all physical. Mentally, he was erecting barriers. She could feel them. Great walls between them.

He was always pressing her to go somewhere else with him, but she felt their relationship was not progressing as she'd hoped. They were marking time, stuck in a rut. Almost, as though he didn't want her any closer.

Jill was feeling a little let down. She couldn't understand him.

Worse, she was afraid she wanted more of Felix than he was prepared to give.

Jill was beginning to feel wound up. Nothing was turning out as she expected. On Monday night, she'd been on call and had been up three times. She'd felt a bit heavy the next morning, but comforted herself with the thought of having an early night.

On Tuesday it was Lois's turn to take night calls. Jill had gone to bed early. She'd heard the phone ring, but turned over and was settling back to sleep again.

Suddenly her bedroom door crashed back and the light was switched on. She was blinking up at Lois.

'I think I've got the flu. I'm all shaky. I can't possibly go out to New Ferry. You'll have to go for me.'

Jill stifled a groan. 'What time is it?'

'Two o'clock. I'm not well enough, I don't think I'd manage the drive. Here's the name and address. It's a child, a temperature and abdominal pain.'

'All right,' she said, swinging her legs out of bed.

'And when you come back, I'll switch the phone through to you so you can take any further calls.'

As it turned out, that meant she'd had to go out again at five thirty.

Jill didn't mind so much doing the calls, or getting up early to see to Gran before going to work. But Lois was ungrateful and difficult at breakfast, and then as she reached the surgery, her mood swung the other way and she was as lively as a cricket. It left Jill feeling like a zombie all day.

At home, she and Nat were treating Lois with kid gloves; at the surgery, everybody seemed wary of her.

Jill was going to have another meal with Felix. Dad had recommended a bistro in Oxton Village. This time she booked the table and arranged to meet him there.

She was parking her Mini at the kerb when she saw the dark green Triumph Stag in front. Felix was locking it.

His face lit up when he saw her and he came striding across with the supple agility she recognised so well. He took her arm.

The bistro had once been a shop and was in the middle of a parade. The window was filled with pot plants and curtained in gingham.

'I've got something to celebrate,' he told her. 'The *Times* wants a weekly article from me. Things are looking up.'

'Champagne?'

'I don't know that I can run to that.'

'Then let me.' But there was no champagne on the wine list.

'Let's settle for claret, it'll go better with the steak.' He smiled and told her more about his work. It was giving her an insight into a wider world.

The food was really good, each dish cooked to order. Felix made it ll seem fun. She was mesmerised by his eager smiles, while all the time, his brown eyes held hers across the table. There were golden lights in their depths and they were telling her what she wanted to know. He was as smitten with her as she was with him. At moments like this she felt very close to him.

She didn't want him to put space between them again. For her, Felix was very special. It didn't make sense to let their relationship drift on, getting nowhere.

The more she saw of him, the more certain she was that he was right for her. She wanted to pin him down, know where they stood, and she knew there was one way she could force his hand.

She finished off her rich chocolate pudding, and looking him in the eye, said: 'Felix, don't you want the things other men want?'

It took him a while to empty his mouth. 'Women too, you mean?' He was sparring with her. Putting her off.

'Sex is what I mean.' He'd filled his mouth again and almost stopped chewing. 'Well, don't you?' She was exasperated.

''Course I do. I really miss my own flat. Here it's so hard. The set-up, I mean.'

'Can't you get a place of your own?'

'No, my father . . . I have to stay with him. For the time being, anyway. What about you?'

Jill thought about having a place of her own. She let the drawbacks and advantages run through her mind.

'Apart from everything else, I'd love to get away from Lois. I see enough of her at the surgery.'

But it would also take her away from Dad, and she had to sort him out. Then there was Victoria to consider.

'Difficult for me, too, just now. We could go on holiday. You haven't had one this summer, have you?'

'No. Haven't got round to it.' He was toying with his glass.

'Would you like to? I think, if I asked, I could get a few days off.'

He was staring at his glass, swirling the wine round as though that was the most important thing in the world to him.

'We should get away on our own, Felix. Perhaps book a holiday cottage not too far away?' Somewhere they could do more than kiss each other. Privacy was what they needed.

She also needed a break from the worries at the surgery and at Links View.

She wasn't sure what Felix needed to get away from, because he wasn't forthcoming. In fact, he was downright secretive, never talking of his own affairs. But in the right circumstances, she was determined that he would.

'I don't think I can go away.' His voice sounded stiff and somehow unyielding.

She recoiled, feeling rejected. She'd not expected him to turn her down.

'It's because I'm working freelance. For myself now.'

She protested, 'Surely that should make it easier? You don't have to tie in with other people to do the job.'

He sighed again, ruffled his wavy hair, uneasy now. 'I haven't achieved the income I once earned. I need to stay at my desk.'

She had to try again. 'Wouldn't a change of scene give you new ideas? Refresh you?'

'I'd love to, but not at the moment. I only wish I could.'

'A weekend then? Surely to be away for a weekend wouldn't hurt?'

He looked thoroughly uncomfortable and wouldn't meet her eyes. It could only mean that he didn't want more of her company.

When the meal ended it was not late.

'I don't feel ready to go home,' Felix told her.

Jill wasn't so sure. If it had been anyone but Felix she'd give up on him. She seemed to be spending her life trying to gain the confidences of those she cared about. It was hard work. Outside on the pavement, he hung on to her arm.

'There's no promenade to stroll along here,' he mourned.

'Having two cars doesn't help.' Now she was sounding grumpy.

'I should have walked, I live quite near.'

She hesitated, half tempted to say she'd like an early night.

'Take yours home then,' she suggested. 'I'll follow you.'

It seemed barely a mile along well-established, wide residential roads before she saw the Triumph turn into a driveway. Jill stopped on the road, switched off the engine and looked up at his home. Like most of the others they had passed, it was a large, solid and mature semi. Lois would dismiss it as being social class two or three. Inferior to Links View.

Felix came crunching back across the gravel. She half expected him to ask her in for another cup of coffee, but he got into the passenger seat. He must have seen her looking at the house.

'It could do with a coat of paint. Inside and out. Dad's done nothing to it for years.'

In the gathering darkness she hadn't noticed. 'How is your father? Is he better?'

It took him a long time to answer. He seemed to be struggling to make up his mind.

'I'm worried about him.'

'Where shall we go now?' She was reaching to turn the ignition key but he put a hand on her arm.

'Would you give me your opinion on something? Your medical

215

opinion?' His face was only a few inches from her own. His eyes shone with intensity.

Jill felt immediately wary. She'd asked for this. She should have kept a closer watch on her tongue. Her voice sounded unnatural.

'This is about your father? The treatment he received from Lois?'

'Yes. You already know?' His face lit up with eager relief.

'No. No, nothing.'

She straightened up, moved herself a few inches away from him. This was what she'd been trying to avoid all along.

His eagerness had faded. 'We've got to talk, Jill. Have this out.'

'I don't see . . .'

'Please . . . Let me tell you about it.'

She made herself say: 'All right.' It sounded grudging, but it made him lean forward and kiss her cheek. 'Who does he see?'

'It used to be your stepmother.'

'I gathered that.'

'He consulted Miles Sutton once or twice. Now he sees Cuthbert Meadows.'

'Why don't you ask him, then? If he's been looking after your father, he'll have all the facts at his fingertips.'

'I have, and he won't tell me.'

Alarm bells were ringing in her head. She pushed herself free of his arm. Opened the window wide. The night air was cold.

'He won't discuss anything your stepmother did or didn't do. He's expansive enough about the treatment Dad's having now and what the future holds, but that isn't what I want.'

Jill was suddenly seething inside. Was she making a fool of herself? Felix had laughed and told her she was sweeping him off his feet. She'd tingled with excitement and believed him. But was he deliberately turning on the charm to get her on his side? So that he could use her?

'Let me explain it to you. It's been worrying me, Jill.'

'Go on.' She was on her guard now. She hoped he wasn't going to ask her to spy on her partners.

'My father saw your stepmother over many months. He had frequent boils on his arms and face, and he was given penicillin to clear them up.'

'That's usual.'

'But he also told your stepmother he was losing weight and generally feeling tired and unwell. He was given a tonic for that.'

'How old is he?'

'Fifty-five. He complained of indigestion and nausea. A dry, sore tongue and a constant thirst. For all of which he received prescriptions.'

'Did he have any tests?' Jill could feel her stomach tightening with tension. The words 'constant thirst' would have made her test his urine for sugar. If sugar had been there, and perhaps even if it hadn't, she'd have organised a blood-sugar tolerance test for him.

'No, nothing. Then he had acute pains in his right leg and a terrible infection in his foot. He went down to the surgery and showed it to Lois. He was given more penicillin.

'I'd come up to Birkenhead for the weekend. Dad was in so much pain from his foot, I called the surgery and asked for a visit on Saturday night.

'Cuthbert Meadows came and put him into hospital immediately. He had diabetic gangrene. He's had his leg amputated and is now on insulin.'

Jill felt her skin crawl with horror. She was appalled at what she was hearing. What Felix had been describing was the usual and frequent symptoms of diabetes.

'Naturally, I feel very aggrieved about this. I can't tell you how my father feels. If his diabetes had been diagnosed earlier, would you agree, medically speaking, that the amputation could have been avoided?'

'This is what you were trying to discuss with Lois at the retirement tea?' Jill felt sick.

'I had to try. She refused to see me in the surgery the week before. We could have talked about it reasonably in private, but she wouldn't. To my mind that confirms her negligence.'

Jill put her arms over the steering wheel and rested her head on them. She could understand Felix being bitter, but he was putting her in a terrible position.

'I know, Jill. I know what I'm asking is difficult because she's not only your stepmother but your partner too.'

She felt too choked to answer.

'What I want to do is look at his medical notes. Could you arrange for me to see them? Let me make copies.'

'Felix!'

'I have to make sure of the facts. If I'm right I'll write an article exposing both her and Miles Sutton.'

Jill felt hot with fury. 'I suppose you think it would make a good story? Exposing the underside of the medical profession.'

'Too good for the local paper. I'd sent to the *Times*.'

'I can't do it,' Jill gasped. 'I'd like to help. I know how you must feel, but . . . No, I can't.'

'They shouldn't be allowed to practise, not after what they've done to my father. If the facts support it, I'll bring a case against them for damages.'

Jill lifted her head to look at him. 'It's difficult to prove medical negligence, Felix.'

217

'It certainly is when I'm not allowed to see the records, and the doctors won't even talk to me.'

'If it wasn't my own practice, and my own mother . . .'

'But then you wouldn't be able to help. Not in the same way. I don't want to make trouble for you, Jill. It's the last thing I want.'

'I know what you want. To get your own back on Lois. You feel your father's been badly treated. Felix, every case presents differently. In your father's . . . It might not be as straightforward as you say.'

'Diabetes is fairly common, isn't it? You see plenty of it?'

'Other things can cloud the diagnosis. Possibly the signs and symptoms didn't add up.'

His brown eyes searched hers. They were no longer filled with affection.

'You won't help me?'

Jill sighed and shook her head.

'I thought you might be different.'

'What would my partners think of me? They expect loyalty. If I let you . . .'

'You're worried about what your partners think? Worried about your career? But my father's whole life is ruined. He's only fifty-five.'

Jill was shaking. 'People expect doctors to treat every case successfully. Do detectives always get their man? No! Doctors don't always get it right either.'

Felix's eyes were suddenly burning with resentment.

'You're like the rest of them, closing ranks to cover the mistakes your colleagues have made. All you doctors do it. You get away with murder and I know why. You do it because you've all felt guilt at first hand. You all know that something you did, or something you failed to do, has harmed a patient. You've all killed or maimed for life. Haven't you?'

Jill could hardly breathe. She couldn't believe Felix was turning on her like this.

'Not yet,' she retorted. But what he said was true. Hadn't she felt that herself?

She'd never forget that most awful moment. It had come in her first weeks of being junior house officer, and had given her nightmares for months. It had taught her to keep a firm grip on her tongue when talking to patients.

She'd been trying to explain to a newly married woman that because her husband had a psychiatric history going back many years, it would affect the outcome of his present bout of depression. Take longer for him to get back to work.

'He's never had anything like this wrong with him before,' she'd

218

assured Jill. 'He's been in the navy. Until now, he's hardly ever had a day off work.'

Jill glanced down at the hospital notes before her. She wasn't wrong. 'This is his fourth admission.'

'You mean he's been like this before? He's been here in this hospital?' The poor girl had been horrified. 'I didn't know!'

For Jill, it was only too obvious what she'd done. She'd destroyed for ever any trust that girl had had in her husband. It was all too easy to do. Often there were no warning signs along the way.

Felix told her angrily. 'If you haven't done it yet, it's because you're just starting. You will.'

'I hope not.' Jill was struggling to control her tears. She hated fighting with him like this.

'Your mother knows all about it. Your partners will have discussed it between themselves and decided to keep it under wraps. You did say she didn't like you coming out with me. That's all part of closing ranks.'

Jill pulled herself together. 'There's not much love lost between her and Miles Sutton.'

'That doesn't matter. One doctor will always protect another. Even if they hate each other's guts.'

'No,' Jill protested.

'For God's sake! It's what you're doing now. You're protecting Lois against me. You're putting her interests above mine.'

That reminded Jill of what Gran had said about protecting Lois. Felix was right. All doctors did cover for each other.

'I was going to ask you to come in and meet Dad.' His voice sounded strangled. 'I don't suppose you want to now.'

'No,' she said. 'I'm not in the mood.'

'I'm sorry,' Felix said stiffly. 'I rather hoped you'd put my interests higher.'

He got out of the car, shut the door gently and went striding up the drive to the house.

CHAPTER NINETEEN

Jill didn't sleep well. She had a tormented night thinking about Felix and his father. The last thing she wanted was to intervene between them and Lois.

She was finding Lois difficult enough without giving her another reason to dislike her. She couldn't afford an open rift.

She told herself she was an idiot. She'd known all along that Felix had this problem. She'd deliberately turned her back on it. Fool that she was, she'd thought it wouldn't affect their relationship. Well, she was wiser now.

Hadn't she been cross with Dad for saying: 'I turn my back on Lois's problems. That's my way.'

She'd told him tartly enough: 'It's the wrong way. If you do that they'll resurface and cause more trouble. I think problems should be faced, discussed and sorted out. That's the only way to settle them.'

Then she'd made exactly the same mistake. It left her feeling unsure of Felix. Unable to get close to him.

She'd attached herself to him like a lovelorn schoolgirl. He'd seemed so eager, so taken with her, but there had been things they couldn't talk about. Things that were important to Felix. What she'd done had kept the relationship superficial.

Even worse, if what he'd told her was true, she could understand his feelings. It sounded as though he did have a case for negligence. And by his own admission, he desperately wanted to get a sight of his father's records. She didn't want to think he'd been using her to do that.

In the morning, she set out to the surgery five minutes earlier than usual. She wanted to get there before her partners. There was one way the problem might be resolved. She was hoping she could assure Felix that he was wrong. That Lois had acted with reasonable care.

She went straight to the office. She was glad to find Selma busy on the phone, her head bent over the appointments book. Jill slid open the drawer in the filing cabinet that held the records of Lois's patients, and flicked through the names beginning with K. The envelopes were jammed in tight.

She heard the phone go down and felt a shiver of guilt. It wasn't unusual for her to check something in a patient's notes. But Peter Kingsley wasn't her patient.

Perhaps Selma wouldn't notice whose records she was reading. It took her some time to find what she was looking for. The envelope was stuffed full of notes.

She checked, too, that Felix was not a patient on the practice. He wasn't.

When she looked up, Selma's lush brown eyes were on the envelope in her hand.

'I wondered how long it would take you to get round to that. There's been a bit of bother about him recently.'

Jill resisted an urge to hide the records behind her back. 'What sort of bother?'

'A clash. Just before you started, I thought the four of them had fallen out for good.'

Selma's lashes swept down. They'd been expertly groomed with mascara. 'Things went wrong. You know.'

'So I gather.'

Jill ran upstairs to her room to read the notes in private. It didn't please her that what Felix had told her was essentially correct. It seemed that Lois had missed a fairly obvious case of diabetes.

She shivered, hoping such a thing would never happen to her. It would be on her conscience for ever.

She was late finishing morning surgery. Because Lois had missed an obvious diagnosis she found herself checking everything twice. Lois and Miles were finishing their coffee when she went down to the kitchen.

'Has Titch gone?' she asked.

'No, had a long list this morning. Still one patient in the waiting room.'

Jill had another cup of coffee when Selma and Polly came in to have theirs. By the time Titch came for his, Polly and Selma had gone to file away the records used that morning.

'Titch,' she said, 'I need some advice. What would you do in my position?' She pushed Peter Kingsley's notes across the table to him.

'Oh, dear.' He sat down beside her. The chair seemed too small to support his weight.

'I'm afraid Lois dropped a clanger over this patient. Handled it badly too. Disastrous for the poor devil.'

Jill told him of her friendship with Felix. Of what he'd asked her to do. Sympathetic eyes behind horn-rimmed spectacles regarded her seriously.

'So you're caught up in it on a personal level? That's never easy and you're not going to like what I say. We doctors have to stand apart from our patients.'

222

'Peter Kingsley is not my patient. I've never even met him.'

'But he's a patient of this practice. And you're getting involved with him through his son.'

'Yes.'

'You'll have divided loyalties. Stepmother and practice on one side, boyfriend on the other. My advice would be to cut yourself off from the Kingsleys.'

Jill felt a surge of pain. 'You don't understand. I'm fond of Felix.'

'I understand all right. I said you wouldn't like it. I take it you don't want to cut yourself off from the practice.'

'Of course not.'

'Jill, you could find yourself in the centre of a maelstrom if you let yourself be persuaded. If you talk to this fellow about the case, you could be called as a witness – against us. Could even be subpoenaed to appear in court.

'Whichever way it goes, you'll get in deeper. You'll be torn apart. You'll feel sympathy and have loyalty to both sides.

'You must explain this to him. Refuse to show him the records. Without seeing them he can do nothing. Even if he saw them I doubt he could prove anything. Lois was full of explanations as to why it happened. What the man complained of didn't add up. He never mentioned having a thirst.'

'She didn't ask the right questions.'

'Perhaps not, but we all get patients who don't conform to the norm. We're all kept guessing from time to time.'

'It seems so obvious. If she'd tested his . . .'

'Jill, we all get the odd case that slips past us. We don't think quickly enough. Or we haven't seen it before, or it's rare. Nothing will bring Kingsley's leg back. We must concentrate on helping him all we can in the future.'

Jill swallowed. She didn't doubt what he said. It was good advice.

'I told Lois she should have talked to the son. Admitted negligence and apologised. If you agree with somebody who's angry, it takes the wind out of their sails.'

He smiled gently. 'He probably wouldn't have sued.'

'Thanks.' It didn't please her, but it was what she'd expected him to say. She'd tell Felix he was on his own with this. That was, if he ever came near her again.

Titch took off his spectacles. Polished them, blinked at her myopically.

'We doctors can get into terrible difficulties. One way or another.'

Jill still felt raw about Felix, and was worried stiff about Dad. Then Lois was bickering with Victoria, bickering with everybody if it came to that, and Victoria was growing more agitated.

'Throwing them off is never easy.'

After all these years, she felt the dust should have settled on Titch's problems, but he seemed to want to talk about them.

'Sometimes we have to learn to live with them.'

'What else could you have done, Titch? You had to earn a living and there was nothing else you felt you could do. When you're struck off the register . . .'

His chair creaked a protest as he eased his bulk round. 'Not struck off any more. I was reinstated. Years ago.'

Jill sat up straighter. 'I don't understand.'

'After three years I applied to have my name put back on. It was refused. But when I re-applied two years after that, they thought I'd been adequately disciplined.'

Jill frowned. 'Then why are you still using the name Cuthbert Meadows?'

'It's not that easy to change your name. Not for a man. A woman can get married and do it. But I have three thousand patients who know me as Meadows. Not to mention the Family Practitioner Committee.

'Couldn't just announce that I wanted to be known as Sinclair in future, could I? Not without admitting what I'd been doing for the past five years. I'd have been promptly struck off again for that.'

Jill stared at him. 'You could have packed up here and gone some-where else, another town where you weren't known.'

'I meant to. It was always my intention. Couldn't wait to be reinstated so I could be off. Then when I was, I was settled here. It didn't seem strange to be addressed as Meadows any more.

'I'd married Esme. She was settled in her part-time public health job. I'd bought a house and I was a partner here.

'There was nowhere else I wanted to go. All my friends are here. I still meant to, of course, I just kept putting it off. I'd dug a comfort-able rut for myself, and I didn't want to make the effort.'

'What a tangle. You could have gone back to Ekbo when you were first struck off. Few would have heard of your troubles there.'

'That isn't allowed either, of course, but I almost did. I wrote to them, but there was nobody left that I knew. Bertie's trouble cleared us all out in a rush.'

'Would that have mattered?'

'Probably not, they were always desperate for staff, but I didn't enjoy it the first time. I should have gone, all the same.'

'You could have worked there until your name was put back on.'

'I wasn't thinking clearly by then. When something like that blows up in your face, you soon find out who your friends are.'

'Victoria?' Jill said. 'And the mutual support group.'

'Victoria was still in Hamilton Square then. She rang me and said: "Come and stay with me. You know there's plenty of room here." It seemed like an offer of sanctuary at the time. I had to get away from the press.

'She was wonderful. She held me together. Her and old Bill Goodbody. It's good to have friends at a time like that. I suppose you think it's stupid to lose one's head over a woman? No matter how beautiful.'

Jill said: 'I expect you were tempted.'

'I was always tempted.' He half smiled, pulled a face.

'It wasn't the first time?'

'You must know it wasn't. The old newspapers will have told you that. All my temptations were chronicled.'

'Victoria says you were always one for the ladies. A bit fast. Janet thinks so too.'

He sighed. 'Too old for that now, of course, and if I had my time over again, I'd be stronger. It ruined everything for me.

'I was big-headed, Jill. Doing wonderfully well. Enjoying myself. All private patients in Harley Street. I was making a mint. Bought myself a Rolls. Thought I had it made.'

'What happened?'

'You read about it. All blew up in my face. Very embarrassing all round. Even Georgina couldn't take it. I thought we'd survive anything, but no.'

'Why not?'

'All the horrible facts coming out in court. Some of them were being proved. She was accused of attempting to poison her husband. I was accused of helping her.'

'You didn't?'

'Of course not! I was guilty of having improper relations with a patient, but innocent of that. I wouldn't have dreamed of it. We're all trained to save life, not extinguish it.'

Jill felt he was transparently honest.

'I believe she took it from my bag.'

'She did try, then?'

'She denied it, but I think so. We were both found not guilty on that, but how could I trust her afterwards?'

'You must have had a terrible time.'

'The stress was dreadful. There were other reasons too. Georgina was used to the bright lights. London restaurants and expensive clothes. She didn't care for Birkenhead, she wanted to have a good time.

'Didn't care much about me, once I could no longer afford it. She wasn't cut out for a life of privation.' He took off his glasses and polished them.

'Some people make an awful mess of their lives, Jill. You must make sure you don't.'

He smiled. 'My wife, Chloe, wanted a divorce. Not that I blame her. The other women turned her off. That and having every detail of our private life emblazoned in the papers.'

'You married again, though.'

'Yes, Esme's father was a doctor who died out in Ekbo. Not in my time, but Victoria knew the family.'

'She introduced you?'

'We had to go to Gretna Green to get married.'

'Very romantic.'

'Not really. Had to use my own name for that. Couldn't do it here, too many people know me as Meadows. Scared I'd be rumbled.'

'Titch, you've come out of it all right. Both feet on the ground. I'd say you were well adjusted.'

He snorted. 'I'm not out of it. That's the problem. The fear is always lurking at the back of my mind.'

'You have to take a bit of needle from Miles.'

'About the drug company lunches? At first, I avoided my fellow GPs, but not now. Miles is just prodding me.

'We've all aged. Altered so much. I know in my mind it's most unlikely I'll meet somebody who knew Bertie well enough to recognise that I'm not him.

'But when I'm feeling stressed or tired, I get anxious, and I find myself looking over my shoulder. Scared the past is going to resurface.'

'You can still move and practise in another town.'

'I don't suppose I will now. I'll retire in a few more years.'

'Then forget it, Titch.'

'I wish I could. Too much to remind me.'

Jill tossed and turned in bed again that night. She felt that the atmosphere was becoming as charged as a pressure cooker, both at home and at work. Everything was getting on top of her.

Because she couldn't sleep she had plenty of time to think things over. She was missing Felix's company, and made up her mind that tomorrow she'd ring him and apologise.

She also decided that Selma knew a lot more about what went on in the practice than she did. She should try and draw her out. It wouldn't be hard. She could, given the right opportunity, ask about her men friends too. Selma was the sort to let it all come out. She wouldn't have secrets.

Instead of starting her surgery, Jill hung around in the receptionist's room, waiting for a chance to have a word with Selma. But the phone never stopped ringing, and Selma was kept busy answering it.

Titch was leaning against the filing cabinets drinking coffee. Behind his spectacles, his eyes were still uneasy.

Jill was about to give up until later, when Polly, the red-haired receptionist bustled in and rammed her handbag in a drawer.

'Good morning. Sorry I'm late. Is it today we're going for a pub lunch?'

'Yes.' Selma's face lit up at the prospect. 'You coming with us, Titch?'

'No,' he said. 'Too much girls' talk.'

'How about you, Jill? We have a lunch out once in a while. We're going to the Queen's Arms.'

'With you and Polly?'

'Edith will be there too, and some of the district nurses. Perhaps the health visitor. Anybody who can find the time.'

Jill didn't hesitate. It looked like the opportunity she needed. 'You're on.'

'See you there, twelve thirty.'

When Jill found her way to the Queen's Arms, she found Selma in the bar ordering orange juice for herself.

The group had pushed three tables together. Jill was introduced to those she hadn't yet met. There were the three receptionists, three district nurses, the bath nurse and the health visitor.

Against the background noise of the bar, Jill couldn't always hear what was being said down the other end of the circle, but it was girl talk.

'Selma, you look very elegant. Where do you find all these clothes?'

'Clothes are my passion. I work at it.'

'You've got the figure to show them off.'

Selma laughed. 'I've lost a stone and a half. Had to work at that too.

'How did you do it?'

'Went to Lydia's slimming club and ate less.'

Lydia was the health visitor. She said: 'I hold her up as an example to every class. If you want to look like Selma, at the doctor's, I tell them, just take my advice on healthy eating and exercise.'

'Did you take Lydia's advice, Selma?'

'Still do. All the time.'

'You'd never believe she was older than I am.' Lydia laughed.

Jill studied them both. Lydia was middle-aged and dumpy, Selma seemed decades younger.

'I wish there were more like you, Selma. Too many give up.'

'I don't know what I'm doing here stuffing my face again.'

Polly was all giggles. 'Lydia, if you know how to turn yourself into a sylph, how come you're still a bit of a pudding?'

'I can't stop eating, not if I have to work. I've got to keep my energy levels up. And I've given up smoking because of the health education I do. Couldn't be seen lighting up. Not when I have to come out so strongly against it.'

227

'It's nothing to do with health education.' Selma laughed too. She always seemed to sparkle in company. 'There are seven deadly sins. If your failing is gluttony, you'll never be slim. If, like me, your fault is vanity, then you will.'

'My advice is good.'

'Your cucumber slices aren't doing much for the bags under my eyes.'

'You haven't got bags under your eyes.'

'I'd like to try cosmetic surgery, but I don't dare. I'm scared of the knife.'

'Selma, you don't need it.'

'I've got bags in the mornings. I look terrible when I first get up.'

'We're none of us at our best then.'

Jill laughed. When she'd first joined the practice, Lois had told her that Selma was forty-four years old. She found that hard to believe.

She'd said: 'She looks more than a decade younger than that. No sign of wrinkles or grey hair.'

'She dyes it,' Lois had retorted cattily. 'Selma owes a lot to the art of hairdressing.'

Dad had been with them. He'd said: 'She looks more glamorous now than she did twenty years ago.'

Jill was reminded that Selma had known her family over many years, and that long ago, she'd baby-sat her when Lois and Dad had gone out.

'She owes a lot to artifice of all kinds,' Lois had said. 'And it's taken her time to get her act together. She didn't always do it so well.'

Jill ate baked potato stuffed with prawns. She and Selma declined a pudding. Nobody drank alcohol.

'Why don't you all come back to my place for a cup of coffee,' Selma urged when they'd finished. 'I live quite near.'

Some decided they couldn't spare any more time, but Jill discovered that Selma lived in the complex of flats where she had a visit to make that afternoon, so she went along. The party was reduced to four.

'I moved here after my husband was killed,' Selma told her. 'Decided I'd feel safer up on the third floor like this. The house I lived in was too big for one and it had too many memories.'

Selma was proud of her flat. She led them through the living room, which was bright and sunny, to the kitchen to put the kettle on. Jill felt quite envious. She'd love a place like this of her own, so that she could get away from Lois.

Because she showed interest, Selma said: 'Would you like to see round?'

'Love to.'

'The others have been before.'

What Jill saw made her even more envious. Selma was not only good at presenting herself, she also had a flare for interior decorating. Her style was plain and elegant. She had the flat beautifully furnished.

The bathroom was small. The proliferation of soaps, talcs, jars and bottles of oils, shampoos and conditioners amazed Jill, as did the display of heated rollers, electric crimpers, face and body creams, toners and moisturisers on the dressing table in the airy bedroom.

She laughed, counting up the jars. There were fourteen, and that was without the bottles.

'I once asked a consultant dermatologist who was lecturing us what he considered was the best treatment to keep wrinkles at bay, and skin in prime condition,' she told Selma. 'He said: "Keep it well lubricated with grease." '

'What else?'

'That's what I asked. He said: "More grease." '

'What sort of grease?' Selma's interest was captivated. 'Did you ask that?'

'Yes. He said: "Any sort." He thought petroleum jelly would be as good as anything.'

'Petroleum jelly?' Selma's face registered disgust.

'I see you've got some here.'

'That's for putting on my brows and lashes. To make them shine.'

Jill studied her brows. They did shine. As she stepped backwards to leave, she almost trod on an instrument that had fallen to the carpet. She picked it up, wondering what it was.

'For curling eyelashes.' Selma was laughing at her. 'You stroke on a touch of Vaseline and make them bend up like this.' She demonstrated its use. 'You've got long lashes, they'd show up much more if you got yourself one of these.'

'They're too fair.'

'Use a bit of mascara. Or have them dyed professionally.'

'I'm a babe in arms when it come to make-up.' Jill laughed again. 'I've spent so much time honing the brain cells to pass exams, I've never got round to honing the body for beauty.' Perhaps, if she tried, she could make herself look more experienced, more sophisticated?

But this wasn't what she wanted to talk about. She looked up to find Selma's brown eyes studying her in the mirror. She must try and get something out of her while they were alone.

'Does it ensure a good social life? Putting on the glamour?'

'No. But it makes me feel better about myself. More confident.'

That wasn't leading where she wanted to go. Jill tried again.

'You said you didn't think I'd turn out as a doctor. What was I really like as a child?'

Selma sat back on the edge of her bed.

229

'Nervous. I remember you having terrible nightmares. You'd wake up screaming and there was nothing I could say to comfort you.'

Jill shivered. She felt as though a ghost had stepped over her.

'You clung to your dad.'

She'd known that. 'Dad's lovely. Always has been.' She waited for Selma to rise to that, but she didn't. She had to add: 'What about with Lois?'

Furrows appeared fleetingly on Selma's forehead. 'You seemed terrified of her.'

'Didn't that strike you as odd?'

'I was terrified of her too. Still am.' Selma laughed. 'Lois has a forceful personality. She'll deliver a kick if things don't please her.'

That was the way Jill had seen Lois at first. Now she knew better. It didn't take much to reduce her to a jelly.

'Lois is a nervous wreck,' she said. 'What's going on . . .'

But Selma had had enough, and was leading her back to join the nurses in the living room. They had already made the coffee and were gossiping about the surgery. Jill might hear something interesting from them.

She was listening avidly when in front of her on the coffee table, she noticed the gold fountain pen lying on top of a shopping list.

Her father's pen? Somehow, a liaison with Selma seemed less likely. She was too fond of a giggle for him.

'Another cup of coffee?' Selma looked round at her guests but the nurses were getting up.

'We've got to go or we'll never finish tonight. Work calls, unfortunately.'

Work was calling Jill too, but she ignored it.

'I'd love some more.' Her heart was pounding as she stood to hand her cup to Selma. To start with, she had to make quite sure the pen was Dad's.

As soon as Selma disappeared into her kitchen, she flicked it over with her finger to see the initials.

She let her breath hiss out through her teeth. There were initials, but they read G.J.C. not N.J.R. It was an exact replica, but not Dad's pen at all!

She'd been working herself up for nothing. She didn't know whether to be relieved or otherwise. She'd been coming up with all the wrong answers.

'I should have put that pen out of sight.' She hadn't heard Selma coming back with the coffee. She jumped guiltily.

'I might have known you'd recognise it. Your dad has one exactly the same, hasn't he?' Selma smiled disarmingly. 'But the story's all round the surgery anyway, so what the hell. You know who it belongs to, don't you?'

'No,' Jill said. 'Who?'

'Graham Challoner. The new man in my life. He left it here the other night. He was Lois's first husband, she gave it to him. Lois doesn't put much original thought into her gifts, does she? The same pen, exactly the same model, to consecutive husbands.'

'So that's why she's got it in for you?'

Selma shook her curls back from her face. 'I could have flattened Miles Sutton for telling her. It's just the sort of thing he likes to do, make mischief. It was Lois he wanted to wind up, not me, but the result's the same. Trouble all round.'

'How did Miles know?'

'He introduced us. I went into the bar at the Queen's – where we've been today. Miles was there having a drink with Graham. He bought me a drink and invited me to join them. Graham and I took it from there.'

'How does Miles know Graham Challoner?'

'Used to work on his firm at the General. Graham says they were friendly once. That's a long time ago now, but he still sees him around from time to time.'

Jill grinned at her. 'For a moment I thought my dad was the man in your life.'

'My goodness! I wouldn't dare. Lois wouldn't think twice about knifing me.'

Jill swallowed hard. Knowing what she did about Lois, Selma was probably closer to the truth than she realised.

As she went to make her visit in a nearby flat, she thought over all she'd learned. The trouble was, it didn't make the picture any clearer.

Jill had finished her visits by mid-afternoon, and the rest of the day was her own. She went home, feeling tired after her sleepless nights. She was looking forward to spending an hour in the garden. It was another hot day.

As she drove her Mini round by the garage at Links View, she could see Lois stretched out on a garden lounger in a shady spot on the back lawn. She took another lounger from the garage where they were stored and set it up near her.

'I've been looking forward to doing this all day,' she said. 'How's Gran? It would do her good to come out here.'

'She'd rather stay where she is,' Lois said from behind her copy of the *Lancet*.

Jill changed into a sun top and a pair of shorts and then looked into to see how Victoria was. Her lunch tray had not been cleared away. She was struggling to fasten her bra.

Jill slid the hooks into place. 'You should have let Lois help you,' she chided.

'I wish I could get her to help me.' Victoria's voice was sharp. 'I asked her twice. The first time she pretended not to hear, and the second she said she'd be back in five minutes.'

'Never mind, I'll give you a hand. Which dress do you want?'

'That blue cotton. It's cool and loose. It's nearly an hour since Lois was up here changing. I tried ringing my bell, but Mrs Moon has gone now.'

'Lois is out in the garden.'

'That's where I'd like to be.' She pushed Jill's fingers away irritably. 'I can manage the buttons as long as they're at the front. I don't need much help.'

'Of course you don't.' Jill carried Victoria's book, sunglasses and cushion, and as she installed her on the chair she'd set up for herself, she saw the look Lois shot in her mother's direction. Her black eyes were heavy with dislike.

'You've decided to come out after all?' She seemed anything but welcoming.

'I was waiting for you to come and help me dress.'

'Mother dear, you said you preferred to stay where you were.'

Jill got another chair for herself and erected it at some distance from the others. It seemed Lois had taken the news that Clive was not her father very much to heart. She'd not forgiven Victoria.

'What about a cup of tea?' Jill suggested.

'I'm still waiting for the one Lois was going to make,' Victoria retorted.

'I'll put the kettle on.'

Jill hurried off to do it. Up to now, it had seemed Lois couldn't do enough for her mother, but all that had changed.

As the afternoon drew into evening, Lois became noticeably more combative towards Victoria.

'You're over your fall now, Mother. Time you pulled yourself together and made more effort.'

Nat was cutting Victoria's roast lamb into bite-sized pieces as he carved. 'She should be able to do that for herself, Nat. Don't coddle her.'

'I don't think . . .' Nat began.

'She's just attention-seeking. She must try, or she'll never manage to feed herself again.'

Victoria accepted her plate with dignity. 'Thank you, Nat. I have difficulty cutting up meat. Pressing on the knife hurts my wrist.'

'You do fuss so, Mother,' Lois exploded.

'It's no trouble,' Nat said easily.

'I think Victoria is doing very well.' Jill added her support.

Lois scowled round the table at them all. It didn't make for a comfortable atmosphere.

CHAPTER TWENTY

After supper that evening, Jill was in the kitchen, measuring coffee into the pot, when the phone rang.

'I'll get it,' she called. The rest of the family had gone to the sitting room. She picked the receiver up.

'Jill?' Pleasure spurted through her as she recognised his voice.

'It's Felix.'

'Hello.'

'I want to see you again.'

She said as calmly as she could: 'I can't help you, Felix. I can't do what you ask.'

'I know. I've accepted that. We won't talk about Dad. But I want to see you anyway.'

She could see his impish smile in her mind's eye. She'd missed him over the last few days.

'I'm a fool, Jill. Here I am falling for you, and I . . .'

She felt her pulse quicken. 'What did you say?'

'I'm falling for you. In love.'

Jill felt a spark ignite within her. He was saying he loved her.

'I was a fool to complicate things with Dad's problems. It's keeping us apart. That's the last thing I want.'

She was bursting with happiness, glowing with warmth. Staying apart was the last thing she wanted too.

'How about it? Can you come for a drink? Just for an hour.'

He didn't have to plead. 'Now?' she asked.

'Yes, wonderful. Jill, we were getting on like a house on fire, I should never have doused it down.'

'Where shall I meet you?'

'In a pub . . .'

'The only one I know is the Queen's Arms.'

'That'll be fine.'

'In twenty minutes then?'

He was waiting when she got there. Eager, but a little wary. He kissed her cheek as though she were his maiden aunt. They settled into corner seats. His eyes wouldn't leave hers.

'I want you to know I've given up all idea of revenge. I'm not going

233

to try to get my own back on your stepmother. Not now.'

He'd seemed desperate for revenge last time she'd seen him. 'Why?'

'Had time to do some soul-searching over the last few days. Asked myself what I wanted most. Decided you're more important to me. I'd be a blockhead to cut myself off from you in order to make Lois Benbow eat crow.'

That made Jill feel better. She smiled.

'Even if I did what you asked, there's no guarantee you could prove anything. Going to court is very stressful, you'd be thinking about it for months on end. Living with it. It's better for you to write it off. Forget Lois if you can. How does your father feel about it?'

'All he wants is his leg back. Seeing Lois get her comeuppance might help. Compensation might too, but I doubt it. He'd rather have his leg. He's fed up all round.'

'It's more important that you concentrate on making him feel better.'

'Been trying to for months. I'm not helping much.'

'Sorry, Felix.' She put her hand over his. 'I haven't been much help to you on this.' She wished she could have been.

He was smiling at her. 'Incidentally, I'd love to go on holiday with you. I'm bowled over by the idea. I just can't leave him on his own just yet. He'd slip back and do nothing.'

'In the autumn?'

'Definitely by Christmas. If I haven't got him up and going by then I might as well give up.'

Jill laughed. 'That's cleared the air between us.'

'It's been there like a brick wall. All the time I've known you. Keeping us apart.'

'I've felt it too.' She knew she ought to kick herself. This disagreement had been largely her fault. She should have known better.

She couldn't have secrets from Felix, and she didn't want to think she couldn't share all his worries. If you loved somebody you had to do that. Hadn't she been railing against secrets at home and at the surgery?

He snuggled down on the seat beside her. 'It's that practice,' he said. 'I wish you hadn't joined it. But I promise not to ask questions. If I do pick up any pointers, I'll keep my mouth shut. Now can we take up where we left off?'

Jill laughed. 'I hope we're going to get a bit further than that.'

'I've told you how I feel about you. We're going a lot further. How would it be if I took you home to meet Pa this evening?'

'Fine.'

'It's high time he met his future daughter-in-law.'

'Not so fast. I haven't quite made up my mind. Not about that.'

234

'I have,' he sighed.

Jill smiled at him, feeling much better. At least something was working out right for her.

Victoria finished the last of her tea, then eased her breakfast tray out of her way.

For her, it was always a bad moment when everybody left for work and the house went quiet. It made her feel old and useless to be left behind. But that was the least of her worries this morning.

She heard the back door slam and the third car go slowly down the drive. Nat was always last.

She eased herself off the bed. She wouldn't wait for Mrs Moon. She must try to dress herself. She couldn't ask Lois to help her ever again. Her eyes burned with such hostility.

She couldn't get Lois out of her mind. She was worried about her. She'd been on edge for some weeks and noticeably worse since the day Victoria had broken her wrist and Jill had come home. She'd tried to calm her down but hadn't succeeded.

She'd warned her daughter never to let Jill come back, but after all these years Lois thought it no longer mattered, that she was safe.

Victoria had always known she mustn't tell Lois that Clive had not been her father. But she hadn't been able to help herself, she hadn't known what she was saying. She'd been hallucinating in a high fever.

Lois had been like one possessed when she first got the gist of her mother's ramblings. That alone had brought Victoria a moment of clarity so that she'd understood what she'd done.

She was afraid the shock was more than Lois could take. It hadn't come at a good time for her.

Victoria's bruises were turning yellow now but she was still unclear as to what had actually happened. She'd been wet with sweat in her rumpled bedclothes when she realised her daughter was bending over her again, pinning her down on the bed with a hand on each arm.

'Tell me,' she had grated, her face ugly with rage. She'd tried, but already Lois had pummelled out of her every detail about Jonathon Pine. Now she wouldn't leave her alone.

'I've never heard of anything more selfish. Did you think what it would do to your husband? Couldn't you have spared a thought for your own child?'

Victoria had cringed down in terror. She'd never imagined Lois would attack her physically. Her words had been hurtful and unfair. She'd tried, all her life, to do her best for her daughter.

Lois had had one breakdown after another. Done terrible things she'd had to hide. Poor Lois, she'd had dreadful emotional problems. And all of them the consequence of her affair with Bertie Meadows.

But Lois herself was the consequence of Victoria's affair with

235

Jonathon Pine, so in a way she must blame herself for all these troubles. She could feel the sweat breaking out on her brow now. No child of Clive's would ever have turned out like this.

Victoria always knew when her daughter was heading for another breakdown. She'd done it often enough for it to leave no doubt in her mind. One thing she'd learned, with Lois, there would always be another time and another crisis.

She could feel it like thunder in the air before a storm. It was coming and there was nothing she could do to help Lois this time.

The beam of sunlight across her room was growing brighter. It was going to be another hot day, and it stretched before her, long and empty.

Victoria knew she had to get out of the house, and forget Lois. She was sure she'd feel better if she did. She'd ring for a taxi and go to the library.

She found it was unbelievably difficult to press her straw hat down on her hair. She had to raise her other wrist in its plaster cast to hold it steady before she could push her hat pin through.

She was going slowly downstairs when the telephone began to ring in the hall.

'I'm glad you're up.' It was Esme. 'I was afraid I'd be too early. I was wondering, do you feel well enough to come and have a bite of lunch with me?'

'Yes. It's exactly what I need, thank you.'

'I thought lunch here at home. Less tiring for your first trip out.'

'Lovely. I'm better this morning.'

'I'm going to buy something nice to eat and go to the library. I'll pick you up later.'

'Esme, can I ask you to take me to the library with you? I've nothing to read.'

'Of course.'

'I'll stay there while you shop. Plenty of magazines and papers. The change will do me good.'

'When will you be ready?'

'Five minutes?'

'I'll come right up then.'

As she collected her books and her bag, Victoria comforted herself with the thought that she still had her friends. They'd all rally round to help her and Lois, should she need them.

CHAPTER TWENTY-ONE

It was Saturday morning. Jill was late getting up because she'd been out with Felix again. She put on jeans, and a yellow T-shirt. Lois was already downstairs.

'Good afternoon, Jill.' Her voice was heavy with disapproval.

Jill stifled a yawn. 'Where's Dad?'

'He's gone to the factory.'

That made her feel guilty. She'd promised herself she'd spend more time there. Even arranged with Dad that she'd go in on Saturday mornings. She mustn't let other things crowd that out.

She made herself a slice of toast and decided she wasn't doing enough about Dad's problem. Today, she must get to the bottom of it, whatever it was.

She hurried through a few chores, took Gran's tea and toast upstairs, and then went down to the factory to see Dad.

The silence seemed strange. For once, nobody else seemed to have come in. Dad's office was empty. She went past the still and silent conveyor belts, and found him alone in the slit of a room he called his laboratory.

'Just trying out a new flavour,' he smiled when he saw her. 'Here, taste this. What do you think?'

She took a mouthful of gooey pink crème.

'Not bad.'

'But not good?'

'It tastes . . . strongly scented. Too sickly for me.'

'Can't be much good then. You'll find some chocolate ginger over there. Rejects.'

'Great, ginger is more to my taste. What's the matter with them?'

'Not enough chocolate in the bath when they were dipped. Not uniformly covered.'

'Do you count this as work? Looks more like a labour of love.'

'It's work. It has to be done.' He smiled again.

'Both perhaps?' Jill bit into another chocolate. 'The business is all right? You are making a profit?'

She felt the change in atmosphere immediately. He was mentally backing away from her.

'You've asked me that before.'

'And you said it was doing fine. But is it? You're uptight about money. So's Lois. Victoria too, come to think of it.' He wasn't smiling any more.

'Dad, can't we talk about it? I know something's worrying you.'

She felt in her shoulder bag and brought out the letter he'd sent her months ago.

'Look, you wrote that you wanted me to come home. I think you even told me why. Then you had second thoughts and tore it up, but the indentations are here on the paper.'

He couldn't bring himself to look at it. 'Let's go to the office. I could do with a cup of coffee.'

Jill filled the ancient kettle and plugged it in. When she turned round she saw he was writing with his gold fountain pen.

'I thought you'd lost that?'

'Ena found it.'

'Here in the office?'

'In the filing cabinet. Must have fallen in when I was looking for something.'

Jill grinned at him. 'I saw Selma using a pen just like that. You know what I thought? That you'd left it in her flat.'

'Why would I go to her flat?' Nat frowned. 'Oh no, not Selma. Not me.'

'She's very friendly, Dad. And very good-looking. Still, that isn't what's bothering you. So what is?'

He wouldn't look at her again. His tongue-tied reluctance had come back.

Jill tried again.

'Dad,' she said, 'my patients come into the surgery and start relating their problems almost before they sit down.

'They don't always tell me exactly what they should. Often there's a lot of beating about the bush, but I don't have to wheedle their confidences out of them. Come on now, tell me what's bothering you.'

He was staring down at the register he'd been filling in.

'You're very sensitive about money, Dad. The business can't be as profitable as you're trying to make out.'

'But it is. Here,' he reached into a drawer, 'take a look at last year's accounts. See for yourself.'

Jill turned to the last page. The business had indeed made a healthy profit for the year.

'Can you read company accounts?'

'Not really, not the finer points.'

He began to explain. She grasped most of what he told her, but realised, too, that there were things he was holding back.

'Do these figures show a sudden improvement, a turnaround? Did you make a loss the year before?'

238

He shook his head.

'Well, there's something fishy going on here. If you aren't worried about your business . . .'

'Jill, what I'm worried about is telling you it's your business, not mine.'

That stopped her dead in her tracks. 'What?' She knew her mouth had dropped open.

'It's your business. Always has been.'

'But, Dad . . . I thought it was yours?'

'No. The Lambournes were your grandparents and Sarah's parents. She was named in their will as their beneficiary.'

'Then surely you . . .?'

'No. In the event of Sarah's prior death, their will carried the usual proviso that everything was to go to her children. She died in the air crash that killed them. You were her only child.'

It was almost more than Jill could take in. She stared into her father's lined, tired face.

'I didn't know.'

'I've always felt I was acting as trustee. I've been trying to build the business up. It was all for you.'

Jill felt the heat run up her cheeks. 'Why didn't you tell me before?'

'I wasn't trying to make a secret of it.'

She stared nonplussed into his harassed face. 'But Dad, you didn't tell me.'

'How do you tell a child she owns a business like this?'

'But when I was older?' She felt he should have done.

'I tried to tell you when you were sixteen and started saying you wanted to be a doctor. I wanted you to know you would have this to run. You wouldn't listen, Jill. You'd made up your mind. You wanted to do medicine.'

Had he tried? There was no mistaking her father's sincerity, it shone in his face.

'Did you mind very much?'

He sighed. 'Yes, I did mind then.'

'And there seemed less point when I didn't want it?' Jill said softly. 'I'm sorry, Dad.'

'I suppose I expected you to take after Sarah rather than Lois. I was disappointed in a way. But more than anything, I wanted you to be happy. If you wanted to be a doctor, rather than work here, I didn't think I should dissuade you.'

'Dear Dad.' She got up and gave him a hug. 'You gained nothing from being Sarah's husband? I can't get over that.'

'She had a half-share in our house. I inherited that from her, of course. The business belonged to her parents. It's the usual way wills are worded.'

'But you took over the running of the business. Kept it going. Without you . . .'

'I went on paying myself a salary.' He smiled. 'Increased it too, a few times. The business has done well over the years. Accumulated quite a bit of capital for you.'

'It has?' She was surprised.

'Well, yes, it's your business, Jill. It paid your fees, and an allowance . . .'

'I thought that was from you.'

'No, from the profits of the business.'

'And this is why you invested money in my name? I hardly know what to say. Thank you, Dad.'

'No need for that.' He looked uncomfortable.

'I think there is.'

He said with a half-smile: 'I suppose I ought to go through the books with you. Explain it all?'

'Not now. I'm too much up in the air. Can't get over the shock of owning it. You know, I'm beginning to realise just how little I know about making chocolates.'

His tired eyes were seeking hers again.

'I've got a confession to make, Jill. This time I'm to blame. There should be more money here than there is. Much more.'

He paused, and Jill said nothing. There seemed to be no end to the surprises she was getting.

'Aren't you going to ask what I've done with it?' He raised his eyes to hers. They were filled with misery.

'What *have* you done with it?'

He was still searching for the words.

'I'm shocked to find I own all this, Dad. Grateful to you for looking after it so well on my behalf. I'm not bothered that there should be more. It'll be all I can do to cope with this.' She thought her father looked worn out.

'I gave it to Lois,' he said in the same tone a man uses to admit to murder. 'It was not mine to give, but I gave it.'

He looked ashamed of what he'd done. She couldn't understand his anguish. 'Why?'

'Because she asked for it.'

'You wanted to give Lois everything money could buy?'

'To start with, yes. I suppose I thought I could buy her affection then.'

Jill put her arm across his shoulders. 'Dad, don't worry about it. But I still don't understand. Was it to buy Links View?'

'No, that's on a mortgage. We pay that jointly from our salaries.'

Jill was still puzzled. 'What does Lois want money for?'

'All her life she's been helping Althea. The poor woman whose husband was murdered by the leopard society. They all have. Victoria, Bill Goodbody, Titch. They've helped support her family.'

'So it was going to a good cause?'

'Jill, I was cheating you.'

'But I didn't know any of it was mine.'

'That makes it worse. I should have told you once you were old enough to understand. Certainly, you should have known once you were of age.'

His voice dropped. 'At that time, I even withheld a solicitor's letter that would have told you.'

Jill didn't know what to say.

'I could be convicted of fraud. I've broken the law. I've given money of yours to Lois without telling you. Misappropriated funds that I was handling on a professional basis.'

'But it doesn't matter . . .'

'It's a relief to hear you say that. To get it off my chest. All the same, it was very wrong of me.'

'Dad, it doesn't . . .'

'That's why I put off telling you the business was yours. I'd have had to show you the books going back over the years. I'd have had to confess to this.'

'Forget it. The point now is what does Lois continue to need money for?'

'Althea . . .'

'Dad, she's given freely over the years. Far more than anyone should expect, and Althea's family must be grown up now.'

'The youngest, the son, is a doctor. They put him through medical school between them. The girls went to college too.'

'When people give money to that extent,' Jill said frowning, 'they don't get desperate if they can't afford to give more. Besides, Althea is no longer in need.'

'They pay her nursing home fees.'

'Good Lord! Surely her own children could afford to do that?'

'It wouldn't be all that much from Lois's earnings.'

'Then this is something else?'

There was horror in Nat's eyes. His voice dropped another octave.

'Both she and Victoria have always kept jewellery in my safe. In the study, you know?'

She nodded.

'I noticed, last year, that some of it had gone.'

'Did you ask Lois about it?'

'She said it was Victoria's, that she wanted to sell it. But I don't think Victoria bought anything else. And anyway, she'd sold her flat in Oxton. She shouldn't be short of money.'

'Does Lois have any debts?'

'Jill, I've asked myself that. I don't think so. She's not a big spender. Oh, I know she likes expensive cars, and expensive clothes, too, but she doesn't buy in excess.'

Jill put a hand on his arm. 'Blackmail then?'

She heard her father's sudden intake of breath. 'That had occurred to me. She's desperate to get money. It's not for her own needs. She's not spending on herself. And she's afraid.'

'She's not afraid of Althea?'

'No, she despises her. Thinks she should do more for herself.' Nat sighed. 'It had to be blackmail. I think it's probably been going on for years, but with her giving to Althea I didn't realise. I mean, where else could all this money be going? Once or twice a year she presses me for more. I know she asks Victoria too.'

'Lois still has jewellery in the safe?'

'No. She said she wasn't the type to wear jewellery, and that it would be safer to keep it in the bank.'

'If it is blackmail, then Lois must have broken the law. Done something she wants to keep very quiet.'

Her father was shaking his head. 'A mistake with a patient?'

'Nothing like that. We all pay insurance in case we're charged with negligence. Victoria wouldn't let her pay out on that.'

'She tried to knife Graham, she can go berserk.'

'Too long ago, and he'd given her good reason. There would have to be something more than that.'

Jill thought of Lois and shivered. This was why she hadn't come home very often once she'd passed the age when she'd had to. She could imagine Lois capable of . . .

'Nobody can exhort money without a reason, Dad. She'd just refuse if she didn't want to pay.'

Her father was shaking his head miserably.

Ena was clumping heavily up the passage. 'Hello, boss. Hello, Jill, nice to see you helping here again.'

She beamed at Jill. Ena's plump, middle-aged face showed all her feelings.

'I don't know about helping.'

Jill felt she needed to think. Lois being blackmailed?

'No, gossiping then.' Ena pretended to be severe. 'Not when I've come to work on a Saturday. This isn't an ordinary work day.'

'Ena's come to help me make up my monthly list,' Nat said wearily. 'Buying requirements.'

'Buying orders, boss. Let's get on with the job and get the orders in. We ran out of vanilla last week, would you believe? And only because we were late with last month's orders.'

'Ena's better at this than I am.' Nat sat down at his desk. Ena brought another chair in.

242

'Not much different from doing the household shopping,' she laughed.

Jill made more coffee all round and watched them. Ena was providing the energy. She was consulting the lists from last month and from the same month last year, and making suggestions.

Dad was deliberating, slowing down the decisions rather than making them. It was Ena who was moving the job along. Jill thought her father would be better to let her get on with it. This was a job he could delegate.

One thing was certain: now Jill knew the business was hers she'd have to do more to help Dad. Take more responsibility for it.

She couldn't let him go on worrying about it and tiring himself out. He had more than enough worry with Lois.

On Monday, Jill did evening surgery again. She'd discovered that it was her lot to do three evenings a week. Lois and Titch Meadows each did two.

When she got home, Bill Goodbody's car was on the drive, and she could hear the rise and fall of voices from the sitting room. She put her head round the door.

Bill looked up and said: 'You must have had a heavy surgery, Jill. You're late.'

She had. 'They never stopped coming. How's retirement?'

'It's great.' His smile wobbled, and she thought he looked depressed.

'He should have given up work years ago.' Janet was trying to jolly him along. She'd had her hair permed again. It was set in tight grey waves and curls.

'A drink, Jill?' Lois asked, as though she were another guest. They were all having gin and tonics.

'Better not, I'm on call for the rest of the night.' She felt tired and hungry. 'I'll see to supper, shall I?'

Tonight, it was meant to be Lois's turn to cook supper but Jill had come in through the kitchen and knew she hadn't started it. There was an uncleared trolley, showing that the visitors had been here for afternoon tea.

'We'd better go,' Janet Goodbody said, getting to her feet.

'Not yet, it'll take another half-hour,' Lois persuaded. 'Plenty of time for another drink. Bring us some more ice, Jill, will you?'

'I shall miss you both so much,' Victoria was saying when she went back with the ice. 'I can't imagine not having you close.'

'Are you going away?' Jill asked.

'To Spain,' Janet said. 'We're going to buy a place there. See the sun again. I'm quite excited.'

'They've sold their house in Oxton,' Victoria lamented. 'What will we do without them?'

'We're going right away,' Bill added. Jill thought he didn't look all that keen at the prospect.

'Away from Birkenhead? From all your friends? For good?' Jill was very surprised. If they'd already sold their house, they must have had this planned for some time. She knew Victoria was going to miss them.

'The winters are a bit of a drag here, and now I'm not working . . .'

Jill found it hard to believe. Friendship had brought them here from the other side of the world. She'd thought them well settled.

Back in the kitchen, she discovered the plaice all prepared and ready to go into the microwave. She had got as far as lighting the gas under the potatoes when she heard her father's old Wolseley pull up outside. He was making a habit of working late now whenever she did.

'Hello, Dad. We've got company. Why don't you go and have a drink with them?'

'Victoria's friends, rather than mine.' Nat took a buttered scone from the abandoned tea trolley and sat down at the kitchen table. 'Well, hers and Lois's. They'll be talking about old friends and old times. Or else it's practice gossip.'

'Not this time. It's a farewell visit. The Goodbodys are moving to Spain. The magic circle's about to be broken.'

'Never! I don't believe it.' The scone was an inch from his mouth but he didn't bite. She could see him thinking. 'Why?'

'They say for the climate. It's warmer in Spain.'

'Lois hasn't upset them? They haven't fallen out?'

'I don't think so. Lois is sorry they're going. Victoria is devastated. I heard her say: "I can't believe you're deserting us now." '

'They'll be back,' her father declared. 'They're like one big family. Can't let go of each other.'

'Not according to Bill. I overheard him say: "It's the only way. We've got to cut ourselves free." '

'That's very strange. I mean, they came to Birkenhead to be near Victoria, and they're getting on a bit to emigrate. They can't speak Spanish, can they?'

'I don't think so.'

'Is something driving them out?'

Jill shook her head. 'If it isn't Lois, I don't know. You're closer to them than I am.'

'I've always been on the edge. Never been to Ekbo and not in the profession.' He reached for another scone.

'Dad, you won't eat your supper if you stuff yourself with scones now.'

He put it back and said: 'Being together in Ekbo bound them all

244

closely. The horrific experiences they had there made them cling. It's all still fresh in Victoria's mind.'

'Mine too,' Jill said ruefully, 'after listening to her going on about it the other night.'

'But they're even closer now. They seem chained, almost. Something else is binding them.'

Jill tried to think. 'Lois and Victoria have fallen out, Dad. And not everybody at the practice is close.'

'Not a happy place?'

'A very troubled place. Do you know what Selma told me?'

He raised his eyebrows and smiled. 'If it's about her liaison with Graham, that isn't a secret. Lois has been sounding off about it for weeks. Though why she should be bothered when it was all over so long ago, I don't know.'

'Lois has her secrets, and she's kept them hidden for aeons. On the surface, she pretends everything's fine but just below . . . Well, the water's murky.

'Victoria can't keep quiet about her secrets any longer, but Lois is desperate to keep what she's done hidden.'

'I told you what she did. She attacked her first husband with a knife.'

Jill shook her head. 'That happened twenty-five years ago, after he'd told her he had another woman, and she didn't really hurt him, did she?'

Dad's tired eyes stared back at her.

'There has to be more to it than that.'

'Do you think so?'

'Dad, she went over the top when I first mentioned Phoebe. Tears from Lois? About something that happened ages ago? That's abnormal behaviour.'

'Perhaps I should ask her. Try and find out.' He pushed his thinning hair off his forehead. It stuck up in an untidy coxcomb.

Jill said: 'We've got to get to the bottom of what's going on.'

There were sounds of departure from the sitting room. They both went into the hall to say goodbye.

'Now you must be sure to write.' Victoria was kissing Janet's cheek. 'Do let us know your new address.'

'As soon as we find a place, we will,' Bill assured her.

Jill stiffened. So they were not leaving a forwarding address? Not even with Victoria, their greatest friend? Dad's eyes met hers across the hall. He was thinking the same. It could only be that they wanted to disappear.

Lois closed the front door behind them and turned round. She looked bereft.

'Supper's ready,' Jill said. 'They timed that well.' She wanted to

245

calm them both, get them back to their usual routine.

She was eating quickly. She was always hungry by supper time, and tonight it was later than usual. She could feel the cold consternation in the atmosphere.

She looked round the table. Victoria's shoulders were sagging. She wore a formal silk suit in soft green, classy wear for a professional woman forty years ago, and still elegant. Her soft white hair with its yellowing streak was drawn up into an immaculate bun. Her wrist in its plaster cast was still anchored by a sling to her neck.

She was barely over her bout of flu, and she looked as though she'd been wound several notches tighter by the news of the Goodbodys' departure.

'Where will it all end?' she asked, and her frightened eyes met Jill's.

Lois was even less in control of herself tonight. Usually she enjoyed members of her inner coterie coming round on the spur of the moment, but she too was upset by their going.

'You've overcooked this fish,' she complained to Jill. 'It's almost inedible.'

'Mrs Moon's note said nine minutes on high, and that's what it's had.'

'Don't be silly, Lois,' Victoria said irritably. 'There's nothing the matter with the fish and you know it.'

'I think it's very nice,' Nat added.

Jill shivered. Both Victoria and Lois were very upset.

Jill had looked forward to meeting Felix all day. She wanted to go out. The atmosphere at Links View was continuing to get her down. It was fraying her nerves to see the effect Lois was having on Victoria and her father.

'There's a new restaurant opened up in Hamilton Square,' Felix said. 'Let's try it.'

She felt closer to him now they'd managed to put their difficulties behind them. But it was still taken for granted that Felix would not come anywhere near Links View. Just to see him come up the drive and Jill run out to his car infuriated Lois.

Last time she'd done that, Lois had railed about it all evening. Her father had said that seeing Felix was like a red rag to a bull to Lois.

As Jill drove into Hamilton Square she saw him standing on the pavement waving to her. She pulled to the kerb so he could get in beside her.

'You're always so punctual,' she laughed. 'I never have to wait for you.'

'I make a point of being early so you don't have to. There's room to park just round the corner in Cleveland Street.'

As they walked back, she pointed out the house which Victoria had once owned.

'She hates to come down here now. She says, like everything else in her life, Hamilton Square has changed for the worse.'

'I like it, pleasant gardens kept neat by the council, fading grandeur, Gothic town hall. Can't imagine families living in these houses, though.'

'For my grandmother, everything was better in the old days. I expect we'll be just the same when we're her age.'

When they were sitting at the table and trying out a first course of antipasta, Felix said: 'I've a favour to ask.'

'Oh yes?'

'I know you're against me writing articles about your family, but . . .'

'Felix! You promised!'

'Your father this time.' He grinned at her. 'I'm doing a series called "The Changing Face of Industry". How heavy industries like coal and steel are in decline, and small new businesses like your father's are growing.'

'Lois is making my nerves fray a bit. I thought you were on again about the practice. Dad's business isn't new.'

'I've been looking up Chamber of Commerce statistics. It only started up after the war.'

Jill's fork paused halfway to her mouth. 'I never asked him when it started. Never thought about that. Dad tells me often it was started by my mother's family and that he worked for them.'

'It wouldn't have been possible to manufacture luxury chocolates during the war.'

'No, of course it wouldn't. I've never thought about it, but if I had, I'd have said it started well before the war, that it marked time then and opened up again afterwards.'

'No. It only started up in 1947.'

Jill frowned in concentration. 'Then it's Dad who has built up Lambourne's?'

'Yes. Would you ask him if he'll show me round and let me write an article?'

'I'm sure he'd be glad to.'

'This series is being syndicated through local newspapers all round the country. It'll be good publicity for him.'

'Then he'll probably jump at the chance.'

Jill felt she'd not appreciated how much her father had achieved. She'd been conditioned by Lois. It was part of Lois's technique, to present herself as confident and successful while belittling what everybody else did.

'Poor Dad,' she said. He wasn't the sort to boast of his own successes. 'He looks tired. Hasn't much energy.'

'If he's running the business efficiently he must still be ticking over well himself.'

'I suppose so.'

'If he's tired,' Felix's impish smile lit up his whole face, 'it's because he has to cope with Lois's problems as well as everything else.'

Dad seemed pleased when she asked him if he'd do it.

'A good idea all round,' he said. 'It will give me a chance to get to know Felix.'

Two days later Jill met Felix outside the shop in Grange Road. She showed him round inside before taking him to the chocolate factory.

'I didn't see my patient, Mrs Dunne, in the shop,' she said to her father.

'Off sick again. You haven't cured that.'

'I saw her in surgery only two days ago. She said she was feeling much better.'

'Better perhaps, but not well enough to come to work,' Nat said drily. 'Phoned in this morning to say she had a stomach upset. Like I told you, she only works a four-day week at the best of times. Often only three. Can't run a business with a manager like that.'

'You've promoted somebody else?'

'The little dark girl, Sandra. She's always there. On her toes, that one.'

'Oh dear. Poor Mrs Dunne.'

'Sorry, Jill.'

'But she's still got a job?'

'For the moment. It depends how often she comes in to do it. It isn't fair on the others. It throws her work on to them. A business is different, Jill. Can't afford to ladle on the sympathy like you.'

Jill knew he was right. Knew he could be tough when he needed to be.

She trailed round behind them for a while, listening to her father explaining the processes, while the conveyor belts rattled and clanked.

'You didn't tell me you'd built all this up yourself, Dad.'

'Some of it,' he said diffidently.

'It could hardly have been off the ground when you took it over in 1950,' Felix added.

Jill thought that Felix appeared to know quite a lot about factory processes already, and seemed interested in every aspect of chocolate-making.

They both sampled a good deal of it as they went round.

'I have to go back to the surgery,' she said. 'A clinic this afternoon.'

'We'll manage very well on our own now,' her father told her.

'It'll be a good article when it's written, Dad,' Jill assured him.

'I'll make sure it's a cracker.' Felix winked at her, then popped another strawberry crème in his mouth.

A few days later, Felix was carefully folding the pages he'd typed and sliding them into an envelope. He'd been working on an article all day in the bedroom he'd taken over as a study. Now he'd finished, he was looking forward to taking his father to meet Jill. She was going to bring her father, and they were all going to have a meal.

He stretched himself and went over to the window, looking down at the front garden. The leaves were beginning to fall from the sycamore and were gusting about in the wind. Autumn was on its way.

His father's new grey Escort was coming down the road. It nosed carefully between the gateposts and pulled very slowly on to the short drive.

He watched his father get out. He was slower than he used to be, much slower, but he was taking tentative steps towards the front door, without using a stick. His artificial leg gave him an uneven gait, he seemed to swing it forward. On gravel, it couldn't be easy for him.

'You're walking very well, Dad.' He went downstairs to tell him. 'I knew you could do it.'

'It's damned hard.' His father was panting when he reached the sitting room. He collapsed on to an armchair and closed his eyes.

Felix knew just how hard it had been. They'd both been excited when they heard his new leg was ready for him to try on. But when he first started to wear it, it had rubbed against his stump and made it sore. They'd eased that for him and he'd persevered. Now he was going to walking school regularly and taking the practice they recommended.

Felix went to put the kettle on. He'd been afraid that Dad would never cope, but he was doing better than he'd expected.

'You'll find it easier as time goes on.'

'That's what they keep telling me at the hospital. It looks all right, though, doesn't it?'

'Yes, most people wouldn't know it was artificial.'

Felix smiled to himself. Now that his father felt his condition wasn't obvious at first glance, he had more confidence. He was making more effort, going out more and meeting his friends.

Felix had taken him out for a drink once or twice and his leg hadn't rated a second glance from anybody. that had cheered him no end.

He opened his eyes and said: 'I called in at the school this afternoon. Saw Griffiths. I told him I'd be ready to come back after Christmas.'

Felix felt a surge of pleasure. 'So soon?'

'I sat in the common room at break time. It gave me the taste for it. Yes, I think I'll be ready by the beginning of January. If you keep me at it.'

'You can bank on that.'

'The boys will probably call me Pegleg Pete.' He was trying to flex it.

Felix grinned. 'Will you mind?'

'Does it matter what they call me? I'll be glad to get back in the classroom. That's normal life for me.'

He drank the cup of tea Felix gave him in silence. Then he said: 'Thanks for keeping my nose to the grindstone, son. I nearly chickened out of this. You made me do it.'

Felix said awkwardly: 'We all need a bit of support at times.'

He went out to post the article he'd written, enjoying the stroll in the afternoon sun. He'd promised Jill he'd do nothing about his plans to get even with Lois. And of course, he wouldn't. But he still felt angry when he thought about it. Still went into fantasies about exposing her. He had the articles all planned out in his mind.

He'd even thought he might approach a television producer. A programme going out in mid-evening would really embarrass her and Miles Sutton. It would scare off most of their patients too.

But he knew he'd never be able to do any of these things if he was going to marry Jill Ridley. He'd had to ask himself which was more important to him.

It was no contest. Jill was.

Felix made up his mind, that if his father could get over his problems then so could he. He'd put Lois and all thoughts of revenge out of his mind for ever. Stop dwelling on it. Accept what had happened. It was better for everyone that way. Particularly for himself.

He felt more cheerful now he'd made up his mind about that. His dad was going back into teaching and his life would be more normal. It made him think of his own future.

He'd stay with Dad for a few more months until he was really on his feet. But he wouldn't have to stay for good. He didn't have a permanent invalid on his hands.

He'd always intended to go back to London when he'd reached that point. Now he wasn't so sure. Jill wouldn't want to leave Birkenhead.

His plans were fluid at the moment, depending on what Jill wanted to do. His step quickened; he felt quite excited when he thought of the future.

CHAPTER TWENTY-TWO

The next morning, for the first time, Jill finished her surgery before her partners. She went down to the kitchen. Usually the receptionists made the coffee, but they too were still busy with patients. She filled the kettle and got out the mugs.

Two fridges buzzed in unison: one held drugs, vaccines mostly, the other held two pints of milk and a salad that Selma had bought for her lunch. The noise didn't cover the occasional cough from the waiting room, or Selma's voice directing the next patient to the appropriate door.

She sat down, thinking what a dismal place the kitchen was on this sunny summer morning. Even after the long spell of hot weather it seemed dank and airless. The tap dripped over an old-fashioned porcelain sink.

Selma came rushing in to take a tin from the cupboard. She put out a plate of digestives on the large scrubbed table.

The phone rang on her desk and she whisked off again to answer it.

Jill heard the front door open and high heels come clicking up the hall. A fruity voice asked: 'Is Cuthbert Meadows free?'

Selma cleared her throat: 'He has a patient with him at the moment.'

'Tell him I'm here.'

'He's not quite finished surgery. He's one more . . .'

'Tell him I'm here.' The voice was imperious.

'Right. Would you like to take a seat for a moment?'

Her cluck of impatience was clearly audible. 'I'd like to see him as soon as he's finished with this patient. You can tell him I won't keep him long.'

Jill had recognised the voice. She went to the kitchen door. Rosalie Sutton's mustard-coloured blazer brightened the dark hall. She was blazing with determination.

Through the hatch, she could see Selma talking to Titch on the phone. Her face told Jill she wanted Rosalie take off her hands.

Jill said: 'Would you like a cup of coffee? I'm sure Titch won't be long.'

Rosalie came into the kitchen, looking elegant and beautifully

251

groomed. She seemed to move in a cloud of expensive perfume, strong enough to vie with the smell of disinfectant.

'Have a seat.' Jill pulled out another chair at the table. China-blue eyes looked disdainfully round and then fastened on her.

She added: 'I'm Jill, I don't know whether you remember me? The tea party? The new partner?'

'Yes, of course, Lois's daughter.' She sat down then.

Jill switched the kettle on again and got out another mug.

'If that's for me, don't bother. I don't think I can face instant coffee. Do you think you'll like working here?'

'When I get used to it.'

Jill wanted to be friendly. Rosalie didn't seem all that much older than she was. They ought to have something common. Her pale-blonde hair was cut in a becoming feathery style. She would have been beautiful if her mouth had not been set in such a hard line.

'This is a depressing place, a real dump. I don't know how you stand it.'

Selma's head came round the door. 'Titch said to send you in before his last patient, Mrs Sutton.'

Rosalie got up without another word, pushing past Polly who was coming in.

Lois came out of the new extension in time to see the mustard-coloured jacket disappear into Titch's consulting room.

'Who was that?' Jill saw apprehension on her face.

'Rosalie Sutton,' Selma said with a wink of satisfaction in Jill's direction.

'Oh my God, not again!' Lois slid on to a chair. The colour had gone from her cheeks.

'Coffee, Dr Benbow?' Polly put a cup on the table in front of her.

'Are you all right?' Jill asked.

'Why shouldn't I be?' she flared at her. That caused an uneasy silence.

Selma broke it to ask: 'What's Rosalie come down here for?'

'Don't be nosy. It's none of your business.' Lois's anger boiled over. It made her bark at Selma again: 'And what are you grinning at?'

'Not grinning, not exactly. Smiling. Just trying to keep cheerful.'

'There's nothing to be amused about. Don't be ridiculous.'

Selma shook her glamorous dark curls away from her face and said: 'Rosalie is an out-and-out snob. Lays it on so thick she can hardly talk to me. Sees me as class three and well beneath her.'

'Can't see me at all,' Polly said, helping herself to a biscuit. 'Only deigns to speak to people in class one and two.'

'She doesn't seem to like any of us,' Jill added.

They all heard Titch buzz through to the receptionists' room.

'Hadn't you better see what he wants?' Lois snapped in Selma's direction.

'Just going.' Selma was already on her feet.

From the reception office she called: 'He wants you to go in too, Dr Benbow.'

Jill watched Lois's face twisting with tension. At first she made no move to go. Then suddenly, without a word, she jerked to her feet and tore down the hall.

As she went in, they heard Rosalie say: 'Hello, Lois, I thought it was time I called to see you again.' Then the door slammed shut.

Polly's eyes were out on stalks. She was holding her ginger head at an angle to hear as much as possible.

'What's all this about?' Jill asked. 'What's going on that I don't know about?'

But she was too late, Miles Sutton was coming to join them. Selma followed him in. Polly got up to make more coffee.

'Your wife's here,' Jill told him. 'Did you know?'

His contemptuous gaze settled on her. It took him a moment to reply.

'I knew she intended to come. Rosalie has a bit of back trouble. She wants Titch's opinion. Doesn't entirely trust mine.' It rolled off his tongue too easily.

'Wants Lois's opinion too, by the look of it.' Jill pushed her empty mug away and stood up. 'I must get going.'

Miles followed her down the passage and went into Titch's consulting room too.

Jill decided there were things going on here that Lois wanted kept quiet. It wasn't just at home that she could feel a secretive atmosphere.

On Selma's desk she found four neat piles of records topped with lists. Jill took hers and went back to her room, leaving the door open. Ten minutes later, she heard the door of Titch's consulting room opening again, and the Suttons coming out.

'We'll leave it like that, then,' Rosalie was saying. 'I'm sure you'll do your best. A week . . .' Titch's voice said something.

'All right, I'll leave it for two weeks. Goodbye.'

Jill went to the window of her room. Below her, Rosalie was getting into a pearl-grey Jaguar, and her husband into a dark-blue one. His-and-hers Jaguars? Both almost new. Her own red Mini had been parked between them. It looked a toy by comparison.

She sat down to write out repeat prescriptions. She could hear Lois's voice from the kitchen, rising and falling in a whine of complaint. Five minutes more and Titch's last patient went out, slamming the front door.

Above the subdued chatter from the kitchen she heard Lois's voice: 'Let's take our coffee upstairs, Titch.'

There were footsteps coming up. The room next to hers had been furnished with bookcases, easy chairs and a low table.

253

'I don't know why we don't have our coffee here every day.' Lois swept inside. 'It's a lot more comfortable.'

'Kitchen's nearer,' Titch grunted.

'We've got to have privacy sometimes. It doesn't do to let the girls know everything.' She was stirring her coffee with noisy vigour. 'Rosalie – has she got a nerve? And as for Miles, he was so insolent, I could have slapped his face.'

The solid door clicked firmly behind them and their voices were reduced to indistinct murmurs.

Jill pursed her lips in frustration. She'd hoped to hear enough to find out what was bothering them. She was fed up with all the whispers and the secrets.

She was ready now to start her visits. On her way out she deliberately looked in on Lois and Titch, opening the door without knocking.

They jerked apart. Whatever they were discussing, it was very important to them. Lois's cheeks were crimson. She stopped speaking in mid-sentence.

Jill said: 'Lois, thought I'd better let you know, I'll be out for dinner tonight.'

'Not that Kingsley fellow again? Really, Jill, I think you ought to have more sense.'

Jill ignored that. There was a moment's silence; she knew they were waiting for her to go.

She asked: 'What's Miles done to upset you? I heard you carrying on about him.' She thought they both looked a little taken aback.

'We wish we'd never given Miles a partnership,' Lois said stiffly. 'His mind isn't on what he's doing.'

Jill raised her eyebrows. 'Is this something new?'

Again there was the momentary baffled silence. It surprised her to find Titch was equally involved in this. His gaze met hers, she could see he was upset.

He jerked to his feet, paced to the window, rattling the change in his trouser pockets. But she already knew that Titch had his own secrets.

She tried again. 'What's he done, exactly?'

'Causing trouble for us.'

Jill didn't like Miles either, but there was a difference between what she felt and the venomous hate Lois was radiating.

'We can't rely on him to do anything right. I wish we could get rid of him.'

There was a silence. Jill had the feeling they would both give their back teeth to oust him. She'd swear they felt threatened in some way.

'What did Rosalie come for?'

Lois expelled her pent-up breath noisily. 'You get out and do your visits, Jill,' she said. 'This is our problem.'

'But if I'm a partner . . .'

'You're not involved in this.'

Jill went slowly out to her car, feeling baffled. She felt that what Lois had said about Miles's mind not being on his work was to throw her off the scent. It was Rosalie who had upset them. Whatever she'd come for, she'd looked as though she expected to get it. Was even in a position to demand it.

As Jill started on her home visits, she found it an effort to keep her mind on the job. She was glad she had only five calls to make. She'd done three; the other two were in the newly built houses on the Tranmere Hall Estate. Her route took her back past the surgery.

She'd used up the last of the antibiotics she kept in her bag for a sick old man who lived alone. This, she decided, was an opportunity to slip in and restock.

She was slowing down when she saw Lois accelerating towards her like a mad thing. She caught a glimpse of her face stiff with tension, her fingers clamped on the steering wheel. Lois didn't see her.

Jill pulled in alongside Titch's old Austin. She'd been out almost an hour. Usually, everybody was away smartly after coffee. If they'd carried on discussing Miles all this time, then the problem must be greater than she'd first thought.

Titch almost bumped into her in the hall. He still seemed troubled.

'What's going on, Titch?'

He looked at her for a moment as though he didn't know who she was. The phone rang. Through the hatch, she saw Marina's dark head bend as she picked it up.

'Come in here for a minute.' He was pulling her into his consulting room, shutting the door.

'You might as well know, Jill. I've decided to leave the practice.'

'Leave? You can't!' She was horrified at the thought.

'Only the other day you were telling me it was my best option.'

'I didn't mean right away. Anyway, you said you wouldn't.'

'I've changed my mind. I'll retire.'

'You're not old enough.'

'I'm sixty. I don't want to drag it out like Bill.'

'But that'll leave me with Lois and Miles.'

'I'm afraid so.'

'Lois is cracking up, I'm doing half her work as it is, and Miles won't do a stroke more than he has to.'

'I'm sorry.'

Jill was indignant. 'I'd never have come if I'd known you were leaving. I've hardly found my feet. I still get lost when I go out visiting. Why didn't you tell me this was on the cards?'

'It wasn't then.'

'I've only been here seven weeks.'

'Yes, I'm sorry. Something's come up.'

'What, for goodness' sake? Titch, it's not impossible to guess. Has Miles threatened to tell the world that your name is really Sinclair? Or is it Rosalie?'

Titch wouldn't look at her. He was stroking his moustache.

'You're dropping me in it.'

'You can get a locum to take my place.'

'I need more than that. You're the one stable person here. I thought I could rely on you.'

'That's the way it is. I'm sorry.'

'But where are you going?'

'I don't know. A long way away.'

'You can't ask Miles Sutton to leave, so you're going yourself. Is that it? It came to a showdown, a battle of strength?'

He glowered at her.

She wailed: 'You could go on working for years yet. You're at your peak, why stop now? I need you.'

He picked up his bag and was heading for the door.

'When? When are you planning on going?'

'As soon as I can.'

'I have to give three months' notice if I want to leave. You'll have to too.'

The door slammed behind him. Perhaps he wouldn't? It depended on whether he'd given a similar undertaking. Jill looked round Titch's room, appalled.

She'd thought him settled. Yet suddenly on the spur of the moment, he'd decided to up and go. There could only be one reason. He was afraid he was going to be exposed.

Jill felt cold. First Bill and Janet, now Titch and Esme. Victoria's circle of friends was breaking up. They were like rats leaving a sinking ship.

Jill was fuming. Her mind whirled with apprehension as she set about restocking her bag. She refused Marina's offer to make her a cup of coffee. Refused to be drawn into conversation about Rosalie's outfit. Went out to do her last two visits.

She got lost in the maze of streets. Her mind wouldn't concentrate.

She was thinking of Gran. This was going to come as a shock, but she'd have to tell her. The old lady would miss Esme popping in to see her every other day.

Perhaps Gran would talk him into staying a bit longer? Even six months would give Jill a chance to find her feet. But it couldn't happen all that fast, could it? Titch would have to sell his house.

256

It was two o'clock when she drove up the drive of Links View, her work finished for the day. She rounded the corner of the house and found Esme's yellow Mini parked outside the garage.

Good, she'd be able to tell them both together. Get them on her side. If this was going to come as a shock to Victoria, what about Esme? Jill was sure it hadn't entered Titch's mind until this morning when Miles had stirred something up.

Mrs Moon was in the kitchen making some sort of a pudding as Jill rushed through to the hall. The sitting room was empty, the door wide open.

'They're in the study.' Mrs Moon's voice followed her.

That door was firmly shut. Jill threw it open. Gran was perched on the edge of one of the red velvet chairs. When she looked up in surprise, Jill could see tears glazing her dark eyes.

Esme Meadows swung round from the window, looking decidedly nerve-racked.

'You know already? That Titch is leaving?' Jill could see they did.

'He doesn't want to go.' Esme's face was screwed up with stress. 'Neither do I. But we must. It's the only way.'

'Why? What's happened? I don't understand.'

'You don't understand any of it,' Victoria said in a flat voice. She blew her nose, sat back in the chair.

Jill slid on to the chair on the other side of the gas fire.

'Gran, you've got to tell me. I don't want Titch to go. I depend on him.'

'I can't believe he will. Not him. I helped him when he needed it, didn't I, Esme?'

'Yes,' she said grudgingly. 'You try to help everybody.'

'And now, when I'm getting old and need help myself, he's deserting me. Taking you away too. Haven't we always stuck together?' Her eyes swung round to Jill. 'Do you know what I did for Titch?'

'He told me.'

'Did he?' Esme was amazed. 'You must take after your grandmother. A shoulder for everyone to cry on.'

'You asked him to stay with you, Gran, in Hamilton Square. When he was in trouble.'

'Yes, he brought his lady friend, Georgina Scott-Temple. I could see what she was. Out for a good time. That's all she wanted.

'After she'd got him truly in the muck, Georgina packed her bags and went. He couldn't work so he had less money to splash about, and Chloe, his first wife, wanted a divorce and a fat settlement.

'Titch was always a philanderer. I'm sorry, Esme, but he was.'

'You did warn me.' Esme sat down in front of Lois's Carlton House desk. 'He promised never to look at another woman if I'd marry him, and he hasn't.'

'He'd had enough of the glamour girls by then. He wanted you, Esme.'

'You were staying with Gran too?'

'Not at that time. I had a place of my own, but I was always round there. I was another of Victoria's lost lambs.'

Gran said, 'I wouldn't say that.'

'Perhaps not as lost as Althea.'

'But you said she was happier, once she had a job,' Jill reminded her.

'What Althea wanted was to get married again,' Victoria said slowly. 'She wanted another husband and a father for her children.'

'She proposed to Titch, you know.' Esme's nostrils flared with distaste. 'He was terribly embarrassed, poor lamb. Didn't know what to say. He'd done his best for Althea. Tried to be supportive. She read more into that than he intended.'

'By then, Titch was interested in you,' Gran said.

'And this was the one time you didn't help, Victoria. Titch told me you were matchmaking for Althea. Throwing them together.'

'I'm sorry, I thought they'd be good for each other,' Gran said. 'I didn't know he felt like that about you.'

'Didn't think I was his type, you mean,' Esme grimaced. 'Too plain. You didn't see me as being of interest to Titch.'

'I was wrong,' Gran said. 'You're exactly right for him. He'd learned by then that looks aren't everything.'

'The trouble was, knowing that Titch had turned Althea down increased the burden of guilt we all felt for her.'

Esme's little dog pushed a cold nose against Jill's hand. She stroked his head absent-mindedly.

'So Titch too has helped her over the years? With money?'

'We all have. Not just money; in other ways as well.'

'Do you still see her?'

'Yes, of course,' Esme said. 'Poor Althea, she's an invalid now. Motor Neurone Disease.'

'You can't blame yourselves for that.'

'All the same, it increased the guilt factor and the sympathy,' Gran admitted. 'We tried to do more for her. We started paying school fees for the children then. Bertie would have wanted them to have a decent education.'

'Gran, I can see now why you worry about not having enough money for yourself.'

'We all worry about that.'

Jill took a deep breath. 'You've handed over money for school fees, nannies, nursing home charges, as well as cash. Althea's been blackmailing you for years. Is that what you're saying?'

'It wasn't like that!'

'No! You don't understand,' Esme said. 'We gave because he wanted to help her.'

'We did it as a kindness,' Victoria added.

'Then why does Titch want to get away? And the Goodbodys too? Did something go wrong?' Jill asked.

She saw her grandmother shudder. 'It was the worst thing that could have happened.'

'We all felt terrible about Althea.' Esme's voice sounded tight. 'She didn't know that Lois had had an affair with her husband.'

'Terrible to find that out after he was dead. She asked me how Bertie came to be doing the bush clinics again. She knew it wasn't his turn.

'I had to make some excuse. I told her the Nigerian doctor had been taken ill with a sudden fever and that Bertie had offered to take his place. I couldn't tell her that Bill sent Bertie into the bush to keep him away from Lois.'

'You warned me,' Esme reminded her. 'Never to mention Althea to Lois. Or Lois to Althea.'

Her grandmother looked ill. 'I didn't want them to come face to face. I was afraid it would upset Lois to see her again. Remind her, you know. Make her feel guilty.'

'But Althea came,' Esme said.

'Yes,' Gran said sadly. 'She came when I didn't expect her.'

It had been a hot Saturday afternoon. Victoria had given a celebratory lunch with all the trimmings for Titch and Esme, who had just announced their engagement. They'd drunk quite a lot of wine.

She'd been thrilled to have Titch back in good form, the débâcle with Georgina well behind him. After staying with her for seven months, he'd moved into a place of his own a few months previously.

She'd been thrilled, too, to see Esme so happy. They'd all been in high spirits, except for Lois.

Victoria had been worried about her. Lois had been spending the day with her because Nat had gone to Jill's school. It was sports day there, and Jill was running in the hundred yards and taking part in the swimming gala.

When the front door bell rang, she and Esme were in the kitchen on the ground floor, setting tea trays to take upstairs. She went to answer it.

It came as a shock to find Althea on the step, her small son swinging on one hand, and her eldest daughter sedately holding on to the other.

'Hello, Victoria.' Althea had been smiling. She was wearing high-heeled sandals and a pink cotton dress, cut with a low neckline, all very pretty. This was how Victoria remembered her in Ekbo.

259

But she was very conscious that both Titch and Lois were upstairs. Titch had told her of his toe-curling embarrassment when he'd turned down Althea's proposal, and she didn't know yet that he and Esme were engaged.

And if that wasn't bad enough, Lois was having a bad day. She'd been so tetchy, they'd all gone for a blow on the ferry after lunch.

Victoria had encouraged Althea to visit from time to time. If she were alone, she quite enjoyed their little chats. She'd even encouraged her to come and see Titch when he'd been staying here.

But this was not a good moment for Althea to arrive, and Victoria didn't know how to turn her away without hurting her feelings.

'Come in, Althea.' She knew she sounded unwelcoming, and added: 'Lovely to see you.'

'And my goodness, Rosalie, you're shooting up fast. How old are you now?'

'Twelve.'

She was leggy, and growing prettier. Her blonde ponytail ended in a curl and glinted with golden lights. She presented Victoria with a posy of flowers.

'Thank you. They're lovely.'

She put them in water, fussed about setting out more cups. Found some chocolate biscuits because the Swiss roll wouldn't be enough for them all.

Esme's engagement ring seemed to be flashing fire. Victoria saw her momentary alarm, but she recovered well. Esme had always been friendly with Althea, visiting her often. She'd said she would try not to let what had happened change that. Althea needed friends.

Now she was greeting Althea with apparent pleasure, swinging the little boy up in her arms with easy familiarity. Telling Rosalie how pretty her new dress was. That it exactly matched the colour of her china-blue eyes.

'It does me good to get out without the whole brood once in a while.' Althea smiled at Victoria. 'It's so kind of you to make it possible.'

Victoria had continued to pay the nanny's wages for Althea. She had meant to stop after doing it for the six months she'd promised, but she couldn't bring herself to suggest it while Althea still had children under school age. Her little son was due to start full-time school this month.

'I was planning to come and see you all,' Victoria said. She'd meant to put it to Althea that she ought to be able to manage without a full-time nanny now. That if she felt she still needed help, it would be more economical to employ a young girl just leaving school.

'Myrtle sends her regards.' Althea smiled sweetly. 'She says she's so happy with us and feels so settled. I really feel she's part of the family now.'

Victoria was pleased to see Althea more confident, happier than she had been. Recovered from the set-back Titch had given her.

'And I wouldn't be able to work if I didn't have her. I do appreciate all you do for us, Victoria.'

That had made Victoria's spirits sink. She was wondering if it would be possible to give them tea in the dining room, without Althea knowing that Titch and Lois were upstairs.

At that moment, Titch's voice boomed down from the landing. 'Can I do anything to help, Victoria?'

Esme gave Victoria a reassuring smile, then, picking up the heaviest tray, she headed up to the sitting room.

Althea had lost some of her composure. Victoria gave her the tea pot and water jug to carry and led the way up.

Lois leapt out of her chair. Victoria could see her face working with tension. Titch leapt to his feet too, stiff and awkward. She could feel his unease.

'Hello, Althea. How are you?'

Victoria clattered the tea cups on to their saucers. She knew Althea must feel their unease too. She was talking too quickly.

'I'm fine. All my tribe are fine.'

'Good, good.'

Althea seemed to draw confidence from their discomfort. She looked Titch in the eye and said: 'I want you to know I'm back on an even keel again. Over it all. Looking to the future now.'

Lois uncurled herself from an armchair and said languidly, 'You've heard of Titch's engagement? Show Althea your ring, Esme.'

Victoria saw the colour drain from Althea's cheeks.

'This isn't quite how I meant to tell you.' Even Esme was awkward, but she held out her left hand.

'Congratulations,' Althea managed, her blue eyes burning with intensity as she looked round at the rest of them.

She said, with an edge of defiance: 'I've made myself put it all behind me. Bertie's death and the other bad things. Had to, for the sake of his children.'

'A dreadful thing to happen,' Esme sympathised.

Lois pushed herself forward. 'You didn't see much of Bertie, so I don't suppose you found that too hard. You preferred to stay here while he was in Ekbo.'

This was worse than Victoria had expected, but Titch was covering up.

'At least you have his children,' he was trying to comfort. Victoria was afraid it was the last thing he should say in Lois's hearing.

Althea was holding her head high. 'Bertie wanted a son. I still get a thrill when I look at him.' She fondled the child's soft, pale curls.

'What have you called him?'

261

Victoria cringed. She knew what was coming. Deliberately, she'd never mentioned it to Lois.

'Cuthbert, after his father.'

'How ridiculous,' Lois burst out. 'It's a terrible name. Fancy saddling another child with that.'

Althea looked taken aback. 'I thought I should. It's history repeating itself, you see. He's been born after his father's death too, just as my Bertie was. Comforting in a way.'

'I don't know why it should be,' Lois bristled.

'Losing Bertie like that, I feel I've produced somebody to take his place.'

'Take his place?' Lois's face was flushing with anger. 'Nobody can take Bertie's place.'

'I didn't mean . . .'

'You wouldn't say that if you'd loved him. Anyway, you're the one person who benefited by his death.'

'Lois!' Victoria could see Althea's face crumpling, the colour draining from her cheeks. Esme was trying to turn Lois towards the door.

'Bertie was in love with me,' Lois spat at Althea. 'You'd have lost him anyway. You should be glad he died when he did. This way, you didn't lose face.'

Althea's mouth dropped open.

'And everybody's make it easy for you,' Lois went on furiously. 'Running round after you, helping out, doing what they can. Not to mention paying your bills.'

Titch said quickly: 'Lois doesn't mean it. She doesn't know what she's saying.'

Victoria's mouth was dry; she said: 'Lois is under a lot of stress at the moment.' Esme had taken her as far as the door.

'I can't believe . . .' Althea's face had hardened. 'But yes, I can see it's all true.'

Her young son was clutching her legs, burying his face in her pink skirt. Rosalie had lined herself up with her mother, her face horror-struck, no longer that of a child.

'It's your fault my father died,' she screamed at Lois. 'You tried to steal him from us.'

Lois was sobbing. 'It was Bill Goodbody's fault. He sent him into the bush. He'd be alive today if Bill hadn't done that.'

Althea had backed up against the wall, an arm round each of her children. Her blue eyes, burning with a terrible intensity, went slowly round the room. She was in command of herself again.

'I thought you were so kind and generous, Victoria. That you wanted to help me and the children. You didn't tell me the truth about how he died. You didn't tell me of Lois's sordid seduction attempt.

'I should have guessed. I saw you panting after him, Lois, but I didn't think it would come to anything. Bertie loved his children too much.

'I hold you all responsible for Bertie's death.' The contempt in her voice was like a whip. 'It's conscience money you're spending on me, isn't it?'

Victoria was appalled. That was too close to the truth.

'I want you to know that the help you've given me doesn't make up for what you've done. Not by a long way. Before I've finished with you, you'll all wish you'd never heard of me and Bertie.'

She pulled her children closer and swept off to the stairs.

Victoria sank on to a chair and closed her eyes. She heard Esme run after Althea, and hoped she'd manage to make peace.

CHAPTER TWENTY-THREE

Supper at Links View that night was eaten almost in silence. Jill looked round the table warily.

Lois was frowning at her plate and eating quickly. Victoria was not far from tears and just moving her food around. Very little was going into her mouth.

Nat whispered if he had to ask for a dish to be passed to him, as though afraid to speak in case he upset somebody.

That Titch and Esme had said they intended to go, as well as Bill and Janet, had brought despair.

Gran went up to her room as soon as the meal was finished. Lois went to read the newspapers in the sitting room.

'Let's sit outside,' Jill suggested to her father. 'It's a lovely evening.'

The day's events weighed heavily on her. She knew they'd continue to go round in her head all night if she didn't make an effort to fix her attention on something else.

'It is, but you'll find the gnats are biting,' her father told her. 'Always are at this time after a hot day.'

'I want to talk to you about the business, and I'm bringing a note-book and pencil,' Jill whispered as she dragged him out.

The chairs were still out under the old oak. Her father dragged them into the last of the evening sunshine.

'Felix says you've built it up from almost nothing. If you had sold it when the Lambournes were killed, instead of taking it over, I'd have virtually nothing today.'

'That's as maybe. The legal position is . . .'

'Yes, you've told me. You've also told me it's getting too much for you.'

'It's growing. The greater the sales, the more work there is. And the whole thing is becoming more complicated.'

'That's because it's such a success. You've done wonderfully well,' Jill told him, and then sighed.

What was the matter with her? She ought to be thrilled to find she owned a business like Lambourne's. At any other time she would have been. Now it just seemed another responsibility.

'I feel I've got to help. I can't let you go on like this, Dad. Not if the business is mine.'

'That's always been the whole point, Jill. I did it for you.'

'Yes, but it's time you were taking things easier. You'll be sixty-five next year. You should be thinking of retiring.'

'A bit difficult under the circumstances.' His tired eyes smiled into hers.

Jill made an effort to pull herself together. She wished she had more energy for this. 'But not impossible. I can't leave everything to you as I have done.'

'Surely you aren't thinking of giving up doctoring to run it? Not after all that training?'

'No!' Now she'd upset Dad. 'Certainly not yet. Felix says . . .'

'Ah, so he knows how to run it after two visits?'

'Dad, don't start bristling, I'm only trying to help. Just listen. What I want you to do is to think how this business will be run over the next decade.'

'Oh, I'll probably manage another ten years.'

'Two decades then. The next quarter-century if you like.'

He was blinking at her, nonplussed. She said more gently, 'You can't go on for ever. None of us can. And I won't be able to do much.'

Her father was still staring at her. 'It would go down the drain, Dad, if something happened to you and I had to take over. I wouldn't know where to begin.'

He asked quietly: 'You don't want it? Would you rather it was sold? You don't want to be bothered with it?'

Jill felt things were going from bad to worse. She'd really upset him now.

'It's not that, Dad. It's always fascinated me. It gives me a buzz. But right now, it's a question of what you want. Do you want to be rid of it?'

Her father's face was grey. He looked numb. It took him a long time to reply.

'I've spent all my life building it up. The thought of selling, well, it would be like cutting off my arm. What would I do all day? What would I think about when I can't sleep at night?'

Jill smiled. 'Then there's no question of selling it. We'd both miss the challenge. The excitement.'

'But you . . .'

'If at any time in the future we change our minds, we call sell it then. Right now we need to work out how we can ease the burden on you.'

He was looking at her warily.

'I want you to think carefully. Break the work down into sections. Production. Packaging. Sales, retail and wholesale. There are the books to do, and the office to run.'

Jill scribbled headings. 'You could delegate a lot of the work you do. I want you to appoint a factory manager and a sales manager, and let them get on with it. The same for the packaging.'

'And what am I going to do?' he demanded. 'I don't want to be washed up high and dry wondering how to fill my days. Not yet.'

'You're going to make sure that everybody does what they should. Keep an eye on things generally. Have time to think of new markets and new products. This way, you won't have to be there every minute of every day.'

She could see he was thinking this over.

'Come on, say you'll think about it. Ena, now, could do more than secretarial work. She could do a lot of the accounting for you.'

'She does already.'

'Well then, let her take more responsibility. She could buy in the ingredients.'

'I knew you were going to say that. My mind wasn't on it then. I was so full of relief to have . . .'

'Yes, Dad. Why don't you let her get on with it? You could just run your eye down her list afterwards, make sure she hasn't forgotten anything. You don't have to do all the donkey work.'

'You're trying to tell me she'd have done it quicker without me the other day.'

'I wouldn't dream of telling you that.' Jill smiled. 'Why don't you let me and Felix come in and we'll help you think through everything you do. Three heads are better than one. What about next week? I'll have to fix it with Felix first, but perhaps Tuesday and Wednesday.

Nat groaned and pushed his grey hair back from his forehead. 'All right, I suppose I am running round in ever-decreasing circles,' he admitted.

'You're too close to it. We'll help you take a more objective view. Dad, if it's mine I've got to do something about it before you run yourself into the ground. What's George Simms like? The man who runs production?'

'He's reliable. A good worker.'

'Could you make him factory manager? Would he be capable?'

Nat sighed. 'Yes, I suppose he would.'

'Well then, let him try. You can't go on doing everything. It's getting too big, for one thing.'

'Perhaps I could cut down the time I spend there.'

Jill smiled. 'Think about it.' She leaned over and kissed his cheek.

Jill hadn't slept well, and she'd had butterflies in her stomach all morning about Titch going. He had a day off today. It seemed a foretaste of what was to come.

Miles had filled the kitchen with cigarette smoke and told her he wasn't going to do home visits in future. His patients must come to him. Every extra job, many of which Titch would have done, had been heaped on her.

She was worried about Lois too. She'd continually heard her step-mother's raised voice in the surgery, finding fault with Selma.

Jill was on her way home at lunch time for a bite to eat. As she turned into the drive of Links View, she saw Esme's yellow Mini coming round the corner from the garage.

She knew Esme had seen her when her car paused in front of the house. The drive was wide enough for them to pass there. Jill drew abreast, pulled up, and shot out to have a word with her. This was her chance when Gran wouldn't be able to put in her oar.

'Is Gran feeling better?'

Esme's good-natured face was worried. She switched off her engine, and gave Jill a full run-down on Victoria.

'Esme, we're both bothered that you and Titch are leaving. I don't understand why you have to go.'

Jill could see by her face that Esme didn't want to discuss it.

She went on: 'All this talk about giving Althea money doesn't make sense to me. You don't have to give it if you don't want to, surely?'

Esme's hand hovered over the key in the ignition, but Jill kept on.

'Is she always pressing you to give her more? Is that it?'

'She's always very grateful for everything we do.'

'Yes, but . . .'

'She used to ask us round for afternoon tea. "It's the only way I have of showing my gratitude," she'd say very prettily. "You're all so wonderful to me."

'She'd send us thank-you cards. Tell us how generous we were. Say how thankful she was that she had such good friends.'

'But she's always asking for more than you want to give. Is that it?'

'She has a way of asking for money. So that we can't refuse.'

'What does she say?'

'Oh, something different every time.'

'Tell me one of them. Go on.'

Esme's hand pressed against her mouth. Agonised eyes met Jill's.

'She had a bad time with the children one year. All ill with whooping cough, one after the other. It went on for months. We could see it was pulling Althea down. She brought them all round to our house one afternoon.

' "Poor little Catrina," Althea said, cuddling her on her knee. "I've been so worried about her. She's been really poorly. What she needs now is a holiday."

'Well, Titch and I couldn't argue with that. They all looked a bit wan.

' "What I'd really like to do is to take all my little brood away," Althea went on. "For some sea air. Not far, nothing expensive. It would get them back on their feet before winter comes."

'We agreed she should go to Scarborough for a fortnight. Althea booked herself, the nanny and all five children into an expensive hotel. That was the first time I thought she'd taken advantage of us.'

'Did you tell her so?'

Esme shook her head.

'And Victoria paid for Althea's nanny for years?'

'About twelve. She died – cancer, I'm afraid – or she'd probably still be there now. Althea nursed Myrtle at the end. Gave up her job to do it. She was that sort. Very generous herself.

'But of course, Victoria went on paying Myrtle her salary. They needed the money when she was ill.'

'Althea's your friend, isn't she?'

'Yes, I was very fond of her.'

Jill noted the past tense. 'And now?'

Esme sighed and studied the roses in the border.

'I think, with hindsight, that she had a way of getting money from us. That she deliberately played on our guilt to get more. It was all done very gently and sweetly.'

'And Lois and Victoria were still very willing to give it?'

'We all were. Perhaps we were too generous. Clive's missionary influence.'

'But now her children are grown up. After the expensive education you provided for them all, they should be capable of earning their own living.'

Esme shook her head.

'Do you still see them?'

'Oh yes.'

Jill knew from the change in Esme's voice that she'd arrived at the answer. 'Tell me about them.'

'Good-looking girls, all of them. Not like Althea, though.'

'And Rosalie's taken over from her mother.'

'She's tougher. Cold-blooded. Hard-boiled. Much harder to say no to her.'

'She won't let you say no?'

Esme shook her head again, and started her engine.

'Then it is blackmail?'

Esme rammed her car in gear and hared off down the drive.

Later that day, Jill was driving home after evening surgery. Lois had been the other doctor on duty with her. She could see her step-mother's dark-green Rover up ahead when she stopped at the lights at the bottom of Bedford Avenue. Lois streaked away as soon as they turned green.

Jill felt worn out. She let the Mini amble up the hill to Prenton.

When she pulled up beside the garage at Links View she could hear Lois's voice already raised in protest in the kitchen. As she went in, Lois turned to her, outraged.

'Mrs Moon didn't turn up for work this afternoon and Mother has done absolutely nothing about it.'

'I didn't notice the time.' Victoria was harassed and upset. 'I meant to ring Jill . . .'

'I expect you've been asleep most of the time.' Lois was cross. 'Surely you could have given some thought to supper?'

'Gran isn't fully over her flu,' Jill said quietly. 'What have we got here to eat?'

'Mrs Moon usually makes a casserole on Mondays,' Lois said. 'But of course, she hasn't. The meat's still raw, we can't eat that tonight. Why haven't *you* done anything about it, Nat?'

'I've only been home fifteen minutes myself.'

'Long enough to get a beer inside you. I'm glad I went out to lunch today. At least I'm not starving.'

'I am,' Jill told her, opening the fridge door. She hadn't eaten at lunchtime. She felt she had to get something inside her now.

'We always keep something in the freezer to fall back on,' Victoria worried. 'Just in case this should happen. Now what was it?'

'How about eggs, bacon, sausage and tomato?' Jill was bringing packets out of the fridge. 'I'll do it in the oven.'

'You could have come to lunch at Thornton Hall too.'

'Was it one of the drug companies?' Nat's arm reached past Jill for another tin of beer.

'Yes. I'll have a gin and tonic, Nat. The lunches are always worth going to. You should come, Jill, and meet the other GPs in the district.'

Jill had met Felix at lunch time. She'd poured out all her anxieties about the practice.

'The best thing for you is to get away for a couple of days. You need it. Shall I make the arrangements for that weekend you suggested?'

Later in the afternoon, he had telephoned to say he'd made a booking and all was in order. She'd begun to feel a bit better after that.

'Lois, I'm going to go away for my next weekend off. That's a week on Friday.'

'Going away? By yourself?' Lois's suspicious eyes went from Jill to her father, as though expecting to hear he was going too.

'No, with Felix Kingsley.'

'I don't think you should!' Lois turned on her furiously. 'I don't think he's a suitable person for you to know. I've told you I want you to drop him.'

Jill was making an effort to stay calm. 'I can't do that, Lois.'

'If you want to live in my house I think you should consider my

270

wishes.' Lois slammed down her glass so that her drink spilled over on to the table.

'My house too, Lois,' Nat reminded her gently.

Jill felt she needed to have it out with Lois. 'Why do you object to him? Come on, let's talk about it.'

Lois said nothing, but there was hostility on her face.

'It's no good trying to keep it under wraps.'

Lois snarled aggressively: 'His father made trouble for me. I know what sort of a family he comes from. He'll make trouble for you too.'

'Lois, I've discussed Peter Kingsley's case fully with Felix and with Titch. I've read through all his notes and drawn my own conclusions. You needn't be afraid of what Felix will tell me. I know it all.'

'Why did you want to talk to Titch about it? You should have come to me.'

'But I did. You just said he was making trouble for you.'

'I don't know what's got into everybody. Nobody believes a word I say any more. You're all turning against me.'

'No we aren't, Lois,' Jill said. 'If it'll put your mind at rest I can assure you that neither Felix nor his father is going to make trouble for you.'

'They're making defamatory remarks about me, that's what I'm objecting to.'

'No, Lois. They've put the whole sorry business behind them. Felix won't write any articles about what you did. He's given up all idea of exposing you.'

'There's nothing to expose. They have no grounds on which to complain.'

'Please, Jill, drop all this,' Gran said, putting a hand on her arm. 'Please don't upset Lois.'

'I hoped I was reassuring her,' Jill flared. 'That's what I was trying to do. Why don't we all forget you had any connection with the Kingsleys?'

'There you are Lois, what could be better than that?' Nat asked, as though appealing for calm.

'You're all against me.'

'We aren't,' Jill said. 'But I intend to go away with Felix, so please don't make a fuss about it.'

Lois looked as though she would explode with fury, then she stormed out of the kitchen without another word. They heard her rushing upstairs.

Victoria collapsed on a kitchen chair with a thump. She looked exhausted. 'I do hope she'll be all right. She's getting quite worked up.'

Nat went to the fridge to get himself another tin of beer. 'What about you, Victoria? A gin and tonic?'

'Yes please. I need something after that.'

271

'Me too,' Jill said wearily. 'But I'm on call tonight. You'd better make mine a weak one.'

Victoria could see her hands shaking. Lois's behaviour sickened her, but it wasn't new. How had she managed to ignore it for so long? But she knew what would come next if she didn't calm things down.

'Here, get this down you.' Nat was pushing a large gin and tonic in front of her.

'Jill that's not the way to handle Lois,' Victoria moaned. 'You rubbed her up the wrong way.'

She knew she wasn't handling this right either. She should try to get the girl on her side.

'I'm sorry, Gran, but I didn't start it. I knew she wouldn't like me going away with Felix, but I have to tell her. I can't just disappear.'

'She's just het up,' Nat said. 'Everything's getting to her at the moment.'

'Nat, you must calm Lois down or she'll do something she shouldn't. You know what she's like.'

Jill said earnestly: 'I was trying to calm her down, Gran.'

Victoria knew that. 'You know what to do for her, Nat.'

He pushed his wispy hair back from his forehead. 'It's taking me all my time to stay calm myself, Victoria. I do my best for her.'

'She's always so aggressive,' Jill said.

'She can get manic.' That's what Victoria had to get over to them. Lois would blow up on them if this went on. 'Get her started on tranquillisers, Jill. For goodness' sake.'

She could feel tears stinging her eyes. She knew all the signs, she couldn't ignore them again. Lois was building up to another crisis. She could see the tension tightening. She'd been through it too often not to recognise the signs.

'She won't take them, Gran.' Jill's worried green eyes were searching hers. 'I did suggest to her . . . But you know what she's like, she doesn't give much credence to my medical advice. Why don't you suggest it to her? She'll take it better from you.'

'I already have,' Victoria said. 'Several times. She won't hear of it.'

Lois had been furious and had screamed at her: 'If you really want to help me, you'd give me the money. Just five thousand. Surely that's not asking too much?'

Victoria felt helpless. She'd given her daughter money countless times. Hadn't begrudged it at first. Now she knew better than to believe it would ever end. And anyway, she had no more to give.

'Jill, promise you'll try. To get her on tranquillisers.'

'All right, but . . .'

'It's helped in the past. I'm sure it's the only way.'

She wished Bill were still here to help. He understood Lois and knew how to handle her. They were all leaving her, the people she'd relied upon for years. Her circle was disintegrating.

She felt too old to help Lois. She couldn't do it again.

Nat went up to Lois's room with her supper on a tray. He knew it would do her no good to miss any more meals. She was already too thin.

He said with a brightness he didn't feel, 'I thought you'd like something to eat up here. More peaceful for you.'

She was sitting on the edge of her bed, staring into space. She'd made no move to undress; she hadn't even taken off her shoes.

He tried to work out how long she'd been sitting there alone. Twenty minutes? Probably nearer half an hour.

'Nat, you've got to help me. I've got to have some money.' Lois's face was twisted between embarrassment and fear.

Nat felt his heart begin to pound. 'I told you never to ask me again. You know I've got to refuse.'

'It's only five thousand this time. You could spare me that, you know you could.' He could see the desperation on her thin, sharp face. 'You said yourself the business is doing well.'

'I've told you, Lois. It isn't my money to give.'

He looked round for somewhere to put the tray down. In the end he pushed the books off her bedside table.

'I'll ask Jill then.' That made him see red.

'Don't you dare ask Jill! Don't you even mention money to her.'

'She'll give it to me, I know she will.'

'Don't! It won't do any good. I hold her securities. I won't let her give you anything.'

'I've got to get it from somewhere,' she sounded desperate.

'It's Rosalie, isn't it?' He'd had plenty of time to think about this. 'It has to be, and I'd say blackmail, but what can she possibly have on you?'

Lois stared back at him stony-faced. 'Don't be ridiculous.'

'Go to the police. Tell them what's happening.'

'I can't,' she wailed. 'You know I can't.'

'I don't know anything. How can I? You won't tell me. You expect me to give you money without knowing what it's for. So don't tell me I know.'

'It's for Althea.'

'You can't be saying you want to make a gift of it? You've done enough for her over the years, and I'm sure she's very grateful. But why go on giving her money. Why should you?'

'You know we always have. It's a family thing. Ask Mother.'

'Althea doesn't need it now. Her family has grown up. I've got to stop you bankrupting us all.'

Nat took a great agonising gasp. Victoria had asked him to try and calm Lois down. He was doing the opposite. He was winding her up.

He started again more gently: 'Come on, Lois. Eat something, it'll make you feel better.'

'It won't.' She was dabbing at her eyes with a tissue but she moved closer to the tray.

Nat sank down on the bed. 'You've bottled this up far too long. Why don't you tell me what it's really about? Two heads are better than one. We'll see if we can sort it out.'

Lois's sloe-black eyes boiled with wrath as she turned them on him.

'I haven't bottled anything up,' she said angrily. 'All I need is the money to sort it out. If you won't give me that, there's nothing else you can do.'

Nat felt he couldn't stand her malevolent gaze a moment longer. He'd tried, and he'd failed. He shot out of her room. He didn't slam the door, but it took all his self-control not to.

Victoria and Jill were eating at the kitchen table.

'I put your egg and bacon in the oven to keep warm,' Jill said.

Nat ignored that and raged at Victoria.

'You ask me to try and soothe Lois but you won't tell me what the trouble is. I've had enough of the secrets in this house. You know what it's all about and you aren't saying. Now come on. If you want our help, we've got to know.'

'Dad,' Jill murmured. 'No point having a go at Gran.' She got up and put his supper in front of him.

'You're not going to put me off, Jill. I've just tried to get Lois to confide in me and she says Victoria knows all the answers.'

He was hungry, he pushed egg yolk into his mouth. It burned his tongue. 'Come on.'

Victoria looked terrible, grey-faced and shaking. The tears were even closer tonight.

Jill said: 'Somebody's blackmailing Lois. Blackmailing you all.'

Victoria didn't deny it.

'What has Lois done? What can she possibly have done? It must be something she's got to hide at all costs.'

'Nothing like that.' Victoria was aghast. 'You know anyway. She wants it for Althea.'

Nat said firmly, 'Victoria, I can't believe that.'

'Poor Althea. We're all very fond of her.'

'You've got to tell me.'

She laid down her knife and fork. 'Better if you don't get involved. For your own sake.'

Nat sighed. 'I can't help unless I know what it's all about.'

'You can't help anyway. It's gone beyond that. Stay clear, that's the best advise I can give you.' Victoria dabbed at her mouth with her napkin and pushed herself to her feet.

'I'll go up now. Good night.'

'You'd like some malted milk?' Jill asked. 'We'll bring it up.'

Nat watched Victoria go upstairs feeling full of frustration. Without her, the kitchen was more peaceful. He watched Jill tidying up and making coffee. They drank it at the kitchen table in friendly silence.

She asked: 'Will you take Gran's malted milk up? I've taken so long to make it, I'm afraid she'll be asleep.' He picked up the beaker and went upstairs.

'Come in,' Victoria called when he knocked.

He pushed her door open. She'd already drawn her curtains and switched on the lamp by her bed, but she seemed far from sleep. She was more agitated than ever.

'Such good friends they've been, Titch and Esme.'

'You've known them a long time,' Nat tried to soothe, putting her beaker within her reach.

'Over forty years. I don't know what I'll do without them. Without Bill and Janet, too.'

He'd been about to leave. Instead he paused at the bottom of her bed.

'They're all going, just when I need them most.' He could see her fingers trembling. 'Janet has been a lifeline to me in the past.' She seemed crushed, just one step from panic.

'When Lois was in difficulties, you mean?' he asked.

'Yes, with her first husband.'

Nat tried to put his mind back. In what way had they helped with Lois? Of course, Bill had been sent for on the night Phoebe died.

He looked round for somewhere to sit. The chair by her bed was piled high with embarrassing garments he couldn't move. Corsets and wrinkled stockings and worse. He sank down on the foot of her duvet.

Victoria gave a sad little laugh. 'Dear Bill. I've always thought of him as being young because he is younger than I am, but I looked at him when he was saying goodbye, and saw those tortuous purple veins snaking across his temples. He's looking older.'

'He's seventy-four, Victoria. What can you expect? When you think he was working until recently. It's a good age for that.'

This wasn't what he wanted to talk about. How did he get her back on to Lois?

He watched Victoria pull herself up in the bed. A glamorous night-dress, all lace and satin, looked incongruous against the withered flesh.

The claw-like hand reaching for the beaker certainly looked old. Her rings were loose enough to turn easily, so that the solitaire diamond Clive had given her all those years ago was now almost always in the palm of her hand.

Nat said: 'We're all getting old, Victoria.'

Where did he go from here? Victoria wanted to talk. He should encourage her, but how?

She said: 'I've always done my best for Lois.'

'So have I. A husband has to try.'

'Not all husbands do.' She spoke with more force.

'I knew Graham, I'm sure . . .'

'Oh, Graham!' Her lips tightened and dark, uneasy eyes surveyed him. He'd got her going now, but were they heading in the right direction?

'We expected more of him. Expected too much, I dare say.'

Nat was sure Graham had tried in the early years, even if he'd given up later.

'Lois is never satisfied, that's her trouble. She's always afraid she's missing out on things other women value. She wanted a career, and when it was barely off the ground she wanted a husband and family as well.'

'Nothing wrong with that, Victoria.'

'What was wrong was she couldn't cope with it all. He was the wrong man for her. I blame myself.'

'How can you blame yourself?'

'You know how things were done in those days. I blame my mother too. She said she knew him well. We invited him to dinner to meet Lois. Just as we invited Robert Montgomery to meet Jill. But Lois and Graham hit it off from the start. We thought he was very suitable.'

Nat already knew exactly how things had gone wrong.

'Graham insisted on staying in Birkenhead because he'd just had promotion here. He wanted her to take a part-time job so she could do more in the house. Graham was too set in his ways.'

To Nat's mind, Graham's ways could have done with being more set. He'd gone chasing after another woman.

Victoria was roused to anger. 'She'd have been all right if he hadn't encouraged her to have a child. Then none of it would have happened.'

Nat knew all about what had happened, he'd been there.

He remembered how sick he'd felt when he'd heard Lois scream like a wild thing. He'd followed Graham as he'd run over the road. He'd seen her fly at him with a knife.

He'd known Graham was cleverer than he was. As a surgeon, he was used to keeping his head and thinking calmly in fraught situations.

He'd surpassed himself at that moment. Nat had been an onlooker. The problems were not his, but he'd felt on an emotional knife-edge all the same.

He remembered Graham standing over the child, nursing his bleeding arm.

'A cot death,' he'd said immediately, giving no indication that there could be any other explanation. Lois had been incoherent and in paroxysms of tears. He'd injected her with something to calm her and make her sleep.

Graham had been afraid of scandal. He'd kept his head and covered up, even from Nat.

Nat had stopped Lois knifing Graham. He'd thought that was what they were covering up. Now he sighed heavily. 'Not Graham's fault, that the child died.'

'Partly it was. Poor Lois, I think she found the marriage hard going and she never cared for housework.

'Bill Goodbody took her into the practice, and did what he could for her after that. I think things were better for a while.' Victoria seemed lost in a world of her own. Nat almost got up and went.

'But then she had the baby. Graham knew she wasn't cut out for motherhood, that she was finding it difficult to cope. Not every woman can.'

'But it was what she wanted?' Nat straightened up. This was new to him.

'She'd wanted to be a paediatrician. He believed baby care to be her speciality, and left everything to her. He didn't realise just how much she had to do.'

'She had help in the house,' he reminded her. Sarah had managed on her own.

'She couldn't cope with it all. She telephoned me. "I've made a mistake, Mother," she said. "I hate babies. This isn't what I want from life at all. I meant to be the best doctor in the family, and just look at what I've landed myself with." '

Nat sat ramrod-stiff, hardly daring to breathe. Victoria didn't seem to know he was here now.

'Poor Lois, I told her several times that she must get a live-in nanny and more domestic help. She needed to get back to work.

'I should have helped her more. I was too engrossed in my own job. And my mother was really past helping her further.

'Lois couldn't stand the endless crying or the fact that she was at the child's beck and call day and night. She felt cut off from real life.

'And Graham should have known the time wasn't right to tell Lois he was leaving her. He should have known it would send her over the edge.'

Nat froze. As he understood it, it had been Phoebe's death that had sent her over the edge. His mouth was dry. He got the words out in a whisper. 'What did she do?'

277

'She felt she'd made big sacrifices for nothing and that she'd be better off alone.

'She said Graham drove her to it, that she didn't realise what she was doing. It was only when she lifted the pillow from the baby's face and found her blue and lifeless that she came to. The pillow was in her hands but she didn't remember pressing down on it at all, and the whole thing was over in a flash.'

Nat's head was spinning. He was tingling all over. Victoria's anguished face looked up into his.

Lois had suffocated Phoebe!

He remembered Graham's guilt and Lois's hysteria. Remembered how, later on, Lois had hovered on the edge of a nervous breakdown with her confidence in shreds. It all added up now.

Nat felt the heat coursing through his body again as he thought of Lois. He was aghast that he'd only known half the story, and that she'd married him knowing that. She'd hidden it from him for years. It made him feel sick.

CHAPTER TWENTY-FOUR

Nat's fury swept him across the landing to Lois's bedroom. It was empty, but the curtains were drawn and the bedside light was on. He could hear water running in the adjoining shower room. He snatched the door open.

'Lois?' He rattled the shower curtain back. Some of the hooks slid off the rail. Water was cascading over her hard, thin body. 'I want to talk to you.'

'Not now.' Imperiously she waved him off and dragged the curtain back.

Nat tried to swallow his frenzy and retreated to the bedroom. Flung himself down on the king-sized bed he used to share with her. He'd moved to another bedroom some years ago. He didn't know why he'd stayed in the same house.

His rage at Lois was building up. He could hardly contain himself by the time she came out, tying the sash of her towelling dressing gown.

'Really, Nat, do you have to come bursting in like that?' She was more irritable than ever.

He was beside himself with bitter resentment. Could barely grind the words out.

'You didn't tell me you'd smothered Phoebe.'

She stared at him. Stilled now, as though turned to stone. Her face had been pink from the shower; now it turned crimson.

'Did I not have a right to know?'

She didn't answer but groped instead for her hair dryer.

'I'm your husband, for God's sake. Don't switch that damn thing on, we're going to talk.' He could hear the shock, and the fear, in his own voice.

'Keep your voice down!' Her eyes were suddenly venomous. 'Jill will hear you.'

'Does it matter? Everybody else knows. Everybody else has always known. Graham, Victoria, Bill Goodbody. Everybody knew but me. You let me marry you without knowing that. Did you think I wouldn't go through with it if you told me?'

He could see Lois shaking. He knew she'd never seen him in a blazing temper like this before.

She choked. 'You don't understand. I didn't want anybody else to know. Would you in my position?'

'I kept telling you I loved you. Didn't you trust me enough?'

'Mother thought it would be better if you didn't know.'

'Damn it, Lois. You were old enough to think for yourself.'

'I wasn't myself. I couldn't be responsible for my actions. Even the law says that.'

Nat felt cold. His anger stilled. The law. He'd forgotten the law. Lois could have been convicted.

'You committed murder,' he whispered. Now he knew what Victoria was protecting her from. Lois was cowering back.

She seemed such a strong and competent person. It had taken him all these years to realise it was a front she adopted to maintain her ego.

'It wasn't murder. You can't call it that.' Her voice was a whine; he hardly recognised it as Lois's.

Was he being too hard on her? 'Perhaps not murder,' he allowed. Hadn't he read somewhere that in this country, no woman would be charged with murdering such a young child? 'Manslaughter at the most.'

'Not even manslaughter.' Her laugh had no mirth in it. 'Not when I had postnatal depression.'

'That's so much hogwash, Lois, and you know it. I heard Graham say you showed no signs of it. That he'd been watching for it because of your previous breakdown. He was a doctor, he'd have seen it if it was there.'

She was staring at him, breathing heavily. There was hate in her eyes now.

'You found you didn't like babies. You didn't want to spend your time on that poor child.'

Her worldly-wise face crumbled. 'It wasn't like that, Nat.'

'You should have told me. How do you think I feel, finding out about it now?'

'I couldn't risk it. I didn't want anybody to know. I was afraid I'd be struck off the register. I had to work. Work is what keeps me going.'

Understanding came in a flash. 'You were in too deep by then. Bill Goodbody had signed the death certificate for you. Phoebe was officially labelled a cot death.'

He pulled himself to his feet.

'Don't go,' she pleaded. 'You don't understand.'

'Go on then, explain it to me.'

'I was depressed. Perhaps not before Graham left me, but afterwards.'

'I know you had another bad bout then. But it took a long time for your divorce to come through. You were over that by the time we got married.'

'No,' she insisted.

'You seemed happy enough to me. Engrossed in wedding arrangements and buying this house.'

'That was to take my mind off . . . I still needed help to cope with it. My grandmother came . . .'

'Ah, so Evelyn knew too?'

'Mother wanted Evelyn to come and live with me. To help me. I needed her.'

'You didn't have her for long.' Evelyn had died very unexpectedly.

Nat felt himself break out into a cold sweat as another thought came.

Lois's dark eyes were staring back at him, pleading for his sympathy.

He couldn't get to the door quickly enough. He managed to choke out: 'I understand now why you can't bear to talk about Phoebe.'

Nat slammed across to the room he used and tossed himself on his bed. He was on his feet again in moments, pounding to the window. He couldn't keep still. The night sky was just deepening from blue to black. He could see right across the golf course, to the Dee and beyond. Lights were twinkling for miles around. All was tranquil outside, but his mind was on fire.

Had Lois . . .? He felt strongly that if a person had killed once, to do so a second time would seem easy.

He hadn't wanted Evelyn to move in with them when they were first married. But Lois had. She'd told him that Evelyn didn't want to live alone, and she'd be a built-in baby-sitter for Jill.

Had she come to resent Evelyn's presence in the house?

Nat had been uncomfortable with Evelyn being there all the time, but had tried not to show it. And he had the feeling now that perhaps Lois had not been so keen as time went on. After all, it had been Victoria's idea that Evelyn should live with them. To keep an eye on Lois?

Evelyn had had supper with them the evening before she died. She and Lois had bickered about something. Not exactly a row, but the atmosphere had been strained.

At breakfast time, everything had seemed normal. Lois had taken her grandmother's morning tea in, and he'd heard the old lady saying she'd had a bad night. But often she didn't sleep well. He'd gone to work as usual.

Lois had rung him at mid-morning to tell him Evelyn had had such a massive heart attack that she'd died before the ambulance had arrived to take her to hospital.

281

Apparently she'd got up to take a bath and been taken ill. She'd managed to telephone the surgery herself to let Lois know, though the daily cleaning woman and Jill's nanny had both been in the house at the time.

Suddenly, Nat felt his neck crawl with suspicion. He felt the hairs on his arms stand erect. He'd seen Lois attack Graham with a knife. There had been murderous intent on her face that night, of that he was sure. And now that he knew the truth about Phoebe, it wasn't hard to believe she could have done it again.

Had Lois killed Evelyn? For a doctor, it couldn't be hard to do. Poison in her morning tea? Lois knew all about poisons and had access to some. She could persuade Bill Goodbody to cover up anything.

Nat knew he'd got the creeps. He'd felt it coming on ever since he'd heard Bill and Janet were leaving. He mustn't panic. Evelyn could just as easily have died of a heart attack. He hadn't questioned it at the time.

He couldn't rest. He had to settle his mind about this. He slipped of his shoes and let himself quietly out of his room. The house was silent now. He crept downstairs to the study without putting a light on. They'd had a small safe installed there, hidden in a cupboard.

He closed the door before putting on any light, then, dialling in the combination, he swung open the heavy door.

He kept all their personal papers in here. He was sure he'd seen a copy of Evelyn's death certificate amongst them. There were also papers relating to his business and share certificates into which he'd invested Jill's money. He riffled through the papers until he found what he was looking for.

The cause of death was stated to be a cardiac infarction. Lois had explained that as a heart attack, but was that the truth? His eyes came to rest on the signature.

He didn't recognise it. Bill Goodbody had not certified Evelyn's death. He was filled with relief.

A moment ago he'd had a gut feeling that Lois had killed her. This seemed to prove that she had not. He'd let his fears run away with him.

Fool that he was, he only remembered now that Evelyn had been taken to hospital. The post-mortem had been done there. There had been no question of calling in Bill Goodbody to sign her death certificate.

'Oh God!' he said aloud. It took him a moment to pull himself together and start putting everything back. His mind was still boiling with doubts.

The creak on the stairs was unmistakable. Was Lois coming to see what he was doing? His heart was thumping as hard as if he'd been caught thieving. He locked the safe as quickly as he could. Retreated to the door.

Jill was crossing the hall in a red velvet dressing gown.

'Dad! I thought we had burglars. What are you creeping about down here for? It's after midnight.'

He felt relief that it was Jill, but was still fearful that Lois might come. He took Jill's arm and led her into the kitchen.

He closed the door carefully before putting on the light. They were no longer under Lois's room. Jill was blinking hard in the sudden glare.

'What's going on?'

He had to tell somebody. 'Victoria says Lois smothered Phoebe. That she killed her.' Every time he thought of it he felt sick.

Jill's jaw dropped. 'Lois smothered Phoebe? Does she deny it?'

'No.'

Jill gave him a hug. 'It scares me just to think of it. I'll make us some tea.'

'Jill, I had the most awful feeling, that Lois had done it a second time. It made me think about Evelyn's death.'

Jill's green eyes were wide as saucers. 'Surely not!'

'I think I could be wrong about that.'

'What do you mean?' He saw her moistening her lips.

'Evelyn's death certificate wasn't signed by Bill Goodbody.' Another thought came. 'But Lois knows a lot of the doctors around here. Even those working in the hospitals.'

'What do you mean, Dad?'

'They might have helped her cover up what she'd done.'

'No, no, not something like . . . Not murder.'

'They might,' he said grimly.

'Would Victoria know if Lois had killed Evelyn? But she wasn't here then, was she?'

'Victoria wasn't with her when she smothered Phoebe, but she knew about that. Perhaps I'll ask her when I get the chance.'

'Dad, are you trying to frighten me?'

'I'm frightening myself.'

'Would Victoria have kept quiet about that? A second murder?'

'She was very fond of her mother.' Nat was choking on the ball of horror filling his throat. 'But she'd never let Lois down. She loves her. She'd look after the living.'

He could see the horror he felt reflected on Jill's face as she tried to think it through.

'Perhaps we'll never know.' He shivered.

'Look, Dad, I can see what happened now. Goodbody signed Phoebe's death certificate as cot death syndrome, and in exchange, Lois kept her mouth shut about Tom Sinclair.

283

'He'd been struck off the register and couldn't work as a doctor. Goodbody allowed his friend to join the practice under the name of Cuthbert Meadows. They didn't know whether Meadows had been killed or not. It's logical to suppose his name had never been removed from the register.

'Tom got the job he needed. Lois got what Graham thought was best for her. Bill Goodbody looked after his friends.'

Nat swallowed hard. Jill was right. Everybody seemed to have something to hide.

'It's not just friendship that binds them together,' he said. 'They are in the mire together, up to their necks.'

'We ought to go back to bed,' Jill told her father.

'We'll feel terrible tomorrow if we don't get some sleep.' It was gone one o'clock.

She could see his hands shaking as he tried to warm them on his mug of tea. He was totally fraught, still in a state of shock.

'We've been married over twenty years and I never knew. She's kept it from me all that time. I can't get over that. I was honest with her.'

Jill was letting him do most of the talking to get it off his chest.

'Lois held a pillow over her own baby's head until she died.'

She couldn't take her eyes from her father's agonised face.

'She said she didn't realise she'd been pressing down on the pillow . . .'

All this was making Jill's imagination work overtime. Dad's nerve-racked state was certainly communicating itself to her.

'What are we going to do about it?'

'What can we do after a quarter of a century?' She'd never seen her father so tense. 'What proof is there now? As far as the law is concerned, she's got away with it. It's left its scars on her mind, though.'

'So we pretend we don't know? Pretend Lois doesn't terrify us? Pretend we want to keep it covered, too?'

Jill felt drained. She had to go to bed. As they climbed the dark stairs she stayed as close to her father as she could. The darkness seemed to hide a thousand terrors.

'Good night,' her father whispered on the landing.

She'd left her light on. Her bedroom seemed a safe haven as she went in and shut the door behind her.

But the next minute she was bending to look under her bed, than yanking the wardrobe door open. She was looking for bogeymen, just as she had done as a child.

She kept her bedside light on for the rest of the night. It took her a very long time to get back to sleep.

At breakfast, Lois acted as though nothing out of the ordinary had happened. She ate muesli and drank orange juice. She disappeared behind her newspaper without speaking to either of them.

'I can't believe it,' Jill whispered to her father, as Lois collected her medical bag to set off to the surgery. They were both finding it hard to get their breakfast down.

'We feel worse about it than she does.' Jill felt a nervous wreck.

'She's lived with it for a long time.' Nat was distressed. 'It's all new to us.'

Before morning surgery started, all four doctors squeezed into Selma's office. Miles and Titch were discussing a patient who had been admitted to hospital during the night.

Lois was tapping her fingernails against the metal filing cabinet. Jill couldn't take her eyes away from her. Lois kept grimacing, and there was a nervous twitch in her cheek.

When Titch made a move towards his consulting room, Jill followed him: 'I'd like a word.'

'I've made up my mind.'

'Not about that. Something else, and it's urgent.' She had to get it off her chest. She needed a clear head to work. She shut the door carefully behind them.

'It's Lois,' she told him. 'Whatever made you decide to leave has upset her too. Victoria's very worried about her. We all are at home. She's giving us an appalling time. Victoria wants her to take tranquillisers, she thinks it might help.'

'A good idea.' Titch's dark eyes were wary behind his heavy spectacles.

'But Lois doesn't want to take them.'

'Why not?'

'Doesn't believe they're necessary. Not for herself.'

'What does she say?'

'I'm perfectly calm. You need tranquillisers more than I do. You've got a very nervous disposition.'

'Have you?' Titch was trying to smile.

'You'd have a nervous disposition if you had to live with Lois. She's driving us all up the wall.'

'I know she's got her problems, but . . .'

'I want you to persuade her. We can't.'

The black memories crowded back on her as she tried to convey what Lois was like at home. 'She's at fever pitch.'

Jill thought she saw a look of panic in Titch's eyes. 'We'll get her in here now. Have a go.' He was on his feet.

'Better if you try on your own, Titch. I carry no weight as a medical adviser. Not to Lois.'

He smiled then, gently, and opened his case. He tapped a sample bottle. 'I'll stand over her while she takes the first dose, and give her the rest of these. How will that be?'

'Great. Thanks, Titch.'

'Provided she keeps taking them long enough for them to have any effect,' he said. 'You can lead a horse to the water, and all that.'

'I don't see what more any of us can do.'

Jill went slowly upstairs to her own room. All day, it was an effort to keep her mind on what her patients were telling her.

She couldn't get the fact that Lois had killed Phoebe out of her mind. Or that her family and friends had covered up for her. Or that Victoria thought Lois was building up to another crisis.

Jill didn't sleep very well again. The problems were going round in her mind. She felt heavy-eyed at breakfast, and a little under the weather during morning surgery. Not ill exactly, but disinclined to exert herself and vaguely headachy.

As the afternoon wore on she began to feel worse. Her head throbbed and her limbs ached. She felt shivery, although it was a warm and sunny day.

At tea time, she rang Felix and told him she couldn't meet him for supper. She found that her temperature was up when she took it. By then, she was asking herself whether she was in for a bout of the same summer flu that Gran had had.

'A good job it's Friday, though it's my weekend on call,' she told Lois.

'I'll ring Miles and tell him he'll need to cover for you tomorrow,' Lois told her. 'I don't feel up to it. Let's hope you're better by Monday.'

Jill was hopeful that she might be. She had only a raised temperature, not all the flu symptoms. It was looking more like one of the many virus infections she'd seen recently. She was glad, because they were of shorter duration and she just had to be over it by next weekend. Nothing must stop her going away with Felix.

She flopped in front of the television and ate only half her supper. Dad was sympathetic, shooing her off to bed and bringing her up a cup of Gran's malted milk.

That night seemed never-ending. She tossed and turned and couldn't get to sleep. She had strange, half-remembered dreams and woke in a lather of perspiration. She looked at her clock fifty times in disbelief. She heard the birds singing in the dawn before she fell into a heavy sleep.

She woke up to find her father standing over her with a cup of tea.

'It's mid-morning,' he smiled. 'I was afraid you'd be thirsty. How are you?'

'Better,' she said. Every bone in her body seemed to ache, but her temperature was down, so she got up and had a bath.

When Nat came to tell her that lunch was on the table, she went

286

down in her dressing gown and slippers. She wasn't hungry but she knew it would worry him if she stopped eating altogether. She had a small bowl of chicken soup.

'I'm glad you haven't caught flu from me,' Victoria said. 'That would make me feel terribly guilty.'

'A good job you're better,' Nat said to Victoria. 'One invalid at a time is enough.'

'Too many,' Lois said crossly. 'I'd have thought you'd have more resistance, Jill. A young girl like you.'

After lunch, Jill went to the sitting room and turned the pages of a magazine. Gran brought some needlework to a nearby chair, but there was no peace once Lois joined them.

'It would do you good to sit outside, Mother. It's another lovely day.'

'It's not warm enough. Too late in the year. No heat in the sun now.'

Jill kept her head down, but Lois couldn't leave her alone either. 'You should be in bed.'

'I feel like staying down here for a bit.' She'd been so restless last night, she'd had enough of bed. 'I'll sleep better tonight if I do.'

'You're a source of infection to the rest of us. I'd have thought you'd have more consideration.'

To get away from Lois's hectoring, Jill dragged herself across to the study, where Nat was working at his desk. Her headache was worse and she was feeling decidedly off again. She collapsed on the big red velvet armchair, tucking her feet up under her.

'Come to keep me company?' Nat looked up and smiled companionably. 'Just like old times. You used to creep in here to be with me when you were small.'

'Comfortable old chair,' she said, settling back between its wings. She felt reassured by her father's presence. She always had done as a child.

'Old-fashioned and rather charming. Both these armchairs came from Victoria's old home.'

Each was furnished with a gold satin cushion. Jill drew hers out from behind her back and let it fall to the floor. It was more comfortable without it.

She felt as though her temperature was up again. Really Lois was right, she ought to be in bed. She'd go when she'd summoned the strength to climb the stairs. She drowsed on, barely half awake, the silence broken only by an occasional sigh or a rustle of paper from the desk.

This room, more than any other in the house, seemed haunted by some dreadful happening. Something that had plagued her in the past; that lurked in her mind just out of reach of conscious memory.

She cast about for it, as she had done before, but it stayed

287

tantalisingly out of reach. She knew only that it had frightened her.

Jill heard the door behind her open, and swift footsteps coming in. She felt threatened. Suddenly the gooseflesh was standing up on her arms and she had the most awful palpitations.

She half roused herself to peer round the wing of the chair, and saw the gold satin cushion being held over her face by two strong hands with long, elegant fingers.

There was a tiny tear in the corner of the cushion. It was coming down. She felt the cool satin slide across her cheek, caught the wafting smell of old cloth.

The sensation was fresh and real. Jill was gasping for air. Bursting for breath, fighting off a pillow that was being held over her face by strong arms. She knew now, this had happened to her years ago.

She'd fought and screamed with her child's strength until she'd managed to push the pillow far enough aside to gulp for air. She'd caught a glimpse of Lois's face screwed up with determination. Ugly with tension.

'No!' Jill shot out of the chair, terrified to find that it was Lois doing this to her. Her own stepmother was trying to suffocate her!

Her scream was like that of an animal caught in a trap. It went on and on, higher and higher. She felt her father's arms go round her and pull her against him.

'Jill, love. What's the matter? You're all right.'

She was panting with horror, but knew that this time she was safe.

Lois looked panic-stricken. She still had the cushion in her hands.

'Whatever is it?' Victoria was in the doorway, her eyes wide with fear. 'I thought something dreadful must have happened.'

Jill tightened her grip on her father. She could feel herself trembling.

'Lois tried to kill me.' She lifted her eyes to her stepmother's face. The colour had left it.

'The cushion,' Lois managed to choke out. 'I only wanted to put it back on the chair. I didn't see you there.'

'Not now. I know not now. When I was a child.'

'Don't be silly, Jill.' Lois was blustering.

'I remember now, you tried to kill me.' Jill felt light-headed and a little sick. 'I was eight years old. You turned on me because . . .'

It was all flooding back now. Her mind was swamped by the full horror of it.

'You were going on at me. Telling me I was naughty. Slapping my legs. You got me so worked up that I said something I shouldn't have. That you did naughty things too.'

'No,' Lois denied hotly, but her eyes were wild and frightened.

'You didn't believe me, did you, Gran?' She looked beyond her.

Victoria had turned to stone in the doorway. 'I tried to tell you.'

'No, what a lot of nonsense.' Lois's face was grey.

Jill loosened her father's arms to look at him. His face registered horror and disbelief. 'I kept it bottled up for years, but it all came out that day.'

She went on, her voice flat: 'I saw her kill Great-Gran Evelyn. She was old, she hadn't the strength to fight her off. I was behind the Japanese aspidistra. Lois didn't know I was there.'

'She's taken leave of her mind,' Lois was saying, just as Victoria slid to the floor in a crumpled heap.

'She's only fainted,' Jill said as Nat went to help her. Then she sank back on the chair, covered her face with her hands and burst into tears.

'Victoria will tell you it's true,' she sobbed. 'She saved my life, she knows all about it.'

CHAPTER TWENTY-FIVE

Jill wanted to put her hands over her ears and shut out the clamour. Lois and Nat were shouting at each other. Victoria had come round and was sobbing her heart out. They were tearing themselves to bits. The atmosphere was explosive.

They were all frightened. She had to get away from them before she too was possessed by fear.

She dragged herself slowly up to her room. What was the matter with her? She couldn't think properly any more.

Why hadn't she realised until now that her family were held in an iron grip by what they had done years ago?

Curiosity had started her asking questions, but the most dreadful secrets were coming out. Nothing would ever be the same after this.

Her head was throbbing but she couldn't stop thinking about what had happened that day. They were arguing about it downstairs. Every single detail was flooding back into her mind, driving her crazy.

It had been the school holidays, and Gran had gone to lie down on her bed after lunch. She hadn't been feeling all that good and had reached the stage when she needed a rest in the afternoon.

Jill had been feeling a little bored with her own company. Her dad had come home early but he'd been writing at his desk. He knew she was in the room with him. To keep her occupied, he'd twisted pipe cleaners to make men and dogs for her. She was playing with them in her secret garden while he worked.

When he began putting his books together, she was pleased. This was the time she liked best. She came out and tried to climb up on his knee.

'I have to go back to the factory for an hour,' he told her.

She felt a rush of disappointment again now. 'Can't I come with you, Daddy?'

'No, pet, better not. With all the machinery there, it isn't safe to turn my back on you.

'Anyway, I'll be quicker if you stay here. Victoria is up in the guest room and Mother will be home any minute now. See you later.'

She knew Lois had arrived before her father left. She'd heard them talking in the hall. Then his car had driven away.

She'd crawled back under the Japanese aspidistra to get her pipe cleaner men. The plant was half hidden by the red velvet chair. She didn't hear Lois come into the room. It was the sound of the cupboard door being opened that made her peep out.

Lois was engrossed in what she was doing. Even as a child Jill could sense the intensity with which Lois was going about opening the safe.

She knew her stepmother was doing something she didn't want Daddy to know about, and that she thought she was alone. That brought a surge of excitement that lifted Jill out of the doldrums. She kept her eyes glued on the safe.

Lois was tutting with annoyance because she hadn't put the combination in correctly. She tugged at the heavy door, but the safe wouldn't open. That made Jill realise she'd never seen her opening it before. It was Daddy's safe. She'd seen him take things in and out many times. He'd explained to her what a safe was for.

Lois stopped to listen, and it made Jill hold her breath. Lois was trying again. This time the door swung open and her stepmother was rifling through the papers that were kept there. She brought out a whole bundle and sat down at Daddy's desk to study them.

Jill could smell the secret, airless odour of the safe from where she was. She knew her stepmother would be furious if she discovered she was being watched, and she was finding it hard to keep still.

She'd been sitting on her legs for some time and was getting pins and needles in her feet. Slowly she stretched one leg out, but her shoes caught the copper planter.

She saw Lois turn and peer in her direction. She felt a flutter of fear and took in a great shuddering breath. The next instant Lois was striding towards her.

She jerked back against the wall. A hand snaked in, clamped itself on to her arm and dragged her out. She was shaking, and couldn't swallow the great ball of panic in her throat.

'You little devil! What are you doing behind that plant?' The shocked fury twisting Lois's face was ten times worse than she'd expected. 'You've no business to be hiding there.'

'You're hurting me,' Jill said. Everybody knew she had her secret garden here.

'You're spying on me.'

'No! I was playing.' Jill wanted to justify herself. 'I didn't know you were going to come in and look through everything in Daddy's safe.'

Lois raised her hand and brought it down hard across Jill's legs.

'He knew I was here,' Jill wailed. 'You ask him, he'll tell you. He made me new pipe cleaner dogs so I would play here.'

'He wanted you to stay there?'

'Yes, of course. I always do.'

'He asked you to spy on me?'

'No! He didn't know you'd be coming in.'

'Don't you dare tell him!' Lois was shaking her, then in another eruption of temper, she flung her back against the red velvet chair.

Jill's legs were stinging, and her arm hurt where Lois's fingers had dug in. She clambered up and huddled in the chair, terrified but angry too. If Daddy approved of her playing in the corner, why should Lois object?

'You're a naughty little girl. Prying into what doesn't concern you.' Lois was bundling the papers back together and returning them to the safe.

'Daddy doesn't think I'm naughty.' Jill sniffed. 'I'll tell him when he comes back. I'll tell him you've been counting his money.'

'What do you mean?' Lois was standing over her again. 'I wanted to get my rings out, that's all.'

'You haven't looked at your rings, only his money.'

'I might have glanced at some of his papers. He won't mind my doing that. He shows them to me when he has time.'

'Those papers are money. Daddy told me so. That's why he keeps them in his safe, because they are valuable. And you were going to take them.'

'Of course I wasn't. Only Daddy can get the money out of his share certificates. You don't know anything about it.'

'I'll ask him. He'll explain it to me. He always does.'

Lois's hand shot out, lifting Jill off the chair. Her other hand slapped against her legs again. Jill tried to sink down on the carpet to cover them, but Lois was dragging her to her feet again. Jill remembered the panic that had engulfed her.

'I'm sorry,' she wailed. She knew she'd made Lois angrier. She'd said all the wrong things and made matters worse for herself. She had to stop Lois's thrashing hand.

'It won't matter what I tell Daddy,' she screamed. 'He won't believe me. Grown-ups never do.

'Gran didn't believe me when I told her you were unkind to me. That you often walloped me.'

'What was that?' Lois was screaming at her now.

Jill knew she'd said the wrong thing again. Lois's face was savage.

The next instant, Lois had jumped at her, knocking the breath from her body, and she felt the gold cushion being pressed against her face. She couldn't get her breath. Strong hands were holding her down.

She kicked and writhed and did everything she could to escape Lois's vicious strength. Turning her face sideways, pushing up against the cushion so she could get some air into her aching lungs. Screaming in panic when she could.

'Shut up, keep quiet, can't you?' Lois grated through her teeth.

The cushion lifted, and she was thankfully gulping air. For a second she saw Lois's face twisting with hate above her. Then her head jerked backwards as a strong hand swiped viciously against her face, knocking all the breath out of her again.

She couldn't give up. By then, she understood that she was fighting for her life. She twisted her head to sink her teeth into one of those hands, and knew she'd succeeded when Lois screamed and relaxed her grip. It brought more blows to her head. Everything was going black, and the hateful, smothering cushion was back with all Lois's weight behind it. Terror was slicing through her.

The next thing Jill knew, Victoria was with them, and she was coughing and spluttering and drawing great gulps of air into her aching chest. Her head was ringing and her face was wet with tears.

'Lois! For God's sake! What are you doing?'

She was aware then of Lois collapsed in the chair on the opposite side of the gas fire. Of Victoria injecting something into Lois's arm. Of Victoria using the phone on Daddy's desk to talk to Selma at the surgery. Jill was shivering and yet her cheeks were on fire.

'You've cut your lip,' Granny Victoria was saying as she dabbed something on it that made it sting. 'You must have done that when you fell downstairs. We'll put you to bed now and you can have supper up there if you're a good girl.'

'I want my daddy!' she'd screamed.

'He'll be home soon,' Victoria had soothed. She'd pulverised some tablets on a spoon for her and covered them in jam to help them down.

'These will make you feel better.' Then she was holding a beaker of hot milk to Jill's lips so that she could drink.

'You settle down and have a little rest.' She'd tucked the blankets round her. 'You'll be as right as rain by supper time.'

Jill had felt herself drifting off as Gran tiptoed out of her room.

All had gone quite downstairs. Jill's head still throbbed; she was sweating and her mouth was dry.

She knew at last what had been wiped from her mind all those years ago. What had left such a deep-rooted fear of Lois, a black cloud at the edge of her conscious memory.

For the first time, she was able to wonder what her father had done about it.

He'd gone out that day when Lois had tried to suffocate her, but he'd said he wouldn't be long. Surely he must have known that something dreadful had happened? She was left with the sickening fear that Dad had failed her.

Now she heard his step on the stairs, and when he opened her door she was glad to see he'd brought the tea pot and two cups. He put the tray down, then sat on her bed and hugged her.

'I didn't know, Jill! You've got to believe me. I didn't know what Lois tried to do to you.'

His eyes blazed, she'd never seen him so angry before. 'I must have been blind not to realise . . .'

Jill felt disorientated. She told him all the details that were coming back to her. She wanted now to get things clear in her own mind. 'You must remember what happened that day?'

'I've been trying to. Victoria was here to look after you, it was the school holidays. But she was tired, she'd been doing too much.

'Because she wasn't feeling too good, she rang me at work and asked me to come home early. I'd had a big order in that morning, and I wanted to make sure it was being made up, so I went back to the factory late in the afternoon.

'The house was full of doctors when I returned. Miles Sutton was just leaving, but Bill Goodbody was here too.

'Victoria told me she'd phoned Selma during evening surgery because you'd fallen downstairs. Miles Sutton was on call that evening. He'd dropped everything to come to see you.

'I knew Lois was in a nerve-racked state. She'd been edgy for months. Victoria said she panicked when you had the accident. She was afraid I'd blame her.'

'You'd hardly be likely to do that. Any child can fall down stairs.'

'I thought Lois was feeling guilty because she'd gone out with Bill Goodbody. They were planning the new extension and wanted to see architects.

'I was shocked when I saw her. She was in a terrible state and Bill Goodbody said she'd already had tranquillisers.

'He fixed up for her to go into a private clinic that same night. He told me she was on the verge of another nervous breakdown, that she was trying to do too much.'

'Did she have treatment?'

'Yes, sleep therapy. They kept her asleep night and day for a whole week. She was better after that for a while.'

'What about me?'

Her father hugged her again. 'Oh goodness, Jill, I'm sorry. I knew you were quiet and a bit withdrawn, but Lois's sudden crisis upset us all.

'It never occurred to me to question Victoria's explanation. You didn't say you hadn't fallen downstairs.'

'I didn't know what had happened to me by then.' Jill moistened her lips.

'I'd blotted it out of my memory. It's a psychological protection, Dad. My stepmother had tried to kill me and I couldn't handle it.'

'If I'd had any inkling, I'd have been frantic.' She felt Nat shudder. 'A terrible thing to do to a child.'

'Horrific,' Jill agreed. It was fresh in her mind again. She wasn't sure she could handle it now. But it all added up.

As a result of that, fear of Lois had lingered. That was why she'd been nervous about coming home again, though she hadn't realised it before.

Nat groaned. 'And I didn't even know what you were going through.'

Jill could feel the sweat on her forehead. 'What made you decide to send me to boarding school?'

He was frowning, trying to think back.

'You didn't want me to go, did you? I remember hearing Lois suggest it and you saying no.'

She'd seen that as proof of his love all those years ago.

'It wasn't to protect me from Lois? Get me out of the way, where it couldn't happen again?'

'No!' Her father's eyes were filled with horror. 'Honestly, Jill, I didn't know she'd done anything.'

'It's classed as child abuse today.'

'If I'd known, I'd have called the police.'

'Physical abuse.'

'Not just a physical walloping. Lois tried to kill you, and you understood her intention. So it was mental abuse too.'

'At eight years old I was too strong for her, not like Phoebe.'

'Lois could have damaged you for life.'

'Fortunately I've come out of it without any hang-ups.'

'No thanks to me.'

She hugged him again. 'I can quite see why you accepted Victoria's explanation. You were hardly likely to ask if Lois had been violent towards me. It's not the first thing anybody would think of. It's so horrible.'

'But Victoria,' he was still quaking, 'she could have done more for you.'

Jill felt thoroughly churned up when she thought of what Victoria had done. She'd stood firmly by Lois. They'd kept it from Dad as they'd kept so much else.

'Was it Victoria who persuaded you to send me to boarding school?'

'She was all for it.'

'She must have felt it would be safer. Both for me and for Lois.'

'Now I think about it, it was Bill. He said it would make it easier for Lois to cope.'

Nat pushed his fingers through his sparse grey hair, making it stand up in a thin quiff.

'I'm continually surprised at how much Victoria and Bill will do for Lois. Whatever she does, they stand by her, help her cover it up and carry on.'

'They were protecting themselves too,' Jill said slowly. 'And no doubt Victoria played all this down. Perhaps Bill didn't know Lois had tried to suffocate me.'

'They're very close. They trust each other. Not that Lois ever seems grateful for anything that's done for her.'

Jill poured herself another cup of tea. 'She wasn't grateful for what you did? What did you do for her, Dad?'

'I gave her your money.'

'As long ago as when I was eight?'

'Yes, and several times before that. I'd agreed to give her money for the new extension. Not a lot, because they were getting a good grant towards it and a loan on very favourable terms, but there were expenses.

'She'd asked me for more a few days before this and tried to pretend it was for the new extension too. But she'd shown me the plans all costed out so I knew it wasn't. I refused to give her more then. That was the first time I'd ever refused her anything.'

Jill had drunk the tea pot dry. She felt on fire again. 'Was that why she was looking in the safe? To see what funds you had available to give her?'

'More than likely.' Nat grimaced. 'Another confession to make. Eventually I did give it to her. I was so sorry for her. Having another breakdown and having to go into that clinic.'

'Dad!'

'We were all programmed to rally round Lois. She expected it of us.'

Jill shuddered. 'That's changed now. The balance of power has changed. Victoria's old and frail, and there's war between her and Lois. I don't think she'll ever rally round her again.'

Jill slept soundly that night and woke on Sunday morning feeling much better. She rang Titch because she should have been on call.

'I've asked the deputising service to cover for us,' he told her. 'We're all a bit on edge. Couldn't cope with anything extra. I'll let the arrangement stand. You take it easy today.'

Take it easy? It seemed the last thing she could do. Just facing Lois after what she'd found out made her feel apprehensive.

Lois hadn't denied she'd tried to kill her. That had been impossible when Victoria had fainted. Her secrets were coming out and Lois would hate her and Dad knowing. It was like stripping her bare. Jill half expected Lois to take to her bed, but she heard her go downstairs.

Jill felt outraged when she thought of what Lois had done. She wanted to accuse her of it, rail against her, yet if she did, she'd destroy what little self-control Lois had left. Make matters worse at Links View for all of them.

297

She was tempted to move out, find a flat of her own. She could solve her own problem that way. But it would mean leaving Dad behind. And Victoria too. They were less able to cope with Lois than she was.

Once again, she supposed things would be covered up. She'd have to pretend she knew no more than she had the day she'd returned. They all would.

On Sundays, they usually had a big lunch – a roast and a pudding eaten at leisure. Jill knew she'd have to face Lois then, but she stayed out of the way in her room until nearly lunch time.

When she went down, Lois was in the sitting room with the Sunday papers and a gin and tonic.

Victoria and her father were banging about in the kitchen, trying to cope with the joint.

'I'm sorry, Jill,' Victoria said. She looked as though she'd had a bad time. She was grey-faced and her hands were shaking. 'I protected Lois, but I did nothing to help you over the shock. Didn't even talk about it to find out how you felt.'

'Nature protected me, Gran. Wiped it from my mind. I'm all right.'

Lois stayed out of the way until Jill called to tell her the meal was ready. She came strutting to the dining room then, her angular figure stiffer than ever. Jill expected her to be withdrawn, ashamed, sorry for what she'd done. She seemed none of those things.

They talked about how tender the beef was and how well Nat's courgettes had grown in the garden.

Lois dropped a plate. Her hands twitched, and her face showed signs of strain. She was pretending nothing untoward had happened, and they were all following her lead.

Jill had telephoned Felix before lunch. He was coming round to collect her at two. She went upstairs to get herself ready as soon as she decently could.

Because she didn't think it would help if Lois were to see Felix, she was down by the front gate watching for the Triumph Stag when it came along the road.

It was a relief to get away from the house. It was another mild autumn day and Felix had the hood down. She relaxed the moment she saw his wavy brown hair blowing in the breeze, and his mouth break into its wide smile.

He leaned across and opened the car door for her. She got in. 'How about a trip to Chester?'

With the breeze fluttering at her own hair, she felt she was beginning to live again. 'I'd like that.'

'You still look a bit peaky,' he told her. 'Are you sure you're up to it?'

'I wouldn't survive if I had to stay in the house with Lois all afternoon.'

Haltingly, she started to tell him what had happened, and then the whole story came flooding out. Felix stopped the car in the next layby. She felt his arms go round her in a sympathetic hug.

'What you must have gone through as a child. I knew Lois was evil. I felt it.'

He kissed her gently and Jill was soothed.

They hired a boat and spent an hour rowing on the river, then walked the city walls until Jill felt tired. Then they sat in the sun. Jill banished Lois and all her other troubles from her mind for the rest of the day.

Jill told Felix she wanted an early night, so it wasn't late when he took her home.

'I'll drop you at your gate,' he said, 'and wait till I see you're inside.'

'It isn't what's outside that frightens me,' she laughed. 'Anyway, Lois has already gone to bed.' The light was on in her stepmother's bedroom; Jill could see the glow lighting up her balcony.

She also knew that her father was still up. The light was on in the study.

'You've got visitors.' Felix nodded towards the two cars parked on the drive.

Jill said: 'Why don't you come in and have a cup of coffee? Leave your car here, on the road.'

'What if Lois . . .'

'I don't recognise the cars, but they'll belong to people Dad knows. Lois has gone to bed to avoid them. She need never know you've stepped over her threshold.'

He was walking up the drive on the grass verge. 'The door to her balcony is open,' he whispered. 'Don't want her to hear me.'

She led him in through the back door and via the kitchen. She could hear voices now from the study, and went to see who was there.

Ena's bulk occupied the chair in front of Lois's elegant desk. George Simms was with her.

'Hello, Dad, I thought it would be safe to bring Felix in tonight.'

'Safety in numbers?'

'Something like that.'

'I hoped you'd be back in time. These two have been working all afternoon. I took them out for a meal and then we came back here for a drink.'

'Easier to discuss things here,' George added.

'Hello, boss.' Ena's plump face was wreathed with smiles. 'I'm delighted with my new job.'

'Are you calling me boss?' Jill laughed.

'We understand you are.' George was grinning now. 'Always thought Nat here was the gaffer, but it seems we were wrong.'

'I find it hard to believe myself. But that's what Dad tells me.' Jill smiled at her father.

'It was Jill's idea to change the way I was running things.'

'To take some of the weight off your shoulders.'

Last month, she and Felix had spent two evenings down at the factory, helping her father sort out exactly what responsibilities Ena and George should take on. All Dad had needed from them was to have the way forward pointed out, and the push to get started. They'd left him to draw up job descriptions and approach the people he'd chosen.

'I'll keep responsibility for finding new sales outlets for the time being,' he'd told them. 'But I'll keep an eye open for somebody I can train to do the job.'

She'd been surprised at how strong Dad's grasp on the business was, and how much enthusiasm he still had.

'This will give me time to think about other things,' he said contentedly. 'What I've really set my mind on are new premises. We're bursting out of what we have. We can't possibly expand any further there.'

'Dad! I thought you wanted less work?'

'I got a bit bogged down,' he smiled. 'Couldn't see my way forward. Got worried about everything.'

'What I'd like is a factory designed for our own needs. With packaging being made and printed on the same site. And easy access, instead of having to drive through the town centre. That wastes so much time.'

'You're not going to stop him working.' Ena smiled as she pushed a black box towards Jill.

'This is what you suggested we make for the Christmas trade. A novelty for children. It looks good, doesn't it?'

'The paintbox?'

'We decided to go with that rather than the crayons,' her father explained. 'Easier and cheaper to simulate.'

Jill reached for the box. 'It's empty?'

'Just the rough-up,' Ena said. 'Cardboard copy of the real thing.'

'Don't be disappointed.' Her father raised his eyebrows. 'These are some of the paints that will go inside. Filled squares wrapped in different-coloured foil. Ten to a box. Very easy to make. Not expensive. You can eat these.'

He said to George Simms: 'What the boss values most about her business is being able to eat an unlimited amount of the product.'

'Very pretty.' Jill took red foil off an oblong of chocolate-covered Turkish delight and bit into it.

'You'll end up like me if you carry on like this,' Ena laughed.

'Tastes lovely.'

'She's thin enough yet,' Felix said.

Jill fitted the other chocolates inside the box, ate another and then passed it round. Only Felix and Ena accepted.

'If you eat as much as I have,' George said, 'you'll find you go off chocolates.'

'I taste them,' Nat said. 'But it's duty, not pleasure now. I've had too many.'

'I'm addicted,' Ena said. 'I'm going to take myself in hand soon.'

Her big moon face beamed at Jill. 'I'm delighted with the way things are going at the factory. I feel as though I'm getting a chance to show what I can do.'

'So do I,' George added. 'I'll do my best for you.'

Her father said: 'Felix has been a great help. He looks at things in a very different way.'

'Felix is good at helping fathers.' Jill smiled at him.

'Getting plenty of experience at the moment,' he grinned.

As Jill got dressed on Monday morning, she felt that Sunday had been a brief respite. Dad was much happier about the business and she felt closer to him. But other problems were crowding in on her this morning.

She was wondering whether Lois should go to work. She didn't think she'd be up to dealing with other people's problems in the surgery. But before she was ready to go down herself, she heard Lois's footsteps running downstairs.

Her father had told her last night that Lois hadn't lifted a finger in the house all day, that she'd been restless and irritable.

Jill went down to meet the scent of coffee coming from the kitchen. Dad was eating toast. There was less of the sparkle she'd seen about him last night.

Lois seemed a different person this morning. She was excited, agitated, almost frenzied. For once she didn't sit down to breakfast or open her newspaper.

'What a lovely morning this is,' she said from the window, then jerked back to the table. She had a glass of orange juice on the work top and a cup of coffee on the table, and she took a mouthful from each alternately.

She never stopped talking, but not about anything of importance.

'This coffee tastes strange. What's the matter with it? Do hurry up, Nat, or you'll be late.'

She started to hand-wash a recently bought cardigan. Talking to them all the time from the utility room that adjoined the kitchen.

'Can't trust Mrs Moon not to felt woollens. She's no good at this sort of thing.'

301

She dropped at least a pint of water on the floor as she rushed the cardigan to the washing machine to spin it.

'She's in a bad state of nerves this morning,' Nat whispered.

Lois was off to work before either of them, her Rover racing faster than usual down the drive.

Jill was unlocking her Mini when she heard the crash. With her heart in her mouth, she ran round the front of the house to see what had happened.

Lois's car had clipped the gatepost. She'd been cutting the angle too close as she moved out into the road. With only a brief gesture of impatience, she put her car in gear again and drove straight on. The sound of metal scraping on metal made Jill wince.

Jill stood looking down at the gatepost left standing at a crazy angle, with half the ornate metal gate swinging on one hinge. Nat came out to join her.

'Lois has certainly got the jitters this morning, Dad,' she said.

At the surgery, things were no better. Jill felt in a state of ferment herself.

She started work straight away. She knew that to focus her mind on her patients' needs would blot out the problems of home. It was what she was used to doing. She wanted to make the morning feel normal.

She had the last patient in her room when she heard Lois shouting downstairs. It shattered the calm she was building up.

'Not another blasted penny,' she was raving. 'Not another one.'

Selma's voice was lower and more controlled. It seemed that Lois was having a row with the receptionist now.

Jill's patient left her to clatter downstairs. Morning surgery had finished. She heard Titch's voice, raised for once. Then Miles's.

When she went down to see what repeat prescriptions she needed to sign up, Selma's cheeks were flushed, but the work for each of them was efficiently laid out in four piles as usual.

Polly's eyes were wide with apprehension. 'Selma asked her to buy a flag for the Lifeboat Fund,' she whispered. 'That's all.'

The flags and collecting box were on her desk. Jill felt for some coins to contribute. By the looks on their faces, nobody would ask her.

The kitchen door was closed but Lois's feverish voice was clearly audible from the passage. Jill decided to give morning coffee a miss.

The state of jitters had spread from home to the surgery.

CHAPTER TWENTY-SIX

The next morning, when Jill arrived at the surgery, Miles was already in Selma's office. Jill didn't want to talk to him, so she took her coffee upstairs and sat at her desk. She was getting more jittery by the minute.

She could hear the patients gathering in the waiting room below. She knew Titch had arrived, his voice boomed up the stairs. He sounded less genial than usual. Lois was railing at Selma again.

Jill decided she'd had enough. This was not a practice she wanted to work in. She'd made a big mistake.

No, she told herself, it wasn't her mistake. She'd been deliberately misled into believing it was a normal practice, where everything was legal and above board.

She lifted the phone on her desk and asked Selma for an outside line. Then she dialled the solicitor who was handling her purchase of Bill Goodbody's share of the practice premises.

'Has the money been paid over yet?' she wanted to know.

'Not yet, we have to clear your cheque. I'd like you to come in and sign . . .'

'I've changed my mind about it,' she told him. 'I want to withdraw from the arrangement. Don't hand over my money.'

If Titch could withdraw, so could she. She didn't want to work with doctors who were being blackmailed. And having tried it, she knew she couldn't work with Lois.

She ran headlong down the stairs, and just managed to beat Titch's first patient to his door.

She let it all come rushing out. Not only was she not going to take Bill's place but she and Victoria were worried stiff about Lois. He was her GP, he had to do something.

'I tried hard to get her to take those tranquillisers, Jill. She refused point blank. I can't make her.'

As she'd suspected, Titch knew that Lois had smothered Phoebe, and all about the cover-up.

'She's over all that,' he tried to placate. 'It happened years ago.'

'My father didn't know until the other night. Neither did I. Everything here is driven underground, kept under wraps, and I can't stand any more of it.'

She could see Titch didn't want to hear any of this. He kept looking at his watch. He wanted to put her off so he could start his surgery. They were both behind with their appointments now. That usually meant they'd be behind all morning.

'We can feel Lois winding up tighter and tighter. You've got to do something. This place is like a pressure cooker. I can feel it building up steam, and soon it'll go off. For Lois, it's too late for tranquillisers. She needs hospital treatment.

'I want her out of the house. She's having a hate session against Victoria, frightening her. I'm afraid she'll turn against me or Dad. She could be dangerous.'

'Oh, I don't know . . . She doesn't seem that bad here.'

'She is. You don't see as much of her as I do. I want you to refer her. Get a consultant to treat her.'

'Jill, you know what Lois is like, I'll have to ask her if she wants . . .'

'She won't want it, but we've got to settle her down. I'm terrified she's going to do something desperate.'

'I'll talk to her, of course, if you think it necessary, but . . .'

Jill sighed with frustration.

'This came in the morning post.' He was pushing a letter across the desk to her. She snatched it up, almost too fraught to read.

'Take it upstairs and study it,' he said, ringing the bell for his first patient. 'You'll be interested.'

Jill knew she'd been dismissed. She went slowly upstairs.

The letter was from the Council to say that the Town Planning Committee had decided to redevelop a further area of Rock Ferry on the edge of the Tranmere Hall Estate. And that property and free-holds in the area shown on the attached map would be subject to a compulsory purchase order.

Jill paused under the landing window to study the map. It applied to the surgery. Several streets would be flattened and then rebuilt.

Jill thought it was the best thing that could happen to it. It would break up this evil practice once and for all.

Seated outside her consulting room were Mrs Cathcart and Mrs Dunne. She signalled to the first to follow her in. She felt involved with these two, and wondered what would happen to her list when she went.

Frustration with Titch bubbled up again. She should have laid it on more thickly. Should have told him that Lois had attacked Victoria the other night, and she was afraid she'd do it again. That he'd have to have Lois sectioned if that was the only way to get her in to hospital.

That they were all living on their nerves at Links View.

Jill's last patient had just left her room. She could still hear her clumping downstairs when the intercom on her desk buzzed.

Selma's voice said: 'Would you mind seeing one of Titch's patients? He's been called out to an emergency.'

'Yes, all right.'

'There's two here actually, and they don't want to wait for him to come back. Miles isn't here. He finished and shot off out as though he knew this was coming.'

'Send them up, Selma.'

'Your mother's still here. I'll see if she'll do one.'

'Fine.'

Titch's patient was an old man who took an age to get upstairs. He was long-winded in telling her what ailed him, and she didn't know his history. When she'd dealt with him, she was glad to find that Lois had taken the other patient and she was free to have her coffee.

The biscuits were out on the kitchen table and Selma and Polly were having theirs when she went down. The front door opened and high-heeled sandals came clicking up the hall.

Polly shot out to see who it was. Jill had guessed even before she heard the plummy voice.

She felt the strength drain from her knees. She guessed, too, that Rosalie had come for more money.

Everybody in the practice had given money to Rosalie's mother. She'd used a softly-softly approach. They'd all had a long guilt trip about the harm they'd done to her. It had made them give generously and frequently.

But Rosalie had taken over now. They had less reason to give to Rosalie. She'd had to resort to threats, make demands to get what she wanted. But she was tougher than her mother.

And Rosalie had plenty to threaten them with. Things they wouldn't want exposed. Titch Sinclair had assumed her father's name when he'd been struck off the register. Lois had killed her child, and Bill Goodbody had known these things and helped cover them up.

Perhaps Rosalie wanted more than money? Jill knew just how strong the urge for revenge could be.

Lois had lured her father away from her mother. Tom Sinclair had taken her father's name, and Bill Goodbody had sent her father out into the bush to be killed.

Rosalie's revenge was to make them pay more than they could afford. She was bleeding them dry. Jill wondered if for her, exacting revenge was sweeter than the money itself.

'I'm afraid Titch has been called out to an urgent case,' Polly was saying.

'I told him I'd be coming this morning.' Rosalie's voice was impatient. 'He said he'd be here.'

'He'll be back, but we don't know how long he'll be.'

305

'Is Lois here?'

'She'll be free in a moment. Just finishing surgery.'

Selma was craning her head to look up the passage. 'She dresses beautifully.' she whispered. 'Navy and white cotton this morning.'

Jill craned forward too. Rosalie was wearing a short-sleeved summer dress. She ought to stop her going in, but how?

At that moment the door to Lois's consulting room opened and her last patient came out. Rosalie was inside before Jill had got herself going. Polly came back to finish her coffee.

'You go home, Polly,' Selma told her. 'I'll do the filing. It's past your time. We're late this morning.'

Jill was filled with dread. She knew that Lois had no money to give Rosalie, and the last thing she needed was to have Rosalie threatening her. It was bound to make her worse. She felt she should be doing something to help her stepmother.

She switched the kettle on to make more coffee. Helped herself to another biscuit she didn't want. Selma's lovely eyes were staring into space.

They both heard Lois's voice. It was so charged with emotion Jill hardly recognised it.

'I can't do it. Can't possibly afford . . .'

Jill held her breath. Rosalie's voice was lower and more controlled. She couldn't catch her words. She could see that Selma was all ears too.

'There's no way I'll be able to get it. When will you learn you can't get blood out of a stone?'

Rosalie was answering, but again Jill couldn't catch her words.

Lois rasped out: 'You've drained us all in this practice.'

Jill was straightening in her chair. Her mind was on fire. She found that Selma's eyes were searching her face. She said carefully: 'Everybody complains about shortage of money. Do they ever think of anything else in this practice?'

Lois's voice came again. 'If I can't, I can't. I've given you all I can.'

Selma smiled over her cup. 'That's the trouble with the new extension. Walls too thin. They should have put in more sound-proofing.'

She drained the last of her coffee and smiled again: 'Especially considering the carrying quality of Lois's voice.'

'We're at the end of our tether. You've got to stop it.'

'Rosalie twists them all round her little finger.' Selma couldn't stop smiling. 'She's giving Lois the run-around. Her comeuppance. Rosalie decides what goes on in this practice. Haven't you noticed?'

Jill took a deep breath. When Dad had suggested blackmail, it had seemed almost a figment of his imagination. Now she was hearing Rosalie in action.

'They're all dying to oust Miles. But of course they can't. Rosalie won't let them.'

Selma's voice dropped even lower. Her tone was confidential.

'They don't seem to be able to throw her off their backs. Good job she doesn't come near us.'

The phone was ringing on her desk. 'Rotten timing,' Selma muttered, getting to her feet.

Jill could no longer hear anything but the shrilling phone. She followed Selma into the hall. Then through the hatch, she saw her beckon.

'It's one of your patients,' she whispered. 'Wants a word.'

'As you said, rotten timing,' Jill grimaced.

To Lois, morning surgery seemed endless. She felt she was in a flat spin. Her desk was a shambles of empty record envelopes and loose paper. Somehow she couldn't get anything organised and put away. She'd upset a box of syringes on her trolley, some had fallen on the floor. She'd crushed one under her foot.

As soon as Rosalie's head came round the door, she felt her heart race. It seemed the last straw.

It didn't help that Rosalie looked beautifully groomed, as though about to model for *Vogue*. She wore a smart navy and white dress, not the sort you saw many of on Merseyside. She didn't look the type to cause trouble, but Lois knew she was.

Automatically, Lois rose to her feet. She mustn't let Rosalie look down on her.

'You know why I'm here, Lois.' Rosalie's tone seemed pleasant enough.

Lois was heavy with dread. 'You're wasting your time. I told you that last week.' Over the years, Rosalie had conditioned them all to give in to her demands.

Lois went slowly round her desk to perch on the corner. The blood was pounding in her head. She felt strapped down. Cornered.

Rosalie ignored the chair provided for patients. Instead she paced back and forth and pretended to be interested in what she could see through the window.

'Stephanie, my youngest sister, is getting married. You remember Stephanie, don't you? Mother and I were sure you'd all want to give her a wedding present. After all, she needs a house of her own now.'

'I can't do it, Rosalie. It's impossible. Neither can Titch.'

Lois felt a spurt of anger. Had Titch really had an emergency? Or had he deliberately left her to deal with Rosalie by herself? The girl didn't know when to stop.

'Of course you can. Mother says you've always been very generous. You always say you can't, but you come up with it in the end.' Rosalie's smile seemed to radiate confidence that this would happen again.

307

'Not any more. You always promise it will be the last time you'll ask.'

Rosalie laughed. Lois wanted to put her hands over her ears to shut out the sound. It infuriated her to see how sure Rosalie was that she was going to get what she wanted.

'You've given wedding presents to the rest of us. It wouldn't be fair to leave Stephanie out, would it?'

Lois could feel her wrath rising. 'I haven't . . .'

'I told you I wanted it by today. You knew I was coming.'

Rosalie's pert manner incensed Lois. She felt a terrible urge to scratch her eyes out, deface her blonde beauty for good. But physically she'd be no match for Rosalie, though she was much the taller. Rosalie was more than twenty years younger.

'Don't let's beat about the bush. I'll take a cheque, as long as you understand what will happen if it bounces.'

Lois felt the surgery eddy round her. 'Miles won't let you say anything defamatory about us. It would ruin the practice. It's his livelihood too.'

'He can turn his back on this any time, Lois.'

'I suppose he can, with what we've given you over the years.' It rankled that she'd had to hand over so much.

'And he's not so enamoured that he wants to spend the rest of his life working here. You must know that.'

Lois moistened her lips. Of course she knew it. 'You've asked once too often. I can't . . .'

'Get your cheque book out.' It was a sharp order now. Rosalie's china-blue eyes were like cold steel. Lois sat on her hands. She mustn't give in to her.

'If you don't, I'll make sure no patient will ever trust you and Titch again. I'll get the police here to ask questions. Then there's the Family Planning Committee and the General Medical Council. I'll get them all interested in what you and Titch are up to.'

Lois swallowed the bile in her throat. What a bitch this girl was.

'If you don't want to use your own cheques, I've brought you a couple of blank ones from the bank. I'll fill in your account number for you.' Another malevolent smile.

Lois saw her push a form along the desk towards her. She slid away from it.

'You don't understand. I've no more money to give.'

It was the gospel truth. She'd started by handing over her own money. But Rosalie's demands had become insatiable. She'd had to ask her mother, and then Nat, for more and more.

'You wouldn't want to disappoint Stephanie? Somebody has to provide for her. It's only fair you should help. Think of what you did to our father.'

'I hate you.' Lois's voice was thick. 'Hate you. Hate you.'

Rosalie had the look of a nanny whose patience was being tried.

'I know you hate me. We've been through all this before, haven't we? Be assured it's mutual. You ruined our lives. My mother never got over it. It was just an affair for you, wasn't it? A whim. Something to enliven your visit to Ekbo.'

'No.' Lois felt anguished. 'I loved Bertie. I keep telling you that.'

Where was Titch? Why didn't he come?

'You didn't give a thought to his four little children, or that our mother might be pregnant with a fifth, did you? It wasn't much fun being brought up on a Widows and Orphans Pension.'

Lois was trembling. The hate, the vindictive need for revenge on Rosalie's face were terrifying.

'Given time, he'd have seen through you. But he didn't get the chance, did he, Lois? You sent my father to a horrible death.'

'I didn't want him to go out in the bush. You know I didn't.'

'It sickens you to think of his body being defiled? Used in juju rituals. Eaten by cannibals. It does me too. How do you think my mother feels about that?'

'He'd be here with us today if you hadn't set your cap at him.'

Rosalie pushed the cheque in front of her again. Her set face told Lois she was in deadly earnest.

'It's only right you should pay. We have to be compensated. Come on, get on with it. I'm not waiting all day.'

Lois could feel the sweat running down her back. She was boiling with rage. 'Have you no mercy?'

'Mercy? Did you have any thought for my mother? She's not wearing as well as you are, Lois. She's had a harder life, with nobody to look after her and her big family. You've never shown any remorse for what you did.'

Lois felt desperate. Her voice rose an octave. 'You've got to believe me. You've had all I can give. My mother and I, we've even sold our jewellery.'

'Poor Victoria,' Rosalie sneered.

'My mother has no more to give. You've had the money from her house, everything Clive left her.'

She'd given Rosalie her own inheritance, Lois knew that. It brought the gall to her throat every time she thought of it.

'Ah yes, the saintly Clive. It must be wonderful to have a father you can be proud of. Your husband makes plenty of money from his chocolates. He'll give you more if you ask.'

'No he won't,' Lois wailed bitterly. It had hurt enough that Nat had refused. To admit it to this fiend was humiliating.

'You've got to give until it hurts. I'm going to make sure you do,'

Rosalie sneered. She knew all about keeping the upper hand. She was pushing a pen at Lois now.

But Lois was determined. 'I can't. I won't be able to meet it. I won't.'

Out of the corner of her eye, Lois saw the box of scalpels she'd left open on the trolley. She'd used one earlier to lance a boil. The rest were tumbling out. Each sterile and sealed in cellophane.

'You've got to stop . . .'

Lois hardly knew what she was doing. She snatched at the nearest scalpel, ripped the cellophane from the blade with one deft movement and lunged at Rosalie's heart.

But Rosalie saw her and flashed back out of the way. The knife caught her bare arm. Blood came spurting out and Rosalie started screaming.

Lois could see she'd barely nicked the flesh. She went for her again.

'I'll mark you for life,' she grated through clenched teeth. She was going for Rosalie's face now. Slashing at it. 'I'll make you suffer after all you've done to us.'

Half blinded with fury, Lois lurched at Rosalie's firm and well-cared-for body, jabbing again and again until the disposable blade snapped away from its flimsy plastic handle. The scalpel was meant to be used once and thrown away.

She turned and grabbed another from the box, but that gave Rosalie time to lift the patient's chair. She was holding it in front of her like a shield, and Lois could no longer get near enough.

Rage gave her superhuman strength. She wrenched the chair from Rosalie and flung it out of the way. Rosalie continued to scream and was backing against the door, trying to open it to get away.

'Shut up! How dare you come here with your incessant demands?' Lois jabbed again, through the navy and white dress.

Suddenly the door was pushing against Rosalie, and she was falling, the door slamming back against the wall.

Selma's face stared incredulously into Lois's. It brought home the enormity of what she was doing but she couldn't stop. She kept on jabbing at Rosalie until that scalpel snapped as well.

Selma was screaming too: 'Jill! Jill, come here!'

Panic lifted her voice to a shriek. 'Jill! Oh my God!'

Jill couldn't take it in. There was blood splattered all round the consulting room. A chair had turned over. Rosalie had collapsed on the floor in a state of shock, bleeding from countless small wounds.

Lois threw herself across her desk in a paroxysm of weeping.

'She asked for all she got.' She was hammering on the desk with her bare fists. 'The bitch, I ought to finish her off.'

Jill was fighting to stay calm. Goose pimples were standing out on her arms although she was sweating. She grabbed a roll of cotton wool off Lois's trolley and bent over Rosalie. She didn't know where to stem the blood first.

Lois had done this? It was the work of a maniac. Jill could feel her own teeth chattering.

'Better call for an ambulance,' she was saying to Selma when she heard the front door slam and Titch walked in, blinking behind his heavy horn-rims. She'd never felt so relieved at the sight of anyone before.

'No ambulance,' he countermanded. 'We'll see to Rosalie ourselves. What's happened?'

'She's losing consciousness,' Jill gasped. She and Selma were both talking at once, trying to tell him what had happened.

'Just fainted. All small wounds, Jill. Hopefully not deep. Done with a sterile blade. Help me get her up on the couch.'

'Several deep cuts on her palms.' Rosalie had used her hands to defend herself. Jill was still trying to stem the flow. 'A bad one on her arm too.'

'Hold her arms up in the air, Selma. Let's see if we can stop some of this bleeding. Cut up the bodice of her dress, Jill.'

'No,' Selma protested. 'It must have cost a fortune.' She was already opening the buttons down the front, pushing the cloth back. Rosalie's white cotton slip had a large red stain on the lace edging her bosom.

'We've got to see if there's damage underneath,' Titch overruled irritably, tearing at the slip. 'Is that cut deep?'

'Nothing dire,' Jill reported. 'A small nick at the top of her left breast. Saved by her bra. Another nick over her ribs here. Could be worse.'

'Nothing on the abdomen?'

'Can't see anything.'

'No tears in her clothes,' Selma agreed.

'Thank goodness.'

'She's coming round.'

'She's severed a couple of tendons on her left palm, probably on the right too.'

'I'll see what I can do later when the bleeding stops.'

'You're not going to repair them here?' Jill had only ever seen it done under a general anaesthetic in a hospital operating theatre.

'Best place, if we're going to keep this quiet.'

'But here? Can you?'

'Yes, Jill. Conditions here are good compared with what we put up with in Ekbo. Nothing like a few years' experience there. Taught me to cope with everything.'

Selma squealed hysterically. 'She's a terrible grey colour.'

311

'Shock, that's all. She'll be all right.'

Rosalie's eyes flickered open. She turned her head to look at Lois, who was still sobbing noisily. Jill saw her colourless lips form the words: 'You won't get away with this.'

Titch was trying to soothe Lois. Jill was glad she hadn't been asked to do that. She could barely bring herself to look at her.

Dad had told her how Lois had gone berserk and attacked Graham all those years ago. Now she'd done it again. Rosalie hadn't realised just how dangerous it was to bait her.

'You'll pay . . . pay for this,' Rosalie groaned.

It made Lois weep more loudly. Her eyes when she lifted her face were red-rimmed and wild.

'You shouldn't have left me to deal with her,' she shrilled at Titch. 'She wouldn't take no for an answer. You can't blame me.'

Titch was giving Lois an injection. 'Largactil,' he whispered to Jill. 'And we'd better start her on oral therapy straight away.'

'Shall I phone the police?' Selma wanted to know. 'I mean, this is grievous bodily harm.'

'No,' Titch barked. 'No, and you must keep your mouth shut about it. We don't want any of this to get out. Good job it didn't happen in the middle of surgery when the place was full.'

Jill knew he was as frightened as she and Selma were, he just had it more under control. He was drawing up local anaesthetic. 'I shall have to probe deep into her right palm. Where did Miles go?'

'Out to do visits,' Selma said. 'I bet he wanted to get out before Rosalie came. He'd be expecting trouble.'

Titch straightened up, frowning. 'Which of his patients asked for home visits? Can you remember?'

'Not off hand.'

'Ring round them, Selma. If he hasn't called yet, leave a message for him to phone here urgently.'

'Not all of them have phones, and I don't know in which order he'll visit.'

'Just try, Selma. Do your best. The sooner we get her out of here the better.'

Jill marvelled at the steadiness of Titch's hand as he tried to repair the tendon to Rosalie's index finger.

'Sliced clean through it.' He glanced up at Jill. She could see the horror in his eyes. 'But you'll be able to use your fingers, Rosalie, when it all heals.'

'Her left hand is worse. Tendons gone in three fingers, I think.'

'Yes, I know.'

'My face?' Rosalie moaned. 'It feels awful.'

'Just shallow scratches,' Jill assured her. Two weals ran for six

312

inches from temple to chin. 'Don't worry about them. They should heal without leaving any mark.'

'We'll use skin closer strips to draw most of your cuts together,' Titch said in his gentle voice. 'But some will need a few stitches. Mostly on your hands.'

'She deserves all she got,' Lois croaked behind them. 'Leave her to rot in hell, can't you?'

'Jill will take you home in a few minutes, Lois,' Titch told her calmly. 'You must go to bed and rest. I'll be in to see you this afternoon.'

'She'll be all right,' he added to Jill under his breath.

Selma came back. 'I managed to speak to Miles,' she reported. 'He was with Mrs Pickles in Hampden Road. He's coming straight back.'

'Good. I'd like the signs of mayhem removed from this room, Selma. Would you mind cleaning the blood off the floor?'

'The wall too,' Selma said. 'I'll see to it.'

'In case somebody comes in. Wouldn't want them to see this.'

'I should have finished her off,' Lois ground out. 'I wish I had.'

Jill couldn't stop herself shaking. There was a huge ball of horror in her throat.

Even after this, Titch wanted to keep it quiet. He was still protecting Lois. He was going to sweep all this under the carpet too.

Where would it all end?

CHAPTER TWENTY-SEVEN

Miles was back before they had finished dressing Rosalie's wounds. Jill looked up to find him watching in appalled silence.

'What's happened?' He was moistening his lips.

'A spot of bother, Miles,' Titch said. 'I assume you know the cause?'

Jill saw him swallow. 'Is she . . .?' He came closer and saw the hand they were working on. 'Good God! Are you all right, Rosalie?'

'Slashed through a few tendons,' Titch replied for her. 'But given average luck, she'll still have the use of her fingers.'

'I suppose we've got you to thank for this?' Miles turned angrily on Lois. 'You must be sick. It's the work of a mad woman.'

Lois lifted her head to glare at him. 'If I'm mad, it's because of you. You and that bitch. You've brought this on yourselves.'

Titch stitched carefully under the glare of the Anglepoise. Selma was watching Miles, open-mouthed.

'Get out,' Lois snarled at him. 'Get out of this surgery and stay out. We don't want you as a partner, not after this. Any agreement we had is dissolved. Null and void. Do you hear? If you ever come back, I'll do the same to you. Don't think I won't. You've both been asking for this for a long time.'

Jill swallowed and looked round. After the wall of silence everybody had maintained, this was unthinkable.

For once Miles seemed stunned. His air of disdainful superiority was gone.

'Take her home, Miles. We've done the best we can for her.'

'Titch has made a wonderful job of her tendons,' Jill assured him. 'Nobody could have done better.'

'Come on, Rosalie, can you walk?' Titch was sliding her down from the couch. He said to Miles, 'I'll help you get her out to your car.'

As Jill went to the kitchen and put the kettle on, she heard him add: 'Lois is right. You find your own consulting rooms. We don't want you as a partner, not after this. We're all going to have to move out of here anyway, but you stay away from the rest of us.'

'I can't do that overnight. It'll take time.' Miles sounded frightened now.

Jill's last cup of coffee had gone cold on the table. It seemed an age since she'd taken the first sip from it. She couldn't get over what Lois had done. Titch came back and slumped on to a chair.

'What are we going to do about Lois?' she asked him. She was worried about taking her home.

'I'll see if I can get her back into that clinic.' Titch looked beaten, as though hope had left him. 'She'll need psychiatric treatment again, of course. Bill kept her notes locked in his desk. Mine now. I had them out the day we wrote her up for tranquillisers. I'd better see which consultant she was under last time.' Titch took his cup of coffee back to his consulting room. 'Let him know.'

All thoughts of routine work had been crowded out of Jill's mind, but it had to go on.

'What about Lois's home visits? If I take half, will you do the rest?'

'Sure.'

Jill went to sort that out. She hoped she'd be taking Lois straight to some clinic.

Ten minutes later, Titch came to tell her there would be no bed for Lois until tomorrow, but her consultant would come and visit her at home this afternoon.

'Let's get her into her own car,' Titch said. 'You drive it home and I'll follow in mine. We'll get her safely into bed, start her on oral Largactil and then I'll bring you back here to get your car.'

'Thanks, Titch.'

'Will there be somebody at home with her?'

'Victoria, of course. And Mrs Moon.'

'I'll try and get a nurse from an agency.'

Jill was grateful for the help Titch was giving. Lois had fallen silent and was reluctant to move. She'd gone stiff and seemed to be having difficulty putting one foot in front of the other.

It took all Titch's strength to get her on to the back seat of the Rover. Jill drove it home carefully. It felt like a bus after her Mini.

Titch was waiting at the front door when she got there. Victoria was hovering on the step, white-faced, panic barely under control.

'I've been so afraid something like this would happen.'

'Would you ask Mrs Moon to make some sandwiches, Gran?' Jill asked, to give Victoria something to do. 'For Titch too. We're not going to have much time for lunch today.'

She wouldn't have got Lois upstairs without Titch's strength.

'No,' Lois kept saying. 'No. Not bed.' Considering how much Largactil she'd already had, she was still very restless and agitated.

'Leave me alone,' she railed at Titch. 'I'm not going to bed now. Father says I don't need to. Not unless I want to.'

'Who says that?' Jill asked, feeling the chill spiral through her stomach.

'Father.'

316

'Clive isn't here, Lois,' Titch said. 'We think you should go to bed.'

'Of course he's here,' she burst out irritably. 'Who is that over there then?'

Jill turned to look in the direction Lois had indicated, and shivered anew. Her stepmother was seeing ghosts. She'd felt them in this house herself.

'She's hallucinating,' Titch whispered. 'Not unusual with this sort of problem.'

Between them, they got her to lie on her bed, but she refused to take her clothes off. Titch closed the curtains to make the atmosphere more soporific, while Jill got a glass of water from the bathroom.

Lois was reluctant to take the tablets. It took them a long time to persuade her to have them in her mouth. They both stood over her while she gulped at the water.

'Come on, Jill.' Titch was pulling her out on the landing, leaving the bedroom door open an inch. 'She'll go off in a few minutes, you'll see.'

'She's in a right state.' Jill's mouth felt dry with fear.

'After what she's just done, I'm not surprised.'

Lois lay back against the pillows and closed her eyes. She hated the way Titch and Jill were whispering to each other about her.

'She'll be all right now,' Titch said, as if she was witless and deaf as well. Lois could barely control her rage. It was tearing her apart.

'Go away,' she grated out at them. 'Leave me alone.' She had to get rid of them.

She watched them leave, waited until they'd gone downstairs, then spat out the tablets she'd kept in her cheek in front of her teeth. She stared at them on her palm, sodden and disintegrating, and felt herself gripped by another surge of rage. They were trying to dose her with another hundred milligrams! She flung the pills under her bed.

They must think she was going off her head. It was far too much! She'd have expected Titch to have more sense. How dare he dictate what should happen to her? He should have discussed it with her first.

They'd all turned against her. Nobody wanted to help her any more. No, but they'd run to help Rosalie Sutton. Rosalie Meadows that was.

She couldn't understand how darling Bertie could have sired such a demon as Rosalie. Probably he hadn't. It would be another story like her mother's.

Lois knew that Titch was frightened Rosalie would let it be known he was still practising under her father's name.

Back in the fifties, the media spotlight had been thrown on him. He'd seen lurid details of his sex life splashed on every front page for weeks. There would be another sensation if his present circumstances

317

were made public. It would probably mean another passage through the courts for him. That he'd worked soberly in the practice all these years would count for nothing.

Titch had paid for Rosalie's silence, over and over, just as she had, yet he'd still repaired her slashed tendons. It had sickened her to see that.

She couldn't understand it. He must hate Rosalie Sutton as much as she did.

Lois heard footsteps outside on the landing. Her door was creaking open. She closed her eyes, feigning sleep. Shortly afterwards she heard the engine of Titch's old Austin start up.

That brought another stab of displeasure. He'd been downstairs with Jill all this time. Talking to her mother no doubt, telling her what she'd done. Blaming her instead of Rosalie Sutton.

She didn't like the way Titch was siding with Jill. Jill was of no account. Never would be. Lois had felt the difference in her attitude. Jill was treating her like she'd treat a bomb about to go off. Her eyes had shone with fear. Fear of her.

She'd said: 'You'll feel better in a little while, Lois. Come and lie down on your bed.' Patronising her. It had made Lois feel sick.

'They're treating you like they treat all their patients,' Clive's voice told her.

Lois wasn't sleepy. She pulled herself up from the bed to sit on the edge. She felt light-headed. Unwell. Wretched, really. Even her own bedroom seemed to have changed. The house was as still as the grave.

Nobody cared what happened to her. They would leave her here to rot. She began to cry again as the feeling of desolation came back.

She had nobody left who would help her. Victoria was downstairs but she wouldn't come near her. Even her own mother had turned against her.

Nat spent more time with Jill than he did with her. He didn't want her any more.

Even Bill and Janet had gone away and abandoned her. Lois felt crushed, defeated and very lonely.

She'd been trying to cope with Rosalie on her own, but what was the use? There was no way she could curb her demands.

'I'm here,' Clive said gently. 'I'll always look after you, Lois. You know that.'

He came to sit beside her on the bed, the way he used to when she was a child. He was wearing his crumpled linen suit and Panama hat.

She didn't know how to tell him: 'Mother says that . . . that you aren't my father. That she had a lover who fathered me.' She saw his face sag with hurt.

'I don't believe her.' He put an arm round her shoulders and pulled

318

her closer. 'You mustn't either. We know how we feel about each other. Nobody can make me believe you aren't my daughter. Haven't I always watched over you? Loved you? Nothing can change that.'

Lois could feel herself sweating with relief. She was opening up to Clive's fatherly love like a flower opens its petals to the sun.

'Victoria has turned against me,' he said. 'Just as she's turned against you. You're all I have left.'

That made Lois snuggle closer to him. 'I hate her. I hate my mother.'

'But we'll be all right. We'll stick together, won't we, Lois? You're clever. Haven't I always told you that?'

'Always.'

'You can do anything you want to. Just set your mind on it and go ahead. You'll succeed.'

'I want us to get our own back on Mother.'

'You can do it. I know you can.' His gentle eyes were smiling down, encouraging her. 'Victoria has betrayed us both. Do it for me, Lois.'

She stood up. The room seemed to eddy round her. She found her slippers and went downstairs. She needed to find the medical bag that was never far out of her reach.

She was crossing the landing when the telephone shrilled in the hall below. She drew back as she heard Victoria coming to answer it.

'Dr Willsden? Good afternoon. Yes, we're expecting you. Oh, delayed?'

'Lois was looking down on her mother's white head. The yellow streak was very noticeable from above.

'I don't think an hour or so will make much difference,' Victoria was saying with all her old self-confidence. 'Between four and five? Yes, she's heavily sedated at the moment. See you later then.'

As the phone went down on its stand, Lois bent double with fury. Victoria's manner was positively condescending. How dare she treat her like this? As though she was totally in her charge.

Her mother went to the kitchen door and said: 'A cup of tea, I think, Mrs Moon. Out in the garden? Yes, that would be lovely.'

Mother would find out she was wrong. Lois wasn't sedated and she was going to show George Willsden that his hour or so delay would make a lot of difference.

She crept down to the study to look for her medical bag. It wasn't where she always left it, She felt herself whirled up in frustrated rage again. She had to have her case.

She tried to think what she'd done with it. But she knew only what she normally did with it. She kicked at the waste-paper basket. Kicked at the copper pot that held that hideous plant. The noise boomed up the hall, and she followed it out.

Mrs Moon came to the kitchen door.

319

'What are you doing down here?' Her metal curlers were standing up like knobs under her red headscarf; her face was working with nerves.

At that moment Lois caught sight of her case. It was on the chair near the hall telephone, together with her handbag. She'd never left her things there before, but to see them was reassuring. She drew herself up to her full height.

'You can go, Mrs Moon. We won't be needing you again today.'

Mystification showed on the woman's flabby face.

'Jill asked me to stay on, Dr Benbow. I think I better had.'

Lois knew she was screaming at her: 'When I tell you to go, you go. Do you hear?' The woman was backing across the kitchen.

'Don't tell me what other people want you to do. I want you to go.'

Lois felt puffed up to see Mrs Moon reach the back door and feel for the cardigan hanging there. Terror was showing in every movement she made. She'd got her domestic on the run.

Then her mother was crowding into the doorway behind Mrs Moon; taking off her sunglasses, coming forward to the kitchen table, with that look on her face which said she was totally in charge and would soon have her daughter under control. She said calmly: 'Lois, we thought you'd gone to sleep. Would you like a cup of tea?'

'Don't try and humour me,' she snarled. 'If anyone has reason to be afraid, it's you.'

Victoria couldn't control the shaking of her hands. She'd been trying to relax in the garden, trying to damp down her apprehension. She'd been sickened and appalled to hear what Lois had done at the surgery.

There seemed to be no end to it. She'd been trying to tell herself that all could still be well. Lois would be given more treatment and recover again.

She'd been trying to read a book to keep her mind off Lois when she'd heard her shouting at Mrs Moon. It sliced through her gut, leaving her fluttering like a leaf in the wind.

She knew there was nobody else here to deal with Lois, and that she would have to do it. Very slowly, she got up from her garden chair and went towards the house.

'Lois is well sedated,' Titch had said. 'She won't give you any trouble.' How could he have been so wrong?

By the time she reached the back door she was in a total lather. Mrs Moon, in a panic disappeared behind her.

Lois's face was defiant; Victoria could see frenzy simmering just beneath the surface. She steeled herself: 'Come back upstairs with me.'

She took Lois's arm and tried to lead her to the stairs. Lois shook

320

her off in the hall and rushed at her medical case. Threw the lid open on the chair. Snatched at some syringes. She had two medium-sized ones in her hand.

'Come on, dear.' Victoria was trying to quell the turmoil she felt inside. She knew she must appear calm. Lois had a volcanic temper. 'You don't need anything from your bag now.'

Lois was closing the case methodically. Placing her handbag back on top.

'I do,' she said. There was cunning on her face. 'I'm going to kill you.'

Victoria felt horror stabbing at her. Lois didn't know what she was saying. Of course she didn't.

'Come in here.' Lois headed into the sitting room.

Victoria took comfort from the fact that Lois had nothing but syringes in her hand. She'd fastened down her case with all those dangerous drugs still safely inside.

If she came rushing at her with a syringe full of something dangerous, there would be nothing Victoria could do about it. She'd feel better if that bag was somewhere Lois couldn't get at it.

Very quietly, she put it into the hall cupboard behind the carpet cleaner, locked the door and put the key in her pocket.

'Come here, Mother. Come here, damn you.'

The sound of shattering porcelain sent Victoria rushing to see what she was doing. Fragments of a Chelsea figurine were scattered over the hearth. Lois was whirling the other one of the pair over her head.

'Put that down, Lois.' She hadn't meant to sound so authoritarian. Lois's dark eyes swung to hers, smouldering with hate. Miraculously, she obeyed, putting the figure back on the table.

Victoria hovered in the doorway. She mustn't leave her. Goodness knows what Lois might do when she was like this.

'Perhaps you'll be just as well off down here,' she said, when she felt capable of keeping her voice steady. 'Lie down on the settee, Lois. Stretch out and make yourself comfortable.'

Why had she told George Willsden his visit could wait? She wanted him now, this minute, before Lois did anything else.

'You lie down, Mother.' Lois's manner was threatening, her eyes clouded and evil-looking. 'On this settee will do fine.'

That made Victoria take a step backwards. Lois went to the door and closed it behind her. A grip like a vice on her bad arm steered her towards the settee. She collapsed backwards on it.

'I'll just sit, dear,' she said, as firmly as she could. She was determined to keep her feet on the carpet. Lois pushed an easy chair in front of her and sat down too.

'I'm going to kill you,' she said. 'The way I killed Gran, when she turned nasty.'

321

Victoria felt icy fingers crawling up her neck.

'You didn't kill her, darling.' She forced a laugh. It sounded hysterical. 'Your grandmother died of a coronary. She'd had cardiac atheroma for years so it wasn't unexpected. You know that as well as I do. We both saw the terrible attacks of angina she had.'

'Conveniently, we all saw them.'

'Poor Mother.' Titch had been here one night when she'd had an attack. Even he had been moved by its severity.

Lois looked as though she was explaining something to a dim child.

'Mother, you must know that the easiest way to kill anyone is to inject air into one of their veins? When the blood carries it up to the heart, that's it. Instantly.'

That brought Victoria up short. Was this possible?

'I can assure you it works.' Lois's sloe-black eyes held hers. This was beginning to feel like mortal combat.

Victoria was in no doubt it would work, but had Lois done that to Evelyn? She wanted to throw up at the thought.

'There's no poison for a forensic pathologist to find.' Lois was leering at her. 'If it's done properly, there's just one tiny prick on the skin that can easily be missed.'

Victoria's heart missed several beats. She was cringing back into the cushions.

'All doctors know how to do it properly. We all have boxes of syringes at our disposal.'

Victoria was clutching at the pearls around her throat. Evelyn had been living here when she died. There had been other people in the house, but all the same . . . She'd never even doubted that her mother had died of natural causes.

'It worked wonderfully well for Gran. You got her here to spy on me, didn't you, Mother?'

'To help you, darling. You were edgy, not settled into your new marriage. Not quite recovered from . . .'

Victoria remembered then. It was all flooding back. Evelyn had been shocked and upset just before she'd died.

Lois had asked her for money, and for the first time, Evelyn had refused. Her mother had been frightened of Lois.

Victoria felt the back of her neck prickle as she recalled how Lois had turned on Evelyn, accused her of spying on her.

Lois's eyes levelled with hers again. She said vehemently: 'Clive says I must kill you.'

Victoria went rigid. 'Who?'

'Clive, my father. You know Clive.'

'He's . . . He's dead, dear.'

'No. He's here.' Lois waved as though indicating that he was behind her. Victoria felt the goose pimples lifting on her arms again. She had to look despite herself.

'Clive wants me to kill you. He says I must. He hates you too.'

'No.' Victoria felt icy fingers clutching her gut. It was ridiculous to protest. Lois was hallucinating.

'He says you deserve it. You treated him despicably. Just as you're treating me.'

Lois was slowly peeling the cellophane off one of the syringes. Victoria could feel everything swimming round her. She must pull herself together.

She said vehemently: 'Grandma wouldn't lie down and let you inject a syringe full of air into her vein. Of course she wouldn't.'

'She had an attack of angina, Mother. A bad one. I'd prepared her, telling her about the latest drug for heart attack victims. How it had to be given intravenously. She believed me. She let me do it.'

Victoria was trying to think. Surely it wasn't that easy?

'It would have shown up at post-mortem.' Evelyn had been taken to hospital. A post-mortem had been performed because of her sudden death.

'No poison to be found.' Lois was smiling, basking in her own cleverness now. That frightened Victoria too.

'Air takes up space, there wouldn't be enough blood to fill the cardiac arteries.'

Lois shrugged. 'Blood congeals after death. Who's to say whether it would be that obvious? Especially in the presence of other physical findings.

'Don't forget, Grandmother had an enlarged heart and atheromatous changes in the valves. I knew it was perfectly safe. Not even a forensic scientist looking at a suspicious death would be likely to come out and say: "Cause of death is an air bubble." Not when he could see the physical changes of heart disease that Grandma had.'

Victoria gasped again in renewed horror. 'But you didn't know . . . Nobody did, until . . .'

'She'd had symptoms for a long time. I was banking on the probability.'

Victoria could feel the bitterness of bile coming up her throat.

'You loved your grandmother. You wouldn't have done such a thing.' It was unbelievable.

'She turned against me. As you have, Mother.'

Victoria could feel her scalp prickling. 'You wouldn't do that to me. You wouldn't get away with it. There's nothing the matter with my heart. It's healthy, a pathologist would have to search further for a cause.'

'We all know they don't always find one. It's just a bubble of air, after all.'

Victoria couldn't take her eyes off the syringe. Keep calm, she told herself. Don't let her frighten you. Lois would never be able to manage it if Victoria were fighting her off.

She leapt to her feet. 'And I'm certainly not going to keep still and let you get into one of my veins with that.'

Lois's fist shot out with the force of a heavyweight boxer and her mother fell back on the settee. It knocked the wind out of her body, left her gasping.

She was leaning over her, her face a few inches from Victoria's, leering at her. Victoria opened her mouth and screamed. She was afraid she was defeated. She hadn't the strength to fight Lois off.

A click from the hall distracted Lois's attention. Victoria pushed with all her might, but Lois was already moving away to crash the door back on its hinges.

She caught a glimpse of Mrs Moon with the telephone to her ear, cringing back against the wall.

'Don't you dare!' Lois was screaming, as she yanked the telephone wires off the wall. 'Don't you . . .'

Victoria couldn't listen to any more. She got to her feet. Her legs felt weak but she had to take this chance. She rushed out to the hall, grabbed Mrs Moon by the arm, and pulled her into the study. She slammed the door and turned the key in the lock.

'I'll get you.' Lois's shoulder hit the door moments later, jerking it on its hinges. 'Come on out.'

Victoria felt she was at the end of her strength. She staggered to Nat's desk and lifted the phone. It was working. She dialled the surgery, praying that Titch was there.

Polly's voice answered, sounding calm, reminding her of the ordinary world where things like this didn't happen. 'Dr Meadows is out doing his rounds.'

Lois's shoulder thudded against the door again. She was roaring for them to come out. Victoria hoped the doors at Links View were solid enough to withstand this.

'Get Titch, it's urgent. Or Jill. Anybody. Try Dr Willsden, tell him to get here as soon as he can. It's Lois . . .'

Victoria felt overcome with terror.

When Jill found herself going round and round the Woodchurch roundabout lost in thought she knew she ought to give up and go home. She was finding it almost impossible to keep her mind on her job.

She had to convince Titch that he couldn't go on like this. For the best part of half a century, he and Bill and Victoria had stood by Lois. Surely she would be classed as criminally psychotic?

At enormous cost, they'd shielded her, covering up her heinous behaviour. They'd striven to find her the best possible treatment and then get her back to work.

But life brought emotional upsets to most people and Lois couldn't take them. She broke down time after time. She was getting worse; surely she couldn't always have been as savage as she'd been this morning?

Lois was downright dangerous. Sooner or later she'd kill somebody. Jill had to convince Titch of that.

Four more visits to make. They'd all had long lists today, and this was one of Lois's patients.

She turned her red Mini off the roundabout and into the estate. A right turn here, this was the road. She was looking at the numbers and pulling up. The notes now. Kelly Chesters, aged six, high temperatures with a rash.

Forget Lois, she had to get on with this. Was it another case of measles? She'd already seen two this morning.

Lois staggered back from the study door. It was locked, she couldn't burst her way in. Pain was shooting through her shoulder. She clenched every muscle until the moment of agony passed. Then, stoically, she picked up the syringe from the carpet where she'd dropped it.

The pain brought a moment of clarity. She was aware that there was a real world where people didn't do the things she'd done.

She couldn't go on like this. She remembered again the first sobering moment when Selma's face had come round her consulting room door. The appalled disbelief on it when she'd seen Rosalie on the floor, covered with blood.

It was only when Selma's horrified eyes had come up to meet hers that she'd realised she was responsible for the bloody mess. To grab for a scalpel had been instinctive. It wasn't easy to stand up to women like Rosalie. Nobody else would do it.

Yet they blamed her. She'd seen revulsion on Jill's face. Condemnation on Titch's. They all thought what she'd done was beyond the pale.

And they'd seen to it that Rosalie would recover to make bigger demands. Lois couldn't understand them. They were letting her down. What she'd done, she'd done for Titch as much as for herself.

Slowly she climbed the stairs. She had to pull herself up now, her strength had gone. What was she to do?

All she'd ever wanted was to bask in their approval. To be thought a good doctor and a clever woman. Instead, this morning she'd felt their censure, their reproach. She couldn't endure much of that. Still, she knew how to end it. It needn't take long.

She went to her bedroom and flung herself on the bed, but this wouldn't do. It was too dark with the curtains closed. She got up to fling them back. Outside, the sticky heat of summer had gone.

Autumn was on the way. Still sunny, but pleasantly warm rather than hot.

The open french window led out to a small balcony over the front door. She'd had two chairs out here all summer. She collapsed on one of them now.

She could see the Mersey in the distance, and beyond, on the far bank, she could just make out the two Liverpool cathedrals in the hazy sunshine.

There was a feeling of peace out here. It was quiet, except for a bee buzzing amongst the geraniums in the box at her feet, and that added to the feeling of somnolence.

She was still clutching the syringe. She relaxed her grip and examined it as though she hadn't seen it before.

She didn't know exactly how much air was needed to kill a woman. It wasn't a subject she felt she could discuss with a pathologist.

She thought even one cubic centimetre would be enough. She'd given Evelyn five. She'd been sure that other, more concrete evidence as to cause of death would be found on post-mortem.

Did it matter how much air she administered to herself? Yes, because if it wasn't enough it could go through the right side of her heart and up to the brain and cause a stroke, yet not be fatal. She could end up as a chronic invalid. That was the last thing she wanted.

On the other hand, she didn't want to be branded a suicide. Only people who couldn't cope with life committed suicide. There was something cowardly about it. She didn't want that said about her.

'Absolutely not,' Clive agreed. She didn't want to let him down.

But were pathologists as bright as they thought they were? Would they see an air embolus? Especially if there were no obvious pointers. Carefully, she pulled back the plunger in the syringe. The safest thing was to put in as much air as possible.

Usually she found elbows and wrists the easiest places for intravenous entry, but on herself? She would have to try a vein on her ankle because she could then use both hands.

She lifted her feet to the seat of the other chair. She still had on the stockings she'd worn to the surgery that morning. They were splattered with specks of blood. Some were quite large, more than specks. She pulled at one of them. The blood spots were on her skin, they'd gone through the material.

She could see a likely vein, but would she be able to get into it through the nylon? She'd never tried such a thing before, but no reason why not. She loosened her stocking.

Plenty of reason to do it. No doctor would think of it as suicide if they couldn't find the site of entry. She would get in as cleanly as she could, but with all the other spots of blood, one more was unlikely to be noticed.

But what about the syringe itself? That would be concrete evidence that she'd injected herself with something.

She would have a moment to deal with it. Here, on the balcony, she could see the slight breeze lifting the leaves of the Virginia creeper that covered the front of the house. They were beginning to turn red, looking magnificent, as they always did at this time of the year.

If she pushed the syringe behind the leaves, it would fall a little and no doubt lodge behind one of the many suckers that held the plant to the bricks. It was light enough to stay there for many years.

She couldn't see anybody being intelligent enough to look for it. And it wouldn't be easy to find if they did.

Lois smiled to herself, because she could still keep them guessing. She was cleverer than most, wasn't Clive always telling her that?

Was she ready to do it then? She took one last look at the red roofs of the houses below, interspersed with the darkening green of mature trees.

She adjusted the plunger carefully. She had to be sure she put in enough. Otherwise it might cause instead a pulmonry embolism. She'd seen patients recover from that.

Of course, it could be any sort of emboli, pulmonary, cerebral, or arterial, but most likely it would mimic a cardiac infarction. She had no way of knowing.

Pull the other chair a little closer. Foot on it. In through the stocking and the skin, a sideways jab into the vein. Ease the plunger back a touch further. The trickle of blood running into the syringe confirmed she was in.

This was the moment. Was she ready? She pushed hard, the plunger went home. Carefully, she withdrew the needle, then flicked the syringe behind the creeper.

Her heart was bounding with the thrill of it. She felt excited, intoxicated even. But otherwise all right. The pain, when it came a moment later, took her breath away, bending her over in one last moment of agony.

CHAPTER TWENTY-EIGHT

Victoria sat at Nat's desk gripped by the most awful palpitations. Her hands were shaking, even the one held rigid at the wrist in its plaster cast.

She could see her diamond flashing fire as it shook. She folded her hands on her lap, kept them below the desk where she couldn't see them.

She wanted to weep for her mother, but no tears would come. Terror was holding them at bay. Lois had killed her!

She couldn't shake off the terrible chill that that knowledge brought. She didn't doubt it was true.

She'd asked Evelyn to come here to anchor Lois to normality, and she'd brought her to her death. If she hadn't done that, Evelyn could have had many more years.

She could remember saying to Nat: 'At least for Mother the end came quickly. She didn't suffer.'

Victoria let out a long, shuddering breath. At the time, she hadn't even considered foul play a possibility. Poor Evelyn, who had loved her family so much, and had sacrificed so much for them all.

Mrs Moon was spreadeagled on one of the red velvet chairs, her face parchment pale.

'Dr Benbow's taken leave of her senses, that she has. Rampaging round like that. Did you see what she did with that vase?'

Victoria could feel the tears coming now, stinging her eyes. The house had gone quiet. She wondered what Lois was doing, but she dared not unlock the door to see. She'd never been so frightened of her before.

She'd felt Lois's hate ever since she'd found out that Clive was not her father. That she might try to kill her had never entered her mind. She hadn't thought Lois capable of such a thing.

Perhaps, knowing about Phoebe, she should have done. Instead she'd gone along with Lois's excuse that she'd been suffering from postnatal depression.

Graham had made it perfectly clear that he regarded it as an excuse. She'd always known it was.

Then there'd been the time Lois had attacked Jill. That should have

329

been a second warning. But it was impossible to think of one's own daughter – a much-loved daughter – as capable of an act like that.

'She's gone off her head, hasn't she?' Mrs Moon was leaning over the chair's arm towards her, her scarf coming adrift now, showing her curlers.

Victoria wondered if she understood that Lois had been trying to kill her. The knowledge left a huge ball of apprehension in her stomach. What could they do for Lois after this? She knew she'd never feel safe living in the same house with her again.

She wished that Titch would come. That anybody would come. She got up and went to the window. Should she ring the surgery again and see if Polly had been able to get hold of him?

A yellow Mini she knew well was nosing through the gateposts and up to the front door. Relief flooded through her. It was Esme. She'd always been able to rely on Esme.

Victoria opened the window. 'Thank goodness . . .'

'Are you all right? Polly rang me at home. She said you sounded desperate and she couldn't get hold of anybody else.'

'We're all right.'

'Thank goodness for that. She's still trying, of course. I don't suppose Titch will be long. She's trying to get Nat too.'

'Nat? Why didn't I think of Nat?'

'Can I come in?'

Victoria's courage failed her. She couldn't bring herself to unlock the study door.

'Lois might be . . .' She was afraid she was still on the other side of the door.

'The back door's open. So is the french window at the back.'

'Watch out for her.'

Victoria watched Esme's dumpy figure disappear round the corner of the house. Listened as her sandals stumped against the flagstones. The house was deathly silent. She was screwed up with tension, listening for something else.

Footsteps, softer on the carpet, were coming up the hall. It sounded like Esme.

'It's me,' she said from the other side of the door. It was Mrs Moon who got up to unlock it.

'There's no sign of Lois,' Esme whispered.

'Perhaps she went upstairs to her room?'

'Come to the kitchen. I'll make you a cup of tea.'

Victoria's mouth felt as dry as bone. Perhaps the kitchen would be safer? They could get out to the garden easily from there. Surely Lois wouldn't do anything outside.

'Come on,' Esme urged. 'She doesn't seem to be anywhere downstairs.'

Victoria crept down the hall to the kitchen. Though she felt safer now that Esme was here, she still couldn't think straight.

Her mind was filled with visions of Clive. He would have been devastated by what had happened today. He'd loved Lois too.

The front door bell trilled before the kettle came to the boil, sending another jolt of anxiety through Victoria.

'I'll go.' Esme went out through the back door and round to the front. When she came back, she had Dr Willsden with her.

Victoria gasped with relief. She felt safe at last. Warmer too. She took him into the sitting room. Esme followed with the tea tray and they both tried to tell him about the terrible thing Lois had done at the surgery that morning.

Victoria tried to tell him something of what Lois had done since. Not all. As was always the case with Lois, there were things that couldn't be told.

The hot tea comforted her. Even though Esme insisted on stirring sugar into it.

'Sugar's good for shock,' she told her. 'You know that.'

Dr Willsden was getting to his feet. 'I'll go up and see Lois now.'

Victoria didn't feel she could face her daughter yet. She asked Mrs Moon to show him up to Lois's room. Esme hovered, undecided whether she should go with them or stay. Victoria pulled at her skirt, to make her sit down again.

She watched Esme pour her another cup of tea, but all the time she was listening, wanting to know what was happening upstairs but too nervous to go up.

She heard Mrs Moon scream, and clutching at Esme she got to the bottom of the stairs.

She felt terrible. Her head was swimming and there were butterflies in her stomach. She knew there was worse to face. She couldn't believe what was happening.

They heard Nat's old Wolseley come screeching up the drive and round to the garage. Seconds later his footsteps came rushing through the kitchen. His face when he came in was wet with sweat and working with anxiety.

Victoria felt it was a nightmare, and there was no one she could blame for all that was happening but herself.

As soon as Dr Willsden came downstairs and told them Lois was dead, Victoria knew she must try to cover up what her daughter had done.

There was so much she felt ashamed of, she couldn't let the whole world know Lois had hated her so much that she'd wanted to kill her. She would have succeeded too, if Mrs Moon had gone home as Lois had told her to.

Victoria wanted to protect Lois, at least limit the damage to her reputation. Perhaps it was second nature. She'd never told anybody more than she thought they needed to know.

The house seemed to fill with people. Mrs Moon had to be soothed. Esme made more tea, and Dr Willsden provided sympathy.

Victoria could see the syringe Lois had dropped on the sitting room carpet, still sterile inside its intact wrapper. With her foot, she kicked it out of sight under the settee, hoping that nobody else had noticed it.

Everything seemed unreal. No longer was anybody worrying about what Lois had done. Now, how and why she'd died was what concerned them.

'Have some tea, Victoria.' Esme put another cup and saucer in her hand. 'It always helps at a time like this. Something very soothing about tea.'

Victoria felt waterlogged she'd drunk so much of it. It no longer helped. She told herself that they all meant well.

'I can't understand what could have happened to Lois.' Titch was frowning into his cup.

He had arranged for Lois to be taken to the morgue at the General Hospital, and he supervised while she was carried downstairs on a stretcher and out through the door.

He didn't let her see that, of course, but she heard it. He shut the sitting room door and they all tried to talk more loudly to drown out the scuffles on the stairs. They were trying to shield her.

'You're upset, Victoria. Understandably so. It all happened so quickly.'

'Because she died suddenly, there'll have to be an autopsy,' Jill explained earnestly. There was nobody present who wasn't already aware of that fact.

'Surely she must have died from natural causes?' Nat asked. Victoria thought he looked ill. The bags under his eyes were bigger than ever.

'Could be natural causes,' Jill supported. 'She hasn't left a note. There's almost always a note if they plan to take their own lives. And I can't believe Lois would ever do that.'

It sounded like wishful thinking to Victoria. After what she'd heard from Lois today, she didn't think she'd ever feel normal again.

At the first moment when nobody was watching her, Victoria took Lois's medical case out of the cupboard and put it back on the chair in the hall. Titch had brought it from the surgery and put it there while they were waiting for Jill to arrive with Lois.

'I think she probably swallowed something.' Titch's kind eyes blinked at Victoria through his horn-rims. 'Or even injected herself.'

Victoria felt her heart thud with alarm. 'What makes you say that?' She knew she had snapped too strongly.

It was winding her up more, trying to keep quiet while they speculated. But somehow she couldn't bring herself to talk openly about it. Not yet. Though she could say more now Dr Willsden had gone.

'There was no reason for her to die. No medical reason.' She could see Titch was convinced about that. 'And she had access to drugs.'

'She could have had a heart attack,' Nat suggested. 'I'm always hearing of people . . . apparently healthy people who collapse and . . .'

'I should be very surprised,' Titch said.

'I think she understood what she'd done. To Rosalie, I mean. Couldn't go on.'

'Perhaps she was afraid Rosalie would tell the police. After all, she'd been threatening to do it for years,' Titch surmised.

'Possibly she was afraid of being charged. She did commit grievous bodily harm.'

Jill's eyes seemed to be watching Victoria. She said: 'The autopsy will tell us. Titch, it's time we made a move.'

'Yes, time to take evening surgery.'

'I'll stay on here and keep Victoria company,' Esme volunteered.

'No need.' Victoria shook her head. 'I'm all right now.'

She was no longer afraid of what Lois might do to her. And what she wanted was to go upstairs and find that other syringe before somebody else did.

'Not a good time to be alone,' Titch said firmly.

She was glad that Nat stopped Esme from making more tea. He poured them brandy instead, and then disappeared into the study. He was allowed to be alone when he wanted to be.

Victoria made an excuse to Esme and went upstairs. She had to see if she could find that second syringe.

Jill felt exhausted by the time she returned to Links View. Her father saw Esme off and then ushered both her and Gran into the dining room.

'Mrs Moon has stayed on to put supper on the table for us,' he said.

Jill was glad of that. 'I don't feel up to doing much more tonight.' Apart from everything else, she and Titch were having to do Lois's work between them. 'Titch is whacked too. He's arranged for a night service to take our calls tonight. We'll be better by tomorrow. We're hoping to get a locum to help us.'

'It's been a harrowing time for everyone,' Nat agreed. 'We all need an early night.'

'Thank goodness everybody's gone,' Victoria said faintly as the back door closed behind Mrs Moon. 'I don't think I could stand much more company. Not today.'

Jill felt almost too exhausted to eat the lamb chops on her plate. She said to Victoria: 'You haven't forgotten you have a hospital appointment tomorrow?'

Her grandmother groaned. 'Just when I could do with an easy day.'

Last week she'd said to Jill: 'Will you take me? I don't think Lois wants to.'

'Of course I will,' she'd agreed.

But now the pressure of work at the surgery was much greater, and it would not be easy for her to get away by half past ten.

'Dad? Would you be able to take Gran? Eleven o'clock appointment?'

'Yes, I'll take you, Victoria.'

'I wish it wasn't tomorrow.'

'You know you've been looking forward to it.' Nat was trying to cheer her up. 'You can't wait to get that plaster off. You've talked of nothing else this past week.'

Jill thought her grandmother looked close to tears.

'I've got something else on my mind now, haven't I?'

'We all have,' Nat said, patting her good arm.

'The worst is over, Gran,' Jill assured her. 'There's nothing any of us can do for Lois now.'

'It's not over.' Jill had thought Gran was weary and sinking like the rest of them, but she was wound up, agitated even. She wondered if Dad had given her too much brandy. 'I only wish it was over. There's a lot to get through yet.'

'There's the funeral, of course,' Jill said, trying to be sympathetic.

'There's the result of the autopsy.' Gran's knife and fork crashed down on her plate. She was weeping.

'Do you know what Lois told me?' she whispered through the handkerchief she was dabbing round her face.

'You didn't say she'd told you anything.'

'You just said she'd come downstairs and acted strangely,' Nat added.

'With all the Largactil we gave her, I don't see how she could even have done that.'

'Lois can be cunning.'

'What did she tell you?'

Victoria looked up, her face ravaged with emotion. 'That she'd killed Evelyn.'

Jill felt her stomach turn over. Hadn't she and Dad discussed this possibility? His tired eyes met hers, his mouth was hanging open.

She swallowed hard. 'Did Lois say how she'd killed her?' They all stopped eating now.

Victoria told them about shooting air into a vein. 'That's how she'll have killed herself,' she said. 'I just know it. She had a syringe in her hand all ready to do it. I haven't been able to find it.'

'We'll have a look.'

'Lois was found out on her balcony. It's nowhere there, I've

334

searched. Yet it couldn't be anywhere else.' Gran was distressed.

'Does it matter?' Nat asked, his face grey.

'Yes, I don't want her branded a suicide. Or a murderer. I don't want anybody else to know.'

'Gran, does it matter now?'

'There's worse – Lois tried to kill me too.' They were both staring at her.

'When?' Nat barked. 'Why didn't you tell us before?'

'It was this afternoon.' Her face was working with terror. ' "I'm going to kill you," Lois said. I know she meant it. She had this syringe. I've never been so scared . . .' Gran was weeping uncontrollably now.

Jill felt sick. Knowing Lois as she did, she couldn't understand why she hadn't thought of that before they'd left her.

'You've been bottling this up,' she said.

'I had to, didn't I? I didn't want Willsden and everybody talking about Lois.'

'You've had too many things to bottle up over the years,' Jill told her. 'Better let it all come out now.'

'But only to the family,' Victoria sobbed.

'That's the nicest thing you could say about Jill and me,' Nat told her. He got up to put an arm round her shoulders. 'Is there anything else you want to tell us?'

Victoria went into paroxysm of tears.

'Isn't that enough? For God's sake, what could be worse?'

Jill met her father's horrified eyes.

'Let Jill take you up to bed, and perhaps she can find something to help you sleep.'

Jill felt dazed as she got to her feet to comply. 'You make her some malted milk, Dad.'

As soon as they'd got Victoria settled for the night, Jill took her father by the arm and led him to Lois's room.

'Let's see if we can find this syringe Victoria was going on about.'

'Do you believe all that?'

'If we find it, I will.'

They searched Lois's room, going over the carpet a foot at a time. They moved her bed. Jill pounced on two crumbling tablets.

'She didn't take these!' Her eyes were wide with speculation. 'Titch said she must have spat them out. To be able to do what she did afterwards.'

'Lois could be quite wily.'

'We both stood over her. Titch and me. I could have sworn she'd swallowed them.'

'The syringe isn't here.'

'She was found out on the balcony.' They searched out there too. Down between the cushions on the chairs. Everywhere.

'If she used it, then she must have thrown it over on to the drive,' Nat said. It widened out here in front of the house.

'It might have reached that rose bed.' The scent of the roses was coming up on the night air. It was dark now.

'Let's go to bed.' Jill yawned. 'We won't be able to see anything, and I'm almost asleep on my feet.'

The next morning, before breakfast, Nat searched the garden inch by inch within the distance Lois could have thrown the syringe.

He went back to her bedroom and out on to the balcony. He ruffled the leaves of the Virginia creeper covering the wall. He peered through them, wondering if she could have lodged it there in some way. He found nothing.

In the following days, as the shock receded, Nat contemplated being a widower for the second time. His feelings were now very different from when he'd lost Sarah.

If he were to be honest, he hadn't loved Lois for a long time. She'd been a source of worry to him for years. He hadn't been able to cope with her, not ever. Even so, the emotional impact of her death was enormous. He felt he was tottering under it.

He tried to tell Victoria that for Lois's sake, he thought it was better this way. That it was safer for both her and Jill. That it removed the feeling of a great hole opening up at his own feet.

But Victoria was locked in horror. She said she was dreading the outcome of the autopsy.

Jill said: 'Titch knows the pathologist. He'll find out as soon as he can. He's as upset about all this as we are.'

Victoria had had the plaster removed from her wrist, but it seemed to bring no relief.

Nat thought Jill was the only one of them to be holding up under the strain. She was going about her work as usual.

'We've got a locum, thank goodness,' she told him. 'He seems a pleasant enough fellow. Titch thinks he'll be fine, if only he's the sort to pull his weight.'

'How's Rosalie?'

'Nobody's mentioning Rosalie. Miles is barely speaking to us. He says he's found himself new premises. A modern semi, but it'll need structural alterations, so he'll be with us a few weeks yet. But the surgery is due to come down in three more months anyway.'

'Have you found anywhere for yourselves?'

'We've had no energy to look. Haven't even decided what we're going to do.'

On the third day after Lois's death, Nat was working in the factory when he saw Jill waving from the door. He knew why she'd come. He hurried her into his office and shut the door.

'You've heard about Lois? The cause?'

'Yes, Dad. Heart failure, but no obvious infarction. No clots or fragments . . . no valvular disease. Nothing definite.'

'But her heart failed?'

'It stopped. For no reason that they can pinpoint.'

'That'll set Victoria's mind at rest.' He felt relief himself.

'Yes. It's what she was hoping for. I'm going home now for lunch. I'll let her know.'

'I'll come with you. It's a weight off my mind too. I think I'll spend the afternoon in the garden, getting my winter cabbages in.'

'How's everything going here?'

'Like clockwork. I feel I can leave things to George and Ena and take the odd afternoon off now.'

'Good. Can I take some chocolates home with me?'

'Jill, the whole place is yours. Take what you like.'

'Any misshaps?'

'George hasn't managed to make any of those recently. Come on, I'll get you a box. Only the best is good enough for you.'

When they told Victoria about the result of the autopsy, a tiny smile hovered on her lips.

'Lois was right then,' she said, her tired, faded eyes staring beyond Jill into the middle distance. 'Somehow she managed it. At least there'll be no scandal.'

Jill felt she was living through a miserable week. The trouble Lois had caused both at the surgery and at home had left her in a turmoil.

She had to keep telling herself that it was over, that they were free of Lois now. She felt as though she'd come through a long black tunnel since she'd been home.

But good things had come of it too. Dad had said to her: 'You've sorted me out. I'm glad you came home.' And she still couldn't believe she owned a thriving business.

Perhaps she should feel satisfied. She'd come home to find answers to her own difficulties too, and she had those.

It was a comfort to know she wasn't a coward or a nervous wreck. She didn't need to look for psychiatric problems to explain her own anxieties. Having Lois as a stepmother explained all those, and now that she knew the whole story, she could put them behind her.

But Jill found that there was no respite from work, and the atmosphere had changed for the worse there.

They no longer collected in Selma's office before surgery started, nor in the kitchen when it was finished. They were all taking their coffee back to their consulting rooms. They were avoiding each other.

Only Selma went out of her way to welcome the new locum. He

337

seemed keen, and was doing all they'd hoped he would and more.

After three days of this, Jill waited for Titch's last patient to go at the end of morning surgery and went to his room.

'Have you heard how Rosalie's getting on?'

He grimaced. 'I haven't asked. Miles hasn't said.'

'I don't think we should ask,' Jill told him. 'I think we should go and see her.'

'What?' Titch's eyes blinked behind their heavy glasses.

'Titch, she'll not be feeling strong at the moment. She got the worst of the encounter with Lois. We need to go in now and lay down the law.'

'I suppose the advantage is with us. At the moment.'

'We've got to make her stop. She can't keep asking for money like this.'

'She's never asked you.'

'But she'd leached it out of my business, and that worried Dad no end. She mustn't go on asking Victoria. Or bothering you.'

'You're being very supportive.'

'I want you to stay here, Titch. It was Rosalie who was driving you away, wasn't it?'

'I suppose so. Yes.'

'Let's go and tell her never to come near us again.'

'Together, you mean?'

She nodded. 'This afternoon.'

'Miles might be there. He doesn't do many visits.' Titch paused. 'Why not wait until he's pinned down in evening surgery?'

Jill shook her head. 'Because by then their little girls will be home from school. We don't want to frighten them. Better if we tackle her and Miles head on.'

'He always sides with her.'

'We've got him on the run too. Wasn't he shocked when he saw what Lois had done to her? Hasn't he said he's found premises for himself, single-handed? You're not aggressive enough, Titch. Much too gentle.'

'I'm not cut out to deal with blackmailers.'

'They don't think of themselves as that. Good Lord, no. They wrap it all up as gifts.'

'To start with I think we all saw it that way,' Titch said slowly. 'Helping our friends while they were down on their luck.'

Jill met Titch at the surgery after lunch. She drove him to Gayton. Titch seemed enormous when squashed into the passenger seat of her Mini.

'What's that pot plant for?' he wanted to know. She had it wedged behind her seat. 'You haven't bought it for Rosalie?'

'Yes. A get-well present.'

'Heavens, what for? We've given her far too many presents, that's the trouble. We conditioned her to expect them.'

He directed her to the Sutton house.

'A fancy place they've got,' Jill said as she drove on to the fore-court. It was larger than Lois's house. Grander and more recently built.

'We've helped pay for all this,' Titch said. 'More fool us.'

They had to ring the bell twice. Jill hardly recognised Rosalie's voice when she called from behind the oversized front door: 'Who's there?' Her self-confidence had gone. She'd lost the bloom that health and good grooming had given her.

'It's Jill. Come to see how you are, Rosalie.'

'I'm fine.'

Jill had to break the silence. 'Titch is here too. We've got a little gift for you. A get-well present. From us all at the surgery.'

'Just a minute.' It took Rosalie a while to open the door with her damaged hands. She kept herself out of sight behind it. 'You'd better come in.'

Jill was impressed by the hall. It reminded her of a church, rising up two storeys and with a wooden ceiling.

She was even more impressed by Rosalie's face when she turned round to look at her. The slashes stood out starkly against her pale skin because they had crimson scabs on them. She had dark bruising round one eye that was now turning yellow along the edge.

She put her hands up to shield her face from their scrutiny. One palm was covered with a dressing; on the other, knotted sutures looked like spiders.

Her china-blue eyes were apprehensive. Jill saw them fasten on the pot plant.

'For you,' Jill presented it. Rosalie's eyes switched to her. There was incredulity in them now.

Jill had to ask herself if Rosalie had expected her to bring the money she'd been demanding from Lois.

'You'd better come through,' Rosalie mumbled, and led the way through the house. Out through a sun lounge filled with more pot plants, and on to a patio. Beyond that, Jill could see the sun glinting on the bright-blue water of a swimming pool.

'We thought we ought to come and make sure you were all right,' Titch said as they sat down.

Rosalie supported the weight of the plant in the crook of one arm. Kept her face down in the flowers in an attempt to hide her disfigurement. Jill was used to seeing her with her chin held proudly.

'You're healing well,' Titch mumbled. 'All nice and dry.'

'What I want to know,' Rosalie said, 'is this the best treatment? Miles says not to cover them up. Let the air get to them.'

339

She was wearing a sun dress that allowed them to see most of her injuries. Only one or two of the deepest were covered with dressings.

'That's right.'

'Will they heal properly?' Rosalie implored. 'You don't think I'll be left with scars on my face?'

'They shouldn't be too bad,' Titch said.

One slash was deeper than the others, the scab wider. Jill thought that could possibly leave Rosalie with a permanent line from right temple to chin.

'But I'll look awful. Like a criminal.'

Neither contradicted that.

Jill plucked up her courage. She had to spell it out clearly. Somebody should have turned on Rosalie years ago. Called her bluff.

'If you are scarred for life, it's your own fault.'

Rosalie gasped. Put both hands up to shield her face again.

'You pressed Lois too hard.'

'I've had to look after my family,' she protested faintly. There was no sign of arrogance in her bearing now. 'Since Mother's been ill, they've depended on me.'

'You've depended on handouts from others. A more normal way would be to get yourself a job. Instead, you've alienated people who've helped your family for years.'

'We lost our father . . .'

Titch's chair creaked as he moved. 'Bertie's death affected us all, you know.'

'A scar might serve to remind you,' Jill went on, 'never to ask for gifts. Never to expect from others more than they want to give.'

She saw Rosalie gulp. She seemed to be casting round for some means of escape.

'You know that Lois would probably be alive today if you hadn't pressurised her? She couldn't take it, you know.'

The china-blue eyes were aghast. 'No! It wasn't anything to do with what I did.'

'You did as much to send Lois to her death as anybody at that practice did to send your father to his. You deserve all you got, Rosalie,' Jill told her firmly.

'No! Lois was always strange. Had delusions, was never quite right.'

'All the more reason not to upset her,' Titch was saying, when they heard a door slam at the front of the house.

'That'll be Miles.' Rosalie swung her feet to the ground with relief. Moments later he was glowering at them. Jill wished they'd got this over with before he'd come.

'I saw your car.' He perched on the end of his wife's sun lounger, looking anything but pleased to see them.

'We called to see how Rosalie was getting on,' Titch explained brightly.

'Both of you?' he asked.

'And to let her know that we don't want her to come near us ever again. Not any of us.'

'Hold on,' Miles said. 'Rosalie isn't feeling too good. She doesn't need this.'

'They're saying it's my fault that Lois died.'

'Did she top herself?' Miles leered at them. 'I bet she did.'

'The findings were inconclusive,' Titch said stiffly. 'What we want is to put a stopper on things at this point.'

'Don't ever come near any of us again, Rosalie,' Jill said. 'We'll refuse your invitations to Stephanie's wedding here and now. Because we'd rather not come. I'll personally make sure nobody in my family or my practice hands over a penny more to you.'

'And that goes for you too, Miles,' Titch added. 'We want to end the partnership agreement. You've found your own premises; now get out.'

'Do you think that'll fix it?' Titch asked as Jill drove him back to the practice. 'Wasn't very strong-arm after all.'

'Strong enough, I think. They've both had a nasty setback. You were always too generous, all of you. Rosalie had only to hint that she needed something and you gave it.'

'Guilt money,' he said.

'Would you have felt guilt if you'd gone away? Abandoned me and the practice?'

'Sure I would.'

'I take it you won't need to go now?'

He laughed. 'I don't want to go. Shall we look for new premises together?'

'I'd like that, and Victoria will be very pleased you aren't going to whisk Esme away.'

'I'm glad the old surgery's going. Helps break it all up. Couldn't carry on there as though nothing had happened.'

Jill turned to smile at him. 'Titch, you're an old softie. Really you are. I'm not surprised Rosalie took advantage.'

He stroked his glossy moustache. 'When Bill Goodbody writes, I'll let him know it's safe to come back.'

CHAPTER TWENTY-NINE

It was the thought of the weekend away with Felix that had kept Jill going. This would be for her, not something she had to do for someone else.

She felt little spirals of excitement every time she thought of it. Two whole days and two nights alone with him seemed an enormous treat.

He had booked a holiday cottage in rural Wales.

'I won't be disappointed if it doesn't come up to expectations,' she told him. 'What I really want is to spend some time alone with you. Without other problems crowding my mind.'

She'd been over to the shops in Liverpool and bought herself two complete sets of new underwear. Something to create maximum allure.

Up until now, her career had absorbed all her interest and energy. She knew it would always be important to her, but life offered other things and she wanted those too.

Friday came at last, and she sailed through morning surgery. She had three visits to do afterwards and then she was free to go. When she got back to Links View she phoned Felix.

'I'm home,' she announced. 'I just want to get something to eat and pack my bag. I'll be ready to leave in an hour.'

'I'm ready now,' he told her. She could hear anticipation in his voice. 'I'll be round to pick you up in an hour.'

'Come to the door. No reason not to now.'

Jill was hungry and it was late for lunch. Mrs Moon had left her a salad. She went to the kitchen and began to eat.

Victoria was pottering about the house doing little jobs again. Jill thought she had more energy. She made coffee for them both.

'The things you girls get up to these days. A weekend away with a man! Just the two of you?'

'Yes, Gran.'

'Without a chaperon? In my day, that would have ruined your reputation for good. Does your father mind?'

'Things are different now.'

'They certainly are. What will you do all weekend? It's out in the country, isn't it? Miles from anywhere?'

343

'We'll walk, Gran. Climb the hills.'

Victoria gave a sniff of disapproval. 'You'd better leave the name of the hotel. In case we need to get in touch.'

Jill forked a piece of quiche into her mouth. She hadn't got round to explaining to Gran that they had rented a cottage and would be entirely alone. She decided it might be kinder to leave her in ignorance.

'Nobody need get in touch. We'll be back on Sunday evening. Whatever happens at the surgery I don't want to know until then. This, Gran, is the first weekend I've had free for ages.'

'Yes, dear. Well, I hope you enjoy yourself.'

As she got ready, Jill watched for Felix's car from her bedroom window. She didn't want any more of Gran's pursed lips.

Already she had a feeling of release. Of being on top of the world. When she saw his Triumph Stag coming up the drive, she picked up her overnight bag and ran down to the sitting room.

'Goodbye, Gran.' She dropped a kiss on Victoria's wrinkled cheek.

'Good gracious, are you going like that?'

Jill laughed. She'd changed into jeans and a T-shirt. This was her off-duty uniform. 'You bet.'

She opened the door to Felix as he put out his hand to the bell. He laughed and kissed her cheek.

'Here we go,' he said, taking her bag. 'For the best weekend ever.'

It was a blustery day of fitful sunshine. He had the top of the car down. Jill gave herself up to enjoying the drive, to not having to think of anything but her own wishes.

She stole a glance at Felix and sighed with contentment. His brown wavy hair was being ruffled by the wind, his face set as he concentrated on the road ahead.

She felt she'd been holding her emotions in check for weeks. Telling herself she liked Felix but wasn't certain she wanted to spend the rest of her life with him. She'd thought it a decision she'd have to put off until she could see her way through all her other problems.

She understood now that it didn't take conscious decision. It had just happened. She knew she wanted him and always would.

The cottage was small and traditional. Quite isolated, miles from any town, and high on a hillside, with the most glorious views.

'It's so peaceful,' Jill breathed. The only sounds were a small stream bubbling down the side of the garden, and the lonely bleat of sheep out on the hill.

Felix unlocked the front door, and then before she realised what he was going to do, swept her up in his arms to carry her over the threshold.

Jill laughed. 'This is for brides. Carrying them into their first home.' His shoulders felt strong, his arms protective.

'This *is* our first home.' He had to lift her higher to kiss her. She could feel the warmth of his body coming through his thin shirt.

'Not really our home.'

'For two whole nights it is.' He swung round to face the stairs. Took a step towards them. They were steep and winding.

'Too narrow. I don't think you'll get me up there,' Jill laughed.

'Wish I could. I'd like to carry you up and show you I don't waste time. You cast aspersions on my manhood, once.' He laughed and set her gently on her feet.

'I want you to know it was a question of waiting for the right opportunity. I mean, you're not the sort of girl for the back seat of a car. Not the right sort of car either.'

Jill took him by the hand and led him from room to room, exclaiming with delight at the open rafters and large stone hearths. The kitchen that provided all the latest gadgets.

'We'll have a cup of tea,' she said, filling the kettle and putting it on to boil.

It was cool inside the stone walls. A wood fire had been laid in readiness in the little sitting room. Felix put a match to it. Orange flames flickered into life, growing stronger and crackling.

'Let's see what it's like upstairs.' Jill picked up her bag and took it up.

There were two simple rooms with low ceilings and white walls. The beds were covered with patchwork quilts.

Felix stood on the landing and asked: 'Which room shall we use?'

'No beating about the bush? No talk of a room each.'

One room was slightly larger than the other. She smiled as she went to the window, to marvel at the open sky and distant fields. Felix threw back the coverlet, and felt the mattress.

'Here? This is fine.' He was reaching for her.

The kettle began to whistle in the kitchen below.

'Don't rush things. We have to build up to it.' Jill pushed him gently away.

'I've been building up to it for weeks,' he teased. 'I'm ready, but we'll have the tea first. Get ourselves unpacked too, if you like.'

'And sort out what we're going to eat for supper,' she said as she ran down to make the tea.

His voice followed her. 'I'm ready there too. It's steaks. I'm going to cook.'

Jill took the tray to the little sitting room. The fire was burning up, brightening the room, filling it with the delicate scent of wood smoke.

She sank down on the hearth rug in front of it. Stretched out. Already she could bask in the warmth of the flames. Felix put on another log and sank down beside her. His brown eyes were full of tenderness.

'It's a lovely cottage,' she breathed, but she knew that it was Felix who was assaulting her senses, making her blood run with heat. 'I wish we could spend a month here.'

'I'd not be satisfied with a month. I want this to go on for ever.'

The touch of his hand on her bare arm sent a thrill down her spine. He put his arm round her, pulled her closer.

'I love you,' he whispered.

She felt the weight of his body press against hers. Felt herself respond.